THE CURER

···

Adam Nichols

The right of Adam Nichols to be identified as the
author of this work has been asserted by him in accordance
with the Copyright, Designs, and Patents Act 1988.

First published in Great Britain in 2001 by
Gollancz
An imprint of the Orion Publishing Group
Orion House, 5 Upper St Martin's Lane,
London WC2H 9EA

A CIP catalogue record for this book
is available from the British Library

ISBN 1 85798 531 1

Typeset at The Spartan Press Ltd,
Lymington, Hants

Printed in Great Britain by
Clays Ltd, St Ives plc

This book is for my uncles,
Bob and Fred, gentlemen both.

PART ONE

I

The world lay silent and dark. Young Pawli hugged himself, perched upon a moss-shrouded boulder, knees up against his chest, shivering in the pre-dawn cold. The forest on the slope a little way below him was an uncertain bulk, like some great dim beast, crouched waiting.

Some great beast . . .

Pawli shuddered, remembering, seeing both the star-shine-and-shadow of the world about him and the bleaker landscape of the dream, in which there had been no stars, no forest, only himself and the Other, a faceless, grim intruder, twice the height of any ordinary man, and no ordinary mortal creature at all, slick-skinned and pale as a peeled bough, with a beast's sharp claws, and only a vague, featureless oval where the face ought to have been. In the dream, Pawli had felt the raw, waiting menace of it as palpably as one could feel the radiating chill from a hunk of ice.

Surging back into the waking world, he had come stumbling out here into the cold dark of the pre-dawn, stricken with the belly-knowing of what he had witnessed. He had known dreams of this sort before – had dream-seen his own mother's death through one such – and there was no mistaking the flavour of it. It was a true *sending*. Something terrible was coming into the world.

Pawli let out a long, uncertain breath and slid stiff-limbed from the boulder upon which he sat. First light was beginning to seep from the eastern sky now, the forest downslope of him emerging from obscurity into limb and leaf and trunk. He walked towards it, needing to move, feeling his cold legs stiff as wood, his feet *kerwishing* softly though the dew-soaked grass.

The trees rose at the verge in a sort of wall, an intricate tapestry of which the eye could make any sort of pattern, seeing a horned beast in a bend of limb and trunk here, a flying creature there, wings poised. And there the figure of a man, standing upright, motionless.

Pawli froze.

'I will have words with him, boy,' the figure in the wood said. 'If you are wise, you will fetch him quick.'

For a long moment, Pawli could not get breath. His skin prickled with goose-pimples and his heart thumped wildly. But he knew that voice, he realised, and recognised the apparition – which seemed to have come into being here like a spirit stepping out of the very air – for what and who it was: a man, one Khurdis Blackeye by name. The recognition held little comfort.

'You're making me wait, boy,' Khurdis Blackeye said coldly, gliding out from between the trees. 'I do not like that. Fetch me your uncle, and be quick about it!'

Pawli straightened his shoulders and faced Khurdis straight on. 'Master Brynmaur cannot see you now. He's . . . busy.'

Khurdis laughed, but there was no humour in the sound. '*Master* Brynmaur, is it? I had no idea he was become such a great man.'

Pawli cursed himself. 'Prouder than a strutting cock, that one,' his uncle Bryn said about Khurdis Blackeye. 'And prickly as a weasel in rut.' Bryn would never have styled himself 'Master'. It was Khurdis's arrogance that had made Pawli add the title.

'Out of my way, boy,' Khurdis ordered impatiently. 'I will go up to him myself. You're wasting my time.' He shook his head. 'Why Brynmaur keeps a skanky, addle-minded lout like you about, I will never know.'

Pawli felt his face flush. Khurdis was dressed all in velvet and silks, spotless and elegant. He wore black leather boots and a wide black belt, from which hung a pair of rods strapped side by side in an embossed quiver, and a long, slim-bladed dagger in a black sheath. The rods were each perhaps two-thirds the length of a man's forearm and two fingers thick, made of brass and silver and ebony, intricate and old. They were like nothing Pawli had ever seen. The dagger had a silver hilt worked into the image of a snarling, unnatural creature. It was a beautiful, nasty-looking weapon, with an aura of age about it, too, somehow – and altogether in keeping with the rest of Khurdis's appearance: rich, soft-cloth clothes, striking colours, the gilt stitching that patterned his clothing gleaming in the soft early-morn light. Even his long black hair, which had been plaited into elaborate rows, was interlaced with glinting gold wire.

Pawli felt like a lout in his stiff, stained leathers. He was all feet and fingers, as Bryn would say, with none of the handsome features or natural grace a man like Khurdis Blackeye possessed. Khurdis looked like a character from some bard's tale, head and shoulders taller than most folk, sinewy slim and handsome as a man could be. Only his eyes gave him away.

'He'd burn his own mother on a stake, that one,' Bryn had once said, 'if she crossed him.'

'Out of my way, boy,' Khurdis repeated. His voice was ice.

Pawli stood as he was, blocking the path with nervous obstinacy. 'Master Brynmaur is . . . he's busy, I tell you. He's not to be disturbed.'

Khurdis stepped forward threateningly. 'Move aside, if you value your own well-being.' He raised one hand and began twisting it in the air in complex, serpentine curves, chanting gutturally in his throat the while.

Pawli tried to meet Khurdis's hard-dark eyes in a defiant glare – but could not. His knees felt weak. Khurdis had touched neither the mysterious paired rods in their quiver, nor the long-bladed dagger, but that was little comfort.

5

Though Bryn might scoff at the stories, folk said Khurdis Blackeye had the true *power*. No telling what he might be capable of. Pawli felt the hairs on the back of his neck prickle unpleasantly.

'Move aside, boy,' Khurdis commanded a third time. 'If you do not, you will regret it all the rest of your days.'

For one long moment, Pawli held as he was. Then he faltered back, knowing no way to meet Khurdis's challenge.

Khurdis snorted in derision, flicked a finger at him in some complex, arcane, menacing sign, and then swept past, heading upslope towards Bryn's cabin.

Pawli stood frozen, his heart thumping in his chest like a crazy drum. He felt as if somebody had tied a length of rope about him and cinched it tight, so hard was it to draw a proper breath. His belly throbbed. His eyeballs did. He hoped desperately that Khurdis had not . . . not *done* anything terrible to him. He felt his limbs, his stomach, his ribs. Everything seemed intact. He took a breath, another . . . and felt a sudden thrust of hard anger.

It was Bryn's fault, this – Bryn, who refused to teach him.

Pawli shivered, his fists clenched, furious and frightened and balked. It was not right that things should be like this. Standing before Khurdis Blackeye he had been helpless as any babe. The *power* was in his blood; he was certain of it. He possessed it as surely as Khurdis Blackeye did, as Bryn himself did. Why else would he experience the *sending* dreams? But Bryn hoarded his knowledge, and the *power* that Pawli felt inherent in himself could find no proper manner of expression.

It was old anger, this; Pawli must have endured the scourge of it half a thousand times over the past years. He felt it move in him like a quick tide. The familiar surge of it seemed to help him feel more his proper self again, somehow. It was easier to breathe. He stared at the hillside

6

– humpy meadow and dwarf birch, with a winding path up which Khurdis had gone.

What did Khurdis Blackeye want here? It had been . . . how many? seven . . . no, eight years, if he had got it right, since Khurdis and Bryn had parted – in anger. Khurdis Blackeye had no business coming up here. Pawli felt his heart catch. Could this have anything to do with his dream of the Intruder? But how?

Bryn ought to have taught him something, he thought again. Anything! There were ways of seeing into the world's hidden patterns, of perceiving the subtle surge and give of the Powers, those great, live forces that moved like strong currents under smooth water – save that the water was the world entire. He had the ability to perceive such hidden movement, he was sure – the *sending* dreams were one aspect of it – but without Bryn's guidance he felt it only obscurely in his guts, in his bones and blood. He *hated* that feeling of groping blindness.

Pawli took a breath, trying to steady himself. He unclenched his fists, swallowed. There was only one thing for him to do: he must go after Khurdis. The way he was likely to be at the moment, Bryn would be quite defence-less.

Defenceless . . . Pawli felt himself burn with shame. Khurdis had thrust him aside like some ridiculous child. He would have to do better, somehow – though he knew not how.

Bryn's cabin door stood open. There was not a sound to be heard save the faint *cheep cheeping* of a lone birch-lark perched on the cabin's eaves. Pawli shivered. Could it be that he was already too late? Did Khurdis have some fell, fatal purpose in coming here? Had he already dispatched Bryn's poor spirit into the darkness of the Shadowlands, wailing?

The very thought of it made him sick in his belly. Almost, Pawli turned and fled. After all, what could he do, all alone, ignorant as a worm, against the likes of Khurdis Blackeye? But in his mind he saw Bryn lying helpless, with none in all the world to aid him save he, Pawli.

Stooping, he snatched up a fist-sized piece of stone – the ground here was littered with such – thinking maybe he could brain Khurdis from behind, or something. Slowly, his heart thumping, he crept towards the open door.

Inside, the cabin was silent and dim. Pawli stood poised in the entrance, awkward and anxious, feeling himself blind and vulnerable, his pulse racing.

There was not a sound. The cabin air was close and musty, overlaid with the sick-sweet, stale tang of starweed. Pawli peered about desperately, clutching his rock, seeing no sign of Khurdis at first, only the dim figure of Bryn, lying sprawled out on his back in the middle of the dirt floor, jaw agape, eyes wide and staring.

'Phawg!' Khurdis muttered

Pawli jumped. Khurdis, he now saw, was standing against the chimney mantel, staring at Bryn's still form. In his hand, he held the silver-hilted dagger, naked blade out now, slim and gleaming and nasty-looking. With the needle tip of it, he pointed at Bryn's sprawled form. 'And so here he lies, the great Master Brynmaur Somnar, far-seer into other realms.' Khurdis shook his head. 'How far the wise are fallen.'

Bryn moaned softly. A thin ribbon of spittle hung from the corner of his mouth. His starweed paraphernalia – the small cedar box, the bone pipe, the little white-fire sticks, the firestone and candle he used – lay scattered on the floor next to him, knocked askew at some point by his out-flung arm. He moaned again. His eyes flickered blindly, staring into whatever fantastical inner visions the starweed gave him.

Pawli drew a relieved breath. Khurdis had not harmed Bryn, then. But Pawli felt himself flush with shame at the state Bryn was in. 'Bryn,' he hissed. *'Bryn!'*

Bryn's eyelids fluttered, but that was all the response he showed.

Khurdis laughed cruelly. 'And I was worried . . . *worried*, mind you, boy, that Brynmaur here might prove a hindrance to certain, ah . . . intentions of mine. Ha! I ought to have known better. He never did have any sharpness to him.'

'That's not true!' Pawli snapped, angered. 'Bryn is—'

'Is *what*, boy? Look at him!'

Bryn lay like an abandoned rag doll on the cabin's hard-packed dirt floor, moaning softly. There was an old blanket draped half over him and tangled about his legs. As Pawli watched, Bryn's head flopped from side to side. More spittle dribbled from his mouth.

'Pitiful!' Khurdis snorted. He lifted the dagger in his hand. 'Easy meat for any who wish it.'

'Don't you dare!' Pawli snapped, the words out of him before he knew it.

Khurdis regarded him, one eyebrow raised. 'And just how would the likes of you stop me, boy?'

Pawli raised his rock.

Khurdis laughed again. 'Oh yes? Bludgeon me to death with your little stone, will you?' Khurdis regarded him for long moments, then laughed mockingly. 'Not to worry boy. Brynmaur poses no threat to me. I see that clear now. Why should I waste my strength on him? He is become pitiful, a mere shadow of what he once might have been. I have misspent my time entirely in coming here.'

Khurdis shook his head, looking down at Bryn. 'The gossip about you, *Master* Brynmaur, falls short of the mark, if anything. I ought to have known better than to worry myself over you.'

Khurdis laughed once more, a soft, cruel sound, then turned on his heel abruptly and made for the cabin's doorway. 'Stand aside, boy,' he ordered Pawli, 'and I will leave the two of you to each other. You deserve each other, no doubt – an adolescent witling and a drug-crazed far-seer. Ha!' He gestured dismissively with the gleaming dagger.

Pawli slipped sideways away from the entranceway.

Khurdis passed to the doorway, paused. 'When he comes to himself – if he ever does – tell him I was here. And tell him . . .' Khurdis fell silent for a moment. With the point of the dagger, he began to carve something into the door's frame. 'Tell Brynmaur,' he said, grunting a little with the effort he put into his carving, 'that he was wrong about me. I am all he said I was not. As you and he shall see. As all the world shall see, soon enough. Can you remember that, boy?'

Pawli nodded, feeling his face hot with outrage. 'I am no witling!'

Khurdis shrugged. He had finished the carving now, and he slid the dagger back into its sheath. 'Witling or no, you will tell him what I said.'

'I will tell him.'

Khurdis stood for long moments staring at Pawli with his hard, dark eyes. 'Perhaps you are indeed no witling. Only an ignorant lout.' With that, he was gone.

Burning, Pawli stepped to the doorway and glared after him.

Khurdis strode the hummocky downslope like he owned it, never once looking back, his movements sure and graceful. The rich colours of his clothing – the green of new leaves, the wine-red – fairly glowed in the morning sun, and the gilt stitching shimmered. Despite all, Pawli could not help but wish Bryn looked more like that. The very thought was a kind of betrayal. But he could not help himself. Khurdis had *everything* – the strength, the skill, the *power*, the looks . . . It was so wretchedly unfair.

A pair of louts they were indeed, he and Bryn, raggedly dressed and foolish. He heaved the rock away in disgust. He must have looked a right fool standing there, clutching the thing as his only weapon. No wonder Khurdis had laughed at him.

Stepping closer to the doorway, he peered at what

Khurdis had carved into the frame there. It was a kind of curlicue, with what looked like a letter in the middle of it. It meant nothing to Pawli, who, beyond his own name, could make out little in the way of writing. He lifted a finger, about to trace the design of it, but hesitated. No telling what sort of thing Khurdis Blackeye might have carved. It could be a . . . a sign of *power*. Or anything at all. He shivered and snatched his hand away.

In the cabin, Bryn still lay as he had. Pawli felt an almost overwhelming desire to kick him. Instead, he hunkered down at his uncle's side and shook him, none too gently. 'Bryn. Bryn! Come back.'

But it was no use. Bryn's eyes were staring and sightless. This close, he smelled, of stale sweat, of urine, of the sharp-sweet odour of the starweed he had been up all night smoking. Khurdis had no such old stench about him, that was for sure.

Pawli sighed, stood up. Bryn would be insensible to the world for the better part of the morning.

And the chores still needed doing, no matter what.

Pawli turned to leave the cabin, but stopped at the doorway, staring uncertainly at Khurdis's carving. Could he pass by such a thing safely? What was its purpose? Perhaps he ought to let well enough alone till Bryn was returned to himself. He could always scramble out one of the little windows in the back to get outside . . .

No.

Suddenly he felt completely fed up with Khurdis Black-eye and his threats and posturings. Making a warding sign with upraised fingers, he brushed past through the door-way. His hair prickled and he felt his heart fair miss a few beats, but otherwise he seemed to make it through perfectly intact. Glaring downslope at where Khurdis had disappeared, he began one of the old curses, 'By oak and ash and bitter thorn . . .' but thought better of it. A man the likes of Khurdis Blackeye might very well turn such a formal curse back upon the sender. Instead, he raised a

11

hand and made the rudest, most insulting gesture he knew how, then moved on across the slope himself, anger slow-burning in his guts like a banked fire in a pit.

II

With the firewood chopped and split and piled, the water drawn from the spring, their few scraggy hens filched of eggs (three this morning – a richer haul than usual), his skin scrubbed raw-clean and his hair washed and hanging in still-damp strands about his shoulders, his leather trousers and tunic scoured with sand (so he would not feel quite such the scruffy lout in comparison to a man like Khurdis Blackeye), Pawli returned to the cabin. It was well past morning by now, with a darkening tangle of rain-cloud piling up over beyond the humped, stony shoulders of old Mount Gim.

Inside, Bryn was sitting up groggily, elbows on knees, head in his hands. 'Wha'dya loogin' ad?' he mumbled, peering sideways through the mess of his tangled hair at Pawli standing in the doorway.

Pawli said nothing.

'You're all scrubb'd like a new potado,' Bryn said, getting his tongue to work a little more properly. 'And you've a face on you would curdle milk. What's going on?'

'Well, *you* certainly wouldn't know, would you?'

Bryn blinked. 'What's wrong with you, Pawli?'

Pawli opened his mouth, closed it again. He took a breath. 'Khurdis Blackeye was here.'

Pawli was not sure what he had expected. Surprise or uncertainty, anger perhaps. Perhaps even fear. But all Bryn did was flop back to the floor and drag the blanket about himself.

'Did you *hear* me?' Pawli demanded. 'Khurdis Blackeye was here. Here! Right in the cabin.'

'And so?' Bryn responded.

'And *so*?' Pawli did not know what to do with himself, jump up and down and shriek or laugh or what. 'Have you lost your mind entirely, then? Has that cursed starweed of yours rotted completely what's left of your brains?'

Bryn sat up, flung back his draggled hair, and glared at him. 'You know nothing about such things.'

'Oh yes? Well, I know *this* much, anyway. Khurdis Blackeye was here, in this very cabin. And he looked at you, sprawled there in the dirt like some witling idiot, and he *laughed* at you. And at me, too. And he . . .'

Bryn rubbed his eyes, shook his head. 'Is there any water?'

'Get it yourself,' Pawli snapped. 'It's outside in the rain-barrel, where it always is.'

For an instant, there was a spark of something like anger in Bryn's eyes. Pawli welcomed it, for Bryn so seldom showed any kind of ordinary feeling these days. But the spark sank away to nothing in a heartbeat. Bryn dragged himself to his feet and headed stiffly towards the door, moving as if he were an old man.

'Careful!' Pawli cried abruptly.

Bryn stumbled, looked askance about the cabin. 'What?'

'On the doorframe.' Pawli pointed at Khurdis's carving. 'There. *He* left that.'

Bryn approached the carving, peered at it, ran the tip of one finger over the design.

'What is it?' Pawli asked uneasily.

'The letter "K". His initial.' Bryn shrugged.

'What's *wrong* with you?' Pawli all but shouted at him. 'Khurdis Blackeye himself was here, waving a dagger about, muttering about dark intentions, carving things into the doorframe. And you don't even seem to *care*!'

Bryn sighed. 'I'm thirsty, lad. Let me drink first, all right? Just let me get some water into me first.'

Pawli shook his head in disgust. In his mind, he heard Khurdis's voice: 'He is become pitiful, a mere shadow of

14

what he once might have been.' Bryn was leaning against the doorframe now – the opposite side from where the carving was – gasping softly. Pushing himself awkwardly off, he disappeared outside.

'You're pitiful, do you know that?' Pawli shouted after him.

Silence.

'Do you hear me?'

'I hear you, lad,' Bryn said, returning into the cabin, the large water dipper in his hand. 'No need to shout. I'm feeling a touch tender right now. Transparent round the edges, you might say.' He took a long swig of water from the dipper, spilling half of it down his front.

Pawli felt like slapping him. After Khurdis Blackeye, Bryn did indeed seem like some might-have-been, pitiful old fool. He was pale and skinny, his cheeks hollow and brown-grey with stubble, his green eyes sunk in their bony sockets. There were dark pouches under his eyes, like bruises, and the left side of his face was crinkled from where he had been lying with it pressed into the ground. His brown hair hung in lank strands down past his shoulders and across his face, veined everywhere with grey and thinning across his scalp line so that his face seemed too much forehead. His breeches were of leather, like Pawli's own, but he wore a linen shirt, horribly wrinkled and shiny with grime. His nails were black with old dirt.

Altogether not a pretty sight, Pawli thought in disgust. He had seen Bryn like this for mornings without count. But today was different, as if he were seeing him for the first time again. He realised how much he had got used to over the past few years.

'You were never like this when I first came here,' he said sadly.

Bryn blinked. 'Like what?'

'Like . . . *this*! Like some flyblown, pitiful old lout.'

Bryn shook his head, took another drink of the water,

15

spilling less this time. 'Tell me,' he said, 'what has happened.'

'I've already *told* you! Khurdis Blackeye was here. Right here in the cabin.'

'And?'

'And he laughed at you!'

'And?'

Pawli stared at him. 'He had a naked dagger in his hand. Don't you care at all that he could have killed you?'

Bryn shook his head. 'Why would he wish to do a thing like that?'

'You were *totally* helpless. He could have done *anything* to you he liked. If I hadn't been here . . .'

Bryn took a last drink of water, dropped the dipper to the floor at his feet, then turned away and went to sit down on the old rocker next to the fireplace. He stared at the ashes of the dead fire, rocking gently. 'I could do with some tea.'

Pawli picked up the dipper. 'He meant you ill, Bryn. I know it. I *saw* it.'

'Khurdis means everyone ill.'

'But what was he doing here? Why come here, now, after all these years?'

Bryn shrugged.

'He said I should . . . should give you a message from him.'

Bryn looked up. 'Oh aye? And that would be what? That he is far more than I wish to give him credit for?'

Pawli blinked. 'How did you know?'

Bryn sighed. 'Khurdis Blackeye was never a very original soul.'

'He . . . he said,' Pawli began, 'he said to . . . to tell you that you were wrong about him. That he was . . . How did he put it? That he was all you had said he was not. And that you would see. That . . . that all the world would soon see. Those were his words – all the world.'

Bryn said nothing.

16

'What did he mean, Bryn? Why was he here? What's he up to? What's happening in the world?'

Bryn shrugged again, ran a hand through his tangly, greying hair.

'Answer me!'

'What do you wish me to say, lad? Khurdis was always full of plots and revenges. He was a right pain in the arse that way.'

'But . . .'

'He never could see properly beyond the end of his own nose, that one.'

Pawli shook his head. Bryn was losing touch with things. That was clear enough. He had a sudden, horrible thought: perhaps Bryn was losing his own *power*. In the nearly five years Pawli had been here, he had never once seen Bryn do anything much beyond the ordinary, unless one counted his curing a few people of ailments. But much of that was done with herbs and touch, and could be done without the use of the true *power*. Pawli had a sudden vision of Bryn as an empty vessel, a deflated sack, sad and wrinkled and dying. It made him feel sick in the pit of his belly.

With a grunt, he drove the image away from him. It could not be. It was too horrible to contemplate. Bryn was Bryn. The finest, deepest Curer in the Three Valleys. He was just dulled by too much overindulgence in the starweed, was all.

Pawli went to stand before the rocking chair. 'You didn't see Khurdis, Bryn. When was the last time you saw him? Years ago! He . . . he has the *power*. I felt it!

Bryn shook his head. 'He has not. And how many times must I remind you? It's a *gift*. Not a . . . a *power*. One doesn't walk the way of hidden paths by bulling along.'

'Don't be ridiculous!' Pawli snapped. 'Everybody knows Khurdis Blackeye has the *power*.'

'*Gift*.'

'*Gift*, then. Whatever. Everybody in Woburn Village, in Bendey, in . . . why, everybody in the whole of the Three Valleys knows Khurdis Blackeye as a true Man of *Power*. He charges outrageously for his services. Folk wouldn't pay all that for nothing!'

Bryn shook his head. 'There's none so blind as they who refuse to see.'

'Meaning what?'

'Khurdis Blackeye *wants* folk to believe he has the *gift*.'

'And you're saying?'

'He has not got it.'

'But . . . How can you—' Pawli ran a hand over his eyes. He did not know what to do in the face of such wilful obstinacy. 'How can you *know*? You didn't see Khurdis. You haven't seen him in years. I faced him. He's . . . there's a . . . a *power* to him. There *is*! I felt it.'

'Just piss and temper is all, lad. That's Khurdis through and through.'

'But I . . .'

'Look,' Bryn said, 'one either has the *gift* or not. Khurdis first came to me for teaching . . . oh, something like fifteen years ago, it must be, when he was five years or so younger than you are now, no more than twelve or thirteen. He was all ranting and bluster, even then. But for all his grand desires and ambitions, he did not have the *gift*.'

'But maybe it's developed in him since then.'

Bryn shook his head. 'That is not the way it works.'

'How can you be so *sure*?' Pawli demanded irritably.

Bryn sighed. 'Because I *do* have the *gift*.'

'And me?' Pawli said quickly. He felt his heart thump. In all the time he had been here, Bryn had never once acknowledged the *power* – the *gift*, whatever one might name it – he was sure was in him. 'What about *me*? Do I not have the . . . the *gift*?'

Bryn looked at him. 'Why all the hunger, lad? The *gift* is more curse than blessing. Believe me. I know.'

'You haven't answered me.'

Bryn turned away and began to rock in the chair. 'I'd like some tea now.'

'Answer me!' Pawli insisted. He was still holding the water dipper and he found he had raised it like a club to strike at Bryn. He lowered it quickly, shamefacedly.

Bryn sighed. 'You understand nothing, lad. You think the *gift* some great empowering wonder, that with it you would be able to do miraculous things, heal the sick, sort out all the wrongs of the world. Well, it doesn't work like that.' Pushing against the floor with his toes, Bryn rocked his chair. 'Trust me, lad. I know what's best.'

Pawli laughed bitterly. 'Trust you? You sit there, looking like some old scarecrow the wind blew in, reeking of starweed, and you give your grand pronouncements about the world and everything in it, and you expect me to believe every word you say just because . . . because—' He did not know how to continue. It was all too ridiculous.

'Listen to me, lad,' Bryn said. 'Just calm down and listen.'

'No!' Pawli snapped. 'You listen to me. Say what you like about him, but Khurdis Blackeye has become a force in the Three Valleys. *You* could have done that. Instead, you rot here doing nothing, smoking your stinking weed. When was the last time you helped anyone?'

Bryn blinked, shifted uncomfortably. 'There was that woman with the lame knee who . . .'

'That was before the winter. It's very nearly summer now.'

Bryn blinked. 'So long ago as that?'

Pawli crouched next to the rocker, dropped the dipper, put his hands on one of the wooden arms to hold the rocking chair still. 'Bryn. Bryn! Look at yourself! You've got to pull yourself together. You need help. I have the *power* in me, the *gift*. I know it! I can feel it in my blood. Tell me the truth, Bryn. Tell me! I can help you. Together we can sort out Khurdis Blackeye if he tries to make trouble. We can oust him from his position. But you must

19

teach me. You must show me how to make the *gift* in me come forth!'

For an instant, Pawli was overwhelmed by a vision of the man he could be: like Khurdis Blackeye, only more, truly gifted, an aid to the weak and sick, an explorer of far realms, a man of substance whom others looked to for aid and counsel . . .

Bryn was looking at him. He shook his head and sighed. 'Get your head out of the clouds, Pawli. Look at me. This is where the *gift* leads. Do you wish to end up like me? For that, surely, is what will become of you.'

'No! It's not the *gift* that brought you to this. It's . . .' Pawli bit his lip.

'Go ahead,' Bryn said. 'Say it.'

'It's that cursed starweed has been the ruin of you. Not the *gift*.'

Bryn laughed, but it was not a funny laugh. 'You understand nothing, lad.'

Pawli glared at him. 'If not, it's *your* fault. I've been here, what? The better part of five whole years now. And what have you taught me in all that time? *Nothing!*'

'I never said I would teach you anything, lad.'

Pawli grabbed him by the arm. 'Bryn. Bryn! I have the *gift*. You know I do! I dreamed last night. A true *sending*. I know it was! I—'

Bryn cut him short. 'Find a life for yourself, Pawli. I'm nobody's teacher. Not any more. Go down into the villages, the Lowlands even, find a girl for yourself, make babies. That's what real life is.'

Pawli's heart lurched. 'Are you sending me away?'

'No,' Bryn said softly. 'No. Of course not. We're blood kin, you and me. I'd never send you off. But, Pawli . . . *think*, lad. What do you expect to gain from following the road that I have walked? The far-seer's way is too hard, lad. The way of hidden paths is . . . it breaks too many of us.'

'It is not a *choice*, Bryn. It's what I *am*.'

Bryn sighed

'Tell me I'm wrong, then,' Pawli challenged him. 'Look me in the face and tell me I have not the *gift*. *Tell me!*'

Bryn regarded him. 'You have . . . you do not—'

'You can't do it!' Pawli cried triumphantly.

'You have not the *gift*,' Bryn said, but he said it weakly and could not look Pawli in the eye.

'You must teach me, Bryn. You *must*!'

'Aiee, Pawli,' Bryn groaned. 'You do not know what it is you ask.'

'I do know. I *do*!'

'Your head is full of foolish, boyish dreams. I had the same dreams, once.'

'What happened to you, then? What happened to your dreams, Bryn?'

'The far-seer's way is a hard path. There's too much in the way of temptation. Too much cost. Too much grief. Too many folk needing too much . . . and hating you in their ignorance for your limitations. And there *are* limitations, lad. I . . . I loved your mother. My small sister . . . I remember her as a little slip of a thing, her hair streaming behind her as she dashed across the meadows. All life and energy and wonder, she was. A marvellous, wise soul. But I could not save her. She wasted away and died, just as all the others did that winter. And nobody has ever forgiven me.'

'No, Bryn. They . . .'

'You don't know, lad. You were just that much too young then to really see what was happening. None comes to me now save in the direst of needs. There's more than a few who believe I allowed folk to die on purpose, for my own dark ends. You've heard the stories, surely?'

Pawli nodded uneasily. He *had* heard the stories: of how Bryn was no true Curer, but a worker of dark magics requiring death and blood. Indeed, two visitors this winter past had come to try to hire him to bring destruction and

21

misfortune upon their neighbours. Bryn had sent them packing with a sharp word.

Bryn sighed. 'My father said not a word to me since the night your mother died. And now he's gone, and my own mother too.' Bryn reached a hand out to Pawli. 'Which leaves just you and me, lad. We're all that's left to carry the name of Somnar now. Find a life for yourself. Find a girl and make fine young babies to carry on the family name. Go. Before you become too tainted with my company. Folk will forgive you your stay here as a youth. But you are boy no longer . . .'

'No, Bryn. No!'

'It's the way of things, Pawli.'

'No! Don't make my life a waste. I'm like a bird, Bryn. I can feel it. I have wings. Teach me to fly! Please. Teach me!'

Bryn looked away. 'I cannot.'

'Will not!' Pawli snapped accusingly.

'You don't understand,' Bryn said.

'It's *you* who doesn't understand.'

Hunched in his rocker, Bryn looked like an old man: a miserly old man hoarding his secrets. 'You're pitiful, do you know that?' Pawli said. 'Khurdis was right! You . . . you're—' There were no more words. Pawli felt his breath catch in his throat. His belly churned in anger.

And Bryn just sat there, rocking.

Pawli wanted to hit him. Instead, he turned and stormed out.

'Pawli!' Bryn called after him. 'Where are you . . .'

But it was too late. Pawli was running, skidding down the hummocky slope away from the cabin and towards the line of the trees below, wanting only to get away, to put as much distance as he could between himself and Bryn, so clotted with anger that he felt as if he might rupture at any moment. Tears blurred his vision as he ran. He tried to fist them out of his eyes and tripped ignominiously, falling hard on his face. Cursing and spluttering, he picked himself up and glanced quickly behind, to see if Bryn had noticed.

But there was no sign of Bryn at the cabin door – where Pawli had felt sure he must be by now. Still in his rocker, most like, Pawli thought bitterly. Rocking his life away . . . oblivious.

Pawli whirled and ran on, blindly.

III

Pawli sat hunched against the great, raspy bole of a gnarled mountain pine, arms about his knees. He was wet and chilled. The rain had stopped now, but water still fell all through the forest, dripping in a steady *krip krip krip* from the limbs and needle-leaves. The air was heavy with the wet, astringent scent of the pines.

Pawli sighed. He felt filled to curdling with anger and shame and ragged frustration. He kept running his conversation with Bryn over and over in his mind, thinking of things he ought to have said, wishing he had not said some of the things he had. He was hungry and somehow hollow-feeling, despite his turmoil, but he did not want to go back. Bryn's cabin was no small distance behind him in any case; he had come a fair ways through the woods, blind and furious, through curtains of frigid afternoon rain – mostly downslope, too, which would mean a weary slog back upwards were he to return.

Maybe he ought just to keep going, as Bryn had said – walk away from everything and begin a new life as any ordinary person would . . . with a woman, children, a farm steading. But no. The very thought made him cringe. Such a life was not for him. He would not concede it. More than that lay in store for him, surely.

Between the trees below he could glimpse the winding ribbon of the Keel Track, the pathway that led up through the Three Valleys. Everyone knew of the Keel Track – it was the sole connecting linkway between the Three Valleys and the Lowlands westwards – but he had never actually seen it before with his own eyes.

It was no more than a few hundred paces from him now; that was how far he had come this day. He could get to it through the pines without difficulty. It would be a simple enough matter then to follow it westwards and so eventually into the very Lowlands themselves. Who knew what might lie away out there? In such faraway places, he might find – the idea made him shiver – a proper teacher, somebody with the true *power*, but who, unlike Bryn, had not thrown it all away.

He imagined for himself how it would be: him lean and hardened from much travel, seeing strange sights and people, passing through far-flung little villages like Woburn as a mountain cat passes through, silent and mysterious, walking, walking . . . till eventually – he had only a hazy notion of the distances involved – eventually he would come through into the Lowlands . . . and there he would meet a tall man with a penetrating gaze who would instantly recognise the nature of the true *power* that lay dormant in him, somebody whose eyes had not been dulled by too much starweed.

Pawli's heart thrilled at the prospect. The world was so huge. He could look in any direction and see mountains stepping off into the distance. And beyond them? The world could hold anything, anything at all. He had done absolutely nothing yet with his life. It was past time he struck out for something larger, something deeper, something more meaningful. He stood up, pushed off from the pine that had been sheltering him, took three steps towards the Keel Track.

And stopped.

Bryn . . .

Pawli sighed. Bryn *needed* him. He should never have shouted as he had, nor stormed off like some silly, mad boy. Bryn had a soul-hurt. That was clear for anybody to see who cared to look. Left to his own devices, he would end up one morning sprawled out on the cabin floor, dead from too much starweed and too little of anything else.

25

But Bryn was *gifted*. No one at all doubted that. And one day, surely – surely – with Pawli's help, the *gift* in Bryn would rise up in him, overcoming the starweed stupor, and he would begin to teach Pawli. Pawli felt his heart thrill at the very thought. It was with Bryn that his life lay, his future.

It was Khurdis Blackeye's fault, all this. He still felt the sting of the man's words. Khurdis was like one of those nasty little blood-ticks; he got under a person's skin and rankled and rankled, till the person did not know what he was doing. Here he was, the day after a powerful *sending* dream – as sure a sign as could be wished of the *gift* inherent in him – and instead of talking it over with Bryn (and having Bryn maybe relent finally and agree to teach him how to properly receive such *sendings*) he was stranded out here on the cold hillside, wet and frustrated and empty-feeling.

With a kind of cold lump growing in his belly.

Pawli saw in his mind the unnatural, faceless face of the Other from his dream. Something terrible was coming into the world. He felt that with an inexplicable, absolute surety. But what? And how? Did Khurdis Blackeye's sudden appearing – him all threat and mutterings about dark intentions – have any connection? He needed desperately to talk to Bryn about it all.

But Bryn would only rock in his chair and ignore him. Or scoff. Pawli shook his head. He could not face Bryn again, not so soon.

How had they ever got to this pass? As a little lad he had fair worshipped his uncle. After his mother had died, he had been shifted about from one uncomfortable relative to another for years, him an unruly, choleric boy, till, finally, Bryn had returned from wherever he had gone off to in the Lowlands and taken him in. Bryn's presence, back then, had been the one saving grace in an otherwise cruelly bleak world, and Pawli would never forget the morning his uncle had come to fetch him, like a wish-dream come true.

But the wish-dream had soured.

Pawli let out a long breath and gazed down at the Keel Track where it curved down across the tumbled shoulder of Mount Gim. It seemed to him like a sort of river, with a hidden current, leading who knew where. One step upon it and that current would take a man's feet from under him and carry him off.

He wished . . .

He did not wish.

Pawli hugged himself. His leathers were heavy with water and he felt chilled and stiff. He craned his head back and glanced up through the interlaced, spiky limbs of the pines. The rain clouds were breaking up into long tatters and streaming away overhead. The sun was well on in the sky. It would take a hard slog to get back up to the cabin before sunfall, even if he followed the straightest route possible. His belly grumbled emptily. He looked downslope. The Track seemed so close.

Pawli clenched his fists. He might not be able to travel that path, but he was suddenly determined to set foot upon it. That, at the very least.

Through the trees he went then, his feet light on the spongy cushion of untold seasons of brown pine needles, skidding over the rain-slicked moss on a ridgeback of stone, till he came at last to the Track's verge. There he stopped, his heart beating hard.

He peered along the Track as far as he could see – not very far, really, for it was hemmed in by the pines on both sides, and it dropped down over the crest of the slope and disappeared from sight only a little distance before him. He lifted a foot, hesitated, put the foot slowly onto the Track's hard-packed dirt surface. Perhaps it was his imagination, but he did seem to feel the faintest of vibrations through the thin leather sole of his boot. What would happen if he let himself go? To what wonderful – or terrible – things might he be led?

He stood staring westwards, the Lowland way, yearning, pulled, wanting to go, needing to stay . . .

And then, round the track ahead of him, a figure appeared.

Pawli blinked in shock. It was still too early in the season for the usual travellers – tinkers and traders and such. For all he had berated Bryn that it was nearly summer, true summer was still long weeks off up here in the high country. So who could this lone figure be, walking slowly along towards him from the direction of the Lowlands?

Almost, Pawli bolted. It had been years since he had faced a human being he did not know. What would this traveller think of him? His leathers were smelly with wet and prickly with pine needles. He ran a hand through his hair and his fingers caught in the tangles. He must look the right bumpkin.

The traveller drew nearer, walking the upslope gradient of the Track slowly, limping a little so as to favour his right leg. He wore loose trousers and leather walking boots – of far solider craftsmanship than Pawli's – and a loose, long-sleeved tunic, the trousers dark brown, the tunic storm-cloud grey. His clothing was dark with water; he too must have been caught in the rain. On his head was a short-brimmed leather cap, from under which a ruff of thick dark hair showed. He had only a little rucksack for baggage. Balanced over his shoulder, with one hand supporting it, he carried a length of pole or something, long as his outstretched arm, wrapped in rough burlap cloth.

He was thin and fine-boned, this traveller, perhaps a hand's breadth shorter than Pawli (who was not especially tall), and beardless – not just clean-shaven, but young enough so as to have the smooth cheeks of a youth. Pawli shivered. It was as if he had somehow conjured up this figure in answer to his own yearnings. This was how he had envisioned himself, walking along through strange territory, meeting odd little folk along the way.

Now he was to be one of those odd little folk.

Pawli burned with envy. Here indeed was everything he

had been dreaming for himself. What wonders had this lad seen, wandering the world at his will like this?

The traveller stopped some little distance from Pawli and looked him up and down. Pawli could feel his face flush, and he shivered under the other's gaze, self-conscious and uneasy.

'Greetings,' the traveller said after a little. His accent was unlike any Pawli had ever heard: a surprisingly high-pitched voice, more nasal than Pawli was used to hearing. The traveller let the length of burlap-wrapped pole slide from his shoulder and set one end on the ground, leaning on it like a walking stick. This close, Pawli saw that his clothes were travel-stained, his trousers rent at one knee, the arm of his tunic patched with mismatched cloth. His face was greyed with fatigue and dirt.

'Greetings,' the traveller repeated, looking at Pawli quizzically now with eyes that were ice-blue and sharp as a bird's.

Pawli blinked, swallowed. 'Gre— Greetings, traveller,' he stammered. He had been gawking like a fool.

They looked at each other in silence for long heartbeats. Pawli felt a cold shiver go through him. Surely this meeting could not be entirely by chance. What with his dream, and Khurdis Blackeye's appearing and all, he felt this day to be charged with significance. Powers shaped the world, and those Powers – great live forces that currented through everything, mountain and man, bird and branch – swayed the lives of human folk, too.

'Would there be a village anywhere hereabouts?' the traveller asked in his nasal, high-pitched, foreign voice.

Pawli swallowed, taken a little aback, in the middle of his grand speculations, by the prosaic nature of the question. 'Woburn'd be the nearest. But it's a farish ways off from here.'

The traveller sighed. He lifted his leather cap, ran a hand through thick, shortish, dark hair, put the cap back on. His sharp blue eyes had a far-seeing cast, it seemed to Pawli, with something of a hawk's long-range gaze. Pawli could not help but wonder what strange sights those eyes might have looked upon.

'And you?' the traveller said.

'Me?'

'You would have come from . . . where?'

Pawli hesitated, then gestured behind him upslope, the way he had come.

'Are you from this . . . village, then?'

Pawli shook his head.

The traveller looked at Pawli, gazed around him at the grey-green mass of the pines, and sat down abruptly on the Track's verge. He laid the wrapped pole, or stick, or whatever it might be, on the ground at his side – it seemed to have some heft by the way he handled it – and drew forth a water flask from his shoulder bag. He took a drink, then offered the flask to Pawli.

Pawli stepped closer, reached out for the proffered flask, and froze. The little finger of the hand that held the flask had been sliced off; all that remained was a stump of white scar-flesh where the first joint would have been. Pawli could not help staring. He had never seen anything quite like it, as if a heavy razor had sliced through the finger, bone and all, in one cruel slash.

The traveller held the flask out, offering it still.

Pawli took it, feeling himself a right, gawking bumpkin, and drank self-consciously. 'Thanks,' he said, handing the flask back.

The traveller nodded. Putting the flask on the ground, he stretched his legs out, flexed his ankles, sighed and began rubbing his right thigh methodically.

Pawli did not know quite what to do. Unused to strangers, he felt the fool, standing there in his rain-sogged leathers, tongue-tied. He sat down, feeling a little less out of step that way. This close, he could see that the traveller was even more raggedy than he had first appeared, and thinner. His face seemed all sharp cheekbones and eyes, his hands all bone and sinew. His clothes were patched and rent everywhere and his skin was ingrained with dirt, his hands green-grey, his nails crescents of black. And he smelled – a mixed odour of old sweat and leather and wood-smoke and wet. He looked worn and most, most weary.

Where had he come from? Pawli wondered. And what was he doing wandering the world alone like this, carrying his queer, wrapped pole, with only a little bag over his shoulder? Was it disaster that had sent him off? Or wanderlust? And how had he got that missing finger?

'You . . . you've come a long ways, then?' Pawli asked, needing to say something.

The traveller nodded.

'From the . . . Lowlands?'

The traveller nodded again. 'You might say. By the long route, though.'

Pawli looked at him quizzically.

'No matter.' The traveller let out a long breath. 'I've been a . . .' He coughed, cleared his throat, reached out and took another swig of water, as if talking were an unaccustomed task for him. 'I've been a wearisome long ways this day. I'll tell you frankly, friend, it's been two days since I last had a proper meal. I'm tired and I'm hungry, not to mention wet and chilled. My leg aches, and I'd relish a soft, dryish place to lay my head this night. I'll pay my way in whatever manner I can. Is there some place not too far from here?'

'You can come back with me,' Pawli said.

The words were out almost before he knew it. Bryn would not like it, Pawli knew. Bryn hated unannounced visitors. Pawli smiled to himself. Tough for Bryn.

Pawli found himself feeling an instinctive sympathy for this traveller. Whether it were chance or no, meeting him here was somehow like meeting a sort of other version of himself that had been conjured up. And though he had not envisioned far-travelling to be like this, it was the natural

31

way of the world, was it not? A body grew tired, hungry, sore and lonely. This traveller might indeed be any sort of fellow – thief, murderer, anything at all – but, somehow, Pawli could not bring himself to believe such. He felt abruptly, breathtakingly glad that he had not taken the plunge himself and gone off down the Track, for he would have ended just as this lad had, alone and weary and asking aid of strangers on the road.

'Come back with you . . . where?' the traveller asked.

'My uncle has a cabin up the mountain here,' Pawli told him. 'I live with him. Just the two of us. It's closer than Woburn Village, and there's room enough for a third.'

The traveller regarded him silently with his blue, far-seeing eyes for the space of several heartbeats. 'Fair enough, then. I thank you.'

Pawli felt the hairs along the nape of his neck prickling softly. There was something a little uncanny about this traveller. Still . . . The more he thought on it, the better he liked the idea of bringing this stranger back with him. A little company about Bryn's cabin would not at all be a bad thing, someone his own age to share the chores with, to talk with. And this traveller must have a wealth of tales, surely. That must be why he seemed a little strange; he had been witness to strange events. Pawli nodded to himself in satisfaction. Having a stranger about might make Bryn a little less likely to over-indulge himself in his starweed habit. And it would surely make his own return less tense, too, for how could he and Bryn resurrect their dispute in the company of this stranger? Besides, it felt . . . *right*, somehow, as if this were what he was *supposed* to do – though why exactly he should feel that he did not know.

'Come,' Pawli said, standing up. 'It's a fair walk, and mostly upslope, but we ought to be able to make it by sunfall if we press.' He stretched a hand out to the traveller to help him up off the ground at the path's verge, where he still sat.

For a moment, the traveller hesitated, then reached up and took the proffered hand. 'Thank you,' he said.

Pawli smiled. 'Name's Pawli.'

The traveller nodded. 'Mine's Roe.'

'Roe? That's a queer-sounding name.'

'No queerer than Pawli.'

They regarded each other in silence for a long moment, then broke into smiles.

'This way,' Pawli said, gesturing up through the pines. Roe nodded, settling his water flask and rucksack, and shouldering the burlap-wrapped whatever it was that he carried.

'What *is* that?' Pawli asked, pointing at the arm-long thing in its rough wrapping.

Roe shrugged. 'Just a thing I carry.'

Pawli regarded him quizzically, then shrugged in return. There would be time enough later to get to the bottom of such – and to hear the stories of this lad's travels. Pawli's heart beat a little quicker as he thought on it. 'Come, then.'

Roe nodded.

Pawli at the fore, they headed off together away from the Keel Track and up into the pines.

IV

It was long past sunfall by the time they finally reached the cabin and both Pawli and Roe were staggering by then. The sky was swimming with stars and the air had a high-slope night-chill to it. Up the last stretch they toiled, panting. Ahead, the cabin showed as a dark bulk, with not a light to be seen.

Seeing the place before him so black and silent, Pawli felt his beating heart falter. He had been anticipating this return, seen it all in his mind: Bryn pacing, framed by light flooding out from the cabin door, staring down the mountainside anxiously, his face lighting with relief when he finally saw Pawli returning. But what if Bryn had gone out searching and got lost or hurt? Or what if – the thought made Pawli's belly curdle – what if Khurdis Blackeye had come back in his absence and . . . *done* something to Bryn?

Pawli hurried ahead, hearing Roe struggle to keep up behind. Rushing onwards, he yanked desperately on the door and . . .

. . . smelled the sharp odour of starweed. A single candle glimmered. There, sprawled on his usual spot on the hard-packed dirt floor, was Bryn.

'Bryn!' Pawli snapped in exasperation.

'Is he . . . all right?' Roe asked uncertainly, coming to stand next to Pawli in the doorway.

'All right as he ever is,' Pawli responded acidly. He lifted the oil lantern from its hook by the door and lit it with one of Bryn's little white-fire sticks. It was warm in the cabin, after the chill of the night-air, and Pawli was all too aware that it smelled – a musty-dirty odour of stale starweed smoke and unwashed dishware and mouldering old clothes. With the softly hissing lantern in his hand, he stared at his uncle morosely. So much for Bryn showing any concern over his whereabouts. It might have been *him* who had been hurt or lost. But did Bryn care? Small chance of that! All that mattered to Bryn was his precious starweed.

'Come on,' Pawli said, gesturing Roe inside the cabin. 'I'll get us something to eat.'

Roe hesitated, staring at Bryn's still form.

'Don't worry about him,' Pawli said irritably. 'He certainly isn't going to worry about us!'

Roe blinked.

'I'm sure you've seen stranger things,' Pawli said, 'in your travels.'

Roe said nothing.

Suddenly, Pawli felt painfully self-conscious. What must this far-traveller think? The cabin's air was rank in the nose. In the lantern's light, it seemed a hovel. 'Come,' he repeated gruffly. 'There's food, at least.'

Hanging the lantern from a beam-hook, he took the last of their good yellow cheese from the small larder and the heel of the loaf of bread he had baked the day before. There was also this morning's three eggs. Bryn had touched nothing all day. 'Fried eggs with bread and cheese?' he asked of Roe.

Roe nodded, glancing about.

'It's not much,' Pawli said deprecatingly. 'And with my uncle like . . . like he is most of the time, it's hard to keep things in proper shape.'

'I've seen worse,' Roe said. He put down his wrapped stick, shrugged the rucksack off and leaned against the cabin wall tiredly, massaging his leg with one hand.

Pawli looked at him, uncertain. But there seemed no edge in what he had said. No doubt he *had* seen worse.

The fire was cold in the grate, and it took Pawli some

little time to get it going. But things went quick enough with Roe bringing wood in from the pile outside, and soon the eggs were spluttering away happily in hot drippings-fat in the old iron pan. Cutting a couple of thick slices of bread – which left only the crust for the morning, but he did not care – Pawli set them to frying in the fat next to the eggs. He looked across at Roe and grinned. Roe smiled back, a quick flash of white teeth in the firelight. It felt good to have somebody his own age to share the chores with.

'Here,' Pawli said, sliding two of the three eggs onto Roe's plate. Roe made to protest, but Pawli insisted. 'You've travelled a far ways more than me this day, I reckon, and need it more.'

Roe shrugged, smiled, nodded his thanks.

Pawli dished out the fried bread and rough slices of the cheese, and the two of them sat companionably together next to the snappling fire's warmth, plates on their knees, spooning up egg and cheese on the crispy-hot pieces of fried bread.

'Delicious,' Roe said in mid-chew.

Pawli nodded, happy.

'Who's this, then?' a voice suddenly demanded. Bryn came stiffly over. 'I thought at first I was seeing things, with two of you at the fire and all . . .'

'This is Roe,' Pawli said. Then, 'He's staying for a while.'

'*Is* he, now?' Bryn replied. He looked none too pleased.

'He is.'

Roe said not a word, merely looked from one to the other. Reaching a hand out, he slid his wrapped stick closer.

Pawli felt a little shiver of unease go through him. Roe was a rough-looking sort, there was no denying it. He had doffed his leather cap. His hair was longer than Pawli had thought, and all tangled with twigs and travel-grime. He looked like he had not washed in a month, and Pawli could smell him, the same odour of old sweat and leather and wood-smoke and wet he had noticed on first meeting Roe on the Keel Track, but stronger in the confines of the cabin.

Bryn rubbed his eyes, ran a hand across his cheek. In the silence that held between them, Pawli heard the soft *rassp* of his fingers against the greying stubble there. Bryn let out a long breath, swallowed, then gestured at what they were eating. 'Is there more of that?'

'There's only enough for two,' Pawli said sharply. 'I tried to wake you, but you were dead to the world.'

'Here,' Roe said. Breaking his piece of fried bread in half and balancing the third egg on it, he held it out with his missing-finger hand.

Bryn took the offering. 'Right generous of you.'

Roe nodded.

Reaching across to Pawli's plate, Bryn filched a slice of cheese.

'Hey!' Pawli snapped, glowering.

'Where'd Pawli here dig you up, then?' Bryn asked Roe through a full mouth.

'I found him on the Keel Track,' Pawli answered. 'He's a traveller.'

'Is that so?' Bryn swallowed the last of his food, wiped his fingers on his shirt – which hung out of his trousers loosely – and set himself down in his rocker. 'Just wandering about the world then, are you?' he asked Roe.

Roe nodded.

'Ah . . .' Bryn said. Rocking slowly, he regarded Roe with one eye, his head titled to the side, as if he were a bird examining something questionable. 'There's more to you than my nephew here thinks, I'd reckon.'

Roe said nothing.

'He was just walking up the Track,' Pawli put in, 'as I was coming down to it.'

Bryn turned his gaze to Pawli. 'You travelled a fair ways yourself today, then, to get that far, didn't you? Nothing like a fit of the black temper to lighten a man's feet.'

Pawli frowned, bit his lip.

'And bringing home strays, too,' Bryn went on, shaking his head. 'The sort of thoughtless-kind thing your mother used to do, that.'

Pawli said nothing and, for long heartbeats, they sat in hard silence.

Then Bryn sighed wearily. 'Too late to argue now, isn't it, Pawli my lad? Don't know about you, but I reckon I've about had enough of argument for one day. Sleep, I'd say, is what we need. We'll all be fresher in the morning.' He looked at Roe. 'We can sort out what needs sorting then.'

Without another word, he got stiffly to his feet and shambled over to his bunk. Wrapping himself roughly in a blanket, he turned his back to them and went promptly to sleep.

Roe looked to Pawli.

'Don't ask!' Pawli snapped.

After a moment, Roe said, 'I reckon he's right, though. Maybe sleep is a good idea.'

'I suppose so,' Pawli agreed. 'We've spare blankets. There's only the two bunks, but you can stretch out anywhere on the floor you've a mind to.

Roe nodded. 'I've slept in rougher places.'

'I imagine you have,' Pawli said, and, for an instant, felt another shiver of unease go through him. Roe sat there with his legs stretched out before him, the burlapped stick on the floor at his side, comfortable, it seemed, in what must be entirely strange surroundings.

Who *was* this traveller he had so easily – so trustingly – brought into the cabin? There were bandits in the wild – everybody knew that – homeless men, desperate men. Bryn had not exactly been welcoming. And Bryn could . . . *see* into things. What had he seen in Roe? Had he, Pawli, made a terrible mistake and brought some poisonous serpent into their home?

But no. Surely not. Roe was just a footloose lad, grimed by hard travel and made a touch strange by the strange things he had witnessed, and with some hidden secrets, perhaps. But having secrets was no crime; nor was being dirty. And he was no threat, surely . . .

What strange things *had* Roe witnessed? With the food done now and Bryn gone to sleep, Pawli would dearly have liked to linger to hear a story or two. There was that odd wrapped stick of Roe's, his bad leg and the missing finger . . . But it was late. Roe looked exhausted. And he too was bone-tired, truth to tell. His knees ached from the weary uphill climb getting back here, and Roe kept rubbing at his right leg where it pained him.

Tomorrow, then . . . And Bryn ought to be better in the morning, too, after a good sleep – so long as he did not rise in the middle of the night and start smoking, as he had done last night.

'Time for sleep, then,' Pawli said.

Roe nodded.

He did a lot of nodding, this Roe, Pawli thought. Not much of a talker, it seemed. Pawli got up, gathered up one of their spare blankets from the back shelf, handed it to Roe, who nodded (again) a silent thanks. Pawli felt awkward. He wanted to say something, but he did not know quite what.

It got lonesome, living all alone up here on the high slopes with Bryn. Perhaps Roe, weary and road-worn as he was, would welcome a place to settle in for a while. Perhaps Roe, too, might feel the need of a friend.

Roe had settled himself in the corner away from the fire near the cabin's entranceway, wrapping the blanket about himself.

Pawli opened his mouth, took a breath. 'Do you . . . need anything?'

Roe shook his head.

'Bryn has some salve, if you want – for your leg.'

'No. Thanks. It's . . . just an old hurt. Not normally this bad. I got it chilled in the rain today, is all.'

Pawli wanted to say more, but all he could think of, finally, was, 'Well . . . good night, then.'

Roe nodded.

Pawli turned, dowsed the lantern – Bryn's lone candle had long since burnt itself out – and crawled into his bed. Taking his boots and day-clothing off, he shrugged into his night-shirt and under the blanket. Bryn was snoring softly, like some animal muttering and grumbling to itself. He could hear nothing from Roe. Pawli lay stiffly, his mind spinning with the day's events, convinced that he would, in fact, never be able to fall into sleep, no matter how achy-weary he might be.

But despite all his mind's whirl, gradually, like sliding down a long, smooth slope, he slipped inescapably into slumber's dark.

Until, out of nowhere, somebody was hammering: *kerwham wham wham! KERWHAM!* Enough racket, it seemed, to make his teeth rattle.

Pawli came up out of sleep as if out of a dark-deep lake, wrenched from a dream about a great mountain cat with ice-blue eyes, like Roe's eyes – entirely human and knowing eyes, and the strangest of sights in the face of a wild beast. It had been an ordinary dream, and no *sending*, but queerly disturbing for all that. His limbs trembled with the remembrance of it.

And now there was this *wham kerwham* hammering.

'What is it?' he demanded with groggy irritation. There was faint, pre-dawn light filtering in through the semi-shuttered windows. 'Bryn?'

But it had nothing to do with Bryn. For an instant, Pawli thought that Roe had somehow brought them harm. His heart lurched. But Roe was a blanket-tangled, startled form on the floor.

Wham! Wham!

Kerwham!

Bryn looked across at Pawli from his bunk, rubbed his eyes blearily, shook his head. 'Go see! It's somebody at the door.'

'At the *door*?' Pawli said. 'Who'd be hammering at our door *this* early?'

'Go see!' Bryn repeated.

Wearing only his ragged night-shirt, Pawli stumbled to the door and unlatched it. Three figures came spilling in. 'Master Brynmaur!' one of them cried. 'You've got to come quick!'

From his tangled bed, Bryn only stared at them.

They were from Woburn Village. Pawli recognised them: Stroud the Smith, his son Kerry, and Manis Mallow. They were ragged and gasping, and Kerry was bleeding all across one side of his face.

'What's happened?' Pawli demanded.

The three men stared at him, their eyes wide and white in the dim, pre-dawn glow that came in through the doorway. There was such a raw bleakness etched upon their faces that Pawli felt it like a blow to the belly.

'What's *happened*?' he repeated.

They surged forwards towards Bryn, who sat hunched on the edge of his rumpled bed, elbowing each other confusedly aside to get to him, all three gabbling at once so that it was impossible to make any clear sense of what they were trying to say. In the confusion, Kerry, the hurt one, let out a little cry and collapsed, white-faced and gasping and bleeding all over the floor.

'Enough!' Bryn shouted. He levered himself from his bed and rushed to the downed man's side, stumbling awkwardly in his haste.

Poor Kerry had a long, ugly-looking gash running from his cheek-bone back across the left side of his head, leaving his ear split into bloody halves. Pawli felt his belly heave, looking at it. Blood welled up along the length of the wound; the whole of the man's shoulder and chest was soggy with it.

Kneeling, Bryn took Kerry's bloodied face in his hands.

'It was too much for him, humping it all the way up here

41

from the village,' Stroud the Smith said. He was a big man, older than Bryn, with a round, protruding belly and arms like tree-trunks from his years at the village forge. He had a short ruff of grey hair and a thick, grizzle-grey moustache which he sucked between his teeth. 'I *told* him he oughtn't to come along, but he wouldn't—'

Bryn motioned him to silence. He was looking into Kerry's eyes, as if searching for something there. Kerry moaned again, his face haggard and white as new bone.

'Can you heal my son?' Stroud asked, hoarse-voiced.

Laying Kerry's head back down upon the floor, Bryn looked about desperately, like a man suddenly lost.

'Can you heal him?'

Kerry groaned. Bryn opened his mouth, closed it, shook himself. 'Water,' he said. 'I need water.'

Pawli snatched up a bucket, rushed out to the rain barrel, came back with the bucket sloshingly full.

Bryn shook back the sleeves of his shirt, lifted his grimy, blood-slicked hands, and dunked them in the water. 'Soap!' he called, gesturing with his chin.

Pawli handed him a cake of the raw lye soap they sometimes used on their clothes.

Bryn soap-scrubbed his hands vigorously, dunked them, scrubbed them again, dunked them a final time, flicked the water off his fingers. All the awkwardness had gone from him now.

'Is there any . . .' Stroud started, but his words dwindled.

About Bryn's hands, a faint, softly-pulsing, bluish radiance had started to grow. Kneeling close, he placed the tip of his left index finger upon the leading point of the wet slit of the wound where it scored Kerry's cheek, showing a little white slice of bone. Next, he put his right index finger on the back end of the wound behind Kerry's split ear, aligning his thumbs so that they pointed across at each other. He began chanting in a voice so breathy and low it could barely be heard.

42

A faint blue aurora seemed to highlight the still-bleeding cut, sluicing softly between Bryn's carefully placed index fingers. Kerry let out a long, soft sigh. Gradually, the welling up of blood ceased.

Bryn stopped his chanting and went immobile. Then, with a slow, careful intensity, he slid the thumb and index finger of his left hand along the glistening pucker of the wound, pinching it together gently. The radiance about his fingers flared. The gapped halves of the slash, where he pressed them, stayed sealed, as if glued. The severed leaves of the ear slid back together like the pieces of a simple puzzle.

When it was done, Kerry lay on his back, pale-faced still, but breathing quietly. The wound was now a puckered, red-pink scar, with here and there a drop or two of blood glistening. Bryn looked down and nodded in satisfaction. Then he fell over backwards, gasping, white-faced, nearly, as Kerry had been.

'Bryn!' Pawli cried.

Bryn motioned at him with one shaky hand. 'Water . . .'

Pawli fetched a dipper-full from the rain barrel and fed it to him.

'More?' he asked when Bryn had done, for most of it had spilled down across Bryn's beard, soaking him.

But Bryn shook his head and sat up shakily. 'I just need a few moments to recover myself, is all. It's been too long since I . . . since I did anything of this sort.'

Pawli was staring at him. They all were. It was true healing they had witnessed here. Pawli had never seen anything like it, had *certainly* never seen Bryn do anything of the sort.

Stroud knelt next to his son. He reached a hesitant hand to the now-closed wound, drew it back.

Kerry sighed, shivered, opened his eyes suddenly. 'Wha . . . what are you all staring at?' he demanded.

There was a long moment of frozen silence, and then somebody laughed, relieved. They all did.

Kerry felt with an uncertain hand at the puckered scar of his wound. 'What's *happened* to me?'

'Master Brynmaur here has *healed* you, lad.' Stroud said.

'What have you lot been up to?' Bryn demanded. He levered himself to his feet, staggered over to his rumpled bed, sat down heavily. 'Who did this to Kerry?'

'It was a sword-thrust,' Manis Mallow started.

Stroud the Smith cut him off. 'They came just as day was ending. Must have been nigh a score of them. Nasty, dirty fellows they were, too. And all armed. And their leader . . . he tells us we all owe him liege-right, and that, from now on, we have to pay him a tithe. Or he'll fire the village fields.'

'Now I ask you!' Manis Mallow exclaimed. A little man, Manis was almost entirely bald, with a pointy face like a rodent's. His left foot was missing three toes, Pawli recalled, the result of an accident with an axe – which Bryn had repaired as best could be some years back. 'Where's the sense in them firing the fields? How's he ever going to expect to get any tithe from us then? The fellow's barking mad!'

'Who?' Bryn demanded. 'Who are you talking about?'

'Bandits,' Kerry, said, getting unsteadily to his feet. He was as tall as his father, almost, but all bone and sinew.

'They'd fired some of the village houses. I . . . I and Frandy and Gussett tried to stop them from burning old man Tine's cottage.' He let out a long, ragged breath. 'Frandy and I got off lucky. Poor Gusset took an arrow through the ribs.'

Pawli did not know what to say. It all sounded so unlikely. Why would bandits attempt such a thing? Woburn Village was not the sort of place to attract such nasty doings, perched as it was way up in the high country. Two or three days' walk away, and there was hardly a soul who even knew where it was.

Bryn sat perched on the edge of his bed, running a hand

through his tangled hair. 'All this happened yesterday, you say?'

'They came just before sunrise,' Manis Mallow answered. 'I was out seeing to the High Field, making sure the young shoots there was all right. Next thing I know, this band of nasty-looking ruffians appears out of the morning mist like so many angry ghosts, waving iron blades at me and making threats.' Manis shuddered. 'Near made me shit myself, I can tell you.'

Pawli felt an uneasy tremble in his guts. These marauding bandits had appeared at exactly the moment he had been out near the forest verge, when Khurdis Blackeye had appeared.

'You've got to help us,' Stroud demanded of Bryn.

Bryn looked at them, silent.

Pawli felt his belly clench up. Bryn could not even help himself much these days. He might have shown a sudden and unexpected virtuosity in the healing he had just accomplished, but that did not mean he had the wherewithal to face up to a gang of violent ruffians such as the Woburners had described. 'What about Khurdis Blackeye?' Pawli suggested, for Khurdis seemed to him the righter man for a dangerous task such as this. 'Can't *he* come to your aid? He could face down these bandits easily enough. Bryn here isn't—'

'Master Blackeye's a tricky weasel of a man,' Manis Mallow cut in, 'and never does anything save for a too-much fee.'

'And no easy person to find, in any case,' Stroud added, 'hidden away up in the heights in that Vale of his. Ghost Vale, folk call it. Those seeking him there can wander for days, lost and confused. We'd never get to him in time.'

'It's Master Brynmaur here who must help us now,' Kerry announced. 'He has *power* enough. We've all witnessed that.' Manis Mallow and Kerry's father nodded vigorous agreement. The three of them turned to Bryn expectantly.

Bryn sighed. 'And just what is it that you wish me to do, then?'

'Drive these ruffians away!' Manis Mallow said, fairly hopping in his eagerness. 'Send them packing, with their tails between their legs.'

'Oh aye?' Bryn responded dryly.

'You're a man of *power*, Master Brynmaur,' Stroud said, 'for all that you . . .' He paused self-consciously, then went on in a rush, 'for all that things may not have worked so well for you in your life. But the *power* does not desert a man – as we've all seen here this morn.'

'We . . . we wasted most all of yesterday dithering,' Manis Mallow said, 'those of us who had managed to get away from the village . . .'

'And it took the whole of the night through to walk here to you,' Stroud finished. 'Our need is desperate, Master Brynmaur. Time's against us and there's none other we can turn to. You must come to our aid. You *must*!'

Bryn sat hunched in on himself, looking very much like he wanted to crawl back into his bed. The three villagers regarded him anxiously. He laughed, a brittle little rustle of sound, and levered himself woodenly to his feet. 'Very well, then. I will do what I can to help.'

The Woburners let out a collective breath of relief. But Pawli felt none of their confidence. Bryn looked too shaky. Pawli watched him stretch, blink, comb his fingers ineffectively through his hopelessly snarled hair. He looked stiff and uncertain in his movements, and there were pouchy-dark smudges under his eyes. Pawli saw him glance down at his paraphernalia where it lay on the floor next to the tangled blanket he always wrapped himself in when letting the starweed take him.

But Bryn drew himself away and went rummaging about for his boots. He had slept in his clothes, so there was nothing else for him to do once he had put his boots on save to take down the worn leather jacket he wore when going outside. With that in hand, he looked across at

46

the villagers who were clustered near the doorway, shifting agitatedly about. 'Let's be off, then,' he said. 'It's a fairish ways down to Woburn.'

'At least it'll be downslope this time,' Manis Mallow said. 'Fair beat the breath right out me, that uphill clamber in the dark.' The others were nodding. They looked a sore and weary group.

'You stay on here,' Stroud told his son. 'That head-wound of yours . . .'

Kerry shook his head. 'I'm coming with you.'

'Now you listen to me, my lad,' his father started. 'The climb up here nearly did for you.'

Kerry's face was set intractably. 'I'm coming, and that's that!'

Stroud chewed on his moustache. 'All right,' he conceded grudgingly. 'Come if you must. You'd just follow along behind us, if I know you, despite anything I said. You always did have too much will and too little brain!'

'Here,' Bryn said, holding up a small haunch of smoked lamb that had been hanging all season.

Pawli almost protested – they had been saving that haunch for their Solstice Feast. But he kept his mouth shut.

'Get some of this into you,' Bryn told the villagers. 'You look like you need the strength.' He pointed at Kerry. 'You especially, if you insist on going along.'

The Woburners made their gratitude clear in a profusion of bows and murmured thanks – and began demolishing the lamb.

Bryn looked at Pawli soberly. 'Mind the cabin,' he said. That was all. Then he turned and walked out. The Woburners spilled out after him, still chewing.

Pawli stared, speechless at such betrayal. Kerry was no more than a couple of years his elder. He grabbed up his leather breeches, struggled hastily into them, jammed his boots on, grabbed his jerkin from its hook and rushed after.

The sky was just lightening in the east over the peaks, and the air was chill. He shivered, pulled on his jerkin and hurried on, skidding on the dew-soaked turf and nearly going down. 'Bryn!' he called, for Bryn and the rest were already some considerable ways ahead, half-submerged, it seemed, by the slope of the hill, the scattered dwarf birch, the knee-high grass.

'Where do you think you're going?' Bryn demanded as Pawli caught up.

'With you.'

'No.'

Pawli bit his lip. 'I'm coming, Bryn.'

'No, you're not. It'll be dangerous.'

'All the more reason for me to come,' Pawli insisted. 'You might need my help.'

'Master Brynmaur,' Stroud called back, for the villagers had pulled ahead. 'Come along.'

'I'm coming with you,' Pawli insisted. 'If you won't let me walk with you, I'll follow behind. And there's nothing you can do to stop me.'

Bryn sighed. 'You're being stupid, Pawli.'

Pawli kept silent.

'Master Brynmaur?' The Woburners beckoned.

Bryn hesitated, shifting uncomfortably from foot to foot. 'Oh, very well,' he conceded grudgingly. 'Let's be off.' Turning, he looked beyond Pawli – and stopped. Roe was striding up out of the cabin, his leather cap back on his head, rucksack slung across one shoulder, the burlap-wrapped stick balanced across the other. What with the commotion about the bandits and all, they had quite forgotten about the traveller, who had stayed most dis-creetly in the background all this while.

'On your way, then, are you?' Bryn said.

Pawli felt a sudden stab of bleak disappointment. There had been no agreement about Roe staying, but he had not thought to see the boy leave so soon . . . and certainly not to abandon them like this, just when it seemed they were in real need of any help they could get.

'Fare you well,' Bryn said.

But to Pawli's pleased surprise, Roe shook his head. 'I'm coming with you.'

'No,' Bryn said. 'This is no concern of yours.'

'Perhaps. Perhaps not. But I think you may need my help.'

'And just what might that help be?' Bryn asked.

'I have had experience with matters such as this.'

Pawli blinked. It was not the answer he had expected from Roe.

'Oh, yes?' Bryn regarded Roe measuringly.

Roe looked him straight back.

'Very well, then,' Bryn said after a moment. 'Come along if you will.' He scratched at his beard. 'All this forms a pattern, perhaps.'

Pawli was pleased with Roe's coming, but he felt a little thrust of unease at the idea of some hidden pattern forming here. What subtle significances might Bryn be seeing? The aftertaste of Pawli's *sending* dream was still strong enough in him to make him feel a little raw, and not for the first time did he curse his own groping blindness about such matters. And the quickness with which Bryn had accepted Roe rankled. Roe was no bigger than he, not very much older, no more likely to be of use in a fight, if it came to that.

'Hoi!' somebody shouted suddenly. The three Woburners came up in a cluster.

'Who's *this*, then?' Manis Mallow demanded suspiciously.

'A far-traveller I met on the Keel Track yesterday,' Pawli replied. In their haste, and preoccupied as they were with their own disasters, the Woburners must have missed Roe in the dimness of the cabin.

'Oh, aye?' Stroud said.

'Scruffy as one of them bandits, he is,' Kerry put in. He glared at Roe. 'Where you from, boy? You one of *them*, now?'

Roe said nothing.

'I'm talking to you, boy!' Kerry snapped. He stepped closer to Roe, his fists clenched. 'You one of them cursed bandit scum, then? Come sneaking round here to spy out the land for them?' Kerry was a full head and shoulders taller than Roe, and considerably more heavy. He pushed forwards pugnaciously, his face white and clenched under the puckered gash that marred it.

Roe stood his ground. He gripped his burlapped-wrapped stick a little tighter perhaps, but Pawli could see no sign of any real fear in him.

Kerry hesitated.

'Leave him be, Kerry,' Pawli said. 'He's no bandit.'

Kerry turned. 'Oh no? How would you know?'

'He's not,' Pawli insisted. But there was a little cold shiver of sudden doubt in him. How *would* he know? Roe could be anything.

'He's a stranger you just met on the road,' Stroud said, coming to stand at his son's side. 'You said so yourself, Pawli. Kerry here's got the right of it, I'd say. This skanky boy comes sneaking around . . . Sheerest *coincidence* is it, then, that he's up here poking his nose into other people's business just as this mob of ruffians shows up to plague us?'

Pawli looked across at Roe, who stood facing the villagers, his wrapped stick held before him in both hands. Roe a bandit? No. He could not – *would* not – believe them. If there was any pattern here, surely it was not that. He stepped forward and stood by Roe's side against them. 'You're wrong! Roe's no bandit.'

'He sure enough looks like one to me,' Manis Mallow said.

'Enough of this,' Bryn began. 'This lad's no . . .'

But the Woburners would not hear.

'I say we take him now,' Kerry rasped, scowling at Roe. 'Then there'd be one less of the bastards to deal with later.'

'Step aside, Pawli,' Stroud said.

Pawli stood where he was.

'Don't be stupid, Pawli,' Manis Mallow snapped. 'Would you side with one of *them* against us?'

'Step away, Pawli,' Kerry hissed. 'Or—'

'Leave be!' Bryn commanded sharply.

Pawli blinked. It had been long and long since he had heard a snap like that in Bryn's voice.

The Woburners froze.

'Roe here is not one of your bandits,' Bryn said.

'How can you know?' Manis Mallow demanded. 'I say we—'

'I *know*.' Bryn said, cutting him short.

The villagers regarded him, uncertain.

'I am no bandit,' Roe insisted, quiet-voiced.

'And we're just supposed to take you at your word, then, are we?' Manis Mallow said scathingly.

'I believe him,' Pawli said.

'He is no bandit,' Bryn repeated.

'How can you be certain?' Manis Mallow demanded. 'Can you . . . can you *see* into his heart or some such, then?'

Bryn shook his head. 'No. But I would know if he were some bandit dissembler sent amongst us to spy things out.'

'For certain sure?' Stroud said.

Bryn nodded. 'About that, yes.'

Pawli felt a little thrill, seeing Bryn like this. He was acting the man of *power* after all, seeing into the hidden ways of the world. He glanced at Roe who, for all he was no big man, stood facing the menace of the Woburners unshaken. Pawli felt his heart beat a little faster. It was good company he was in.

'Roe's coming along to *help*,' Pawli said to the villagers. 'Don't be such ingrates! He and I, and my uncle. We're all here to help you.'

'Why would you, a complete stranger, want to help us?' Manis Mallow demanded suspiciously of Roe.

Roe shrugged. 'I have had . . . dealings with men like these bandits you describe. I may be able to aid you.'

51

'And do what?' Stroud demanded. 'You're just a whip of a lad. My Kerry here tops you by a head, and he couldn't do nothing against them.'

Roe shrugged. 'I am not . . . helpless.'

'But why would you *wish* to aid us?' Manis Mallow insisted. 'You being a foreigner and all.'

Roe shrugged again.

'Time's wasting,' Stroud said. 'If Master Brynmaur here vouches for him, that's good enough for me, I reckon. We've more pressing concerns than this lad. Day's upon us already, and we've a long ways yet to go to get back to Woburn. Let's get along.'

Kerry still glared at Roe in deep suspicion. 'I don't like this. There's something . . .'

Stroud put a beefy hand on his son's arm. 'Let's get along, I say. We're wasting time arguing up here.' He looked at Bryn. 'Master Brynmaur?'

Bryn nodded. 'Let's get along, by all means.'

Together, they all set off towards Woburn Village.

V

As they tramped along, Pawli felt himself brimming with unanswered, uneasy questions.

What would they find in Woburn? Who were these bandits who had so suddenly appeared out of nowhere? Where had they come from? And why had they chosen Woburn Village, of all places, to maraud? And what of Roe? Where was *he* from? And what had he been doing in the past to have confronted men such as these Woburn bandits?

It was all most unsettling. Life went along uneventfully for years, and then, in one abrupt day, there came his *sending* dream of the intruding Other, Khurdis Blackeye, Roe the far-traveller, violent bandits, all piled one atop the other. The world was shifting about him; he could feel it in the pit of his belly, as if he had stepped over the crest of some steep slope and was now beginning to slide irreversibly downwards, picking up momentum. And everything, somehow, was woven together with his feeling of some dire thing aborning. He wished he understood more and cursed again his own ignorance.

But he had no chance at answers. The three Woburners were grim-faced and silent as they plodded along, and Roe was his usual quiet self. Bryn kept his own counsel – whatever that might be.

Pawli caught the villagers sneaking uncertain glances at Bryn as they made their way through the forest. He might have spoken with authority back by the cabin, but now he was far from confidence-inspiring; he puffed and gasped and had to stop every little while to recover his wind. Pawli could not help but share the Woburners' unease. If the simple trip down to Woburn took so much out of him, whatever was he going to be able to do about the bandits?

But Bryn had hidden strengths. Pawli was convinced of it. His healing of Kerry and decisive intervention over Roe had proven that, had it not? Bryn's strengths were just not strengths of the body, that was all. There was surely nothing to worry unduly about.

On they went, downwards and cross-slope, moving as fast as they could, until, well into the afternoon, they finally drew nigh to Woburn Village. They were following a winding hunters' track through the maze of the high-slope pines. As it crested a ridge of blue rock, Pawli could see streamers of smoke below.

'They've fired Bathy's house,' Stroud said, stopping.

'Shit-eating bastards,' Manis Mallow grunted.

They did not yet have a clear view of the village, and Pawli could not tell which house might be which from up here, but he had no doubt the villagers were right. 'But why?' he demanded, outraged.

Bryn said nothing. He was gasping, bent over, hands on his thighs, head down.

Manis Mallow peered about. 'There's been no sign of the others that escaped the village. Where'd they get to, do you think?'

'Fled away entirely or taken, most like,' Stroud said. He turned to Bryn. 'What do we do now?'

Bryn was leaning against a tree bole, pale-faced and panting still.

'What do we do?' Stroud repeated.

Bryn took a breath, shrugged. 'We will do what we must.'

'But . . .'

'Enough.' Bryn pushed himself off from the tree. 'Let's get along now.'

So downwards they continued, till they came through

54

the trees into the clearing in which Woburn was set. There were some half-score or so houses layered across the slope, log-walled, with roofs of yellow-green sod, some set so sharply into the inclined ground that their back walls were half-buried. The two nearest were little more than shattered, smouldering ruins, charred log-ends sticking out like blackened bones.

At the other end of the village, they heard shouting. Blinking in the sunshine after the dimness of the pines, they hurried on. The air was thick here with the scent of burning, and it caught in Pawli's lungs, making him retch. Past the houses they hastened to the village's far side.

At first it was hard to make out exactly what was happening. Folk were gathered in a ragged crowd. Somebody was saying, '. . . you can't – can't expect just to walk off with everything . . . *everything* we've stored. What will we do till the crops come?' Somebody else wailed, 'It isn't *fair!*'

Drawing closer, Pawli began to make things out more clearly. The villagers were all clustered together, like a flock of agitated fowl, facing a smallish group of men – perhaps a couple of dozen or so. They were a rough-looking lot, those men, no doubt of it, dressed in leathers from head to foot, patched and stained, and all were armed. Several had longbows, one an ancient and ugly-looking crossbow. All had knives or axes or blades of some sort.

At the fore of this group stood a short, barrel-chested man with a long beard plaited into two forks. He was dressed in the same rough fashion as the rest, but a broadsword hung from a scabbard at his waist. Pawli stared. It was the first true sword he had ever seen. They were most costly things, and scarce. Where had this hill bandit got such a precious thing? Whom had he stabbed in the back and stolen it from, more likely?

'You,' the man was ordering the villagers, 'will do as you're told, or more of your houses will be burnt.'

'But that's completely *crazy*!' somebody cried. Pawli recognised the voice as old Tomae's – Head of the village. 'You say you want to collect a tithe from us,' Tomae went on, 'and then you destroy our houses and make off with our bearing ewes and our seed grain. How can you expect us to supply you with anything if you take away our means of livelihood? Do you not know the story of the duck who laid the silver eggs? You're mad, man! Utterly *mad*!'

'And you,' the man with the forked beard replied, 'will watch your mouth.'

'Or what?' Tomae returned in exasperation. 'Will you start killing us? Kill us all and see how easy it will be to tithe us then!'

'I grow tired of this, old man,' fork-beard replied.

'It's *you* who—' Tomae began.

The bandit leader lunged forwards, scattering villagers before him, and grabbed old Tomae. He was only shoulder-height to Tomae, but his arms and shoulders were thick as Tomae's thighs. He flung the old man to the ground and kicked him in the belly, hard. Tomae howled. The villagers erupted into shouts and cries.

The man drew his broadsword. It had a long, dully gleaming blade of iron, ground glittering sharp along both edges. The crowd of villagers hushed. Pawli felt the hackles along the back of his neck prickle coldly. It was a fell, deadly-looking thing, that sword, long as a man's out-stretched arm. It could cut a person in two.

'You *will* do as I command,' the fork-bearded bandit said. He raised the iron blade over poor Tomae, who lay clutching his belly, white-faced and cowering. 'You do not know me,' he announced, to Tomae, to the Woburn crowd. 'I am not a man to be crossed. Do you hear? I am Nerys Ironblade. I *will* have what I wish, *everything* that I wish . . . or blood will be spilled. Is that clear?'

The villagers stared.

'Is that *clear*?'

There was not a sound.

Nerys Ironblade placed the sharp tip of his sword against Tomae's sternum. 'And you, old man with the big mouth, lest you think I do not mean what I say . . .'

'Enough!' Bryn cried suddenly.

Fork-bearded Nerys whirled, sword up.

Bryn came forward, Pawli and Roe and the rest behind him.

'And just who are *you*, then?' Nerys Ironblade demanded. Behind him, two of the bandits nocked shafts to their bows.

Pawli felt a shiver of ice go through his belly.

'He is a man of *power*!' Stroud the Smith said from behind Bryn. 'Beware.'

The fork-bearded man stood his ground, but the sword came up a little higher. He stared at Bryn. 'What do you want here?'

'You must stop this,' Bryn said simply.

Nerys Ironblade laughed. 'Just like that? Stop and go home?'

Bryn nodded. 'Aye.'

'Or . . . what?'

Bryn shrugged. 'You must stop.'

The bandit leader stalked towards Bryn, slowly, blade up.

Bryn went to meet him.

Pawli looked on aghast. What did Bryn think he was doing? The man would skewer him like an autumn ram. 'Bryn!' he hissed. But Bryn went on. Where had such a man as this Nerys Ironblade come from? Pawli thought desperately. What had the poor folk of Woburn ever done to bring upon themselves such a calamity as this?

Nerys hefted his broadsword, the iron of it glinting coldly in the sunlight. 'This is a named blade, man,' he told Bryn. 'It came to me through blood and grief. Thorn, it is called. I am not a man who likes to play games.'

'I play no games,' said Bryn.

'Then back away. Or Thorn here will be the ending of you, as it has been the ending of many a man before you.'

Bryn stepped slowly towards him, an unimpressive, tousle-headed figure in rumpled clothes, hands at his sides, utterly defenceless. Pawli felt sick. The bandit leader stood his ground now, feet apart, iron broadsword ready. Almost, Pawli rushed out and tried to yank Bryn bodily away. But such a move might bring complete disaster, for the bandit bowmen still had their arrows nocked and ready, and they were tense as hounds. Pawli felt utterly helpless – and furious. Why must Bryn be so wilfully stupid? Walking empty-handed up to this bandit leader, he did not stand a chance. The starweed would be the end of him after all, addling his mind as it had.

Bryn stood only a few paces from Nerys Ironblade now. The bandit leader stepped forward, closing the gap between them. The sword came up close to Bryn's throat.

'One stroke, man,' Nerys said. 'Only one is all it would take. You are a skinny creature. I could remove your grey head from your shoulders in a breath.'

Bryn said nothing, merely stood as he was.

'Or I could open your belly. Ever seen a man die of a belly wound? I have. It takes days, long, slow, agonising days.' Nerys thrust at Bryn, the sword's tip stopping barely a hand's breadth from Bryn's stomach.

Bryn flinched not at all.

Nerys scowled, drew back, raised his blade.

Pawli surged forwards, stopped, dithered agitatedly. He had to do something. Somebody had to do something!

And then, for no reason Pawli could see, Nerys seemed to falter. For all that he was a ragged and uninspiring figure, Bryn stood solid as any rock, his eyes locked with those of the bandit leader.

Nerys took a step backwards, stopped. 'Don't try any tricks with me, man,' he said, his voice tight. 'I am protected against such as you.' Reaching into his leather jerkin, he produced a little amulet on a chain. 'This has been given me by . . . by one who knows.'

Bryn stayed silent, but his gaze slackened not at all.

'Stop *staring* at me like that!' Nerys snapped.

Bryn said not a word.

The bandit gripped his sword white-knuckle hard. Pawli could see him shiver. There was sweat suddenly glistening on his forehead.

Pawli was astounded. He had never seen Bryn like this, calm and solid as any rock. And . . . *dangerous* seeming.

Bryn and Nerys stood facing each other, poised. Pawli had no idea at all as to which way things might go. He held his breath, fists clenched . . .

And then, abruptly, there came a commotion from the verge of the forest rimming the village. Pawli whirled, saw the bandits there part hurriedly.

And who should come striding out from the trees but Khurdis Blackeye himself, looking tall and regal and immaculate as ever. He wore velvet breeches the colour of blood, a royal blue tunic, and a long, black cloak, all interwoven with the same glinting gilt stitching Pawli had seen the day before. On his head, Khurdis now wore a small, brimless hat made of incredibly complex embroidery, all green and gold and crimson. His long black hair was tied in a single queue down his back, interlaced with gold and silver wire. Compared to those about him, he shone.

Having come a dozen paces or so out of the forest's shadow, he stood silently, arms folded across his breast, regarding them all.

From the tree-shadow behind him, a great mountain cat came stepping, its fur golden, flecked with dark patterns. It was a large animal, long and sleek, its back coming quite up to Khurdis's thighs. Khurdis paid it no more than a passing glance out of the corner of his eye as, with the regal elegance of all cats, it padded silently across the meadow-grass and came to sit by his side, its long tail curled neatly about its feet.

A gasp went up from the assembled villagers. It was not only the sight of this wild creature, large and fierce, trotting calmly out from the trees to sit at Khurdis Black-eye's feet like any house cat. It was the nature of the animal itself: it licked its lips and yawned, regarding them all intelligently with eyes that were . . . that seemed entirely *human*.

Pawli shivered, reminded suddenly of the dream he had had about the human-eyed cat.

Khurdis Blackeye smiled. 'Is there a problem here?'

Old Tomae went towards him with relief. 'Master Black-eye!' he said. 'Thank the Powers you are here. These . . . these men are—'

'I grow tired of this,' fork-bearded Nerys interrupted. He had his eyes still on Bryn, who stood facing him, but he gestured at Tomae with the cold iron blade of his broad-sword. 'Back away, old man.'

'Master Blackeye,' Tomae said again, stepping gingerly sideways away from Nerys's menace and slipping behind Bryn in an attempt to get nearer to Khurdis. 'These men . . . these *bandits* are trying to hold us to ransom. They have already burnt parts of the village. Look! You can see yourself what they have done. They are mad. Quite mad! Help us. Master Blackeye. Use your powers to drive them away.'

At this, the bandits began to surge forward menacingly. Khurdis Blackeye held up a warning hand and they stopped.

Khurdis smiled a thin smile. He pointed towards Bryn. 'You mean you need *my* help, even though you have the great Master Brynmaur Somnar himself here to protect you?'

The Woburners stared about uncertainly at the halted bandits, at Bryn, at Khurdis himself.

'Why did you not come to me first?'

'We would have, Master Blackeye,' Tomae replied. 'But it all happened so quick! And you're no easy man to find.'

'So you went to Brynmaur here when you could not find me. Is that it?'

Tomae shifted uncomfortably.

'And he has been of precious little use to you in this situation so far.'

'Well, I wouldn't . . .' Tomae started.

But the crowd of villagers was shuffling about, muttering and nodding to each other. Pawli felt himself burn with sudden anger. What had they expected? That Bryn would strike this Nerys Ironblade down with lightning from out of the clear sky? He had been doing all right, had Bryn. More than all right.

But with Khurdis Blackeye standing there, tall and regal and shining, nobody was paying attention to raggedy-looking Bryn any more. Those nearby were quietly putting distance between themselves and him. Khurdis's smile broadened. Pawli wanted to hit him.

'So you wish my aid in this now, do you?' Khurdis was saying to the villagers.

'You *must* help us!'

'Oh, yes?' Khurdis responded coldly. 'And why *must* I, then?'

'It's what you ought to do!' Stroud said. 'You are a man of *power*. You must use that *power* to aid us.'

'Ah . . .' Khurdis said softly. 'You admit that I am a man of *power*, then?'

Tomae and Stroud and the rest looked at him in confusion. 'Of course,' Tomae said. 'None doubts it.'

'You are wrong there,' Khurdis said. 'There *are* those who doubt me.'

'No,' Tomae said quickly. 'We all know . . .'

'*He* doubts me,' Khurdis said, jabbing a stiff finger accusingly towards Bryn.

'He . . .' Tomae looked round at Bryn, uncertain. 'But Master Blackeye . . . What does this have to do with anything? None here doubts you. I assure you of that. We need you now to . . .'

'*He* doubts me,' Khurdis repeated, eyeing Bryn coldly.

'No,' Tomae insisted. 'None can doubt you. You are a true man of *power*. All know it.'

'Let him say it, then,' Khurdis replied.

Tomae looked utterly confounded. 'But, Master Black-eye, I don't understand. The *bandits* . . .'

'Let him *say* it!' Khurdis snapped. 'The "bandits", as you name them, will wait.'

It was true; the bandits stayed halted as they were, as if they were obedient to Khurdis's every wish.

All eyes were on Bryn now.

Pawli understood this no better than old Tomae. There had been blood about to be spilled here, and all Khurdis seemed to care for was his old bitterness with Bryn. Pawli saw Roe looking equally uncertain, the length of wrapped pole gripped tight in his hands as he glanced from one face to the next.

'Say it!' Khurdis ordered Bryn.

'You are . . .' Bryn said, 'a pretender. Nothing more, nothing less.'

The gathered villagers murmured in shocked unease.

Khurdis Blackeye only smiled, a thin, cold smile. He looked down to the sleek cat, which had sat quietly at his feet all this while, and said to it, 'So he thinks I am a pretender, does he? Clearly, the man's an idiot.'

The cat nodded. 'Clearrly an idiottt,' it said in a soft, hissing, but altogether understandable voice.

The villagers faltered back, stricken, some covering their eyes and moaning in superstitious shock. Pawli stared. He felt his belly heave, as if he had just been pushed off some great height. He had heard about such beings – the incredible talking animals of the highest wild – but had never in his life expected to actually encounter such. Along with most folk, he had only half believed the tales about them. Semi-magical creatures they were supposed

62

to be, animal of body yet human of spirit, created by the all-knowing Seers of long generations ago, before the time of the great wars of old.

However had Khurdis Blackeye come by such an uncanny companion?

'Would a . . . *pretender* have such a companion as this?' Khurdis demanded of the shaken villagers.

The cat stood up and padded silently towards the clustered, shivering Woburners, who melted back in panic. 'Leave them be, Tigern,' Khurdis said. 'They are ignorant folk and know no better.'

The cat stopped, staring at the villagers with its eerie, humanesque eyes.

Pawli felt an unpleasant shiver go through him. Bryn had been wrong, so very wrong about Khurdis Blackeye. Only a man of true *power*, surely, could summon up and command such an incredible creature as this. It was a beautiful, terrible being, a strange mixture of human and not. It turned and regarded him with those knowing, human eyes . . . and he had to turn away. It made his guts flutter just to think of what such a creature was, or might be.

All about him, the village folk were staring and shivering and moaning. The bandits, too, had backed away, wide-eyed and uneasy, their weapons up. Only Bryn seemed unflustered. Bryn and Roe, too, Pawli realised. Roe stood regarding the cat-creature with interest, but calm as could be wished – as if encountering such an impossible being were an everyday occurrence for him. And Bryn? Had Bryn even seen such before? Pawli felt suddenly over-whelmed by wild surmise. What strange things might Bryn have seen and done in his life as a far-seer?

Roe stepped forward. 'It is a surprise,' he said to the cat-creature in his nasal, surprisingly high-pitched, foreign voice, 'to encounter one of the Free Folk here.'

The cat blinked. 'Itt iss a ssurprisse to meet one who knowss the Free Folk.'

The two regarded each other in silence.

Pawli was utterly thrown. Roe *knew* this sort of creature? And what in the world were the 'Free Folk'?

'Enough!' Khurdis Blackeye snapped. 'Tigern, come to me.'

The cat-creature turned slowly and regarded Khurdis.

'Come to me,' he repeated. 'Now!'

The cat came, but languidly. Khurdis bit his lip, glaring at Roe.

For the space of a dozen heartbeats there was silence. Then fork-bearded Nerys stood forth. 'I grow weary of all this foolishness.' He gestured with his iron broadsword at the shaken villagers. 'I have given you my terms. Will you accept or no?'

Tomae glared defiance at him. 'We will not accept. There is no need to bow to you now. Not with Master Blackeye here to protect us. Do you not have eyes? He is clearly a man of great *power*. Would you pit yourself against the likes of him?'

The bandit leader turned slowly and regarded Khurdis.

'Tell him, Master Blackeye,' Tomae said.

'Send him packing!' somebody cried. 'Him and all the rest of his dirty lot. Send them all packing back down the mountain where they belong!'

Khurdis looked at the bandit leader.

'You like to play games,' Nerys said disgustedly.

'I do what I do,' Khurdis replied. 'And the likes of *you* do not question me.'

'Send them out of here!' one of the villagers cried.

'Master Blackeye, use your *power*. Send them off!'

'Tails between their legs,' somebody else added. 'Send them off like beaten pups.' A general hue and cry went up.

Khurdis raised his arms for silence.

'If you are wise,' he said to the village folk once they had quietened, 'you will do as Nerys Ironblade here orders.'

VI

Stricken silence greeted Khurdis Blackeye's words.

Nerys Ironblade grinned through his forked beard. 'That's better.' He turned to the villagers. 'Do you hear? If you are wise, you will heed me.'

'But . . .' Tomae began. He came forward, staggering, as if he had just received a physical blow, his hands raised imploringly towards Khurdis Blackeye. 'How can you . . .'

Khurdis sneered at him. 'Do you think I *care* about you lot? Ragged, ignorant fools that you are. I have . . . plans. Nerys here is a part of those plans.'

Eyes went from Khurdis to Nerys, back again.

Khurdis nodded, smiling. 'Yes. He is *my* man, Nerys Iron-blade. You will do as he says, for his orders are *my* orders.'

The Woburners collapsed into dismay, groaning and shouting and milling about.

'Quiet!' Nerys shouted. 'Quiet, the lot of you or . . .'

Old Tomae, still standing a little forward of the rest, cried out, 'Master Blackeye!'

'I've had enough of you, old man,' Nerys said. He spat, lifted his iron blade.

'Leave him be!' Roe cried.

Nerys turned, glaring. 'And just who are *you*, then, to be giving me orders?'

Roe said nothing, merely stood his ground.

Nerys regarded him appraisingly, then raised his blade. 'Very well, boy, you with your little bundled stick. Come to me. Come and meet Thorn.'

Roe stepped forwards, gripping the burlap-wrapped pole in his hands.

Pawli tried to reach for him. This was madness, all of it. He felt like he had just received a flurry of hard blows from some invisible attacker. 'Roe!' he called. 'You can't . . .'

But Roe dodged him easily and went towards the bandit leader. The crowd fell back. Pawli felt sick. That silly wrapped whatever it was against Nerys's iron blade. Nerys would cut Roe down like a farmer hewing corn. 'Bryn!' he hissed. '*Do* something!'

But Bryn was facing Khurdis. 'Don't,' Bryn said. It was just the one word, and softly said, but it made Khurdis blanch with fury.

Khurdis had been reaching for something in a bag that hung slung at his hip. He froze, glaring at Bryn. 'What gives *you* the right to tell me yay or nay?'

'I was your teacher, Khurdis. You know that. I know you.'

'You taught me *nothing*!'

'I taught you all you were able for.'

'You hated me,' Khurdis spat. 'You still hate me.'

Bryn shook his head sadly. 'Never that.'

A sudden gasp had gone up from the crowd. Pawli, whose attention had been focused on Bryn and Khurdis, turned to see what was happening.

With a quick flip and yank, Roe had unwound the burlap from the stick he carried. The crowd – villagers and bandits alike – stared in shocked amazement.

It was no pole, no stick, that Roe held; it was a sheathed sword – but such a sword. The scabbard was of lacquered leather, a deep crimson, bound round with an intricate braiding of glimmering bronze wire. The sword's hilt, too, was of bronze, fashioned into the image of a snarling dragon's head, with glittering ruby eyes.

Pawli had never seen – never even *imagined* – anything like it. It made Nerys's iron blade look a paltry thing. No wonder Roe kept it wrapped in coarse cloth as he did; he would never be able to travel with such a weapon without arousing instant notoriety. Pawli felt himself reeling. How in the world had Roe ever come by such a wondrous thing?

Roe hefted his incredible sword, still sheathed, and gestured at Nerys. 'Leave the old man alone.'

Nerys stared. He too, obviously, had never seen anything like the blade that had appeared so unexpectedly before him. He took a step back, another, then halted. Gripping his own weapon more tightly, he sneered at Roe. 'A pretty sheath and fancy hilt does not make a man good with a blade. Come to me, boy, and Thorn and I will relieve you of your little toy.'

Roe looked at him. 'Sheath your own blade and walk away.'

Nerys laughed. 'Come on, boy. Let's see what you're made of.' He beckoned with his blade. 'Come *on*!'

Roe drew his sword from its ornate scabbard. The gathered folk faltered back even further. It was a straight, double-edged blade, like the bandit leader's, though slimmer and somewhat shorter. But that blade . . . it glowed uncannily, like a bar of purest light. Roe dropped the sheath to the ground and took a stance, the shining blade held in both hands, feet braced. He looked like he knew *exactly* what he was doing.

'Whiteblade!' a voice said. The cat's. The creature left Khurdis and sidled over towards Roe. 'Whiteblade,' it said once more, gazing raptly at Roe's incredible, gleaming weapon.

Pawli felt shaken to his bones. He did not understand any of what was happening.

'Come, then, boy,' Nerys said, 'and we will see how your shining wand stands up against true iron.' But though he was clearly trying to brazen things out, his voice had a note of uncertainty to it, and he gripped his sword with a white-knuckled intensity.

'*Yaeiii!*' a voice cried suddenly.

Pawli whirled. It was Khurdis, who stood, his long cloak flapping like a kind of wing, both arms raised high above his head. In each hand, he held a slim rod, ebony and brass and silver, glistening and glinting – the very rods Pawli had seen in the embossed quiver at Khurdis's belt yesterday morning. Between them, an eerie green light arced, like forks of small lightning. Pawli could hear the soft *kruckle* of it. He felt the air shiver. All the hairs on his body prickled.

'Stand away, boy!' Khurdis commanded Roe. 'Lay down your weapon!'

Roe regarded him cautiously, but made no move to lay down his white blade. Instead, he reached inside the neck of his tunic with one hand and brought forth a small bone amulet hung on a leather thong, holding it as if the thing had some virtue he trusted.

'Do as I command!' Khurdis cried. He gyrated his hands above his head, and the small green lightnings that had been arcing between the rods erupted. With a quick snap of the wrists, he hurled a wash of crackling green fire at Roe.

Sword in one hand, bone amulet in the other, Roe stood his ground. The shining blade came up and Khurdis's green fire caught on it, dancing like a live thing. The Woburners fell back, wailing. Pawli covered his eyes and staggered.

The unnatural green lightning coursed along Roe's blade, leaping to the amulet in his other hand and then back again in a kind of sizzling circuit. Roe shuddered, brought the sword up with obvious effort and whirled the blade above his head, slowly at first, then faster and faster, making a spinning green circle . . . until the caught lightnings shot hissing away, like complex, green-shining water from a chute, and slammed into the ground with a loud *ker-rumph!*

Roe stood panting, intact, but clearly shaken. Folk were on their knees all about. The air stank of burning. The last of Khurdis's uncanny green fires fizzled into nothing, leaving a charred spot on the trampled sod. Looking at it, Pawli felt his skin crawl.

'Surrender your weapon, boy!' Khurdis Blackeye cried. He held aloft the rods, between which new lightnings arced.

The amulet still in one hand, the white-shining sword in the other, Roe stepped towards him.

'Don't even think of it, boy,' Khurdis warned. The green lightning *kruckled* menacingly. 'I can strike you down before you've taken three paces.'

'Leave him be.' It was Bryn speaking. He walked calmly across to stand at Roe's side.

Khurdis Blackeye scowled. 'I can strike *you* down too!'

'Then do so,' Bryn returned. He stepped past Roe towards Khurdis.

Khurdis mouthed something so filled with venom that Pawli could make out none of the sense of it. Then, his face clenched with fury, Khurdis flung crackling green fire at Bryn.

'No!' Pawli shrieked. But it was too late. Bryn was suddenly enveloped in emerald burning. The unnatural lightnings danced about him, so that he seemed a man submerged. The air erupted with a long *kaa-raa-raakk!*

Pawli cowered, trying to cover his eyes, his ears. It had all happened so fast. He could hardly believe it. On his knees, his heart thumping so hard he could hardly get breath, he peered between his fingers, expecting to see Bryn on the sod, a pitiful charred form.

Bryn stood erect and calm and entirely unhurt – though all about him the grass was a charred ruin.

Pawli staggered to his feet. 'Bryn!'

But Bryn's attention was all on Khurdis Blackeye. 'You are a mere pretender, Khurdis.'

'No!' Khurdis all but screamed. 'I am a true man of *power*!'

Bryn shook his head. 'A pretender. You know it and I know it.'

'No!'

'Put down your toy, Khurdis.' Bryn pointed at the brass

lightning rods Khurdis still held in his hands – though not so high now. 'I do not know where you have got such things, but, for all their puissance, they do not . . . *can not* change what you are.'

Khurdis raised the rods in threat, the green lightnings spitting nastily. 'You always hated me, Brynmaur. You *envied* me, that's the truth of things. You hated my talent and did your best to keep me down. Well, no more. *No more!* Do you hear me? Your day is done. You're a pathetic, starweed-crazed, ageing man whose life is a ruin, who fights to keep anybody with true talent from rising in the world!'

Khurdis raised the green-fire rods high above his head. 'Your day is *done*, I say! And mine is beginning.' With an inarticulate shriek, he hurled the unnatural lightnings at Bryn once again.

This time, Bryn seemed to somehow catch them in his hands, his fingers sparking with green fire. About his head, his grey hair lifted, sticking straight out in all directions. Pawli felt the air shimmer all about. Then Bryn launched the lightning fire back at Khurdis.

'No!' Khurdis screamed.

The whirling fire wrapped itself around the brass rods Khurdis held, like a mess of spidery, green-shining, frantic serpents. The rods sparked and hissed. Khurdis shrieked and flung them from him, holding his hands to his chest in agony.

Pawli could only stare in shock. He had never imagined such . . . such combat.

But things were not finished yet. From behind him, Pawli heard a shout. Pivoting, he saw Nerys Ironblade hewing at Roe. Like everyone else, Roe had been staring at Bryn and Khurdis, transfixed. Nerys had gone for Roe without warning, and now Roe was on his knees desperately trying to parry a series of vicious, hacking sword blows. Pawli felt sick looking on, helpless as he was. Despite the wonderful sword he might wield, Roe was only a thin lad. Nerys was a heavy-set, powerful, angry

70

man in the prime of his full strength. He roared like a beast with each hewing stroke he took. Roe could not survive much more, surely . . .

But to Pawli's amazement, Roe's flashing blade caught Nerys's heavier one and turned it so that the bandit leader stumbled. And then, suddenly, Roe had bounced to his feet, the white-bladed sword in a two-handed grip.

Nerys rushed him.

Roe met the attack with unexpected assurance, as if he were going through the steps of some intricate, yet wholly familiar dance, his feet going just so, his body weaving, all with astonishing grace and speed and coiled-steel strength. When Nerys struck, Roe was simply . . . not there. The bandit leader's heavy blade swept through empty air and he stumbled, off-balance. The next instant, he lay sprawled on his face on the sod, his broadsword tumbled from his grasp.

Nerys Ironblade struggled to his knees, staring about him, shaken. Pawli saw one of the bandit bowmen draw back an arrow and let fly. 'Roe!' he shrieked in warning, but too late.

The shining blade came up in a quick bright arc and deflected the arrow so that it veered off to *crump* into the turf to one side and behind Roe . . .

. . . leaving Pawli and the rest staring in complete unbelief.

All but Nerys, who grabbed up his broadsword and flung himself at Roe, howling.

Roe whirled and parried Nerys's attack, the two swords *krangging* off each other. Nerys swore and raged, hewing gracelessly at Roe as if he were trying to cut the boy in half with each stroke. But he could nowhere come near. Each heavy slash of his was met by the white blade and turned – all with the incredible speed and dance-like grace that marked Roe's every movement, and all backed by a hard strength that seemed altogether beyond what was possible for one so slim-limbed and light as he.

71

'Lay it down,' Roe said, motioning at Nerys's sword. 'I have no wish to kill you.'

Nerys paused, panting.

'Lay it down,' Roe repeated.

The bandit leader looked about desperately. Seeing one of his bowmen still with an arrow nocked, he cried, 'Shoot him! Quick!'

Roe pivoted to face the bowman, shining blade up. The man lifted his bow in shaking hands, then faltered and backed away, the nocked arrow slipping from his hold and dropping to the ground.

'Fool!' Nerys shrieked.

'Lay your blade down,' Roe said.

'No!' Nerys charged Roe in fury.

Roe laughed. It was a fell laugh, and unexpected, and it made the short hairs along Pawli's neck prickle unpleasantly. Roe's face was changed, lit from within by a bright ferocity.

It was all over in a heartbeat. One moment there was the *krang* of blade against blade and the grunt and shove and whirl of the fighting; the next Nerys lay sprawled on his back on the turf. He lifted himself up on his elbows. 'What have you *done* to me?' he gasped, staring at Roe in horror.

Only then did Pawli become aware of Nerys's wound. It seemed but a little thing, a small slice into his ribs. Events had happened so fast that Pawli had never even seen how he received it. But as he watched, he saw the red blood well up, like water from an underground spring. Nerys looked down at himself and groaned. 'You've *killed* me!'

Roe said nothing, merely looked at him. His bright blade was webbed with blood.

Nerys pressed hard against the wound in his breast with both hands, but the blood welled up through his fingers, soaking his leather jerkin and the sod beneath him. He lunged to his knees, staring about, wild-eyed, his face white and clenched. 'You can't . . .' he said to Roe. 'I will not . . .'

Then he fell over onto his face, heavily. Blood continued to drain from him into the grass and he went limp, like a sack emptying its contents through a vent.

The bandits faltered back.

'No!' Khurdis Blackeye cried. He stood with his burnt hands folded to his chest, his face twisted with pain. 'No!'

Bryn regarded him sadly. 'It's over, Khurdis.'

'No!' Khurdis repeated.

Roe came striding over. There was a look on Roe's face now, the like of which Pawli had never witnessed – a kind of mindless ferocity like that of some hunting hawk's. The small bone amulet dangling at his breast seemed to glow palely. The white blade still dripped blood, and Roe still moved with his uncanny dancer's grace.

As he drew close, Khurdis faltered away, ducking his head.

'What do you wish done with him?' Roe asked Bryn, gesturing at Khurdis.

'Done with him?'

Roe nodded. 'I know his sort. He will not rest till he has caused more mischief.'

Bryn sighed. 'Aye. Perhaps you are right. But what can we do?'

'There is . . . *this.*' Roe said, lifting his bloodied, shining blade. His face fairly shone too, with a fierce fell glee.

'No!' Bryn said quickly. 'There has already been enough blood spilled here.'

'It is the only sure way,' Roe insisted.

Pawli felt inclined to agree.

But Bryn shook his head. 'How can you even think it? His fangs have been drawn, he is helpless now. We need only . . .'

'No!' Khurdis said. 'I will *not* have you pleading my cause.' He stepped in front of Roe. 'Kill me then, and have

73

done.' He glared at Bryn. 'What worse could happen? Kill me, I say. *Kill me!*'

Roe raised his white-shining blade.

'Leave him be!' Bryn grabbed Roe by the shoulder and hauled him off.

For an instant, it seemed Roe would go for him, too. The blade came up in menace.

'No!' Pawli cried, too far off to be of any help.

But Roe let the blade drop.

'You cannot kill him,' Bryn said.

Roe shrugged. 'I can. All too easily.'

'You will not, then.'

Roe gestured at Khurdis, whose face was contorted with fury. 'You are making a mistake. A man such as this . . .'

'You will not kill him. Death is no answer.'

'It is the final answer,' Roe replied softly.

Pawli looked on, appalled and darkly fascinated. It was as if the Roe he had known – had *thought* he had known – had been somehow replaced by another, strong and quick and dangerous beyond belief. Nerys Ironblade had stood no chance against him. The Woburners were all staring at Roe as if he were some Fey out of the furthest wilds suddenly appeared in their midst.

Khurdis Blackeye was shaken and white-faced and utterly furious, cursing and muttering and fuming so that spittle flew from his mouth.

'Walk away, Khurdis,' Bryn said quietly.

Khurdis only stared.

Bryn made a gesture of dismissal. 'I do not know what scheme you might have thought you were furthering with this . . . this treachery of yours against Woburn, but it is over now. Go away.'

'You will live to regret this,' Khurdis snarled. 'I will be avenged for this!'

'Walk away,' Bryn said.

'Do as Brynmaur says,' Roe ordered, gesturing with his white blade, to which a few dollops of sticky blood still hung. 'Walk away.' There was such a raw menace to Roe that Khurdis backed off precipitously, nearly tripping over a little hummock on the ground behind him and getting the long black cloak he wore all tangled up.

Several of the villagers tittered.

Glaring murder, Khurdis caught his balance and drew himself up with a cold dignity. Stiff-spined, he looked this way, then that, his face bone-white and frozen. Then he spat upon the ground three times and made a quick, complicated little pattern with his fingers in the air. 'May you die an ill death and a painful, Brynmaur Somnar,' he said. And then, glaring at Roe: 'You too, you meddling fool of an interloper.'

'Walk away,' Bryn repeated simply, showing no concern over Khurdis's curse.

Khurdis Blackeye looked about him one last time, opened his mouth, closed it so hard that Pawli heard the *snapp* of his teeth shutting together. Then Khurdis turned and beckoned to the cat-creature – which had been sitting silent, solemnly regarding all the fighting and commotion.

'Tigern, come,' Khurdis commanded it.

The cat ignored him.

Khurdis ground his teeth in fury. *'Come* to me!' he repeated, but it was no use. The cat had eyes only for Roe and his white-shining blade.

'Walk away, Khurdis,' Bryn said for the last time.

Khurdis did, slowly, balked and shaking and blindly furious. Into the pines on the village's verge he staggered, disappearing finally amongst them.

'Good riddance,' Pawli heard somebody mutter.

Roe stood, bright blade lowered, staring after where Khurdis had gone. 'You ought never to have let him walk away,' he said to Bryn, shaking his head.

'He is finished here now,' Bryn replied. 'Whatever grand ambitions he might have had are crumbled into nothing. The folk of the Three Valleys will shun him now. Let that be enough. Death is never an answer.'

Roe opened his mouth, closed it again, shrugged. 'As you will.'

There was still that fierceness about Roe, as if, taking up the sword, he had also somehow taken up a new self. Turning now, he walked away from Bryn to where he had left the crimson scabbard. Some of the Woburners had drifted over near where the scabbard lay. As Roe drew near to it they melted back, murmuring amongst themselves and staring at him.

Ignoring them, Roe scooped up the scabbard, carefully wiped the last of the blood from the white blade on the grass, and sheathed it. Pawli was not sure if it were his imagination or no, but it seemed to him then that Roe sagged, and that the fierceness melted out of him. He stood for a long few moments, head bowed, panting softly, one hand gripping the sword, the other the bone amulet on its thong. Then he slipped the amulet back under his tunic and looked up.

The cat-creature stalked up to Roe. 'Whiteblade,' it said in its strange, hissing voice.

Roe merely stood, leaned tiredly on the sheathed sword as if it were a walking stick, silent, panting still a little.

'I knoww of yoo,' the cat went on.

Roe said nothing.

'Yoo arre Elinnor Whitebladde. From the ssoutherrn landss. All wildd folk knoww of yoo and yoor sshining weaponn.'

Roe made a formal, small bow to the cat-creature. 'And all know of the Free Folk in the high wild.'

'Yoo brroughtt rruin uponn the Dark Brrotherss in the ssouth,' the cat said.

Roe shrugged. 'Not me alone.'

'Butt thrrough yoo.'

Roe nodded. 'Through me, yes.'

Pawli understood none of what they were talking about. What did this cat-creature mean by naming Roe . . . What was it? Elinor Whiteblade? The surname, yes. He could see that. But *Elinor*? Unless . . .

No. Crazy thought.

But he looked at Roe suddenly with new eyes: the slimness, the light bones, the smooth, beardless face. Roe's oddly high-pitched voice . . .

Pawli walked up to him uncertainly, skirting the cat-creature.

There were smudges of exhaustion under Roe's eyes, Pawli saw, and Roe's hands quivered where he held the sword's hilt. Roe smiled at Pawli wearily and said, 'I could use a sip of water. I am always drained . . . afterwards.'

'*Elinor* Whiteblade?' Pawli said.

Roe shrugged uncertainly. 'It is my name.'

'But . . .' Pawli started. It was true, then. Looking at her now, he could see it; despite the sword and the man's clothing and the travel-grime, he could see it clearly. This was altogether too much. He felt dizzy, as if the world had dropped suddenly out from under him. All that had happened . . . it was too much for him to grasp properly. Roe a woman? And wielding that terrible/wonderful white-bladed sword like that? Pawli stared at the sheathed blade. He wished, suddenly, that it had been him wielding it . . .

Roe had saved the day here, and the Woburners were staring at Roe and the shining sword with uneasy awe. Pawli imagined himself in Roe's position. Folk would not be hanging back from him as they were from Roe. *He* was no dissembler. And *he* would have saved the day, just as Roe had. With that incredible sword in hand, Roe had been fearless, unstoppable. Roe . . . no, *Elinor*. Pawli took a breath. It was altogether too, too confusing.

Roe-Elinor put a hand out to him. 'It's a long story, Pawli.'

Pawli jerked back from her, tripped over his own feet unexpectedly and sprawled to the ground. Roe-Elinor reached to help him, but Pawli scrambled away, refusing. He got to his feet alone, flushed and confused and angry. He felt like an utter fool, having been so easily deceived. Roe must have been laughing at his stupidity all this time. 'You lied to me,' he said accusingly.

Roe-Elinor said nothing.

'I thought we could be . . . friends.'

'We can,' Roe-Elinor answered.

Pawli snorted and turned away.

'Pawli!'

But Pawli walked on, spurning her, his insides churning. It was too much – everything that had happened, all of it, the whole day . . . too much. The Woburners were all staring, and he felt like he wanted to crawl away into a dark place somewhere and hide. Instead, he squared his shoulders and walked onwards, ignoring them.

Nerys Ironblade lay where he had fallen, with a little cluster of villagers standing around him now, staring. On the ground near him lay his iron sword. On sudden impulse, Pawli went over and snatched the thing up. It was surprisingly heavy. But with it in his hand, he felt suddenly . . . important. The Woburners were staring at him in a different way now.

Dead Nerys lay face down in the dirt, in a pool of congealing blood. The iron sword's scabbard was still hung from his belt, sticking half out from under him. Pawli stooped over the corpse – it smelled of blood and shit and old, sweaty leather – and tried to pull the scabbard free, wrestling clumsily with the belt fastening, which refused to come undone. When he was finished, his fingers were red and sticky, and he felt sick.

The scabbard was a simple thing, sticky as his fingers now with blood, but it was solid, and the iron blade fit into it perfectly when he slid it home. The Woburners stared at him, open-mouthed.

'Pawli! What do you think you're *doing*?' It was Bryn, come over to him, face taut. 'Put that thing down!'

Pawli scowled and clutched the sheathed sword posses-sively.

'You've no need of such a fell thing,' Bryn said. 'It ought to be buried, the blade of it broken in half and then buried deep, so that it can cause no more grief.'

Pawli said nothing. The sword felt good in his hold.

'Give it up, Pawli,' Bryn said, reaching a hand out.

Pawli backed away. 'I'm keeping it.'

'Are you *mad*?' Bryn replied, shocked. 'It's a thing of death.'

'Pawli!' Roe-Elinor called. 'You don't know what you—'

Pawli turned from them. He did not want to argue it or think it through. He barged through the clustered Wobur-ners. With the sword in his hand – even sheathed as it was – none moved to hinder him.

'Pawli!' Bryn cried.

Pawli went on into the pines and away, running.

'Pawli!'

It was a voice, made faint by distance and the trees, and he ignored it easily, scrambling upslope and away, his heart thumping hard with excitement, the iron sword held tight to his breast.

VII

'Where is it?' Bryn demanded.

Pawli frowned. 'None of your business. None of any-body's business.'

'Pawli, you're acting the stupid boy! Such things as that blade have a . . . they have a soul of sorts. Look what it's doing to you. The better part of two days, you've been gone, skulking out there in the wild doing the Powers alone know what by yourself. You've had me sick with worry.'

Pawli turned away.

'Pawli!'

'Leave me be! I'm not a child to be ordered about.'

'You're behaving like one!'

They lapsed into stiff silence, not looking at each other. The cabin was at their backs, Bryn on a rough log seat, Pawli squatting on the turf a little beyond. He had come back in the pre-dawn, trekking the high slopes in the dark, to find Bryn here, staring mutely into the distance. There had been no easy greeting between them.

The long, downwards slope of the mountain lay spread out before them, green-ochre turf and scattered dwarf birch, the thin, twisty branches clothed in a pale green lacery of new leaves. The sun was easing up from behind the peaks eastwards, flooding the sky with soft red-orange all along the horizon. A fresh-cool breeze blew down from the far-away snowy heights. The air rang gently with birdsong.

The world turned on in its ponderous, peaceful fashion about him, but in himself Pawli felt a depth of change that turmoiled his blood. He clenched and unclenched his hands, remembering the solid heft of the sword's hilt.

Alone in a clearing, away in the deep woods, he had first unsheathed it . . . The flat iron surface of the blade was all folded and wrinkled and pitted, as if it had been made of a series of dirty rags folded and pressed together. But where it had been ground to an edge it was sharp as sharp could be and glistened bright silver – almost the way Roe-Elinor's sword glowed.

It was heavy in his hand, like a solid metal bar. He took a stance, trying to remember the way Roe-Elinor had done it, placing his feet, gripping the sword two-handed, raising it slant-ways before him. 'So you defy me, do you?' he demanded of a recalcitrant pine tree before him. Stepping forwards, he hewed at the tree.

The shock of the blow lurched through the bones of his arms right into his shoulder sockets. The blade bit into the side of the tree and stuck, like a badly swung axe. He had to wrench it free, bracing himself with one knee against the tree bole. He stared at the gash he had made, no more than a clumsy hack.

He tried again, swinging the blade first this way then that, chopping and slashing at the pine in an awkward series of blows. The sharp edge of the blade bit into the tree Bole at each stroke with a *krunkk*, and wedges of white pine wood flew. After a little, he backed off, panting, his arms aching, and took a new stance. Slowly, trying to dance on the balls of his feet as he had seen Roe-Elinor do, he stalked the tree. With a sudden rush, he cut leftways, whirled away, aiming to slash from the other side. But in the whirl, somehow, he tripped over his own feet and fell sprawling.

Spitting out brown pine needles, he got up, glad there had been no witnesses to his stumblefootedness. The sword had gone spinning away, and he looked at it ruefully. Wielding a blade had looked so easy, when Roe-Elinor did it . . .

'Pawli?' It was Bryn, prying him back from memory.

'What?' Pawli returned irritably.

'What have you been doing with that blade?'

How could he tell Bryn what it had been like? He would have cut a ridiculous figure, he knew, had there been anybody to watch him trying to wield the iron broadsword. His practising had gained him little save sore arms and stiff joints. And yet . . . yet, standing there alone in the deep woods with the heavy, naked blade in his hand, he had felt like . . . like a hunting cougar, or one of the great brown mountain bears, come down to patrol the forest. He had felt . . . *strong*.

'You must give it up, Pawli. The thing has to be destroyed.'

Bryn's face was closed tight. Bryn would not understand. For him, such a blade was altogether wicked. But it was not that simple.

'What*ever* did you think you were doing, running off with it like that?' Bryn went on. 'Of all the fool stunts!'

Pawli hung his head. In truth, he had to admit that it did seem a fool act, on the face if it. But that nagging, cold lump in his guts that told him something dreadful was coming into the world had never left him, and he felt *pulled* in ways he did not understand. Nothing was the same as it had been. With the sword's hilt in his hands, he had felt less vulnerable. And there was a growing, inexplicable conviction in him that he and the iron blade were somehow fated together. 'Bryn . . .' he started.

'I don't want to hear excuses,' Bryn snapped. 'Just bring the sword back.'

Pawli bit his lip. He felt torn every which way, his guts churning with knowledge he did not understand, his hands remembering the good heft of the sword's hilt . . .

82

And Bryn was closed against him like a wall. He had never felt more alone.

'Pawli, you must give it up!'

'I will not.'

Bryn stared at him. His eyes had a bruised look.

Pawli's heart turned over. He felt like a traitor – and like the one betrayed. It was all so complicated, somehow.

From behind them, the cabin door creaked open and Roe-Elinor came out, the crimson-scabbarded sword at her waist. She yawned, ran a hand through tousled hair, saw the two of them. 'Morning.'

Bryn nodded to her stiffly. Pawli would not look her in the face; he still felt a fool over the way she had deceived him on their first meeting.

Silence.

None of them seemed to know what to say for the moment.

Roe-Elinor coughed. She looked thin and weary, as if what she had done in Woburn had drained her. 'I'm . . . interrupting.' She reached up the empty bucket that stood next to the water barrel. 'I'll fetch some water then, shall I?' When neither of them said anything, she turned and moved off slantwise across the grassy slope, walking slowly and a little stiffly, one hand holding the bucket, the other on the sword at her hip to steady it.

It was the weapon of a great champion, that sword, a weapon as seemingly magical as any found in a bard's tale, and a person wielding it ought to be . . . Pawli did not know quite what. Famous. Respected. Adulated. Certainly not a lone, dirt-poor wanderer, and *certainly* not trudging along like this in the high beyond, doing a country peasant's chore with that wondrous blade swinging at her hip. He did not at all understand her. She seemed like some creature from another realm entirely, where none of the ordinary things he understood applied, and she evoked both resentment and respect in him.

'I'll be glad to see her away and gone, that one,' Bryn said. 'And good riddance to her.'

'She's never done *you* any harm,' Pawli snapped. He found Bryn's comment miserably ungracious. 'You're just peeved at her because she fooled you. Brynmaur Somnar, the great far-seer, duped by a wandering, sword-toting girl.'

Bryn scowled, scratched at his stubbly jaw. 'I don't like dissemblers,' he said. 'Nor murderers.'

'Murderers!'

'I may not have done much with my life, lad. Nor . . .' Bryn sighed, 'nor lived up properly to the promise of the *gift* in me, perhaps. But I've never taken a human life. That girl and her white blade are steeped in blood. I can feel it.'

'But . . .' Pawli shook his head. 'But she was *defending* us! That bandit deserved what he got.'

'The world is too hard, and too filled with griefs, lad. Death is a black solution.'

Pawli glared. 'You're being ridiculous, Bryn. For men like that Nerys Ironblade, men who prey upon others, there *is* only the one solution.'

'Death is never the only solution,' Bryn insisted. 'This Elinor is trouble. I feel it in my bones. Besides . . . who appointed you her champion? You're no more fond of her than I am. I saw the look you gave her when she came out.'

Pawli winced. He had not thought himself so transparent. 'I don't have to like her to recognise what she did for us all. Why do you refuse to see . . .'

'She's like a . . . a storm walking through the world, Pawli. Even when she was just Roe, I knew there was something strange about her.'

'Easy to say now, with hindsight.' Pawli remembered Bryn's assurances to the Woburners that Roe had not been one of the bandits – and of how he would recognise a dissembler. 'You never said anything at the time. You vouched for her.'

Bryn shrugged glumly. 'Events happened too fast. And I wasn't seeing things so very clear.'

And probably aren't seeing them any too much clearer now, Pawli almost said, with your mind addled from all that starweed. But he kept the thought to himself. 'Tell this Elinor to go, then,' he suggested instead, 'if she makes you so uncomfortable.'

'The Woburners want nothing to do with her,' Bryn answered, 'despite all she did for them. She's too . . . strange. The least I could do, all things considered, was offer her the hospitality of our hearth till she's ready for the road again. I won't withdraw that, once given.'

Pawli watched Elinor move off through the dwarf birch and over the crest of the slope some distance away. The hilt of her sword caught the morning light in a soft flash, and then she was lost to sight. 'I don't know why you're so set against her. If this were some bard's tale we were living, she would be a hero now after what she's done, lauded across the breadth of the Three Valleys.'

Bryn shrugged.

'She would have dealt with Khurdis once and for all, too, had you let her.'

'I could not stand idly by and let her *murder* him!' Bryn bristled.

'Letting Khurdis Blackeye wander free to plan his revenge is preferable, I suppose?'

Bryn rubbed at his eyes. He looked most weary. 'Khurdis' he said softly, 'is going to have to be dealt with.'

'By who?'

'Me.'

Pawli shook his head. 'You're not making sense, Bryn! First you prevent Roe – Elinor – from dealing with him, and now . . .'

'I must do things as I must do them, lad, being who and what I am.' Bryn let out a long, tired breath. 'There's something happening, Pawli. Khurdis has . . . done something.'

'Like?'

'When he first came to me, Khurdis was hardly more than a little lad, skinny as a twig and so hungry to learn I hadn't the heart to turn him away.' Bryn shook his head. 'But he hadn't the *gift*. I could feel that, certain sure. It was a terrible thing I did, not sending him away right at the beginning, when I had the chance. But it seemed so . . . cruel. All that boy ever wanted was to be a far-seer.'

Bryn gazed off into the blue distance at the distant teeth of the peaks. 'He had a strength of will, that boy. An *incredible* strength of will. I saw him once actually move an iron pin, make it jiggle along a table top, just with the raw brute strength of that will of his. Almost made me believe he *did* have the *gift* after all.'

'But he doesn't?'

'The only *gift* Khurdis Blackeye has is that obstinate, iron will of his. But he has found . . . *something*. Those fire-rods he produced. Wherever did he get *those*, I ask myself. I don't like the answers.'

'Which are . . . what?'

'I'd rather not speak of it.'

'Bryn . . .' Pawli began, exasperated.

'Enough,' Bryn said. 'There's things beyond you here. I do what I must.'

Pawli's belly went suddenly tight. He felt as if he were looking into a river, seeing vague, dark shapes flitting under the moving surface . . .

'Pawli,' Bryn was saying. 'That sword . . . you must give it up. For your own good.'

'I will not speak of it,' Pawli said. And then, 'I, too, do what I must.'

'Pawli, listen to me.'

'No! You refuse to share anything, and then make unfair demands.'

'There's something moving in the world, Pawli. I can *feel* it.'

'I can *feel* it, too,' Pawli returned. 'No thanks to you!'

'Pawli . . .'

'No! Enough, Bryn. Enough of your selfish secrets.' Pawli lurched to his feet. 'I've spent years – *years!* – watching you sprawled out on the floor in your starweed daze, moaning and dribbling like an idiot, while I waited for the day when you would start to teach me, to acknowledge me for what and who I am. But no! And now you sit here giving me orders, hoarding your secrets as always, making grand, ridiculous plans . . . And in another day or so, you'll be back swooned on the floor again, stinking of starweed and drooling.'

Bryn went rigid.

'I'm done with it! Do you hear? I'm not a little lad any more. And though you may refuse to grant it, I'm no *ordinary* person, either. It's in our family's blood, Bryn. I'm a far-seer, just as you are. I have my own path to walk.'

'Pawli . . .' Bryn reached out.

But Pawli whirled, too quick for Bryn to be able to stop him, and stormed away.

VIII

Rain fell through the forest with a continuous hissing. Crouched under a sheltering pine, Pawli listened to the falling-water music of it and stared blindly off through the wet tangle of the trees, the iron broadsword held securely against him.

He had done it again, stormed off from Bryn in a heat of anger to find himself alone in the forest, his insides all turmoiled.

He felt as if he were perched upon a precipice, with the ground shifting uncertainly under his feet. It was coming. He could feel it . . . some mysterious, terrible thing was coming into the world, like a fell creature emerging out of the depths of a dark lake to crawl up upon the shore.

And what was *he* supposed to do about it?

It felt comforting to have the heavy sword in his hold, but he would be of no use with it in any real fight, he knew. He was no Roe-Elinor, who, through whatever hidden magicks she possessed, danced light-footed as a rabbit and deadly-strong as any hunting cat. No, he had no such magicks as she.

And all the while, that sense of terrible foreboding was growing in him. He was growing heartily sick of the feeling. When was this fell thing – whatever it might be – going to appear?

In the meantime, he had to do *something*.

He tried to search his inner self. If he was sensitive enough to feel this foreboding, then surely he ought to be able also to sense what actions to take. A far-seer read the hidden patterns of the world and acted accordingly . . .

But though he held himself still and focused as could be, straining like a hound searching the air for a faint scent, he could perceive no hidden pattern, no hint of any sort. Just the cold lump of fore-knowing in his guts. Pawli felt like hitting something, hard. What was the use of being *gifted* if all it did was torment one?

He could not suppress a surge of anger at starweed-addled Bryn, who would not share, who would not listen, whose fault it was he squatted here so utterly confounded.

And yet, for all that, if he were honest with himself, he had to concede that Bryn was his only true chance. What else was there for him, besides to wander alone and directionless through the trackless forest? Like it or not, his best path was to return to Bryn, keep his temper better, make Bryn understand. There had to be *some* way to get through to him.

And the sword? Pawli ran his fingers over the cold metal of the tangs and up across the pebbly leather wrapping of the hilt. The thing was, truly, of little practical use to him. Giving it up would be the sensible move – a peace offering to Bryn. But the very notion gave him a pang of dismay. It might be his own imagining, but he could not rid himself of that visceral conviction that this sword and he were somehow intended for each other. And, despite everything, it was still a pure thrill to feel it in his hold, heavy and solid and dangerous.

He wished with all his heart that there were some clear solution to all this, some way to know for certain his right path. Or that some miraculous thing would happen to unlock him, or to reveal the world's hidden secrets, or . . . something. But there was nothing. Just the rain, which had never ceased, and the forest like a black, wet maze all about him.

Slowly Pawli got to his feet and headed away upslope through the trees.

It was well on to evening by the time he got back to the

cabin – and still it rained, as if all the water in the mountains had been siphoned up to be let loose in a long cascade from the clouds. He was soaked to the bone and shivery, and eager to be indoors.

There was nobody outside the cabin – not surprising, given the day. But something was . . . not right. He felt abruptly, inexplicably certain of it. He had left the sword hidden securely just inside the verge in the forest, unable, at the last, to simply hand it over. Now he wished he had it with him. What if Khurdis Blackeye had come sneaking round, looking for revenge, and caught Bryn and Elinor unawares?

He hurried forwards, his heart thumping.

The door was ajar, and he hesitated, not knowing what might lie inside. There was nothing to hear save the steady drumming of the rain on the roof shingles. Pushing the door further open, he ducked in. After the outside, the cabin seemed close and warm and dark. Watery light washed in a little ways from the open door, but not enough to dispel the overall dimness, with the shutters closed against the rain as they were. A lone candle burned, throwing flickering shadows.

Elinor was knelt near Bryn, who lay sprawled out in his old place on the floor. 'Where have you been?' she demanded.

Pawli did not bother to answer. The cabin stank of stale starweed smoke. So much for Bryn's grand plans of dealing with Khurdis, he thought disgustedly. And so ended his own hopes of a meeting.

'I'm worried for him,' Elinor said, gesturing at Bryn's comatose form. 'He's been like this all day.'

'He's fine,' Pawli returned curtly. He looked about, dripping water everywhere, unable to quite dispel the sense of there being something wrong. But there appeared nothing.

Elinor was still hovering concernedly over Bryn. 'Come look at him . . .'

'I've seen him like this many a time,' Pawli told her, feeling his irritation mount. He resented the way she seemed to be trying to take charge here, in *his* home. 'You saw him like this yourself, the night you came here.'

'Not like *this*, surely,' she said. 'I can't seem to get any response from him at all, and I've tried everything I can think of.'

Pawli felt scant sympathy for Bryn. Going to the rear of the cabin, he reached down dry trousers and shirt from a shelf and changed quickly out of his sodden clothing. He hung his old clothes to dry, wrung his wet hair, lit a second candle, and only then went over to Bryn. What he saw stopped him cold.

Bryn lay in his usual place on the floor, his ratty old blanket wrapped half about him, forming a lump, as it usually seemed to, around his legs. All that was normal enough. But Bryn's face was white as new bone, and his jaw hung open in a manner that made Pawli think uneasily of the slack jaw of a corpse. And he seemed to be hardly breathing.

'I've never seen him like *this* before,' Pawli said uneasily, crouching down.

'Perhaps we should get him to his bed,' Elinor suggested.

Before Pawli could say anything, she had leaned forwards and started to disentangle Bryn's blanket. It was a thing Pawli would never have done so unselfconsciously, for Bryn had made it clear long ago that he was not to be disturbed in any way – any way at all – while he was deep in starweed.

'What's this, then?' Elinor said in surprise, lifting something from out of the blanket's dirty folds.

Pawli stared, astonished. 'I have no idea. I've never seen it before.'

Cradled in Elinor's hands, glowing softly in the cabin's dim light, was a perfect crystal globe. The size of a man's skull nearly, it was clear as the purest new ice, without

91

blemish of any sort save for a small trail of what seemed like tiny bubbles spiralling through it.

Where had Bryn ever got such a wonderful object? Pawli felt as if somebody had just yanked the firm ground out from under his feet. How was it that he had never seen the thing till now? And what . . . *what* was it doing wrapped in the dirty blanket under Bryn's knees? Pawli leaned closer and peered into the globe's crystal depths. Clear as clear it was, yet somehow there was a . . . a *strangeness* about it. Gazing through it, it seemed to him that the room looked queerly far away. The little bubble-trail spiralled through the crystal like a diminishing path, leading down, down . . .

'Pawli,' somebody was saying. 'Pawli!'

Pawli blinked. He felt something hard pressing against his back. For long heartbeats he did not know quite where he was, or how. Then he realised that he was on his back on the floor, staring blindly up at the ceiling.

'What . . . happened?' he muttered.

'You fell over,' Elinor told him. The crystal globe was on the floor, and she flicked it with the toe of her boot. 'You looked into the globe and just . . . fell over.'

Pawli shivered. He did not know what to say.

'Let's get your uncle to his bed, anyhow,' Elinor suggested. 'That before anything.'

Pawli got up – feeling tilty-dizzy for the first few moments – and helped Elinor haul Bryn to bed. He was a clumsy load, but not heavy. Under his baggy clothes, poor Bryn was all skin and bones. When he was safely tucked up in bed under the blanket, Pawli stood over him worriedly. Bryn's face was slicked with a sheen of dank sweat, and he felt chill to the touch. He had not moved when they carried him, not so much as the flicker of an eyelid.

Elinor, meanwhile, had returned to the crystal globe. Reaching down a raggedy towel from a wall hook – as if she feared to touch the thing with her bare hands – she carefully lifted the crystal from the floor and placed it on their narrow plank eating table, bunching the towel about its base to hold it from rolling about. 'You've truly never seen this thing before?' she asked Pawli.

He nodded, staring at it. In the candlelight, the globe glowed with a soft, complex glitter. And it seemed deep, somehow, deep without end . . . Pawli blinked, swallowed, looked away quickly. 'It doesn't make any sense,' he said. 'I'd *know* if Bryn kept such a wondrous thing here. I've been here with him for years.'

'He's a man of hidden knowledge, your uncle,' Elinor said. 'The ways of such as he can be most subtle.'

'Meaning?'

'Perhaps he did not *wish* you to know such a thing was here.'

'No. Why would he want to . . .' Pawli stopped. None of this made any sense.

Elinor was gazing down at the globe on the table top. 'Is it this thing, do you reckon, that's responsible for what's happened to your uncle? It certainly seems to be an object of *power*. And it had an immediate effect upon you. Could Brynmaur have used it in some manner and found himself . . . I don't know – entangled by it, or some such?' She turned to Pawli. 'How much do you know about this starweed he uses? Could Brynmaur have simply taken too much of it? Could that reduce him to the state he's in now?'

Pawli shrugged uncertainly. He had grown so used to Bryn's starweed habit that he hardly paid attention. 'I don't . . . don't think so.'

'So it's likely to be this globe in some way?'

Again, Pawli shrugged. He did not know how to know.

The two of them stood next to the table gazing down at the crystal globe uncertainly. It glowed and scintillated. There was something . . . *compelling* about it. Pawli looked away, shivering. 'Do you feel it?' he asked.

Elinor looked at him. 'Feel what?'

'The globe. It . . . draws one into it.'

Elinor shook her head. 'I feel no such draw. Or . . .' She looked into the globe's crystal depths. 'Perhaps just a little, yes. Though not as you seem to. You have a sensitivity I lack. But it does feel strangely . . .'

'Deep,' Pawli finished for her.

'Just so,' she agreed after a moment.

They stood for the space of a dozen breaths, saying nothing. The only sound was the steady drumming of the rain on the roof overhead. One of the candles began to gutter, sending lurching shadows everywhere. Pawli reached the oil lamp down from its hook and lit it. Night was drawing on, and he closed and latched the cabin door. Holding the lantern high in one hand, he went over to look at Bryn, who lay like a corpse in his bed. He had always said Bryn would kill himself one day with the starweed. But surely, *surely*, this was not to be that day.

Pawli felt the cold lump of foreknowing that had been sitting in his belly these past days expand within him, as if something had ruptured, filling him with sudden dread. It was all connected: Bryn and Elinor and himself and Khurdis and . . . and he did not know what. Like a great storm looming. Shadows . . . hints. He was sick of being ridden by such formless things! A sense of dark urgency gripped him.

'We've got to help Bryn!' he said, turning to Elinor.

She was gazing round the cabin. 'Do you reckon there might be other things hidden about here?'

Pawli shook his head impatiently. 'No. I'd know about them. Listen, we've got to—'

'Where persons of *power* are concerned,' Elinor said, 'nothing's simple,'

'But I would have *seen* anything special.'

'Not unless he wished it.'

Pawli opened his mouth, closed it. If Bryn had kept this wondrous glowing globe from him – his eyes kept slipping

94

towards it, and he had to pull his gaze away with an effort – what other secrets might his uncle have? 'All right,' he conceded. 'Let's look. But quickly.'

Elinor nodded. 'Let's.'

They searched everywhere, from the little pit of the root cellar to the musty, web-hung rafters, with no result. 'There's nothing here,' Pawli said, with a certain relief. 'Besides, we don't even know what we're looking for.'

'Let's keep looking, anyway,' Elinor said.

'But we've already looked!'

'So we look again. Sometimes it takes time for the eye and the mind to adjust to a task.'

Pawli wrung his hands in agitation. Bryn lay like a very corpse, and the world was heaving in some deep way he did not understand. They had to *do* something! But, try as he might, he could think of no alternative course of action to pose against Elinor's. And there was a solidity of will to her that brooked no denial. 'All right,' he said. 'Let's look again.'

In the end, it was Elinor who found the little book.

It had been hidden in the most obvious place – if 'hidden' were the right word. Bryn had simply placed it upon the fireplace mantel. It was just the right size to fit the mantel's width, and thin enough to sit flat and unnoticed. There had been an old tin candle sconce set on it. Pawli had missed it entirely.

It was only because Elinor had gone back methodically through everything he had already checked that the thing came to light. A little cold shiver went up Pawli's spine. He must have walked past it a thousand times.

It was a smallish, leather-bound volume, one finger-width thick perhaps, if that. It had a musty, odd smell to it once one got close. Elinor opened it slowly to the first page. Peering over her shoulder, Pawli made out several lines penned in a crawling handwriting. 'What's it say?' He swallowed. 'I . . . I can't . . . read. Can you?'

Elinor nodded.

95

Pawli felt a quick little stab of envy at this young woman who could do so much.

'This is an *old* book,' she said. 'Listen. On the first page here, it says, "The . . . the *talanyr*" – I've never seen that word before. And below that, "being a . . . a guide" – I think. The spelling is queer. "A guide to its use and . . . and properties." '

'That's all?' Pawli said.

'All on this first page.'

Carefully, Elinor turned the page. Pawli saw that the next was packed with dense writing.

' "When properly employed," ' Elinor read, ' "the . . . *talanyr* enables the Seer to . . . to far-travel to realms beyond those en . . . envisioned by ordinary mortal folk." ' She stopped, took a sharp breath. Her eyes flicked down the page, and she read on, ' ". . . when the spirit is properly loosened from the flesh . . ." ' She read on, mumbling the words to herself too low for Pawli to make them out.

'What does it say?' he demanded.

She went over to Bryn's rocker and sat down. 'Give me a moment,' she answered, poring over the little book.

Pawli stood impatiently, shifting from foot to foot. 'Well?'

'It seems that this . . . *talanyr*, as the writer of this book calls it, acts as an aid to loosen the spirit from the body and send it far-travelling into . . . I know not where.'

'What's a . . . *talanyr*, then?'

Elinor pointed towards the crystal globe. 'That's a *talanyr*, according to the description I've just read.'

'You mean . . .'

Elinor nodded. 'Your uncle used that thing to far-travel into . . . some realm or other. And I reckon that he must have got himself . . . stranded.'

Pawli felt sick. 'But why would he . . . Why didn't he *tell* me he was going to do such a crazy thing?'

'He must have had his reasons,' Elinor said.

Pawli frowned, bit his lip. This had something to with Khurdis Blackeye; he felt sure of it. Damn Bryn for not telling him anything!

He looked across at the little book in Elinor's hands, at Bryn, deathly pale, lying still as still on his bed, at the glowing crystal globe – the *talanyr*. It was hard to get his mind round it all: Bryn not merely in a starweed faint but spirit-travelling to some utterly strange realm . . .

IX

'And so?' Pawli demanded impatiently. 'What does it say?'

Her nose in the book, Elinor waved him off. 'There's more I need to read.'

Pawli turned from her and paced impatiently. It was black night. The rain had ceased and the cabin was wrapped in silence. Poor Bryn still lay as one dead. At times, indeed, it seemed he *was* dead, for his breathing was so shallow as to be almost undetectable.

'What *did* you think you were about, Bryn?' Pawli said softly, pausing to stand over his uncle. He was beginning to be gripped by a feeling that they had all passed some kind of ethereal watershed and were headed . . . he knew not where. The urgency he had been feeling had not slackened. He looked across at Elinor. 'Well? What have you found? What purpose did he have in doing this thing? How do we bring him back?'

'There's nothing here to help us answer those questions, I'm afraid,' Elinor replied.

'What *does* it say, then?' Pawli asked in exasperation.

'As far as I can make out, it gives instructions on how to use the *talanyr* to far-travel.'

'And?'

'It says that the spirit must be properly loosened from the flesh in order for the *talanyr* to work. There seem to be several ways of doing this, though I don't understand them all – there's much here I can't make sense of . . . But one of the ways of soul-loosening it mentions is the use of something the writer names *stella munda*.'

'Which is?'

'A plant. There's a drawing of it here.' She held the book out to him, open. 'Is this what starweed looks like?'

Pawli peered at the image on the page. It was neatly executed in brown ink, showing the familiar seven-leaf cluster of starweed. He had helped Bryn pick many a crop down in the sheltered, sunwards slopes of the Jade River Valley, and he recognised it easily enough. 'That's it,' he said.

Elinor nodded. 'So that's my way, then.'

Pawli blinked in surprise.

'He'll die if he isn't brought back soon,' Elinor said. 'And nothing we've done for him has been of any use. I'm going after him.'

'You can't!' Pawli said. 'You're no far-seer. How can you—'

'The book makes it all most clear.'

'If anyone goes, it ought to be me, then. I have Bryn's *gift* in me. I . . .'

'No,' Elinor interrupted. 'I've had far more experience in the world than you, and seen more than a few strange things. Who knows what might lie in wait in this . . . this *other* place the *talanyr* conducts one to? I'm the one to go.'

'What makes you think . . .' Pawli paused. 'Why should you want to do such a thing?' All his confusion and ambivalence about her, all his repressed resentment and the balked urgency in him, suddenly spilled over in an unexpected flood of vehemence. 'Wandering out of nowhere up here into the heights, alone and in disguise, toting a weapon so regal and puissant you must keep it hid, fighting like some unstoppable demon and yet raggedy-poor as any peasant . . . What manner of creature *are* you?'

Elinor looked taken aback.

'What deeds have driven you?' Pawli stabbed a finger at her. 'You're trouble. That's what Bryn said. What are you *doing* here amongst us?'

Elinor laid the book aside and unhooked the sheathed

sword that, as always, hung at her belt. She held it up for his inspection. The bronze wire wrapping the crimson leather scabbard glinted under the candlelight. In the visage of the bronze dragon-head that formed the hilt, little ruby eyes flashed, as if alive. '*This* is what drives me,' she said, soft-voiced. 'It is no ordinary weapon.'

'I have seen *that*!' Pawli replied sharply.

'It is burden and gift,' Elinor said. 'My grief and my joy.'

'And the . . . amulet you wear? What of that?'

Elinor looked discomfited. 'It . . . was given me in a far-away place. I'd rather not speak of it.'

Pawli had had his fill of secretiveness with Bryn. He wanted none from this Elinor now. 'Tell me . . .'

But she had come forward to him, putting the sword aside – one of the few times he had seen her part with it. 'My life has not been . . . easy, Pawli. I will not bore you with the details. You see me as I have become: poor and ragged and without a home. But I am . . . *called*, will I or nil I. Your uncle gave me the shelter I needed when nobody else would, despite his misgivings about me. Folk are not generally so . . . kind to me. I owe him for that. But there is . . . more. Something has drawn me here into your mountains. It is set upon me to do what I do.'

Pawli remembered Roe as he had first seen him – her, rather – on the Keel Track, alone and travel-weary, having trekked the Powers alone knew how far. 'What do you mean . . . *called*?'

'I think you know, Pawli.'

Pawli's scalp prickled. He had a sudden sense of great, depthless currents surging under him. 'Powers move the world.'

Elinor nodded. 'Trust me. I am no enemy of yours.'

There was something in her look, compellingly direct and guileless, that made Pawli believe her – for all that he still had unanswered questions. 'All right,' he said slowly.

Elinor turned and grabbed up the book. 'Let's begin, then. Every moment we delay hurts Bryn the more.'

This agreed with Pawli's own sense of urgency. He fetched Bryn's starweed paraphernalia – the little cedar box, the bone pipe, the white-fire sticks and candle – and laid the things on the eating table, at the far end from where the *talanyr* still rested.

Working the close-fitting lid off Bryn's little box, he took out a pinch of the starweed. It was blackish-green, the leaves of it so finely rubbed as to be nearly powder. Dropping the pinch of it in his palm, Pawli sniffed at it. He had never taken the time to examine it before. This close, the scent of it was so sharp it stung his nostrils and made him sneeze.

'What do I do?' Elinor asked.

Pawli shrugged. 'I'm not sure. I never paid much attention, really. It was nothing *I* ever wanted to try.'

Elinor nodded. She held up the pipe. 'We put the dried leaves in here?'

'Bryn always did.' Pawli tried to recollect. Somehow, he had no clear remembrance of how exactly Bryn smoked his starweed. It was odd. All the years he had been here, with Bryn in starweed trance more often than not in the last couple, and yet he could not recall even the simplest of details. And how had Bryn kept that incredible crystal globe hidden from him? It made no sense. The thought of it lit a smoulder of resentful anger in him. Why had Bryn refused to share even the smallest of things with him?

'Well?' Elinor was asking.

Pawli took the pipe from her and dipped it into the box, tamping the powdered leaf into the pipe's bowl with his thumb. 'Here.'

They settled her on Pawli's bed – that would be more comfortable than the floor Bryn had used – and followed Bryn's lead by wrapping a blanket about Elinor. She kept the sword by her side, saying nothing about it, but being careful to make sure it was tucked securely away beneath her under the blanket. Once she was properly installed, Pawli fetched the *talanyr* from where it still sat on the table, holding it using the towel Elinor had lapped it in, taking pains neither to touch the thing directly nor to look into its queer crystal depths.

Elinor was stretched out full-length on the bed, lying partly on her side, the blanket wrapping her from toes to chin, though leaving her arms free. Gently, Pawli laid the *talanyr* on the mattress close by her head, making a little nest for it with the towel so that it would sit firm.

Propping herself up on one elbow, Elinor held out the charged pipe. Pawli took up one of Bryn's little white-fire sticks, flicked it with his thumbnail the way one was supposed to, and a spurt of bright flame lit the tip.

Elinor took it from him, placed the flame to the pipe's small bowl and inhaled. The first hit of smoke made her cough so hard she fumbled everything, spilling sparks all across the bed and nearly tipping the *talanyr* onto the floor.

'Careful!' Pawli said, grabbing for the *talanyr*.

Elinor stared at him as if he were very far away.

'I'll hold the pipe this time,' Pawli said. Steadying her hand with his, he held the flame of a new white-fire stick to the pipe's bowl. Inhaling the smoke made Elinor cough violently again, but this time he was ready and nothing untoward happened. They repeated the process once more. He could hear the little *krackle* in the pipe's bowl each time Elinor inhaled, and the powdered starweed took light. The air was filled with the pungent scent of the smoke.

When the pipe was emptied, Elinor let it drop from her hold, as if her fingers were gone numb. She began to shiver, little wracking spasms that made her teeth chatter softly.

'You all right?' Pawli asked, concerned.

She said nothing. Slowly, her head fell back onto the pillow. The hand that had held the pipe slipped off the bed, hanging in mid-air. Pawli lifted it back and tucked it under the blanket. Her skin felt chill to the touch. 'Elinor,' he said. 'Elinor! The *talanyr*.'

Her head came round. She blinked owlishly. Pawli held the crystal globe before her eyes. Her mouth opened in an 'O' of . . . surprise, fear, excitement? He could not tell.

'Elinor?' He did not know what he had expected. Some dramatic flare of mysterious light, perhaps, a strange sound filling the cabin, the globe expanding to huge size . . . But nothing of the sort happened. Her face pressed close to the *talanyr*, staring fixedly into its crystal depths, Elinor let out a small moan. Then her eyes rolled suddenly in their sockets and she fell back upon the bed.

'Elinor!' Pawli cried.

But she was gone.

Pawli steadied the *talanyr* and stood looking at her for a long few moments. Had it worked? Was her spirit even now voyaging in some incredible, distant realm? Or was she simply in a starweed swoon? There was no way to tell, except . . .

The first hit of the smoke was like a sharp wire ball being thrust down into his lungs. He gasped and coughed and retched, just as Elinor had. But he was expecting it and managed not to drop anything.

The starweed tasted foul. He hugged himself and spat, trying to rid his mouth of the bitter taste of it. He felt a sudden cold chill go through his limbs.

Placing the little flame of the lighting brand to the pipe bowl again, he put the pipestem to his lips and inhaled. The smoke was like a blow. How could Bryn stand to do this day in and day out? He exhaled, coughing, and watched the smoke shred into long blue spirals. It caught the dancing candlelight and drifted, a delicate webbery ascending.

His head seemed to have grown very big, or his body very small. He was not sure which. He felt himself beginning to shiver uncontrollably, as if a winter wind were suddenly whipping through the cabin – but there was no wind. He blinked, tried to take a breath. The shivers had him in a relentless grip, long wracking waves of them. He hugged himself, trying to make them stop, more than a little frightened – perhaps this had not been such a good idea after all. He felt sick. He tried to wrap himself tighter in the blanket – Bryn's ratty starweed blanket – knowing now why Bryn had always wrapped himself up so.

Elinor had taken three good hits from the pipe. He had one more to go if he were to follow her. He put the pipestem to his lips and forced himself to take another inhalation of the bitter smoke. This time, his lungs did not feel it quite so much. He let the smoke out slowly, watching it ascend through the light in fine, impossibly complex patterns. Slowly, for his head seem entirely huge by now, he turned his gaze to where the *talanyr* lay.

It glowed like a little moon. Pawli stared at it, transfixed. It seemed to throb. His vision seemed to. The cabin was gone, somehow. Dropped entirely away. Only the glowing crystal globe remained. The little track of bubbles inside it trailed off.

He felt himself falling then, a slow, inevitable plunge into . . .

He knew not what.

The bubble trail curved and dipped and shimmered. There was light, and darkness . . . then more light. He felt a great, tearing pain lance through him. Something seemed to snap apart.

And then he was . . .

Gone.

PART TWO

X

Elinor came to herself flat on her belly with her face pressed into cindery dirt.

So much for the great starweed/crystal globe adventure, she thought disgustedly. She had managed to accomplish nothing more than to pass out on the cabin's dirt floor. Her head ached, and she felt sick. Her mouth was foul with the smoky aftertaste of the starweed. Grumbling a curse against the useless stuff, she pried herself up to a sitting position.

And gasped.

She was not, *certainly not*, in the cabin.

There was not much in the way of light, and she found it difficult to make any clear sense of her surroundings. It was like waking up in the dim pre-dawn: there were shapes and forms about, but everything seemed hazy and indistinct. The air had a faint metallic twang to it that bit unpleasantly at the nostrils. And all was wrapped in a silence so profoundly deep that her ears rang with it. Stiffly, she got to her feet. A soft radiance, she realised, did help relieve the darkness a little, almost like starshine, but, though the sky overhead was black-dark, there were no stars to be seen. Elinor shivered.

She could hardly credit that she was standing here, in this dreadfully *other* place, while, at this very same instant, her body lay in the bed in Brynmaur's cabin. She lifted a hand before her face, peered at it, flexed her fingers, and froze.

The little finger of her left hand . . . Almost two years ago it had been severed. Now it was intact. She bent the finger, feeling the joints move. Reaching down to her right thigh, she felt for the long ridge of scar tissue that ought to be there. It was gone – along with the ache that had been in it these past wet days.

She felt her pulse thump, felt cindery-dry air flow in and out of her lungs; she was dressed exactly as she had been when she had smoked the starweed. How was it she had a body here, then? And a body cleansed of injuries . . . How could such things be? This was past anything of her experience.

Yet she was here.

Wherever 'here' might be.

Instinctively, she reached for the reassurance of the sword at her side. But it was not there – of course. It lay tucked under her blanket-wrapped body back in the cabin. Quickly, she felt at her sternum, under her tunic. Yes! Her little Fey-bone amulet was still there. She slipped it out of the neck of her tunic, peering at the familiar shape of it: the small ivory-ochre piece of bone, slender and straight, the length of two finger joints, intricately carved with a miniature tanglewood, all limb and leaf, elbow and crook and shadow of tree. It felt warm in her fingers. A *special* thing . . .

How was it she had this with her, yet not the white blade? She crossed her arms and hugged herself, cherishing the hard little shape of the Fey-bone in her hands. She felt naked and alone, separated from her sword. With it, she had done wonderful things, and terrible too. It had been guide and defence and companion for years now, always to hand or by her side, and she sorely missed its familiar presence in this strange, *other* place.

Empty-handed, she looked about her at the dim, unearthly landscape.

What to do now? However was she to find Brynmaur? There was no sign of him here, no sign of anything human at all, just the dim, uncertain landscape all about, and the oppressive silence.

And her, stranded here alone upon this most, most strange shore.

She lifted the Fey-bone again, remembering how it had come to her . . . the long, pale fingers of the Fey cradling it, the full moon ghosting the sky above, the dark shapes of the great forest Phanta as they danced their slow, ponderously graceful dances, the eyes in Gyver's furred face bright with wonder . . . a painful, wonderful, rich memory.

Elinor shook herself from out of it. The Fey-bone resting in her palm had virtues she could only guess at. Could it be of help here in this *other* place? Was there some way to use it in the search for Brynmaur? But though it pulsed with a soft warmth in her hand, she could perceive nothing in the way of guidance from it. A spasm of frustration went through her, and she yearned for her white blade. That, at least, she knew the virtue of. She would far rather have its solid weight in her hand than the light warmth of this mysterious shard of bone. She wished . . .

If wishes were horses, Jago, her stepfather had been fond of saying, beggars would ride.

She shook herself and slipped the Fey-bone back under her tunic. Enough of memory and confusion. It was time she did something. Peering ahead, she tried to get some sense of the lay of things, but the dim, untrustworthy light made it difficult to distinguish one form from another. There was a darkish rise of something before her, but she could not tell if it were the long back of a distant hill, or the slope of some largish rock formation close at hand. It was all most unearthly strange.

And then, suddenly, she head a voice call 'Elinor,' soft and hoarse. In the great silence of this place, it sounded like a shout. She twisted round, startled, her heart thumping.

It was Pawli, sprawled in the dirt a little distance away.

'What are *you* doing here?' she demanded. It was one thing for her to voyage to this place; she had felt herself channelled here, and she had had experience of more than a few strange things already in her life (and little enough left to lose, really, if all went wrong). But Pawli was innocent as a babe to the wider world's cruel ways, growing up in the isolated mountain hinterland as he had, and vulnerable.

He had got to his feet now. 'Did you think I was just going to sit around back there like some obedient little lad, waiting blindly?' They were conversing in fierce whispers, for there was something about the great depth of the silence here that made them feel uneasy about breaking it. 'I'm fed up to the back teeth with waiting,' he hissed vehemently. '*And* with people keeping secrets.'

'You . . .' Elinor began, but then faltered. There was little point in arguing. He was here now, for good or ill. And, truth to tell, she was not altogether unhappy to have company in this unsettling otherwhere.

Pawli had turned from her and was peering around uncertainly. 'Is Bryn hereabouts, then?'

Elinor made no answer. Behind Pawli she could suddenly make out a wall of dark rock – the first thing she had truly seen clear in this place. She tipped her head back, following the rise of the rock with her eyes, up, up, up . . . There seemed no end to it.

Pawli stamped softly against the cindery ground. 'Is this place . . . *real*? Are we?'

Elinor stepped up to him and put a hand lightly to his arm. 'You look and feel . . . real.' She gestured to the too-tall cliff face behind, the dim landscape facing them. 'So does all else . . . seem so, at least.'

'I don't understand,' Pawli said.

'Nor I,' Elinor agreed.

'It's . . . *ugly*,' Pawli went on after a few moments. 'Whyever would Bryn choose to come to a place like *this*?'

Elinor shrugged. 'Perhaps he did not . . . choose. Or perhaps there is more to this place than we see now.'

They went silent then.

Elinor had a sudden, complete conviction that she did not wish to be here. This was not a realm that felt friendly to ordinary mortal human folk. She stared up at the starless dark of the sky beyond the far-distant top of the cliff, then dropped her gaze to the dim contour of the landscape about her, hummocky and jagged – she could make things out a touch clearer now, as if her eyes were beginning to adjust to this place. But nowhere could she see anything alive. No bird call, no slightest buzz or hum of insect life lightened the relentless grip of the silence. She swallowed, clenched and unclenched her fingers. Her mouth tasted foul. Her head throbbed. Her nose stung from the acrid air. It seemed hard to get a proper breath. And there was no sign of Brynmaur, no indication of where to go or what to do.

She ached to have the white blade in her hand.

Pawli was looking at her expectantly.

Elinor sighed. Like it or not, she was here. Her life had brought her to more than a few strange passes; this was but another. And, as had happened before, there was no denying the task before her.

There were no landmarks in this *other* realm, nothing to indicate one direction as better or worse than any other. But if they were to find Brynmaur, staying here looked to be a singularly useless option. 'I reckon we'd best move on,' she said, speaking softly in the silence. Turning, she scanned the dim landscape, hoping to find something – anything – that might give her a hint as to direction. There was nothing. The only option was to press on regardless, so she led off directly away from the cliff, that being as good a direction as any.

One step she took, another . . . and then stopped.

'What is it?' Pawli asked uneasily.

'I . . . I don't know.' Elinor tried to go on, but could not. It was as if there were some manner of invisible tether pulling her back towards the cliff. She turned and fretted and shivered with it.

'What's wrong?' Pawli asked. 'Let's get along.'

'I . . . I can't,' Elinor said uncertainly. 'Something seems to be pulling me back.'

Pawli stared at her. The darksome light of this place made his eyes seem to shimmer in a soft, eerie manner.

'I feel . . .' Elinor did not know quite what she felt. It was too strange. There was just this *something* pulling on her, like a soft hook in her guts. For good or ill, she simply could not gainsay it. 'I . . . I must go back,' she said, shivering.

'Back *where*?' Pawli demanded.

Not without reason. They had arrived in this realm directly at the foot of the rearing cliff-wall, as if they had been thrust through the very stone of it. There *was* no way back. And yet . . .

The tether – or whatever it might be – tugged at her and she had no choice save to follow, feeling like a blind person tracing a faint, nagging scent.

'What are you *doing*?' Pawli complained.

She made no answer. All her attention was focused now on the stone detritus that lay before her. The cliff reared up and up, as if it rose straight up into the sky for ever . . . if indeed there was a sky in this queer place. The stone face of it was rough and broken and, down here at its base, Elinor now saw, there were many hollows and grottoes created by the tumble of fallen rock from above. They had *emerged* here in the middle of one such grotto and walked out of it, all unknowing. Lucky nothing had come plummeting down on them. She felt her skin crawl and looked up, half expecting to see some huge boulder hurtling downwards . . .

The tether was still tugging at her. Ducking round a dark slab of stone the size of a house almost – what a great crash it must have made in this silent place when it came smashing to the ground here – she caught sudden sight of a faint glow ahead and downwards. She had to get on her hands and knees and crawl through into a kind of cracked fissure-cum-tunnel to follow it. The tether-feeling was clear as clear now. She was being *pulled* . . .

And then, suddenly, there it was: a slender rod of light.

Her blade! Somehow she knew it had to be, though how such a thing might occur, she had no notion. Reaching a hand out, she picked the thing up. It was light – far lighter than her true blade – and not much longer than her forearm. But she could feel the familiar tingle of it in her finger bones. Her heart beat hard. Yes . . . This was her white blade all right, though why it should have the seeming of a slender wand made of softly glowing wood, she did not know.

She looked at it, relieved, comforted, thrilled, utterly mystified. The sword was no ordinary weapon; it gave and it took, making her greater and lesser than ordinary folk, changing her irrevocably. It had a presence, a soul almost, and was an entity to be reckoned with. She had yearned for it. Had it somehow known her need? She held the slim wand up before her, relishing the soft, reassuring glow of it. Let it remain a mystery, how it came to her here. She did not need to know. She only needed to have the familiar thing in her grasp. It made her feel whole again.

'What are you doing?' she heard Pawli demand waspishly from behind her. 'First you start crawling about, and then you just . . . just drop down this hole and— What's *that*?' He was staring at the glowing wand.

'It's my blade.'

'Your *what*?'

Elinor hefted the wand. It felt very light in her hold. 'It's my blade. The white blade.'

Pawli sat on the edge of a boulder and rubbed his thigh. 'It's a stick!'

'But it's my own true blade nonetheless.' Elinor grinned. 'I have no notion how such a thing can be. But it is.'

Pawli stared at the glowing wand in her hand. 'It's a cursed *strange* place, this. Why*ever* would Bryn choose to come here?'

Why indeed, Elinor thought. What would bring any ordinary man to an unnatural realm such as this? She hoped that they had indeed arrived at the right location and that they had not made some terrible mistake. What if there were many such realms as this, like many rooms all leading off from a single corridor, and they had somehow arrived in one that Brynmaur had never gone near? Elinor shook herself. It did not bear thinking on. 'Come on,' she said. 'Let's be off.'

Away from the cliff they walked, Elinor in the lead. There was no path, and they merely followed the route of least resistance, weaving a way through the mess of the tumbled boulders and then, once they had got beyond the range of such things, traipsing along across a curving, empty slope. The ground underfoot was cindery dry. Each step they took rattled and *cruuunched* outrageously in the huge quiet.

Ahead, the view began to open up a little, and Elinor could make out hummocky mounds and mouldering upthrusts of something like, yet not quite like, stone. As they drew close to the first of these upthrusts, thick as a great tree's bole and the height of three men at least, Elinor put her hand on it tentatively. It felt solid enough, but she could dig her fingers right into it. Stone it might appear, but it had no more hardness to it than stale cheese. It cast a soft glow, like a firefly.

'Where do we go now?' Pawli said, whispering still.

Overhead, the sky was a starless, dark void. Elinor could make out no horizon, no light save a kind of faint, directionless radiance. No . . . It was the cheese-stones, she suddenly realised. They cast a soft glow all about.

'Where do we go?' Pawli said. He was crouched next to one of the softly glowing cheese-stone upthrusts, squinting about uncertainly, rubbing his leg.

'I don't know,' Elinor replied. There was no hint, no sign of Brynmaur anywhere.

Pawli snorted. 'My legs feel wrong.'

'What?'

'My legs feel all *wrong*.'

Elinor peered at him. It seemed an odd thing to say. But in this place, who knew what might or might not be? 'Stand up,' she suggested, for he was still hunkered down against the upthrust of cheese-stone.

Pawli did. He looked exactly as he had back in the cabin, same worn leather clothing, same lad. And yet . . . Was he a shade taller? Elinor regarded him appraisingly. Perhaps . . . yes. His legs did seem to be longer than they had been. In fact, now that she looked more closely, they seemed longer than human legs ought to be.

Pawli hunkered down again, drawing his legs up. His knees, now, came well up past his ears. 'I don't *like* this,' he said in a plaintive voice.

Elinor knelt next to him. 'The . . . the *real* us is back in the cabin, Pawli,' she said reassuringly. 'Anything might happen here in this strange place, but when the starweed's effect wears off, we'll be back to our old selves again.'

'What would *you* know about it?' Pawli snapped. 'It didn't wear off for Bryn.'

Elinor had no easy answer for that.

Pawli's face was puckered in distaste. 'I don't *like* it here.'

Elinor looked about her at the darksome landscape, full of uncertain shapes. 'Me neither.' The faint-glowing cheese-stones around them tilted this way and that, some rearing up tall and slender as needles, others squat and mounded. Her eyes ached for a bit of colour, something wholesome and alive and green.

'It gets . . . *inside* me,' Pawli murmured.

'What does?'

Pawli was hunched over himself, rubbing compulsively at his legs.

'Pawli?'

No answer.

Elinor reached a hand to his shoulder. 'Pawli? Is there anything . . .'

He jerked from her touch, blinking furiously. 'Just like some tadpole in a black-deep pond,' he said.

Elinor stared at him. 'What?'

He was scratching himself vigorously under the arm now. 'Only the tadpole doesn't understand.'

'Pawli! You're not making sense.'

He shook his head, blinked some more, like some night creature suddenly exposed to the too-bright day.

'We . . . we need to get on,' Elinor said, thinking – hoping – that movement might help whatever was happening here.

Pawli stopped scratching abruptly. 'Get on? Which way?'

'The direction we've been going is as good as any, I reckon,' Elinor replied, pointing ahead. If nothing else, she thought, the towering cliff-face behind them at least provided a marker they could use to avoid wandering in useless circles. 'Let's get along.'

Pawli stood up on his long legs. He was definitely taller; his head now easily topped hers. 'It gets inside me,' Pawli had said. Meaning what? He was acting so strangely. She sensed no such . . . invasion in herself. She felt quickly at her own legs, her arms; everything seemed as it always had, save for her miraculously cured injuries. She flexed her left hand, just for the simple joy of feeling – and of seeing – her restored little finger move.

Pawli took a step, stumbled clumsily, caught himself against an upthrust of cheese-stone. 'I can't walk.' he said in anguish. 'My *legs* . . .'

Elinor reached a hand to him. He stared at her, his eyes wide and white with fear. 'Just a matter of getting used to them is all,' she said lightly, trying to defuse the growing fright in him. She felt her own heart shiver a little, but she smiled and made sure that her grip – her five-fingered grip – upon him was steady. 'They're your own legs, after all, Pawli.'

'They used to be, at any rate.' He smiled back, attempting to make light of it, as she was. But it was a strained smile, and his hands were shaking.

'Come on,' Elinor said. 'Lean on me till you've got your legs properly under you.'

They started off together, Pawli taking big, clumsy steps with his queerly long legs.

After a little, he shrugged away from Elinor's supporting hold and stood rocking on his feet. Then, slowly, he moved on, one step, another, his legs rising high and slow, almost like he was learning a new dance.

They pushed forward, working their way slowly up a long slope that had appeared before them, weaving through the glowing cheese-stones. At the crest, they stopped, panting, Pawli rubbing his legs and muttering to himself.

The slope they had been climbing fell away beyond them in a series of dropping swells. Seen like this from a distance, the mass of cheese-stone peggery took on the look of an outlandish forest almost, a giant, rolling, soft-glowing, pebbly forest-carpet that swept all the way to the horizon – or where the horizon would be in any normal land. Here, there was only a fading into dimness, with no clear separation of earth and sky at all.

'What we need now is—' Elinor began. But she stopped in mid-word for, suddenly, the Fey-bone amulet hanging under her tunic had become a pulsing warmth. She put a hand to it, surprised.

In the distance ahead, something rumbled.

After all their time in the great silence of this place, the noise seemed stunningly loud. The very ground shook with it: a deep, throbbing vibration, almost like far off thunder, felt in the bones as much as heard with the ears: *KOO-OOM-BAH BAH . . . KOO-OOM-BAH*. Elinor felt her skull begin to shudder uncomfortably with it. The warmth of the Fey-bone increased.

KOO-OOM-BAH . . .

Getting louder.

'What *is* it?' Pawli hissed. His hands were to his ears and he was shaking his head.

There was another sound added now, woven atop the deep-bass thrumming. A kind of high keening it seemed, like the shrieking of some anguished bird – or the wailing of some lost and tormented soul for a demon lover. Elinor tried to cover her ears, but the keening struck right through her hands.

Pawli had fallen to his knees, his head in his hands. Elinor kept her feet with difficulty. The sound was getting louder by the moment, and the Fey-bone had grown hot now, uncomfortably so. She stumbled over to Pawli and crouched with him, pushing the two of them in against the shelter of one of the cheese-stone upthrusts.

KOO-OOM-BAH . . . KOOM BAH! The ground shook under them. *KOO-OOM-BAH . . . KOOM BAH!* Through it ran the painful keening: *sheee-sheiee sheee-eiee . . . sheee-sheiee sheee-eiee* . . . louder and louder, till their very flesh quivered excruciatingly with it.

And then, in the half-lit distance away off downslope to their left, Elinor saw a greenish radiance, brighter than the pale cheese-stone glow, throbbing, as the sound that filled the air throbbed, as the Fey-bone throbbed, as her very flesh and bones did.

They cowered as the green glow grew. Whatever the source was of that great sound and radiance, it was . . . *huge*. There was no easy way to judge things in this *other* place, but Elinor felt the ground dance with the shudder of some great weight as the thing drew nearer and nearer.

And now, faintly, she caught her first glimpse of some . . . thing over the crests of the cheese-stones in the distance. A creature of some sort. A long, undulating . . . back? She was not sure. It had what seemed to be barbs quivering erect along its spine. It came on with a sort of flowing, humping motion, a hairless, slug-like body, the hide speckled with silvery mushroom growths.

It was hard to make out quite how the thing moved, for,

from Elinor's vantage point, it seemed to be wading through the cheese-stone. But move along it did, rapidly, crossing their path from leftwards, passing by them . . . she was not sure how close. Distance was impossible to judge clearly, and the thing was so *huge*.

It was almost opposite them now, throbbing and wailing and making her feel sick in the pit of her belly with the bone-shuddering force of its great presence. The Fey-bone quivered, hot and pulsing uncomfortably against her breast, but it seemed to offer no especial aid, and the little glowing wand that her white blade had become was utterly useless as defence. Even if it were its true, razor-edged self, she thought it would still prove utterly useless. She wanted to leap up and flee. It was a small creature's panicky response to the large, she knew, the mouse's instinctive, terrified flight from the hunting cat.

And what if this creature were such a hunter, then? She shuddered at the thought.

At her side, Pawli began to squirm. She could hear him whimpering. He tried to thrust her from him and scramble away, but his over-long legs betrayed him and he fell in a tangle before he had properly got up. Elinor flung herself upon him. 'Hold still!' she hissed in his ear. 'We're too little for it to notice, unless we thrash about and call attention to ourselves.'

Pawli looked at her wildly, his face clenched in fright, but he nodded, panting, shuddering so hard he was like to shake his teeth loose.

They lay where they were, pressed close, trying to push themselves into the cindery ground under them, while the great *KOOMING* thing moved ponderously past. Elinor peered over Pawli's shoulder, clutching the un-comfortably warm Fey-bone for what virtue it might have, terrified . . . and yet somehow fascinated, too. She remembered the wonder of the night the Fey-bone had first come to her, the radiance of the moonlight, the dark, furred shapes of the Phanta as they moved through their slow, elegant dances, the pale forms of the Fey, like so many silent apparitions in the moon-lit night deeps of the forest . . .

But none of that was as terribly strange as what she faced here. The great creature before her resembled nothing so much as some insanely huge grub. There were what seemed like rings running vertically down its sides. Ribs? She had no idea. It was hairless and mottle-skinned, as she had already seen, but now she realised that its skin was baggy as an old coat, hanging in folds, tattered and wrinkled. Its head – or at least the part of it at the front – was raised a little above the rest of it, and there seemed to be eyes, but she could make out no familiar eye-structure in them, just two soft-glowing globes half-sunk in bloated grey flesh. She had no idea how it might see though such organs – if in fact it could see at all. It made no movement with its head, no side-to-side surveying of the territory through which it moved. She still had no notion whatsoever as to how – or why – it made the noise it did in passing.

Was such a being native to this place? Or was it – the thought fair took her breath away – what if it were a mindful creature and, like she and Pawli, a visitor who had *emerged* here? She had always thought unquestioningly of the world in which she lived as *the* world, the one and only, but she was overwhelmed now by a sudden wild speculation: what if there were other worlds, many others, perhaps. And what if these worlds were populated by all manner of strange beings? She had a vision of such creatures, each utilising whatever method he, she, it could in order to *emerge* here into this place, like so many strange seabirds, flocking from all over a multiform ocean to congregate upon a single island.

Was that what had drawn Brynmaur to this *other* realm? Was it a . . . a kind of meeting place, then? Incredible thought. She gazed at the monstrous slug-creature. However could one meet with such a gargantuan being? And what manner of world could it come from, and how, to visit here?

The great *KOOMING shree-eiee-eiee* of it shuddered through her bones, and Elinor felt terrified and exhilarated, sickened and enthralled, all at once, as the thing made its titanic way along . . .

. . . until, gradually, it disappeared, leaving behind only a diminishing echo of its passage.

'What *was* it?' Pawli asked in a shaken voice.

Elinor did not know how to answer. It had been a great . . . wonder.

Pawli pushed her from him – they were still huddle-tangled together on the ground – and stood up on his over-long legs. 'I *hate* this place!' he grumbled, rubbing at his thigh.

Somehow, Elinor could not quite share his feeling. She stared off in the direction the great slug-being had disappeared. The Fey-bone amulet had cooled and gone quiescent. No harm had come to them. She thought she could still hear – or half-hear – the last, distant-faint echoes of its huge crying. This *other* realm was perhaps a terrible place, but it was also a place of strange wonderfulness. She was beginning to get an inkling as to why somebody like Brynmaur might come here.

Pawli was flexing his legs, scowling. 'I need to walk,' he said. He brushed cindery dirt from his leather trousers, the cuffs of which came no more than halfway down his calves now. 'Let's get along.'

Elinor regarded him uneasily. There was something about him . . . Not just the elongating of his legs. His face seemed to be changing too. His skin appeared to have darkened and become somehow coarser. Were his eyes grown larger?

'You're *staring* at me,' he said. 'I don't like it.'

'Sorry,' Elinor replied and turned her gaze from him.

'Let's get along,' Pawli repeated. He scanned the series of dropping, cheese-stone carpeted swells that stretched before them. 'It's safe now. That . . . *thing* has left us and gone on to wherever it's going. Bryn surely can't be far off.'

Elinor was far from convinced that Brynmaur was any-wheres about here, but, whether he was far or near, they had little choice save to continue onwards. With the great slug-creature safely gone from their path, down the series of slopes ahead seemed as good a direction to travel as any.

Onwards they went.

XI

They made their winding way down through the maze of the glowing cheese-stones, which began to rise up taller and taller about them. It truly was like walking through some kind of outlandish forest for, in all directions, their vision was hemmed in by upthrust pegs and slabs and knobs, coarse-textured and soft to the touch, all giving forth the same eerie, faint radiance. With the slug-thing's departure, the silence had returned and there was no sound save the noise of their own passing – the *kruunch kruunch* of their feet in the cindery dirt, the scrape of clothing, the soft panting of their breath.

Elinor had expected to pass over the track of that great slug-thing – for it had been travelling athwart their way – but there continued to be no sign of it, only the gently dropping slope along which they walked and the cheese-stones and the silence. She gripped tight the wand that was her white blade, feeling it tingle in the little bones of her fingers. It might no longer have the appearance of a weapon, but holding it familiarly in her grasp reassured her.

There was no way to tell how long they had been walking, for how could one gauge time in a place with no sun, no stars, no change of anything? Elinor stared about her. What if the effects of the starweed wore off before they had found Brynmaur? And what would happen when the effects did wear off? Would they swoon away, only to find themselves back in the cabin? What if, like Brynmaur, they found themselves stranded here?

Ahead, suddenly, there seemed a more open way, a kind

123

of cut through the glowing cheese-stone upthrusts. The ground fell away steeply, and they scrambled down. At the bottom, they found themselves in a wide, shallow depression running transversely to the direction they had been travelling. Along the middle of it, lay a . . .

'It's a roadway!' Pawli exclaimed.

Elinor blinked. It was indeed. Made of paving stones, each at least three or four paces to a side, it stretched for as far as the eye could see in either direction, dead straight, wide across as three tall men, the paving stones fitting absolutely perfectly with each other.

Who had built it? Where did it lead? And whence?

Looking more closely, Elinor saw that the paved-stone surface was partially covered in spots with thin drifts of dark, cindery dirt-dust. A monstrous track ran the length of the road, an uncertain imprint that showed most clearly in the deeper drifts. Elinor felt a little cold thrill. This, then, must have been the slug-being's pathway. And the creature had been even huger than she had thought. She stared at its spoor – a massive, complex corrugation filling the whole of the roadway – and shivered with uneasy wonder.

Pawli, however, shook his head, spitting in distaste, and sidled along the verge of the road until he came to a spot where bare paving stones showed clear and there was no trace to be seen of the great thing's passing. Carefully, he tested the stone surface with one foot, as a man might test the feel of uncertain water. He put the sole of his boot to it, set his weight gingerly down, then leaped back.

'What is it?' Elinor said. He was looking odder and odder, was Pawli.

He regarded her out of the corner of his eye. 'Nothing. Just . . . you wouldn't understand.'

She tested it herself, but could feel nothing. Under her foot, the roadway surface felt like perfectly ordinary stone. She looked at Pawli uneasily. He was changed; there was no doubting it. His skin was become . . . greenish, was it?

It was so hard to tell in the uncertain light. He squatted by the road's side, his knees up above his ears, his arms before him, fingers fanned out, just the tips of them touching the ground.

Then, to Elinor's astonishment, he leaped clear across the roadway, landing in an awkward heap on the far side.

'Pawli!' she cried.

Pawli scrambled to his feet, laughing.

'Are you all right?'

He looked at her, blinking his large eyes slowly.

'Pawli!'

'I'm all right, yes,' he called over the road. 'Come on!'

Elinor put one foot tentatively on the road's stone surface, put the other foot on, took a step. Nothing untoward happened. She hurried across, skipping from one bare patch to another, avoiding the slug-thing's track, trying to leave no spoor of her own for others to see; she did not fancy some creature looking at her tracks as she had looked upon the slug-being's – and perhaps following them.

By the time she got to the far side, Pawli stood poised halfway into the maze of cheese-stone ahead, flicking distasteful glances back at the roadway, urging her on, jittery to be away. Elinor paused, turned to look back, fascinated, unnerved, confused.

'Come *on*,' Pawli hissed. 'This way.'

Elinor still hesitated. 'But . . .'

'This way!' Pawli gestured vehemently into the cheese-stone forest, hopping from foot to foot.

Elinor had no idea how he could be so certain, but, having no suggestions of her own to oppose his, she followed him uphill into the cheese-stones once more, leaving the mysterious roadway behind.

They traipsed on. Elinor's throat was parched and her tongue felt like a piece of old leather. She swallowed painfully, feeling stiff and weary. Pawli seemed under no such discomfort, though. He moved ahead with a bouncing gait, his long legs covering the ground more easily than hers, so that she was beginning to have a hard time keeping up.

'I need to rest for a moment, Pawli,' she said.

He slowed, turned, looked back at her. Trailing his fingers across one of the cheese-stone upthrusts, he stood on his left leg, the sole of his right foot pressed against his left knee. 'You can rest later,' he said. 'It's not far now.'

Elinor blinked.

'Come *on*, now,' Pawli said impatiently.

'Come on . . . where?'

'To Bryn, of course.'

'Pawli, how do you . . . How can you tell how far anything is in this place?'

He looked confused. 'Can't you?'

Elinor shook her head.

'But it's so *clear*!' Pawli gestured ahead, the way they were going. He held his hands out, as if he were warming them before a fire. 'Can't you feel it? This way. Not so far now.' He turned and led off with his bouncy, loping gait. 'Come *on*!'

Clutching her glowing blade-wand, Elinor followed, but slowly, feeling far from confident. She did not understand the changes in Pawli. He was nephew to a deep Curer like Brynmaur, and though she knew there had been some dispute about it between the two of them, she reckoned that Pawli had the far-seeing gift in his blood. Perhaps, being what he was, Pawli had a sensitiveness to this place that she lacked. 'It gets inside me,' he had said. Maybe 'it' was this place entire, seeping into him like water into a porous gourd, filling him, changing him . . .

Elinor shuddered. Could she trust this growing certainty in him? What was he becoming?

'Come on!' he called back to her, his voice seeming harshly loud in the great quiet. 'Slowcoach!'

'Not so loud, Pawli,' she urged softly.

He beckoned to her impatiently.

Elinor sighed. She had little choice but to keep on, misgivings or no, so she followed his lead, plodding where he went lightly, tired and thirsty and out of sorts, for each light step of Pawli's seemed to make her own that much heavier.

And then, abruptly, the maze of cheese-stone peggery ended and they found themselves standing atop a high stone bluff.

'See?' Pawli exclaimed excitedly. 'I *told* you!'

Elinor stumbled, entirely taken by the view. Ahead lay a long vale, and in it was a . . . forest. A proper-seeming forest, too; she could make out the tangled webbery of the trees. Far as her eye could see, that forest ran, till it faded into indistinctness at the point where, in her own normal world, there would be a horizon marking the meeting point of sky and earth. As before, though, here there was only a far-off dimness.

'Come on!' Pawli cried. With a hop, he started down the slope leading from the bluff upon which they stood. It was a steep, gravelly incline, but he skipped on down it with ease.

Elinor followed more slowly.

The forest began abruptly, like a great dark wall four or five times the height of a tall man. The trees were not quite like any tree she knew. They were entirely leafless, gnarled and knotted in the manner of ancient oaks, but their trunks tended to split partway up and break out into thick stems which twisted into knobby, peculiar shapes. Their roots spread in complex, humpy tangles along the ground.

Elinor put a hand tentatively on one tree's bole. It was rough-barked and slightly cool to the touch. It felt just like a gnarly tree – nothing more. She was reassured by such seeming normality.

'Come on!' Pawli said. 'This way.' He bounded ahead and disappeared.

'Pawli!' Elinor called after him, once. The trees echoed her call: *Paw-lee-lee-lee* . . . then swallowed it entirely.

She waited where she was for him to come back to her. It was crazy to go barging in here like this. Who knew what might live in such a wood?

But Pawli did not come back, and she did not like to call again. The forest-echo had made her uneasy. There was nothing for it but to follow after him. Hesitantly, she stepped forwards, ducking under a loop of low-lying branch and into the forest itself.

It was a dim maze of limb and bole and branch, like a great mad tapestry knitted from the trees. There were splotchy growths that cast a little light – like a kind of glowing fungi – but their radiance was faint in comparison to that the cheese-stones had cast. She ought to have ripped out a chunk of the glowing cheese-stuff and brought it with her to light the way, Elinor thought. Too late now.

Nowhere was there more than a few paces of moving space in any direction. Damn fool boy, she thought. How was she ever going to track him in a place like this? She stood listening, hoping to hear him in the silence. But all she could make out was a myriad soft creakings, near and far, as the trees shifted their limbs in the way trees did.

Nothing for it but to move on.

The ground was bare cindery earth, with the tree roots showing through it like veins or ropy sinews. She had to take care where she set her feet, for the roots were treacherous; twice, she fell sprawling. Her movements sent echoes skittering through the forest silence. She felt like a stone flung into a pond; everything nearby would know her whereabouts from the ripples she cast all about her.

And then, suddenly, the Fey-bone amulet pulsed against her sternum with a sudden burst of warmth. She froze, remembering how it had responded to the slug-thing's presence. She peered uneasily here and there, trying to make out what might be the cause. Out of the corner of one eye, she caught a hint of movement. Snapping her head about, she could, at first, see nothing. The glowing-fungi radiance was so uncertain. But no . . . There was definitely something there. A shadowy form pressed close to the juncture of limb and bole, more than a man's height above the ground, unmoving now. The Fey-bone throbbed with soft heat. Elinor gripped her wand, though what use it might be she did not know.

She felt a sudden, painful stab from behind and whirled, her heart banging.

It was Pawli.

He had a long, twisty, slim stick in his hands, with which he had stuck her in the back.

'Pawli!' Elinor hissed. 'You near scared me witless.'

'I've got one of my own, now,' he announced proudly, holding the twisty stick up for her to admire. He had it gripped like a sword, tip extended. He made a stab at her again, grinning.

'Pawli!' she said, parrying him with her wand.

He executed a couple of awkward swipes through the air with the stick. 'You shouldn't be stomping about like this. What's the matter with you, anyways? I told you to follow me.'

'You . . .' Elinor glared at him in exasperation. 'You disappeared on me, Pawli!'

Pawli merely shrugged and gestured with his stick. 'Well, come along now, then.'

'Wait.' Elinor pointed up and behind her. 'There's something in that tree over there.'

Pawli squinted upwards.

'There,' Elinor said.

'I don't see anything.'

It was true. There was nothing there now. And the Fey-bone had gone quiescent once more.

Pawli did another swipe with his stick. 'Good thing, too – or I'd run it through.'

'Pawli,' Elinor said uncertainly, 'what are you doing with that . . . stick?'

Pawli frowned. 'You have yours, so why shouldn't I have mine?'

Elinor was not sure what to say to him. He was becoming so strange.

'Come on,' he said brusquely and slipped away through the dim tangle of the trees.

'Pawli!' Elinor snapped in exasperation, but he was already gone on, leaving her no option but to follow or be left behind again.

So onwards they continued, working a way through the intertangled, dark trunks. The air was ashy in the throat. Their passage – hers more than Pawli's – created a flock of unsettling echoes, as if there were a double score of small creatures footing furtively about in the shadows all about them. And everything looked the same. Elinor had no idea at all how Pawli might be navigating – if he was, indeed, doing anything but losing them deeper and deeper into this woody maze.

It was getting harder to see now, the trees larger and more heavily intergrown. Pawli had become a dim figure, flitting in and out of sight ahead of her. Elinor held the glowing wand up, and found that it helped illumine her path – a little, at any rate. 'Where are we going, Pawli?' she demanded. 'Where are you taking me?'

But Pawli made no reply.

Elinor sighed and continued on, having no other choice she could see. She was beginning to hate this seer, dim forest with its imprisoning trees everywhere. Her back ached, for it seemed she could not straighten up comfortably without smacking her head on some low-hanging limb or other, and the roots seemed to clutch at her feet. Her throat felt dry and sore. They had still yet to see any sign of water anywhere. Could one die of thirst here in this *other* realm?

'Pawli!' she called, her voice breaking up into wavering echoes. 'I've got to rest.'

Pawli peered at her from around a tree bole. His greenish face was round and queer-looking, and his eyes were huge. He beckoned her impatiently with his stick.

She shook her head. 'No. I have to . . .' The Fey-bone suddenly pulsed hotly, shocking her. Something was moving up in the crotch of the tree above Pawli and to one side. He craned his neck to peer up into the branches, let out a yelp, and leaped sideways and away, leaving Elinor quite alone.

She ducked behind a tree and squinted upwards into the tangle of gnarly branches, the Fey-bone quivering against her skin under her tunic. There was what appeared to be a bundle of sticks that she first took for a nest – until one of the sticks moved. She realised that it was a creature of some sort, long spiky legs wrapped about itself. As she watched, it unwound itself and began to move from the crotch where it had been roosting.

Elinor shuddered and backed away. Her instinctive sense was that she faced some manner of gigantic insect, like a monstrous great spider perhaps, perched clinging in the tree – waiting for prey? It was hard to see clearly, but the creature's skin was a pale, bluish-grey, mottled with white blotches. It shifted position, and Elinor heard the tree to which it clung rattle dryly. She could see a pair of large, reddish eyes regarding her – there, then gone, then there again. It took her a long moment to realise that the thing had blinked.

It was coming down out of the tree now, long limbs unfolding with the slow, jerky motions a grasshopper might make: one of its arms would come out, halt, quiver, move on. Elinor backed off hastily, the glowing wand held before her in defence. The creature clung sideways now, halfway to the ground, head lower than feet, gripping the tree with long, black talons, staring at her.

'Come away,' a voice suddenly hissed in Elinor's ear. She whirled, cracking an elbow painfully on a tree. It was Pawli, come creeping up behind her.

'Let's away from here,' he whispered. '*Quick!*' He stood crouched, shifting from foot to foot agitatedly, *swishing* his stick through the air in little, sharp, useless arcs.

By now, the creature had unfolded itself to the ground. Though it was not easy to tell for sure, Elinor reckoned that it must be half again as tall as any ordinary man, but it was stick-thin skinny, all bone and raggedy, hairless skin. She could make out sinews, like long cords, running from wrist to elbow, shoulder to skull – though such words as 'elbow', 'wrist', and 'shoulder' were hardly appropriate. It had the same number and placement of limbs as a human being, and so one was tempted to use human labels. But its limbs were not formed like those of a human person. Its 'knees' seemed able to bend in four directions, giving its legs a sometimes sickeningly fluid motion. Its 'elbows' were knobs of bone, like something glued on as a afterthought, and its arms moved in a manner that seemed somehow *wrong* – though Elinor could not quite grasp why.

It was the head and 'face' of it that were the most disturbing, though. The skull was all pointy bone, full of vents and sharp-spiky knobs, covered by sagging, hairless skin. Its eyes were round and large, sunk in pockets of bone. They were in the same place in the 'face' that human eyes would be, but there was nothing human about them. They resembled nothing so much as complexly pulsing bubbles of reddish jelly. For a 'nose' there was a mere slit. The mouth was a long, tapering muzzle, ending in thin white lips, past which the needle points of ivory-yellow fangs protruded.

Elinor felt Pawli tug at her from behind. 'What's *wrong* with you?' he hissed. 'Let's away from here before it's too late!'

Elinor shrugged him off. The Fey-bone was pulsing at her breast with soft warmth, not nearly as forcibly as it had in response to the great slug-creature's passing – it was a rather pleasant feeling, actually, although the creature before her made her belly cramp with a kind of terrified disgust. It was so nearly human in shape, and yet so not, like a horrible attempt at mixing human and insect that had gone utterly wrong.

And yet . . .

Yet it had made no outright threatening move. The Feybone continued to pulse softly, pleasantly. The creature merely stood, regarding her. She remembered the notion that had come upon her as the slug-creature thundered past, of this *other* realm as a meeting place for beings from far worlds. Could this be such a being, then? Appearance aside, it did not . . . *feel* like anything mindlessly vicious or predatory. What did it think of them? Did they seem as ugly and repulsive to it as it did to them? Strange thought.

'Come on,' Pawli urged impatiently. He gave her thigh a stinging swat with his stick. 'Come *on*!'

She pushed him away irritably. There was something here that intrigued her too much. She took a step closer towards the creature, another.

'Are you *crazy*?' Pawli hissed from behind her.

She ignored him.

The creature moved to meet Elinor, walking on three limbs, with odd, insectile grace. Its talons left thin gouges in the dirt. The forth limb it held up towards Elinor in a gesture of . . . What? Elinor could not be certain. The talons in that gesturing 'hand' began to rub together, *kleekk keek, kleekk keek*.

Elinor did not know what to make of this. Threat? Invitation?

Pawli yanked at her. 'Come *on*! That thing's deadly *dangerous*. Can't you see?' He held his stick up defensively, as if he expected the creature to launch itself at him on the instant, all fang and talon and screeching fury.

But the insect-creature just stood there.

Elinor tried to thrust Pawli away. 'I . . .'

A sudden, startling shriek sounded from deeper in the forest.

The insect-thing whirled.

Again came the shriek – a long wail of pain and fear, it seemed. The cry echoed trough the trees.

The insect-creature was gone, up a tree and disappeared in an eyeblink. Elinor stared about her. The wailing was dwindling now, a mere whisper of echo. The Fey-bone had ceased its soft pulsing.

And then the sound came again, louder, ripping through the dark forest quiet, the shriek of some poor soul in an extremity of terror – the cry some hapless fly might make as it is seized by a spider. Elinor ran after it. She did not know quite what she was doing, or why, but that cry was not to be refused.

She plunged through the tangle of the trees until, abruptly, they thinned out and she found herself atop a large ridgeway of naked ochre stone – far too symmetrical and smooth to be natural – like a sort of long wall with a root-shattered stone terrace running before it. The trees might have thinned out, but they were not gone altogether. A network of sinewy, dark tree roots was woven intermittently over the smooth stone, like choking tentacles.

The shrieking had stopped now, and the forest gone silent again. Elinor stared this way and that, uncertain. There seemed to be . . . things set into the stone before her. Carvings? She was not sure. She moved closer, peering ahead. In the clutch of one root tangle she glimpsed what seemed to be a figure cut in stone, about man-sized, but clearly not a man. It had six limbs, like an insect, yet there was a head, too, with large round eyes and an expression queerly human in nature, with the wide mouth open in a scream. The roots had grown around it like cruel bonds.

Could it be this creature that had been crying out? She imagined it thrashing and shrieking in the remorseless clutch of the tree roots while its flesh slowly, agonisingly, was turned into cold stone. No . . . Even for this *other* realm, such a thing seemed blatantly impossible.

There was no sound now in the forest save that of her own breathing and the oh-so-faint creakings of the trees. She felt at the Fey-bone amulet, hoping for a pulse of response from it. But there was nothing.

The nearly-human stone face before her seemed frozen in an extremity of terror. Elinor shivered, gripping the slim haft of her wand. Pawli was nowhere to be seen.

She heard a soft *krunk*, then. The sound of something breaking. Away to her right it was, along the ochre wallway of the stone ridge. She turned that way and heard a moan, so soft as to be hardly audible, but the sound of some creature in great agony. She could feel it in her own bones.

Hurrying onwards, she followed the ridgeway over a low crest and came to a kind of cornice. Here was another 'statue' like the one she had seen behind. But this one was, indeed, alive.

It was more human than anything else she had yet seen in this *other* realm, a man by all appearances, but no ordinary human man. His limbs were too long and too thin, his face too narrow and pointy of jaw, ears too large. His eyes, too, were too big for ordinary human eyes. They filled fully half his face, wide and dark and glistening. He looked almost like one of the Fey – had their same long slimness of limbs and paleness – but he was clearly a creature of mortal flesh and bone, with none of their etherealness.

There was a tangle of roots drawn about him, like a set of great, multi-fingered, clutching hands strangling him. He struggled and twitched, but the roots' grasp on him was too strong. Elinor could see his breast shudder with the effort to draw breath. One of his arms had been caught at a bad angle and broken by the tightening power of the roots. Pale shards of blood-slicked bone stuck up through the root tangle. His feet and lower legs were grey and pebbly-looking, as if . . . as if they were in very truth being metamorphosed into stone in some horrible, slow manner.

A root nobule was pressing against his mouth. He had twisted his head back, gagging, trying to prevent it from thrusting its way down his throat. His big dark eyes were wide with horror and pain – and, seeing her, sudden hope.

Elinor took a step forwards, not knowing quite what she might do, but with the wand held ready before her, gripped as if it were, indeed, her razor-edged blade.

'Don't touch him,' a voice said.

Elinor whirled. Pawli sat hunkered down a little distance away – how long he had been there, she had no idea – watching the poor trapped being's struggles against the strangling roots.

'Stay away from him,' Pawli said. He was looking on like a cat watching a mouse caught helplessly in a trap. The point of his stick trailed in the dirt. 'There's nothing you can do now.'

The root-imprisoned being moaned again, louder, and quivered and twisted and thrashed in desperate impotence.

'This foul, horrid, *impossible* place . . .' Elinor muttered. Stepping in, she slashed at the nearest root with her wand. Nothing happened. She had not known what to expect, but she felt acutely disappointed nevertheless. She did it again, thrusting the tip of the wand against the hard, dark root-wood this time.

'What are you doing?' Pawli demanded shrilly. He vaulted over to her and yanked at her, hard, making her stumble back.

'You shouldn't meddle here,' he said. 'It's *bad* to meddle in things here that don't concern you.'

'How do you know?' Elinor demanded. 'How can you know anything about this place?'

Pawli shrugged sullenly. 'I just know, is all. I just *know*.'

They stared at each other silently.

The root-strangled being moaned again.

Elinor turned and attacked the roots once more.

'No!' Pawli cried. He tried to pull her away and, when

136

that failed, whacked at her with his stick. She shoved him off, hard, sending him sprawling so that he fumbled the stick and lay gasping.

The poor being before her was nearing the end now. He was choking and pale and shuddering. She could see the roots slide tighter about him, like horrible, slow snakes. There was blood about his mouth, where the root was forcing itself into him.

Elinor hacked at the nearest root, again and again, but accomplished nothing. Where was the power of her blade when she needed it? Why was it so impotent here?

In a blind fury, she stabbed and slashed and hit.

'Stop it! *Stop it!*' Pawli wailed from behind her.

And then, without warning, one of the entangling roots suddenly struck at her, like a serpent. She ducked back, slashing at it with her wand. Another came for her, and another after. She stumbled back beyond their reach, for they were still tethered to the tree of which they were a part.

She had not seemed to hurt the roots in any way, but at least they were loosened a little and the entangled being had got a moment's respite. The thrusting root had been shaken out of his mouth and she could see him draw a great, relieved breath.

The roots waved and lashed about, straining blindly for her.

She moved a touch closer.

'Don't!' Pawli hissed from behind.

A root had snaked out, longer than the rest, and struck at Elinor. She parried it with her wand and . . . incredibly, its tip elongated into a shadow image of that glowing wand, and she found herself in a fencing match. The root thrust and parried as if it were the arm of some master swordsman, meeting her own wand with blows of such force that she staggered. It was crazy.

'Back away!' Pawli urged. 'It can't follow you.'

It was true. It was sound advice. But she could not bring

herself to do it and abandon the poor, doomed soul before her. She struck and jabbed, falling into one of the defensive routines that Master Karasyn had schooled her in back in Minmi City – only a few short years ago now, but it seemed like half a lifetime away. Little could he ever have expected she would use her training against such an adversary as *this*.

Jab, guard, thrust . . . jab, guard again. There was a sort of rhythm to it, she saw. The root was . . . she did not truly know what the root – or what the root was a part of – might be doing, but it seemed to her that it was mere mimicry rather than true skill she faced. Her thumping heart settled a little.

She backed slowly away until the root opposing her was stretched to its limit. It came, she now saw, from a great twisted-up tree that grew along the top edge of the stone ridgeway. The tree's bole was wrinkled and split, and there was a kind of opening in it, hung about with the glowing fungi, a moist, moving thing like a working mouth or a beating heart.

Hardly thinking, she parried the sword-root with a neat move Master Karasyn had called the screw-feather, sending the sharp root-tip *krunking* into the cindery ground. Leaping over it, she thrust her wand point-first into the opening in the bole, deep as she could, until she felt a slimy fleshiness against her knuckles.

The tree groaned and cracked. The roots lashed frantically, mindlessly.

Leaping away, Elinor made a one-handed grab for the foot of the imprisoned being. The roots about him were writhing like mad serpents, coiling and uncoiling, but ineffectively. Elinor whacked and slashed at them with her wand, tugging at the being's foot with her free hand in an effort to yank him loose.

'Help me,' she gasped over her shoulder at Pawli. 'Help me!' But he stayed where he was, his silly, twisty stick useless in his hold, looking on sullenly.

The prisoner was thrashing about himself now, trying to help her as best he could. A stone-pebbly leg came free, another. The roots flailed. One thumped her hard across the side of her head, making her vision swim, but she hung on grimly and beat out with her wand and pulled and heaved until, unexpectedly, the prisoner came free all at once, sending her reeling backwards, heels over head.

Snatching up her wand – she had fumbled it in her fall – Elinor scrambled to her feet, ready to beat back any attack by the writhing roots. But there was none. The tree seemed to have folded in upon itself, the bole becoming thinner, limbs and roots shrinking in. Where the predatory tangle of them had been, there were now only a few quivering roots, like old sinews.

At her feet, the being she had freed moaned and was sick, the painful, gasping heave of a dry stomach. He said something too garbled for her to make out. She knelt at his side, rolled him gently onto his back. 'Who are you?' she said. 'What happened here?'

'Pou . . . pou quaeb iki-rem,' he replied.

'What?'

'Iki-rem. Kati, kati!' His voice was surprisingly low-pitched, given the exaggerated thinness of his frame. He blinked his over-large eyes, swallowed. 'Chi nesum echa . . . Li y ud – ud-ruen gnad!'

'I don't understand,' Elinor said to him. 'What . . .'

'Li y ud-ruen gnad!' He struggled weakly. He was dressed in thin, stained garments, a sleeveless tunic, baggy trousers. His feet were bare, his toes long and thin, grey and pebbly like actual stone. He tried to sit up, wincing, cradling his broken arm, but his lower body, where it was stony-grey, was frozen into immobility and he faltered back.

'Ud-ruen gnad!' he gasped with desperate earnestness, gesticulating with his good hand. 'Ud-ruen *gnad*!'

It was no use. Elinor understood not a word.

He looked up at her imploringly with his huge, almost-human eyes, frightened and determined and hurting. Awkwardly, he reached out to her. She took his good hand in hers, feeling the warmth of it, the thin bones, the surprising smoothness of the skin. She looked into his large, dark eyes, looking into . . . she knew not what. Eyes were the windows of the soul, it was said, but what manner of soul lay reflected in the eyes before her? They were without whites entirely, a rich dark brown with a black, elongated pupil. So utterly *strange* . . .

He took a gasping breath, opened his mouth, and then, suddenly, fell back motionless.

'No—' Elinor said. 'No!' She reached to him, but it was too late. His eyes stared sightlessly up at her, his breast still and unmoving.

And then, to her astonishment, he . . . *dissolved*.

One moment, he was there before her, palpable and real. The next, he began to fade, to crumble, like a clot of dirt dropped into a fast-moving stream. Save he was not dirt and there was no stream.

In a matter of a few breaths, he was gone, leaving not the slightest trace behind.

Elinor shuddered, ran a hand over her face, tried to get breath, completely at a loss.

'You oughtn't to have done that,' Pawli said.

She looked at him.

He shook his stick at her. 'It's dangerous to meddle in things you don't understand.'

'Things I don't . . .' Elinor got to her feet, staring at the empty place where the being she had rescued had lain. 'I don't understand *anything* about this foul, impossible place! Those roots would have killed him! Was I to stand by and let him die a horrible death like that while I watched?'

'You shouldn't meddle,' Pawli repeated.

'Meddle with what?' Elinor demanded in exasperation. 'Meddle with whom?'

Pawli shrugged and looked away from her.

'Pawli?'

'This way,' he said, turning.

'Pawli!'

But Pawli was gone off abruptly through the trees, not looking back.

Leaving Elinor no option but to hurry after.

XII

Along the cracked stone terrace that bordered the ridgeway Elinor went, shaken and confused, haunted by the
remembrance of the big, dark, not-human eyes of the
being she had rescued – *almost* rescued, before he had . . .
evaporated into nowhere. None of it made any sense!

Pawli had gone on ahead, skipping down over a series of
shattered stone hulks that had to be the remains of
buildings – what sort of a history did this *other* realm
have? – and thence through to a kind of escarpment.
Following after, Elinor saw that a great tableland of dark
stone lay spread before them, punctuated here and there
with the occasional twisted-up tree, the landscape split and
cracked into a hundred hundred fissures of varying sizes.
Pawli was casting about, like a hound on a scent, prodding
with his stick, nosing into this fissure, then that, until . . .

'He's *here*!' Pawli shouted, whirling his arms madly and
capering.

Elinor hurried over. Pawli was crouched at the lip of the
fissure now, staring down into it. 'Bryn!' he called. 'Bryn!'

There was no response from Brynmaur, who was
wedged down a fair ways into the cleft of the fissure.
Pawli lay on his belly and reached out a long-boned arm,
but Bryn was down too deep to reach.

'Bryn?' Pawli said anxiously. '*Bryn!*'

Brynmaur lay like one dead, curled into a foetal position, arms wrapped tight about his knees, his face pressed
against the dark rock. Pawli leaned down and poked him
with his stick.

No response.

'He's dead!' Pawli moaned. 'That's why he couldn't come back. He came here and did what he oughtn't . . . and he *died* of it!'

Elinor tucked her wand through her belt and carefully lowered herself into the fissure. When she got to him, Brynmaur felt warm to the touch. She did not know for certain if that meant the same thing here as it did back in the 'real' world, but she hoped so. 'Feel him, Pawli,' she said. 'The dead feel cold. He's not cold.'

Pawli scrambled down and put out a hand to touch Brynmaur's curled back. 'Bryn!'

No response.

'Help me get him up out of here,' Elinor said.

It was no easy job. Brynmaur might be all skin and bone, but he was well and tightly wedged in, and as awkward to lift as a sack of beets. After much sweating and straining, they managed it, heaving him out and dragging him across the stone tableland till they came to a little mound of cindery earth – the softest thing they could find to rest him on.

'Bryn, Bryn!' Pawli moaned.

Brynmaur might not in fact be dead, but he certainly looked it. His face was grey and slack and haggard. His jaw hung open. His eyes gazed sightlessly into the void. If anything, he looked worse here than he had back in the cabin. For a terrible moment, Elinor thought he truly was about to die here before them – like the root-imprisoned being she had saved . . . If it was, in fact, death that had come upon that being. Things were *most* confusing . . .

But Brynmaur neither died nor disappeared. There was a slight rise and fall of his ribs if one looked carefully, weak but steady. Bending close, she felt the soft touch of his breath against her palm.

'What's happened to you?' Elinor said, taking one of Brynmaur's hands in hers. This *other* realm was full of dangers and traps and strangenesses, but she would have thought a man like Brynmaur capable of handling himself

143

here. She felt a little sliver of ice go through her. Who – or what – had done this to him?

'Pawli?' Elinor asked. He seemed to know more and more about this place with each passing moment, though how much he really knew, and how, she had no notion. 'What's wrong with him, Pawli? Do you know?'

Pawli glanced at her, looked away

'Pawli?'

He said nothing, refusing to look her way. He picked up his stick, which he had dropped, and began to fiddle with it, like a little boy with a dark secret. 'Pawli, you must . . .'

'Bryn's gone far, *far* away,' Pawli said in a small, cracked voice. 'He's . . . *dead*.'

'No, Pawli. He's not. Feel him. He's still breathing.'

'He's *dead*, I say.' Pawli turned on her, his face white and stricken. 'Don't lie to me. He's gone as gone can be. Dead . . . And it's *your* fault.'

Elinor gasped. 'What? Pawli . . . what are you saying?'

'You killed him. Through your meddling back there. You ought to have left well enough alone. But no. Oh, no . . . You thought you knew best. You always think you know best, don't you?' Pawli was swiping his stick through the air now, *whish whish*, in angry, awkward arcs. 'You with your magic white sword and your oh-so-mysterious past. You who share nothing. Well . . . I have my own secrets now.' He *whished* the stick and grinned malevolently. 'And if you think I'm going to share any of them with you, you can think again!'

'But Pawli, I—'

'Shut up!' Pawli snapped at her. 'Just . . . just shut up! *Murderer!*'

Elinor stared at him, speechless.

'You've ruined *everything*. Now we'll never get back . . . and Bryn's dead and gone and . . .' Pawli threw himself to the ground and fell apart into sudden sobs.

'Pawli,' Elinor said softly. She went to him, reached a hand down to his shoulder.

He wrenched away from her as if she were some dreadful beast. 'Go away! Leave me alone! *Murderer!*' He lurched to his feet, snatched up his stick, and began to skip about, wild-eyed, his too-long legs scissoring madly. 'Murderer, murderer, *murderer*!'

Elinor did not know what to do. 'Pawli, Stop this! You're acting like a mad person. Brynmaur's not dead. Stop this!'

But he never looked at Brynmaur, nor at her, now. He was whirling wildly about, stabbing and cutting at the empty air with his stick, staring sightlessly, moaning and muttering and blowing air. She tried to reach for him, but he skittered away with a little shriek, capering and hissing, leaping across a rock fissure, teetering on its edge so that Elinor's heart was in her mouth, skidding and flailing and wailing . . .

And then he was gone beyond her sight.

Elinor sat down on the hard stone beneath her with a thump, hardly believing any of this had happened. It made no sense. What was *wrong* with Pawli?

What was she to do now?

Brynmaur was not dead. She was certain sure of that. If she could revive him somehow, maybe *he* might have an explanation for the craziness that abounded here.

But she had no luck. Try as she might, nothing she did made any difference.

Elinor sat slumped in upon herself. She put her hand to the wand, which was still tucked through her belt, sighed, let the hand drop to the cindery dirt. She felt weary, parched, confused . . .

The Fey-bone amulet suddenly lit up with an unpleasant pulse of warmth against her breast. Lurching to her knees, she stared about. But there was nobody, nothing. The ragged stone tableland stretched out empty as could be in all directions. She did not understand how or why the Fey-bone acted as it did, responding to the presence of some beings and not others. Neither Pawli nor Brynmaur evoked any reaction. Nor had the root-imprisoned man. And now it appeared that it was responding to nothing at all . . .

It throbbed again, a pulse of heat so sharp it made her gasp.

'Having a *problem*, then, are we?' a voice said from behind her.

Elinor whirled about, still on her knees, her heart thumping, the wand out in her hand now. A man stood there, about ten paces off, in the midst of the empty tableland where there had been no creature only scant moments before.

Khurdis Blackeye.

At least . . . Elinor was not entirely sure. It seemed to be the man she knew as Khurdis Blackeye, but there were changes in him. This man was dressed in the same sort of extravagant finery that Khurdis seemed to favour, but where Khurdis had had a head of thick, long black hair, this man was entirely bald. And Khurdis had had a full, healthy face; this man's was thin to emaciation – a skull-face.

'Well, well . . .' the man said. 'So we meet again.' He smiled, a thin, cruel smile. 'Such a shame about poor Brynmaur here, don't you think?'

Elinor scrambled to her feet. 'What are *you* doing here?' she demanded. 'How did you . . .' She stopped. There was something profoundly unsettling about this man. Not only did he look different from the Khurdis Blackeye she remembered, but his voice did not sound even remotely like she recalled Khurdis's voice sounding. It was far deeper, more ringing, with some manner of foreignness to it.

The Fey-bone quivered against her breast, gone inexplicably cold now. This *other* place could change one; she knew that. But something told her that what she faced here was more than just some *other* change.

'Ah . . .' he breathed. 'I see you have your doubts about me. And so soon. Clever girl.' He smiled at her, and there

146

was something about that smile that made her shudder. 'Oh, I am Khurdis. Make no doubt about that. But I am also . . . more. He was such an ambitious soul, was our Khurdis, so hungry for so many things. But so . . . lacking, don't you think?'

Elinor said nothing.

'If poor Brynmaur here were able to speak, he would agree with me entirely, I am sure.' Khurdis shook his head, reached a hand to her in mock concern. 'But you are confused. Here, let me explain things to you . . .'

The man who claimed to be more than Khurdis walked closer towards her. There was something in his eyes that was serpentine, a depth, a coldness that left her belly clenched. She tensed, feeling her amulet quiver, and brought the wand up, taking a defensive posture.

He laughed softly. 'Oh, do not fear me. Or should I say, rather, do not fear me *unnecessarily*. I have no intention of harming you here. It would be . . . counter-productive.'

Elinor did not know what to say.

The man sat down leisurely on a lump of stone, settled back as if he were relaxing in a comfortable chair – and, indeed, the very stone seemed to accommodate itself to him, shifting and stretching to support him. 'Khurdis was a most ambitious man. And extraordinarily lucky. If one believes in "luck", of course. Myself, now, I have never given much credence to the concept. The world is far too complexly interwoven for events to happen by chance. Don't you think?'

He was smiling again, a thin stretch of lips over sharp white teeth. 'So . . . one might say that Khurdis was lucky, or, more properly, that he was a channel through which the world's currents flowed. And so you see me sitting here before you now. Or perhaps I ought really to say that you see *us* sitting here before you.'

Elinor glanced about uncertainly, but could see only the one man facing her.

'You do not understand at all, do you?'

Elinor said nothing.

The man before her laughed and then made a sort of mocking half-bow from where he sat. 'It shall be my pleasure to explain it to you, then. Ignorance, they say, is bliss. And bliss, my girl, is not what I have in mind for you. Oh no. Not at all.'

The man took a breath, settled himself more comfortably in his accommodating stone seat. 'Khurdis was a restless sort, you see, never content. He wandered the high slopes far and wide, his head filled with magnificent dreams. And in his wandering, one day, he stumbled across a great find. Try to imagine it, if you can . . .

'There you are, alone, far up beyond the normal habitations of men, with only the white goats of the rocky heights to keep you company. You are young still, filled with visions and hopes, and you burn with righteous anger, for you know you are destined for great things, but the world denies you, and folk spurn you.

'You stand upon a ridgetop, one hand against the bole of a lone, last pine. The bark is sticky under your fingers. It has been a long, hard climb, up slopes new to you. You take a breath, turn, look out across the stone shoulder of the slope up which you have just clambered, and you see the gulf of a mountain vale – a vale you have never before laid eyes upon, that no man has laid eyes upon for long, long years . . .

'And then you gasp, blink, rub your eyes. For you are sure, at first, that you are imagining things, suffering a sudden, illusionary vision from the exertion of the climb. But it is no vision. There, distant on the vale's far side, but clear as clear, is a stone tower.'

Khurdis – if it *was* Khurdis – smiled a thin, feral smile. 'How did such an impossible thing get here? you wonder. What *is* it? Clearly, it is most ancient, for even at this distance you can see the stones of it are green with moss and its lines are smoothed by long weathering. You feel your heart leap. Here, perhaps, lies . . . who knows what? Secret knowledge. Ancient learning. Anything at all . . .

'So you set off through the trees and down across the wooded vale, your heart beating with hope. It is a long, arduous clamber to reach your goal, and it is the next morning before you finally feel the cool, rough touch of that old stone against your palm.

'There the tower stands before you, great blocks of red-brown stone fitted precisely together. It is high as three tall houses, weathered and moss-furred and old as old can be. How did such a thing ever come to be built here? you ask yourself. But there is no way to know. Slowly, your heart beating hard, you search for an entrance. There is a doorway, with a small wooden door, black with age. You push against it, all eagerness. It does not budge. You push harder, hammering at it in your impatience to get inside. Then you see the iron handle. You lift it, twist it first this way then that. Something goes *tlick*, softly. The door opens . . .'

The man nodded his bald, skull-like head. 'It was a moment of complete excitement, that. A whole new world opening up before him. Khurdis felt himself truly to be the chosen man at that instant. Now, at last, that which he had for so long felt he deserved had finally come to him.

'So he entered the tower.

'At first, it was hard for him to make sense of anything. It was a dim, cluttered, confusing place, filled with crates and stacks of mouldering old books and odd paraphernalia. Six floors there were, linked together by a spiral staircase of stone, and an open, rooftop courtyard at the crown.

'In that tower, Khurdis found . . . many things. Toys and treasures. And he was not always capable of telling the difference between the two. Brynmaur was right, of course. Khurdis possessed not the true *power*. He did not possess the depth of vision needed to see through the veils of the world and into the final verities that allow a man of *power* to do what he does. But he has a great strength of will, does Khurdis, and vaulting ambition. And those make up for much else.'

The man laughed. 'So he studied and tinkered and used what he could from the treasure trove of that tower, building for himself a reputation as a man of *power*. But as Brynmaur said, he was a . . . pretender. I believe that was the word he used. Yes. Khurdis remembers it well. And all his grand schemes came to naught.'

The man's skull-like face curdled with abrupt anger. 'Thanks to the meddling of you two here.' He stabbed a bony finger at Elinor. 'You, a mere girl – and that rankled all the worse once Khurdis saw it – you with your nasty, shining blade . . . about which you know less than you think. And Brynmaur here . . .' Khurdis regarded stricken Brynmaur with a dark satisfaction. 'He, at least, has been paid his due for that meddling.'

Elinor shook her head. 'I don't understand. Who are you? You speak of "us", and of Khurdis Blackeye as "him" . . . Yet you *are* Khurdis. Or seem to be . . .'

Khurdis laughed. 'Oh, I *am* Khurdis Blackeye all right. But I am more than simply that. You see, once you and Brynmaur had thoroughly humiliated poor Khurdis and driven him away like a beaten cur, he returned to the tower, burning with shame and fury. And that fury led him to . . . something he had shied away from attempting before.'

Khurdis – if it was indeed Khurdis – beckoned to her. 'Do you know anything of history, girl?'

Elinor shrugged. 'A little.'

'You have heard of the great wars of old, then? Of the Seers who once were?'

Elinor nodded.

'Have you heard of the War of the Lords Veil?'

Elinor nodded uncertainly, having no idea where any of this might be leading.

Khurdis smiled. 'Many long lives of men ago, it was.

150

From the lands south of here, they came, northwards in a march of conquest. The Lords Veil were nine in number, and yet were one soul.'

Elinor blinked. 'I don't . . .'

Khurdis raised his hand for silence. 'Wait. It will all be made clear. The Lords Veil had a Seer, you see, a man of great knowledge and greater *power*. Through his arts, this man was able to do many wondrous things, not the least amongst which was that he could replicate human flesh, taking a portion – an arm, say, or an eye – and from that grow an entirely new and complete, completely identical person. Nine times did the Seer replicate the Lord Veil, more than any other great Lord of that time. And the Lords Veil triumphed in the south and, as I have said, marched northwards, victoriously.'

Khurdis scowled. 'But in the north, things began to go wrong. Puissant enemies appeared where none had been looked for, and the great march of conquest came apart in blood and chaos. Even then, the Seer might have been able to save the day. But there were . . . others who became involved.'

Khurdis went silent, his eyes focused inward. Then he blinked and continued, 'The Elders, they were known as, even in those long-ago days. Beings *of* the world in ways human kind cannot know. You would know nothing of such creatures, girl. In appearance, they are almost human-seeming, yet taller, pale of skin, large-eyed . . .'

Elinor shivered. The Fey. It must be the Fey he was talking about. Khurdis was wrong. She did know such creatures.

'These Elder Folk, mistaking charity for wisdom, interfered – as you and Brynmaur interfered on behalf of the Woburners. They . . . *removed* the Lords Veil's Seer from the conflict. And with him gone, no hope remained.'

'I don't . . .' Elinor started. 'What does this have to do with—'

'Patience, girl!' Khurdis snapped. 'As I say, the Lords

Veil's Seer was *removed* from the fray, *removed* from the world, in fact. But the Elder Folk do not kill. Oh, no . . . So he languished, trapped beyond the world. Long, long, very long years was he trapped thus. Until, finally, Khurdis Blackeye, in angry desperation, attempted something beyond what he knew.

'There are, you see, ways of slipping through the hidden layers of the world to journey to . . . *other* places. Your Brynmaur learned one such way.' Khurdis motioned around him. 'And you followed. So we are all here, having this little talk, in a place you must find more than a little odd. No?'

Elinor nodded confusedly.

Khurdis smiled. 'The world is far stranger than the likes of you know, girl . . . far stranger than the likes of you *can* know. In his fury and anguish, Khurdis extended himself very far indeed, diving far-deep into realms few ever visit. And there he encountered the Seer I have mentioned.

'It had seemed like an eternity for the Seer, trapped as he was in that place – in a great darkness and a greater emptiness. The Elders do not kill. But they are quite prepared to strand a man in a realm inimical to his soul and leave him there until the very soul-stuff he is made of unravels and he finds himself tumbling piecemeal into the Shadowland dark.'

Khurdis was on his feet now, pacing, his hands slicing the air. 'Any ordinary man would have long since dissolved into nothingness in that terrible, black place where the Seer had been imprisoned. Like being buried alive, it was, with Death's cold hands ever near, ready to rend him apart once and for all. But the Seer was no ordinary man. He survived.'

Khurdis went silent, shuddering. He bent over, put his hands to his face, let out a long, raspy breath. Then, with a sigh, he straightened. 'The Seer's mortal body had long since crumbled into soil, you see. The Elders had had their final revenge – or at least so they thought – without having to sully their oh-so-perfect hands. For they had not killed him, oh no. They had merely removed him from the fray, separated him, body from soul, then laid his body out in a wood somewhere to die and rot. And laid his soul elsewhere to do the same. But though their plan failed, and the Seer was stronger than they reckoned, without his mortal shape he could never again return to the world. He was doomed to spend all eternity in that place – that, or die. But he would not die.

'And then, after a black, desperate, endless time, Khurdis appeared. Like a sudden light in the darkness, he was. Like a wonderful breath of clean air in a foetid hole. Like a door suddenly opening. Like a little bright fish come shimmering along through dark water. And the Seer, who had held himself poised for so long he was half-mad with the effort, the Seer . . .'

Khurdis laughed. It was a shrill, unfunny sound. His skull-like face was tight, and his eyes seemed to burn. 'Have you ever seen a little fish swim before a bigger? The smaller one darts and shivers, shying first this way then that, slipping closer, flashing away, returning . . . until, in an eyeblink, the bigger fish strikes. There is a quick flurry, the water is clouded for a few instants. And then all is calm again. Except that the little fish is no more.

'Well . . . so it was. The Seer waited, holding himself in desperate readiness, while Khurdis drew nearer and nearer . . . and then the Seer struck! And Khurdis was no longer. Or, at least . . . Khurdis was no longer *alone*.'

The man who had been Khurdis made another little mock bow. 'For now we are two, you see. I and Khurdis Blackeye. Though, in a sense, I have . . . eaten him. Khurdis is . . . disturbed by the arrangement. But he will learn in time. And I . . . *I* have come back into the world!'

Elinor stared, hardly believing.

'I am Tancred, once Seer to the Lords Veil. Look upon me, girl, and despair. You and Brynmaur here defeated Khurdis. He still feels the agony of that defeat. *I* feel it. And

I, Tancred the Seer, am not one to easily forgive, nor forget.' Khurdis/Tancred laughed. 'This is something, at least, in which Khurdis and I are in complete alignment. I have doomed Brynmaur, stranding him twice-removed from his own place. There is no way in which he can extricate himself. And as for you . . . Well, all I need do is strand you here, you see, as I have stranded Brynmaur elsewhere, as I, myself, was once stranded in my way. I have closed the road back to where you came from. Your mortal shape will wither and die soon enough, as will Brynmaur's. And you . . . well, we shall see how long *you* manage to survive here as a castaway. I shall look in upon you from time to time, for curiosity's sake, to see how well – or how poorly – you are doing. There is a delicious irony in it all, don't you think? And a most pleasing symmetry.'

Elinor launched herself at him, stabbing at his eyes with her wand. It was all she could think to do – catch him unawares.

But he dodged her easily, flinging himself backwards and up into the air as if he were attached by invisible strings to the sky. Standing on empty air well above her reach, he shook his head and laughed cruelly. 'Stupid girl. Do you think you can harm the likes of *me*?'

Elinor stood panting, humiliated and angry. She glanced about, hoping to spot a chunk of stone she might grab up and fling at him. Instead, behind and beyond Khurdis/Tancred, she spotted Pawli come sneaking back, his silly twisty stick in his hands. She tried to wave him away surreptitiously, hoping Khurdis would not grasp the significance of her motions, for his back was to the boy.

But Khurdis/Tancred smiled. 'Ah, yes . . .' he said, not turning nor looking back. 'The boy. With his stick. I have plans for *him*. He has the *gift*, you see. And he, too, is ambitious. Brynmaur here, in his boundless, self-involved ignorance, refused to nurture the boy's talents. I, on the other hand, have every intention of bringing them to the fore.'

Khurdis/Tancred gestured, though he still did not look behind to where Pawli came creeping. 'Look at him. *You* come here to this realm and what happens to you? Absolutely nothing. But *he* is most profoundly affected. You, girl, have nothing, *are* nothing. Without that sword of yours – and I know that sword, girl, know who made it and why – you would not even be worth my disdain. As it is, you are a problem easily solved, a simpleton representing no threat, no challenge . . . no interest at all, really. With a single fang that is so easily drawn. But Pawli . . . *he* is something altogether different.

'Pawli is open to the currents of this realm. Ignorant he may be, but there is no doubting his rightful nature. He is truly *gifted*, and will make me a *most* useful tool. He reminds me of another *gifted* young man I once knew, long ago. That one was taken from me, by the meddling of others, before I could mould him properly. Pawli, however, will be mine.'

Elinor lashed the wand impotently through the air, furious and frightened and entirely balked.

From where he stood in the air, Khurdis/Tancred bowed to her a third time, a mocking, cruel gesture. Then he dropped a hand behind him, making a complex beckoning motion with his fingers. Squawking in shocked surprise, Pawli rose up into the air, limbs swirling. 'And now, girl,' Khurdis/Tancred said to Elinor, 'I must make my goodbyes.' He bowed a final time. 'May your sojourn here be long and desperate, and may you soon rue the day that you were born.'

With that, he was gone, taking a struggling Pawli with him. There one instant, simply disappeared the next.

Leaving Elinor entirely alone in the stony landscape except for Brynmaur, who was still comatose, slack-jawed, grey-faced.

Elinor shuddered, kicked the hard stone ground angrily, shook her fist at nothing, furious and helpless.

XIII

Hunkered down next to Brynmaur, Elinor hung her head. It was hard to draw a proper breath. Her lungs ached; her head did. She felt weary beyond measure. And destitute as any beggar.

But very angry, too.

That Khurdis, or Tancred, or whoever – or *whatever* – he was . . . Arrogant arsehole. She had encountered men like that before, men so full of their own importance they thought the wide world itself no more than a little plot of land for their ordering. It made her back teeth ache, remembering the mocking way he had bowed to her. Well . . . She had got the better of men like him in the past. She would get the better of him, too.

Somehow . . .

Almost, she laughed. Getting the better of Khurdis/Tancred did not seem a very likely prospect at this precise instant.

She shook herself and stood up. This was not the first bad position she had found herself in. She had survived so far. There had to be *something* she could do.

But, scanning the horizon she could see nothing to give her much in the way of hope. Behind lay the humpy ridgeback down which she and Pawli had come. Otherwise, the stony tableland went on in all directions for as far as she could see, its dreary sameness only broken by the occasional solitary writhen tree. The sky was still a dim-black void overhead, with no sun, no stars. The sear air bit at her throat. Everything was twilight and shadow, with no colour anywhere. And the silence hung over all like a great, smothering blanket. Her ears, her very skull, throbbed with it.

She felt her heart turn over. Stranded here with no way back . . . *forever*. The beginnings of a creeping panic started chittering at the back of her mind, like a pack of small, nasty creatures chewing at her. What chance did she have in a terrible place such as this?

None at all, she told herself, if she did not pull herself together. Stranded here in the midst of very nowhere, she felt like some helpless little insect. But that, no doubt, was *exactly* how that Khurdis/Tancred wanted her to feel.

She made an insulting gesture with her fingers at the empty air, aiming it at wherever Khurdis/Tancred might be. He could go stuff his own head up his arse, that one. She would not give him the pleasure of tears, or despair, or anything of the sort. By his own admission, he had survived such an exile, and returned from it. So would she, then. And, one day, there would come a reckoning.

Standing there alone, Elinor felt old angers well up with the new. She had served Powers in her day, and the effort had cost her dearly – and nobody had ever consulted her in the matter. Though she had seen the faces of such Powers made manifest, she knew there was no easy appeal to them. The Powers were what they were, both greater and lesser than human images of them, and she could no more argue with them than could a frog argue against the river's current.

But she could not help but be angered. Too often had she felt herself mere flotsam, flung hither and thither by great unseen forces. And now here she was yet again, stranded upon a strange shore, alone and desperate. She was fed up with it.

The Fey-bone amulet suddenly began to pulse against her breast. From behind, she heard the scrape of something against rock. Whirling, she spied the insectoid creature she had encountered in the forest – or another just like it – creeping along towards her across the stony tableland.

She grumbled a curse. Just what she needed . . . to be stalked by such an ugly brute out in the open like this, with Brynmaur comatose and helpless at her feet. Gripping the wand as she would have gripped her white-bladed sword, she took up a defensive posture – the one Master Karasyn had named the Scorpion – in front of Brynmaur's still form. Let the thing come, then. She would teach it a lesson it would not soon forget.

Clearly, the approaching creature was more at home in the tangly closeness of the trees than in an open area like this. It moved with a kind of sideways, crab-like motion, skittering across the rock with the quick nervousness of a cat caught out in the open and trying to flit from one spot of cover to the next, scuttling from one of the few trees that grew here to another, sliding along the lip of a fissure, ducking behind a tumble of rock.

Elinor waited, feeling her heart thump, feeling the anger burn in her but trying to ignore it, to focus, feeling the Fey-bone amulet pulsing softly. As before, the amulet's pulse was . . . pleasant, almost. It made no sense. The creature approaching her was clearly some manner of predator – the long dark talons, the needle teeth, the very way it moved . . . It was as hideous a nightmare image as one could imagine. Yet the Fey-bone gave her no sense of that hideousness.

The creature sidled close, coming to a halt no more than five or six paces off.

Elinor stood tense, ready for the sudden rush, or leap, or whatever it might be – though whether her slim wand would be proof against such a creature, she had no idea. There was a ribbon of glistening saliva drooling from the side of its sharp-fanged mouth. If the thing before her had had a tail, she would have expected it to be twitching like a cat's just before the strike.

But it did not strike. Instead, it crept closer to her, bent partly over, ever so slowly – as if *she* were the dangerous one here. It held out a sharp-taloned hand, as it had before in the wood, rubbing the horn-like talons together, *kleekk keek, kleekk keek*.

Elinor did not know what to think. Was this some weird ploy to get her off her guard? She gripped the wand more firmly, determined not to be suckered in.

The creature made a soft *hroomming* sound in its throat. The *kleeking* talons went still. Slowly it reached forwards, taloned fingers extended.

Elinor batted at the reaching hand with her wand and it flicked back.

They stared at each other. The creature's eyes were large and round, wholly unhuman, pulsing bubbles of reddish jelly set in spiky bone orbits. Elinor shuddered. Insectile body, all sinew and bone and hanging skin, mere slit of a nose, long, tapering muzzle, thin white lips, wet, needle points of ivory-yellow fangs, those glowing red-jelly eyes . . . She was looking upon something utterly strange and utterly terrible.

Once again, the creature made the soft *hroomming* sound. It lifted its taloned hand tentatively, reaching.

Elinor raised her wand to strike at it.

But paused.

It was a terrible-*seeming* creature, this, surely. But the pulse of the Fey-bone amulet at her breast continued to be . . . pleasant, somehow. And the anger in her seemed to have evaporated. She could not explain it. By rights, she ought to have attacked in a mad fury, or fled screaming from this awful, predatory thing. Her heart ought to be knocking against her ribs. But it was not.

The taloned hand came slowly closer. Each of the dark claws – there were three of them, two to the fore and one behind, in the manner of a bird's foot – was twice as long as Elinor's fingers. They were hooked, and pointy-sharp as an eagle's.

Elinor shivered. She stood her ground, the wand up and

ready, but she made no move. The Fey-bone *thrummed* with soft warmth.

The taloned hand was very close now, within her guard. If it struck at her suddenly, she would have difficulty turning the ripping points away from her guts. Her hand twitched where it held the wand. If she thrust quick enough, she might be able to impale one of its red-jelly eyes with the wand's sharp tip.

But the taloned hand made no sudden move. It dropped slowly past the wand and settled upon Brynmaur's still shoulder. With the back of those hard-sharp talons, the creature gave Brynmaur a gentle, slow caress.

Elinor stared.

The talons had slid to Brynmaur's face now, to his death-pale cheek. The creature made the soft *hrooming* sound once again – and now Elinor could not help but feel it was a sad sound. The dark talons – still with their backs pressed against his skin and the sharp points curled up and safely away – passed softly, tenderly, over Brynmaur's cheek.

Elinor did not know what to think.

The creature shifted, lifted its hand away from Brynmaur and brought it back towards Elinor, brushing her face lightly. The horn-like talons felt smooth as polished wood, and surprisingly warm. Elinor shuddered. She reached her own hand out to touch the creature's forearm – if that were the right word for it. The skin was warm and pebbly-feeling and loose, wrinkled into a thousand fine lines. The bony forehead came forwards and touched with hers, softly.

Elinor let out a little sharp breath and thrust away with a cry.

Something *most* strange had happened.

She stared at the creature, which squatted unmoving before her, in no way threatening. When its bony skull had pressed against hers, she had heard – felt, rather – a sort of *voice*.

The creature made the *hrooming* sound again, softly, and leaned close towards her. Shivering, Elinor met it, feeling her forehead press against the knobbly bone of the other's. There was a murmuring, a distant hum that Elinor could feel through the marrow of her skull rather than her ears. It was as if there were some secret sound source deep within the creature's body which resonated softly. Elinor could 'hear' the voice – barely. Like a whisper in a forest. Like a murmur half-submerged in the gushing sounds of a brook. She could hear the rush of blood, the creak and shift of sinew and joint. And the words . . .

'. . . aan -oo arm ild . . . ee oten–mees.'

'What?' Elinor said. She remembered the gobbledegook the being she rescued from the tree roots had spoken to her. What was the use of this improbable 'talking' if she could understand not a word of it?

The voice was coming again, resonating softly in the bones of her skull: 'eece ild . . . een oono arm.'

'My *. . . arm*?' Elinor replied, uncertainly.

'. . . eace child . . .'

There! She almost had it. But what was an 'eace child'?

Eyes tight shut, she 'listened' as sensitively as she could, ignoring her ears and concentrating instead on the soft vibration in her skull – a little insect buzz, a few words interspersed with odd thrums and pulsings, a half-sentence, almost caught and then lost, a word, two . . .

Once she found the knack of it, it was like listening to any normal human voice in, say, a wind-ruffled forest; there were the background sounds she had to ignore, the occasional murmur or unclarity, but nothing impossibly difficult.

'Peace, child,' she heard. 'We are not enemies. Put away your sting.'

Elinor pulled back, shaken suddenly by what she was doing – and a little piqued by the 'child'. She regarded the ugly creature before her for a long, uncertain moment. It *looked* so utterly unhuman, but the words . . . It had been a

161

soft voice, clear, now that she had got the knack of making it out. And if she had somehow been able to erase her perception of the being before her, and the strange manner in which she had 'heard' the words, she could have taken it for an ordinary, human voice.

But this could still be part of some elaborate, predatory feint, could it not? She had learned already some of the complex dangers this *other* realm contained.

But the Fey-bone amulet gave her no hint of danger. It pulsed with a steady, pleasant warmth. She lowered the wand.

The creature before her leaned close and their foreheads touched again. Elinor shuddered involuntarily. Its skin felt warm and rough and pebbly, like a lizard's might.

The voice came to her: 'I mean you no harm, child. Truly, we are not enemies, you and I.'

'I'm no *child*!' Elinor snapped. A foolish thing to say, and she cursed herself the moment after. But she was weary, and angry and frightened by all that had been happening, and it had, somehow, stung her.

For several long breaths there was no response. Then, softly, Elinor heard what might have been . . . laughter.

Elinor flared. 'I will not—'

'Calm, child. Calm. We do neither of us any good if we bicker.'

Elinor took a breath. She was being foolish. The creature had the right of it. Incredible creature . . . 'What . . . who are you?' she asked of it. As she perceived the creature's 'voice' vibrating in her bones, so it must perceive hers. 'Are you – do you live here in this . . . *place*?'

'No, child. Like you, I am come from afar.'

'But . . .' Elinor took a breath, unsure how to continue. 'Why were you . . . Who *are* you? Why did you approach me in the wood, and then follow after? And why follow Pawli and I out here?'

'I was not following you, child. I was *searching* for you.'

'Searching . . . How did you know I was here? How

did you know I even existed? And why . . . *search* for me?'

'I needed your help. Need it now.'

'Need my help for *what*?'

'For my own sake and yours. And for the man's sake,' the creature said. It took Elinor a long few heartbeats to realise who 'the man' was: Brynmaur.

'I don't . . .' she started, stopped, swallowed, started again. 'You know Brynmaur, then?' It seemed a lame question, considering. But she did not know how else to respond.

'Your Brynmaur and I met in this place, more than a little time ago, now – though time is not always easy to judge in the Otherwhere.'

'The . . . *Otherwhere*?' Elinor said uncertainly.

'This realm where we are met. That is my people's name for it. The Otherwhere. It is an . . . unpredictable place. Time here does not pass quite the same as it does in your home world, or in mine.'

'But what is your world?' Elinor asked. 'And where?'

'To that, I have no easy answer that would make any sense to you. The Otherwhere exists as a sort of . . . hub to many wheels. Mindful beings are drawn here from many worlds. The path for each is different – and never simple.'

Elinor gasped. 'Then there really *are* many different worlds?'

'Oh, yes. Many as the twigs in a great wood.'

Elinor thought about that for a moment, remembering the great slug-creature that had crossed before Pawli's and her path. She shivered. 'And you met Brynmaur here, then?'

'It seems long ago now, in the wood back there, where I first tried to contact you.'

'But I don't . . .' Elinor tried to gather her thoughts. 'I don't understand. What is Brynmaur to you, then?'

There was silence for a moment – or, rather, a period of humming vibration, where the bones of their different foreheads touched, that contained no words. Then the creature said, 'What is the man to me, indeed? No easy question to answer, that. He is puzzle and darkness, light and foolishness and anger, wayward mind and beating heart and joy, pain and loss and . . . many other things as well.'

'Who are *you*?' Elinor demanded. 'And what were you to Brynmaur?'

'Your Brynmaur named me Moreena. It is a name I have grown . . . fond of. As for what I was to Bryn. We were . . . lovers.'

Elinor was so shocked that she broke contact inadvertently. She stared at the sinewy, insectile creature so close to her. It seemed blatantly impossible. How could Brynmaur . . . (she hesitated even to use the word) *love* such a creature? How could he ever make love with it?

Moreena, as she had named herself, was squatting patiently on her bony, stick-thin legs, stroking Brynmaur's face again, lightly, with one taloned hand.

It might have been her imagination, but Elinor thought she detected a sense of . . . laughter, when she reconnected.

'You are shocked,' Moreena said.

'No . . . yes,' Elinor admitted. 'I don't see how . . .'

'How two beings so very, very different could ever have been lovers.'

'Just so,' Elinor agreed.

'I have said that the Otherwhere is a strange and unpredictable place. Here one's body is a spirit body, both solid and unsolid, changeable and not. When I first spied Bryn, I was . . . taken with him. I am a great traveller after my own fashion, and have spent much time in this realm, but never before had I seen such an unlikely creature, like a soft, pale bag full of flesh, with little glittering eyes, entirely defenceless and stupid as he blundered about in the wood, blind to the dangers that lurked there – or so he seemed to me. But there was something strangely fascinating about him, nevertheless. So I followed him, slipping along through the trees well above him, as he stumbled about.

'He nearly died for good and all, poor Bryn, on that first occasion. If I had not been there, hovering and curious, one of the wood's less pleasant residents would have . . . well, "eaten" is not quite the right word. Ingested, perhaps. Or acquired – yes, that's better.'

'You mean this *other* realm has its own inhabitants, then?' Elinor asked.

'Yes and no. Nobody knows what the Otherwhere might have been originally. It has been the meeting ground of so many strange beings for so many aeons now that there is no way to resurrect its beginnings. But there are creatures here who have made this their home, who are, for all intents and purposes, this realm's inhabitants. Do you remember the stone ruins you scrambled through to reach here?'

Elinor shuddered. 'Only too well. The one just after the stone ridgeway where I rescued . . . failed to rescue that being? Did you know about that?'

'I was watching from the trees, ready to help if need be. But there was no need. You handled yourself very well, child. Not many beings would have been able to beat back a Hoory as you did.'

'A Hoory?'

'The creature who inhabited the tree.'

'What happened to the poor being I rescued . . . almost rescued. He just . . . disappeared.'

'He remerged.'

'*Remerged?* I've never heard of—'

'It is a vocabulary that your Brynmaur and I devised together. One *emerges* into the Otherwhere. Creatures like the Hoory *merge* with it. Those of us who depart it to return to our own worlds *remerge* with them. The being you saved returned safe in soul and limb to his own world. And only just in time, too. Once a Hoory gets full grip upon you, there is no escape. One *merges* with the Hoory. It is how they feed.'

Elinor shuddered. 'So I *did* manage to save him, then?'

'Oh, yes.'

Elinor sighed. It was something. 'Was it a . . . a Hoory that threatened Brynmaur, then?'

No. Another sort of creature entirely, even less pleasant, if that were possible. Bryn stumbled straight into its lair like a blind kit.' Elinor again had that sudden sense of something like laughter. 'He never knew it was me that saved him, of course.'

'Why not?'

Again, the laughter. 'He was almost as terrified of me as he was of the creature that nearly destroyed him. He fled, thinking, no doubt, that two hideous monsters deserved each other.'

'I don't understand,' Elinor said. 'You say you and Brynmaur were . . . lovers. Yet he *fled* from you?'

'On that occasion, he saw me as you see me now. In something like my true form.'

' "Something" like?'

'The Otherwhere . . . changes one.'

Elinor thought of how Pawli had changed. 'But I'm still the same,' she said.

'Yes and no. Less the same than you think, perhaps.'

Elinor felt at herself surreptitiously. She seemed intact, her old self as she knew it. Once more, she sensed the laughter. 'There is change and there is change. The Otherwhere is many things, but it is never simple. And some visitors here change more than others. The young one with you was most open to the changes.'

'You mean Pawli?'

'The young male that . . . *He* abducted.'

'*He?*' Elinor said, uncertain. There was so much in this conversation that she and this Moreena had to sort out. 'Do you mean Khurdis, or Tancred, rather?'

'*He* has been the cause of much misery, that one.'

166

For the space of long heartbeats, there were no words between them. Then Moreena continued, 'I followed after Bryn that first time, for he was lost and alone and a newcomer to the Otherwhere – always the most vulnerable, those who first arrive. But I knew that I could not show myself to him as I was, for he would recoil from me in horror. So I . . . changed.'

'Changed, how?'

'The Otherwhere has its own currents and ways. One's bodily form here is far more mutable than in other realms – if one knows how. I became as he was in shape. Or very nearly so. I was clumsy at first, learning how to be one of your kind – you are most strange and fascinating creatures, with senses all at once far more shallow yet far more refined than those I was born with.

'Bryn and I spent much happy time together here in this place, and I became most comfortable in my human form. It was a great learning for me, and one I cherish . . . and because of it, you and I are able to converse now – though I must resort to this clumsy method.'

'How *do* you talk like this?' Elinor asked.

'It is . . . not anything I could explain to you in any way that would make sense. I am a stranger being than I seem to you, child.'

Elinor went silent, trying to digest this. 'How much,' she asked after a little, 'did Brynmaur know of all this?'

'Nothing whatsoever, child. He never knew I was anything else than what I seemed . . . until the end.'

'What happened at the "end"?'

'*He* descended upon us and stripped my seeming form from me. *He* has great power and greater knowledge, that one. To my own shame, I underestimated *him*. *He* accomplished *his* designs upon me and locked me into the form you see now – all before I could marshal myself to prevent it.

'Poor Bryn was horrified, seeing me suddenly as I am now, and *he* worked on that horror, growing it like a tumour till it filled Bryn's mind and spirit entirely – till there was no way for me to reach to him. Then, with that horrifying revelation overgrowing in Bryn's mind, *he* forced Bryn's spirit out of the Otherwhere into a realm even more rarefied. The poor soul went, screaming, ripped from everything he knew, and plunged into empty darkness.'

'You mean—' Elinor broke the contact between them, backing away a little. She needed to take a moment to gather her thoughts.

If the truth be known, she had considered Brynmaur as a little pathetic, really – a man of deep knowledge, certainly, but a man fatally hampered by a crippled dependence on the starweed he smoked. She had, without giving it much serious thought, imagined his starweed 'trips' to be self-delusional, indulgent, essentially pointless experiences. As had Pawli, clearly. And she had thought the *talanyr* – that crystal globe – something he had used only once, in some quest after Khurdis, or something of the sort.

But she – and Pawli too – had been wrong.

He must have been using the *talanyr* in conjunction with the starweed to create a . . . a portal to this Otherwhere, as Moreena named it. Brynmaur had been doing far, far more than she or Pawli had ever imagined, far-travelling in ways they never *could* have imagined. For years, apparently. What manner of strange experiences had he undergone? Elinor felt a little stab of envy. She had travelled in her day, seen strange sights, lived more than many her age – and had strange lovers, too, if it came to that. But what Brynmaur had been doing . . . He had a whole *world* to explore here, and such a world. And a guide to show it to him. A guide whom he . . . loved.

It was still more than a little strange to her, that notion.

'He truly . . . loved you?' she said to Moreena, taking up the connection between them once more.

'We loved each other,' Moreena replied.

'And you never even hinted at your true nature?'

Elinor sensed something very like a sigh. 'Not till *he* descended upon us to crack our happiness apart. I should have told Bryn. It was a terrible mistake not to. But I was . . . afraid of losing him.'

Elinor felt a surge of sympathy. This creature might look horrible, and no doubt it was, in fact, a far stranger being than it was appearing to her now, but that fear of loss was so completely human . . .

'But I don't understand,' Elinor said after a little, 'how could Khurdis know about . . .'

'*He* is not simply this Khurdis you speak of. *He* is far, far more than you can know. *He* came upon me unawares, spying and prying as *he* had been, and set a *binding* upon me. I am no weakling, child, nor young and foolish. But *he* approached me first as a human man – seeming hurt and confused – and Bryn was the only human man I knew. I was curious, interested – and off my guard. *He* caught me like any silly kit.

'And *he* is far more than *he* appears, child. Tough as an old star, and so set upon working *his* will that *he* has become mad with it like some poisonous plant whose only thought is to grow and grow, strangling all others, spreading poison till it fills all the world.

'And so I am as you perceive me now, having to resort to this ungainly method of communication, *locked* into this form by one who had the guile, the power, and the *knowledge* to do so – where I looked to find no such things.'

'And you?' Elinor asked. 'You, too, possess such . . . *knowledge*, don't you?'

'I do,' Moreena agreed simply. 'I ought to have known better than to allow myself to be so trapped.'

'You are a . . .' Elinor shivered. It was come perfectly clear to her now: Moreena was a Wise Woman. Elinor had known such before. To see this in Moreena now made her both more comfortable and less so – on the one hand,

Moreena's unhuman form seemed no more than an exotic covering over a familiar soul; on the other hand, her experience had taught her that it was never, ever, easy dealing with Wise Women.

'I am a what, child?' Moreena asked.

'A . . . You're a Wise Woman, aren't you?'

'Those are your words for it, yes. You have had experience with such before?'

'I have met several in my time.'

'Perhaps that explains it, then.'

'Explains what?'

'Our meeting proved far less difficult than I had imagined. You are deeper than you seem, child. Most of your kind would have run screaming from me, or attacked me hysterically, long before we had a chance to build a bridge between us.'

'It was . . . I . . .' Elinor did not know whether to reveal the Fey-bone amulet or not. She hardly understood the thing herself. But she had learned it was always best not to try to hide things from a Wise Woman – there was no easy knowing what they could and could not perceive.

'I have this . . . gift,' Elinor told her. 'Given me by one of the Fey. Do you know of such beings?'

'Not by such a name,' Moreena replied.

'Khurdis – what Khurdis has become . . . he named them the Elder Ones. They are closer to the world than we human folk. More *in* it, if you see what I mean.'

'The Bone People, you mean?'

'I have never heard of such,' Elinor said.

'Those who dwell in the bones of the world. For whom the world's pulse is the very beating of their hearts.'

'Yes,' Elinor agreed, 'that's them. It must be. Did Brynmaur talk to you of them, then?'

'Perhaps,' Moreena said. 'We talked of so very much, your Brynmaur and I. But each world has its Bone People, child. They are part of the weave that holds each world together.'

'Each . . . world.' Elinor took a breath. The image of it thrilled and chilled her: world after world, each stranger than the one before, each with its Bone Folk, looking . . . who could know what form such beings on such utterly strange worlds might take?

'May I look at this gift of yours?' Moreena asked. 'I have sensed something about you, but I would see it with my eyes, if I may.'

Elinor hesitated, then broke the contact between them, stepped back a pace and lifted the little Fey-bone out of her tunic. Moreena leaned her head closer. Her strange, red-jelly eyes seemed to glow more brightly. Elinor's hand shook a little as she held the amulet. She was not sure what she would do if Moreena tried to touch it. Nobody had touched the thing save her since the night it had been given to her . . .

But Moreena merely looked at it for a long, quiet while. Then she motioned with a taloned hand for Elinor to put it back away. 'It is a great gift, this,' she said, once they had re-established contact. 'Greater than the other.'

'The . . . other?'

'The sting you carry, child, that you brought with you from your home place. No simple feat, that. You are . . . no ordinary person, are you?'

Elinor did not know quite how to respond to that.

'You are . . . how should I put it for you? You are like a forked tree through which the lightnings of the world may run. But you know this already, do you not?'

Elinor did. She had been told this before, though the words had been different: an *axle*, she had been named once, by a corpulent old Wise Woman named Tildie she had met in crumbling Minmi City; and *fulcrum*, by green-eyed Gillien of Margie Farm, dead now, poor soul; and *conduit*, and other words, too . . . All amounting to the same meaning: she was a channel through which the world's hidden currents flowed.

But it had brought her no joy, being such a channel.

'I may be a . . . a forked tree, as you put it,' Elinor said, 'but the lightning *burns*, Moreena.'

'I know, child.'

'How would *you* know?' It was hard not to be a little bitter. Moreena had far more than she – great knowledge, and who knew what sorts of powers?

But, 'I, too, after my fashion, am a channel for such lightnings,' Moreena said. 'I, too, have been . . . *burnt*, child.'

Elinor shivered. It was so much to take in all at once: world after world, all so different, yet all, at some fundamental level, so very similar.

'It is a vista to make one's mind and heart reel, is it not, my child?' Moreena said. 'I remember well the first time I saw it all spread before me in my mind's eye.'

'Don't call me child, Moreena,' Elinor said suddenly. 'I am no child.' But she was feeling like one, mortally so.

Something like soft laughter came from Moreena. 'But you are so very *young*, child. Like a little bird just out of the nest, your little veined wings still wet and wrinkled and draggly, trying to see if you can fly.'

'I am not *that* young!'

'You are to me, child.'

'How . . . how old are you, then?'

'It is no easy question, that. There are years, and there are years. And time between the worlds is never quite constant. I do not know entirely myself how old I am. Perhaps . . . perhaps three or four thousand of your years.'

'No,' Elinor said. 'You must be counting wrong. Three or four hundred, maybe.'

'I know well enough how to count. I am *old*, child. The oldest of my kind, and we are a long-lived folk. Even to myself, I feel *old*.'

Elinor broke the contact between them then, shivering. She looked at Moreena and did not know what to think. Three or four *thousand* years old . . .

Moreena beckoned her back with a dark-taloned hand.

'Do not let your mind dwell upon it, child. You have had too much to digest of late – and too strange. Let be. The worlds are what the worlds are, and dwelling too much on the strangenesses will only make your spirit unwell. There is that at hand we must turn ourselves to now.'

Elinor took a steadying breath, another, feeling Moreena's lizard-pebbly, warm forehead pressed securely against hers. 'What is at hand?'

'Brynmaur here must be rescued, and the other young male. You must be rescued. *I* must be rescued.'

Elinor felt her heart skip. With an ancient Wise Woman – human or not – such as this on their side, she and Brynmaur and Pawli stood a real chance. 'What will you do?' she asked Moreena. 'Can you being Brynmaur back, then? Can you defeat that Khurdis, now that you know him for what he is?'

'Would that I could, child. *He* is proven a thorn in my underside I would give much to remove. I do not *like* being made another's utensil. And for what he has done to poor Bryn, I would happily rip his belly open and feed him his own entrails.'

Elinor shivered.

'But such,' Moreena went on, 'is not to be.'

'I don't . . .'

'*He* has me truly and well bound, child. My own fault, all of it. But it has happened. There is nothing I can do to change it.'

'But how . . .' Elinor's heart sank. 'Why have you come to me, then?'

'*He* may have bound me, but I am not a helpless creature. There are ways, and ways . . . and I will not allow *him* to get away with what *he* has tried to do.' Elinor felt Moreena shudder – in anger?

'I am not bound here to this realm, child, as you and Bryn are. That is the one exit *he* has permitted me. And *he* counts on my taking it, expecting me to abandon poor Bryn, to withdraw in defeat. But I will not.'

'Could you,' Elinor asked, 'go after Brynmaur from here? To the . . . place Khurdis has banished him?'

'I might,' Moreena replied.

'Then why don't you?'

'I cannot go after him myself, child. *He* has bound me to this form, no matter what realm I travel. If I were to follow after Bryn, he would still perceive me as he did before, as you see me now – or worse, perhaps. I have made the attempt, but had to withdraw back the instant Brynmaur began to be aware of me. *He* is nothing if not subtle.'

'But if you can reach Brynmaur where he is,' Elinor asked, 'can't you bring him back without him seeing you?'

'No, child. Only Brynmaur can bring himself back.'

'But I don't see . . .'

'It is not easy. There are ways and means and possibles and not. The thresholds are closed in some ways, open in others. And it depends on the nature of being one is. My kind can travel the ways between worlds far easier than yours.' Moreena paused for a moment, then went on. 'And so, we come to you.'

'Me?'

'You, child. I cannot go after Brynmaur. But *you* might be able to bring him back.'

'Me? How? You said yourself only Brynmaur himself could bring himself back.'

'True. But what Brynmaur needs is a . . . How can I explain this to you? He is like a man cast away in a dark sea. He drifts and flounders, not knowing which direction is which, weary and despairing, sinking deeper and deeper. But give him some object to cling to, something familiar, and he stands a chance of gaining his bearings, of striking out on his own, of returning.'

'And I,' said Elinor uncertainly, 'would be that . . . object?'

'Exactly,' Moreena said.

'But how would I . . . travel to this realm where Brynmaur has been imprisoned?'

'I would send you, child. It is no great feat. Though you may find the journey somewhat uncomfortable. And the realm into which *he* has banished poor Bryn is no simple place. You will find it far less comprehensible than this one.'

For an instant, Elinor balked. Moreena was talking as if it were all arranged, as if she had already agreed. But she had *not* agreed to anything. And she did not take kindly to people – human or not – making life-decisions for her.

'It is our only hope, child,' Moreena said. 'You must allow me to send you after Bryn. If there were some other way, I would have taken it long since.'

Elinor let out a breath. How sensible was it, putting herself entirely in the hands – the sharp-taloned hands – of this unhuman being?

'Trust me, child,' Moreena said. 'We are allies in this. Truly we are.'

'If you send me to the realm where Brynmaur is trapped, how do I help him get oriented, or whatever it is I must do?'

'There is no easy answer to that, child. You must do what you must do.'

Typical Wise Woman answer, that, Elinor thought.

'The most I might be able to do is set a *draw line* upon you.'

'A what?'

'You are unfamiliar with such? A draw line is a manner of . . . "spell", you would term it, I think. Though that is a misnaming, really. A draw line helps to . . . to bring into your path that which you need.'

'Like?' Elinor said.

'It is impossible to know that until it happens, child.'

Elinor sighed. More Wise Woman talk.

'I must warn you,' Moreena went on, 'that if you do not allow me to send you after Bryn, there is no escape for you from this realm. *He* has woven *his* webs too well. You will languish and die, first your flesh body on your own home world, then your spirit body here.'

'And if I do allow you to send me after Brynmaur, what then? How do I get back?'

'With him.'

'And if he can't manage it?'

'Then you are stranded with him there.'

The prospect of being sent to another realm even stranger than this one was enough to make Elinor feel a little sick. And to be stranded there forever . . .

'It is a chance, child, no more. But it is our *only* chance at this moment. And the draw line may make all the difference.'

'Only *may*?'

'One never knows for certain sure with such things. There is always the element of the unexpected. And what is drawn to you may help, but also may be . . . not what you looked for.'

There was silence between them for long heartbeats.

'It is all I can offer,' Moreena said.

'And what of poor Pawli, taken by Khurdis as he is?'

'Bryn first, child,' Moreena replied. 'Then we see about the young male.'

'We?'

'I will be waiting here for your return. Then we will see what is to be done. Will you do it, child? Will you go?'

'I—' Elinor broke the connection between them, stepped back. She looked about at the oppressive strangeness of the Otherwhere. It was a terrible place, this, to be stranded in. Moreena regarded her steadily with those alien, red-jelly eyes of hers. It was impossible to recognise any human sentiment in them. Moreena might sound like a human person when they talked, but there was no forgetting her unhumanity when one stepped back and looked at her.

Could she truly be trusted, this strange creature? Elinor did not, finally, know how to know. But the Fey-bone still pulsed with pleasant warmth, and, in her heart of hearts, she could not, somehow, quite bring herself to disbelieve in Moreena.

And what other options lay open for her here in this dreary *other* place?

Elinor stepped close and leaned her forehead against Moreena's. 'I . . . I will do it,' she said.

XIV

It *hurt*.

Her arrival at the *other* place had been like waking from a long sleep. This was nothing of the sort.

It seemed to Elinor that her whole bodily self was being ripped apart, muscles and bones shredded and stretched out in long, dripping strings. She would have screamed – but she had no mouth.

And when she *emerged* . . .

Elinor had not known what to expect. Moreena had described the realm to which she was going as less 'comprehensible' than the one she had been in. But that *other* place was all she had to go by, and she had anticipated something like it, only stranger, darker, more terrifying, perhaps.

It was not like that at all.

There seemed no . . . no clear world here at all. Only a dizzying, confused swirl of currents, pulsing, writhing, flowing. In the *other* place she had been her own natural self in body – or seemed so, at any rate. Here, she had no recognisable limbs at all, merely a kind of flat-smooth torso. There, she had been able to feel her bones and breath. Here, there was nothing like that. She *existed*. She felt herself *be*. But it was not a sense of being like any she had ever experienced before.

And her senses were most unlike ordinary human senses. There was nothing quite corresponding to vision in this place, and no hearing or touch . . . at least, not touch as she had always known it. She could sense the strange currents *sizzle* softly all about her, all through her.

She, herself, seemed to give off a kind of soft force that helped to *illumine* the surging space around her somehow.

She could move about here, she discovered, riding the swifting currents of this place – but what exactly those currents were, she could not say. They were not liquid, nor solid. They moved and shifted, and she shifted and moved with them, like a fish, or a bird, riding and sliding . . . or like a kind of soaring worm, for as an eyeless earthworm might squirm its way through moist dirt, so she slid and dipped through the *sizzling* currents here, yet much, much faster than any worm.

It was horrifying and exalting all at once.

Around her, she could sense only an endless emptiness, and the surging currents. No land, no sky, no water nor trees nor rocks nor . . . anything. How was she ever going to find Brynmaur in such a place?

Onwards she moved, having no other option. The current she followed *sizzled* along like some great river, and she, like a little drifting leaf, swirled and spun with it – though she was *in* it rather than *on* it. It was most difficult to keep any sense of direction, of purpose even. There was only the motion, like an endless, dizzying fall, with her tumbling clumsily at first, like a newborn learning how to walk, but learning it nonetheless, until she began to get a hard-won sense of balance. After a timeless, plunging time, she became aware of something ahead of her.

She felt a flash of excitement. She had no notion as to what it might be, but it *might* be Brynmaur. Moreena had said she would set a 'draw line' to pull into Elinor's path whatever she needed. Could it be so simple – and Moreena so powerful – that she would be drawn to Brynmaur as surely as a river is drawn to the sea? She truly, truly hoped so.

Holding that hope in her mind like a light, she slid in closer, trying to ride the crest of the current like a tiny cork skimming a great wave.

Closer and closer she came, hoping, hoping . . .

179

But it was not Brynmaur, could not be, for there was more than one . . . something ahead.

They – whatever *they* were – lay strung out in a loose, curving line, coasting the crest of a current as she was, off to one side of her, some distance away. Were they native to this strange place then, these creatures? What manner of beings were they?

As she drew closer, she was able to make them out more clearly, though it was not a question of sight or sound. In some manner she did not quite grasp, she was aware of their presences, aware of the way in which they manifested themselves: like sleek, pulsing kites, each different, yet each a sort of slim, flexible-yet-stiff, leaping dart form.

Leaping towards her, suddenly . . .

Elinor shied away in panic. They were sweeping down upon her like a pack of winged wolves. She flung herself away in a desperate surge, skipping awkwardly from the great current she had been riding and plunging unexpectedly into a whirling upswell that took her spinning aloft and away.

The pack of dart-things followed after, moving with far more grace and precision than she.

Elinor thrust herself forwards, feeling her whole form quiver painfully. She had once watched a blue-tailed hawk attack a flock of wood pigeons, screaming into them from above before they were aware, scattering them in a burst of blood and feathers. She felt like a wood pigeon now, hounded by a pack of hawks.

They were gaining on her.

The current she rode was still taking her up – if 'up' were the right term to use in a place such as this with no objects with which to orient oneself – in an ascending spiral, round and round. She could feel the force of it pushing her not only upwards but out as well. Below, the pack came after, swirling in a series of graceful, frighteningly efficient arcs. She thought she could sense a sort of shrieking now – it was not sound, exactly, but her human-shaped mind could not help but interpret it in a familiar manner: like the hunting cries of a pack of fell hounds.

Hardly thinking, she veered herself sideways right to the edge of the upwelling current, and, as she came whirling round at its periphery, she tipped herself over just enough so that the outwards force thrust her shooting away.

Where she hung . . . drifting. To her dismay, there seemed to be no current here for her to ride at all. Even so, for a moment she thought it might work. The pack spun up past her where she hung, whirling, screeching to each other.

But then they shot out above her, one after the other, and the whole swarm of them came spiralling down upon her.

Desperately, she tried to scoot away, reaching, grappling for some hint of current motion, anything. But there seemed no current-movement anywhere about her, and she hung squirming and helpless.

The first of the pack was upon her then, and the next, and the next after, whirling and skimming around her – though how they managed to move so quickly while she floundered was beyond her. She tried to lash out at one of them, to knock it away from her. But it was moving far too fast, and all she managed was to further disorient herself.

Round and round the pack swirled. Any instant, she expected one – or all – of them to fly at her, tearing into her. There was no sign of her white blade here in this place. And even if it were here – in whatever form – she had no hands with which to wield it. Even the Fey-bone amulet had failed to accompany her here. And Moreena's 'draw line' had clearly miscarried somehow. She was entirely without defence.

One of the pack came at her, dipping low, then suddenly rising up underneath her.

It was all too quick. Before she could do anything, the creature had seized her – with something that felt like a net of pulsing, sinewy tentacles – and was up and away, with her laced tight upon its back – if 'back' were the right term. She could feel the creature shivering and shuddering with the effort of its flight in this currentless area. Then it hit a current and, with a jar, leaped away on it, gliding with such speed and grace it fair dazed Elinor's mind.

She jerked and twisted desperately, but the tentacles – or whatever they were that gripped her – held her fast. The creature that had taken her seemed not to notice her struggles. It surged on, riding the energy of the current, gaining speed, the pack darting and swooping excitedly about it.

And then, without warning, it dropped abruptly out from beneath her, releasing her in the same instant, and she found herself launched in a sickening tumble into emptiness.

Or seeming emptiness.

For now, as she gained the beginnings of a little control over her scrumbling, shooting course, she became aware of a kind of disturbance ahead. It was like . . . she did not quite know how to interpret what she was perceiving: it was like a small clot of dirt in a clear stream shedding itself into the water, giving off a muddy cloud that obscured the water's flow – but a clot that refused to dissolve.

What could it be? And why had the creature released her as it had?

She was shooting straight towards this . . . clot. Was it . . . She shivered at the new thought. What if it were some sort of . . . of *something* – she did not know what to name it – that the soaring predatory creatures fed, as birds fed their young. Was she to be *food* for it, then?

She struggled to try to change her shooting course, but it was no use. There was no current here that she could sense, and the arc of her forced flight had too much momentum. She would be borne straight down upon whatever it was that lay before her, will she or nil she.

So much for Moreena's great plan, Elinor thought in

angry despair. So much for the vaunted 'draw line'. So much for *her*. Behind her, she could sense the pack shrieking with . . . satisfaction, was it? Eager to see her gobbled up like some flying titbit?

As she was swept down into the mud-cloudy aura of the thing before her, Elinor perceived a shape in the centre of it, like the creatures of the pack that had taken her, and yet not: a long, slender, central body which diverged, spreading like moth-wings into two quite delicate halves.

Struggling and quivering and . . .

Frightened.

She did not know how she knew. But it came to her clear as clear: the creature awaiting her was caught helplessly in an unmoving eddy between currents, desperately afraid. It thought *she* was the attacker.

And then she was upon it, smacking into it with shocking force, the two of them tumbling and twisting away with the strength of the impact. About them, the pack swooped and darted, shrieking and waiting – though it was still not sounds, proper, that Elinor heard, but a sense of purpose and satisfaction and excitement – and of anger, too.

And at that moment of impact, she was somehow overwhelmed by an abrupt flood of revelatory impressions: they had not been hunting her for food, that pack of strange creatures; she was, to them, an alien, a disturbing presence, as was the creature they had slammed her into. Like a poisonous lump dropped into a clear pool he was to them.

Two alien presences brought together.

Another traveller such as she?

By now, the momentum of her flight had been lost. With no current to oar into, it was difficult for her to get her balance properly. The creature she had smacked against hung a little ways off from her, squirming.

What manner of being was it?

She tried to perceive it – a process like, but unlike,

vision. At first, the cloudy aura about it was too obscuring for her to make out anything much. But, as she persisted, things grew more clear, and she began to have the strangest sensation that, underneath its exotic form, this creature was . . . familiar.

And then it came to her. Against all hope and expectation, the creature before her was . . .

Brynmaur himself!

Elinor felt a long shiver go through her. Moreena's 'draw line' seemed to have worked after all.

The hunting pack was hovering close now, expectant. They had brought her here on purpose, obviously, wanting her to . . . to do what? She could not tell. But it was clear that this was Brynmaur. She felt it, certain sure.

But how was she to approach him?

There was a febrile feeling to him. He hung there like a wounded moth, shuddering. He had all the signs of a mortally shaken creature on the verge of mad flight, hanging tense and quivery-wary, like a fragile small animal expecting, at any moment, to be set upon by some rapacious predator.

She approached ever so slowly, as best she might through the currentless space, trying to emanate friendliness, calm, familiarity, not wanting to scare him further and thus drive him off. All she needed was to have him swing into a current and flee from her as she had fled the pack.

He side-slipped awkwardly away from her a little, his whole form shuddering. The cloudy aura about him seemed to grow thicker, darker.

No! Elinor thought. *Don't go.* But her words, of course, never reached him. His two-halved form shivered and shifted, and he managed to wobble a little way further off.

Elinor held herself still, waiting, imploring him in her mind to stay put. *Brynmaur!* she tried to call out – though she had no mouth to do it with. *Brynmaur, it's me!*

His cloud-aura shrank till it became almost entirely

opaque, and he only a dim form within. He turned, dipping into a sudden, clumsy-desperate dive away from her.

No! Elinor called, though there was no clear way for her to do so. She felt a thrust of despair go through her. To find him like this, to be so close, and then to lose him again . . .

But one of the hunting pack, which was still circling about them, veered in suddenly and tipped Brynmaur back, sending him tumbling closer to Elinor, fluttering and quivering.

It's me, Elinor projected at him, trying to put into it all the comfort and familiarity she could, feeling her heart go out to him, the poor soul. What must he have endured here, stranded all alone for an endless time in this deeply disorienting place, directionless, grieving and stricken, his mind torn by the terrible revelation Khurdis/Tancred had forced upon him?

Then a new and most uncomfortable thought struck her: what if his mind had broken under the strain of everything? What if she could never get through to him? They would both be stranded here for good, till the very stuff of their souls shredded apart and they tumbled piecemeal into the Shadowlands of the dead.

Elinor shivered. It did not bear thinking on. Brynmaur was no ordinary man. He would have ways to endure, surely. There had to be a way to get through to him.

Brynmaur! she emanated, trying to put every bit of energy she could into that cry, trying to make of his name a sort of bridge, a call to memory and focus and presence, a connecting link between the two of them, between Brynmaur and his self, his past, his humanness.

Brynmaur!

The hunting pack whirled about them excitedly, drawing closer. Elinor tried to ignore them, but they were too intrusive. One came skimming in so close she could feel the *ker-wish* of its movement against her side. She tried to shrug it off.

Brynmaur! she called again.

And then she felt a jolt of something go through her. The pack creature smacked up against her from behind. A *thrumming* thrust of . . . she did not know quite what, went through her. Energy, yes. But directed energy. Like a limb, almost. For a terrible instant, she thought she had been dead wrong, that she was prey after all, and all that had happened so far was no more than some cruel pre-kill game on the pack's part.

She squirmed and struggled in a desperate spasm, but there was no ejecting the thing that had entered her.

But the pain and violence she had anticipated never came.

She felt herself filled now with a kind of strength – almost like the feeling when she took up her white-bladed sword. She did not know how or why the creature was doing what it did, but it was . . . helping her.

Brynmaur! she called once more, only now, there was far more force and focus to that call.

BRYNMAUR!!

He shuddered, twisted, went suddenly still. His cloudy aura seemed to clear a little.

Brynmaur, it's ME, Elinor projected, trying to put all of her human self that she could into that 'me'.

And then, suddenly, it was clear that Brynmaur *did* recognise her. He reared up, shimmying, his cloudy aura dissipating. He came towards her, moving awkwardly in the currentless space, still uncertain, like nothing so much as a frightened puppy. It was embarrassing, almost, the naked need in him. Elinor could feel the mix of terror and joy that filled him to overflowing, could almost see him as a small, desperate, lost pup, crawling towards her, belly to the ground, tail wagging madly, whining and yipping.

She went to him, clumsy herself in the no-current.

The touch of him was a shock. The obscuring, cloudy aura had shrunk away from him now. He felt like soft ice. She sensed him trying to communicate with her, frantic and joyous and near hysterical. If he had been a man with a man's body, he would have been laughing and weeping and shouting all at once.

Remembering how Moreena had done it, Elinor gently pushed herself against him. 'Brynmaur!' she said – though it was still not any ordinary 'voice' she was using.

A throb of something went through her where their forms were linked.

'Elinor!' she "heard" Brynmaur say in return. 'Can it really be *you*?' His 'voice' sounded shaken and weak. His whole being seemed shaken and weak. He was shimmying with such force that he tumbled clumsily away from her, breaking the contact between them.

'It's really me,' she said, once they had managed to re-connect.

'But what— How . . .' he stammered. 'Where have you come from? What are you *doing* here?'

'I'm here to help bring you back.'

'But how did you ever manage to come here to this . . . this *place*?'

'It's a long story. I don't . . .'

The hunting pack had drawn in close to them again now, swirling around them. Somehow, without her having been aware, the pack creature had withdrawn whatever it was it had inserted into her. It had meant to help her, that was clear. And now that she had established a link with Brynmaur, it had withdrawn its help. The focusing energy that had filled her was gone away. Strange creature. She could not help but feel grateful towards it.

But Brynmaur, clearly, had no such positive feelings toward the pack. He shrank away from them as they circled. 'Beware,' he said. The cloudy aura that had enveloped him began to re-emerge, to envelope the two of them. 'Stay close! I will protect us. They have been hounding me mercilessly ever since I arrived in this realm. Only just have I managed to elude them.' Elinor felt him shudder. 'They are terrible creatures.'

But they were not. She sensed them whirling about, angry, yes, but intent on something other than the kill. 'Brynmaur! They are strange creatures, yes, but not inimical to us. They just want us to . . . *leave*.' Elinor somehow felt the fact of it from the pack so strongly there could be no mistake. 'You . . . you and I, we are a disturbance to them. They do not like us being here. But they will do us no harm.'

'*Leave!*' Brynmaur returned. 'Would that I could. There is no way out for me from this realm.'

Elinor felt a little thrust of despair. 'There must be *some* way out of this place,' she said.

'None,' he replied, and from him she sensed only defeat.

'Brynmaur!' she said, hotly.

He pulled away from her, the cloud-aura thickening into an almost opaque blob.

But she was not having it. She forced herself upon him. 'Brynmaur! You must know a way. You're a man of *knowledge*. You've explored far realms before this. How can you just . . . just give up?'

Brynmaur gave forth something which, if it had come from a human mouth, might have been a bitter laugh. 'A man of knowledge indeed. Oh yes. And look where it has got me. Everything I've ever touched has come to naught. It's betrayed me, that's what all my much-vaunted knowledge has done.'

'Brynmaur . . .'

'You don't know,' he said accusingly. 'You don't *know*!'

'I know more than you think,' she replied. 'I'm *here*, aren't I?'

That stopped him.

'How did you . . .' She felt him shudder. 'I don't understand.'

The pack was still whirling about them still, screeching and shrieking – or, at least, emanating something that her human mind interpreted as such. Elinor felt a sort of sick

188

dizziness take hold of her middle as the pack swept around and around, faster with each circuit.

And then she had a sudden burst of realisation: Brynmaur had been a disturbance the pack had been unable to deal with; in his fear and black, stricken despair, Brynmaur, man of knowledge that he was, had walled himself away too powerfully. But now, with her coming, and with her having, with their help, broken through the dark aura that had enveloped him . . . now the pack could sense a way to do what was necessary. But he must relinquish the protective aura he had constructed for himself.

'Think of your proper life!' Elinor said quickly.

'What?'

'Just do it!' Elinor insisted. 'Stop trying to defend yourself from them. You've buried yourself in a hole, Brynmaur. They need a pathway.'

'*They?* Who?'

'The . . . the pack.'

Brynmaur began to pull further away from her in confusion, his protective aura throbbing.

'They mean us no harm,' Elinor told him. 'They just want to . . . to send us way from this place.'

'How can you know that? You haven't been hounded by these creatures as I have. You haven't—'

Time was growing short. The pack was circling closer. Elinor could feel an anger swelling in them. She thrust herself desperately at Brynmaur, burrowing through the cloud-aura to contact him. 'Brynmaur!' she said. 'Think of your proper human life. Open the door back into your life for them. That's all they need. Just a doorway, a pathway. They can do the rest now. You must let them do this!'

'No!'

'Yes! Do not defend yourself from them. They are not the enemy!'

'But I can't . . .'

'Just do it!' she cried. The pack was a tight, whirling

189

flock now, circling closer and closer. 'Before it's too late. *Do it!*'

She felt him shiver. The aura about them coalesced, broke apart, shimmied uncertainly. 'Do it!' she repeated. 'It's our *only* chance of escape from this place! Can't you sense it?'

Brynmaur shuddered, twisted, shook. She clung to him, putting all her will into it, felt the whirling pack do the same, a pulsing hammer beat: *do it, do it, do it!*

The cloud-aura about Brynmaur began slowly to unravel, like smoke in a breeze. The currentless space about them seemed to shimmy, and there was a kind of burst in Elinor's mind, images of limbs and light and dancing spirals of brightness, and . . .

The pack *ejected* them.

She had one last instant in which the strange reality of this place was clear to her, the soft-ice form of Brynmaur pressed close up against her, the pack swirling and screeching . . . and then she was filled with a blinding thrust of agony, an abrupt, dark explosion that ruptured her self into broken slivers.

XV

Pawli opened his eyes and breathed. He felt his heart beating quick and strong. He felt so . . . *alive*. His fingers tingled. His whole body did. Rolling over, he kicked the blanket from his feet and got up. The dark little cabin felt close and stuffy. Turning his back on it in distaste, he opened the door and went out into the wider world.

The water in the drinking barrel sparkled and danced as he scooped the dipper into it, and the wonderfulness of the cold liquid going down into him near made him swoon. The sky overhead simmered. The dwarf birch on the slope below him were robed in pale radiance. The very peaks themselves wore glowing, pearly-pale haloes.

So this was what it felt like to be a true far-seer! he thought excitedly. The world about him seemed to waver, to be composed of double images. The familiar surface appearances he had always seen glowed now, as if lit from within, a subtly astonishing, beauteous complexity of soft light. But under that lay something else again, a sense of shadowy movement, as if some invisible sun were casting its light across the world and creating a myriad shadow shapes that had previously been invisible to him. But that was not right, either, for he knew somehow that those 'shadows' were the true heart of everything, not the old familiar forms he had been used to. It was confusing and exhilarating and he felt dizzy with it.

Finally . . . *finally*! He was become what he had always dreamt.

Pawli hung the dipper back up in its accustomed place

and pirouetted slowly, feeling the coolth of the morning air against his skin, the pleasant heat of the growing sun. Little trails of light seemed to arc through the bright air about him, and a subtle currenting underlay all. The world was so . . . *deep*, and he could see clear to the bottom; or would, one day. Now he only sensed those depths, like being on a little skiff on the surface of an unfathomed ocean, feeling the surge of the water, knowing he could dive down at any time.

But not just yet.

He turned back to the cabin – dilapidated, pitiful little place that it was – and went inside. Time to gather up his few things and leave.

The bodies of Bryn and Elinor lay unmoving. He shook his head, looking down on them. A tragedy, no doubt. But no less than they deserved, really. They *would* meddle in affairs that did not concern them.

Pawli felt a great, irrepressible smile lighting his face. Understanding filled him. A far-seer just . . . *knew* things. It was wonderful! No more confusion or vague sensings. No more frustrated waiting. Everything was clear as clear. Poor Bryn had been so very wrong about Khurdis, so very wrong about so much. He had wilfully crippled himself, had Bryn, like a bird that worried and worried at itself, plucking destructively at its own feathers until, finally, it could no longer fly. What a waste for a man like him to do such.

But Bryn's day was over now, and his begun. That which was come into the world must be faced and destroyed. And *he* was to be the one to do it! It filled Pawli with a great pride and an even greater sense of vindication. He had been right all along.

That terrible presence . . .

Pawli shuddered involuntarily. He was glad he did not have to face such a fearsome creature alone. Between them, he and Khurdis would outface it.

Khurdis . . . who was so much more than any of them

had expected. Wiser and deeper and stronger. How could Bryn have been so blind?

Pawli went to the rear of the cabin, took down an old jacket, his wet clothes that he had hung up – still slightly damp, but they would have to do; he had no others beyond them and what he now wore – and made up a little travelling bag. There was a sense of growing urgency in him, as if some invisible cord were set into his flesh, pulling on him. But he wanted something to eat. He did not know exactly how much time had elapsed while he had sojourned in that *other* place, but he could feel a trembling weakness in his limbs underneath the thrill of his new becoming, and his stomach was painfully empty. As he turned to look in the little pantry, a sudden, unexpected spasm of dizziness went through him and he stumbled, put a hand to his head, shook himself . . . and carefully latched the door shut behind him, as Bryn insisted he always do.

Pawli froze. He was . . . outside. He felt his skin lift in a prickle of goosebumps. How had he got here?

It must be part of some natural adjustment process, he told himself. The portal that had been closed off inside him for so many years was now opened. There were bound to be side-effects from a thing like that. Moments of blankness . . . That must be it. Nothing to worry himself about.

He was still hungry, and he saw that he did not even have the little travel bag with him, so he opened the door to go back in. It was a little difficult to do so, as if the cord he had imagined was still set into him, and returning inside the cabin was against that pull. He felt confused in some way he could not get quite clear. There were things he needed to do, and he needed to leave.

He needed food, he told himself. That first. He rummaged up a couple of week-old biscuits from the pantry and a small haunch of smoked lamb he remembered was still hanging from one of the back rafters. Reaching up his bag, he pushed the biscuits in, then hacked a chunk off the lamb and bit into it, relishing the smoky flavour. The pull was still upon him, and he felt his feet twitch, eager to be off. Bag slung over his shoulder, still chewing, he moved towards the door.

Elinor's face was white and drawn. Leaning over her, he could hardly see sign of her breathing. He remember how it had been in that *other* place, watching her grow uglier and more lumpen by the moment, while he himself had become lighter and more comely-strong. But that was to be expected in the likes of her, in one of the blind-deaf ones. There was a music in that *other* place that got into one's blood, if one had the sensitivity. He had heard that music, and it had opened him inside like . . . like a surge of water bursting a dam. It had changed him forever. That, and what Khurdis had shown him, and promised to show him.

Pawli felt the pull still on him. It was time to go. Khurdis waited. There were deeds to be accomplished. That which was come into the world must be destroyed and the world made safe. He remembered the terrible visage of the creature, its blood-jelly eyes, the long cruel talons, the needle fangs. Like a great insect it had been, creeping about the *other* forest, trying to suborn him and bend him to its black will. Far worse than anything he had ever imagined. Worming its foul way into the world to spread terror and destruction. Khurdis had shown it to him clear as clear. It was using that *other* place as a stepping stone into their world, bringing the Powers alone knew what nightmare creatures with it in its deadly invasion.

And he must face it down. There were none others able beyond himself and Khurdis.

Pawli lifted the blanket from Elinor's side and reached in. The hilt of the sword was warm from being close to her body. He pulled the thing out and flipped the blanket back in place loosely. The sword glowed. With his new-found sensitivity, he could clearly sense the strength hidden in it, even when sheathed. To draw it was to be . . . filled, he

194

knew. He felt as a man might, holding some great war-dog on a leash, feeling the line shiver with the dog's strength and eagerness to be freed for the attack. It was like some live thing.

Turning, he hastened out the door and away, not bothering to latch it behind him this time. His responsibilities here were finished.

Only halfway down the slope towards the forest did he realise that he had taken no last goodbye look at Bryn. Too late now. The pull was on him most strongly.

On he went, his feet flashing through the grass, feeling as if he were riding a rushing current. He leaped rocks, skimmed through clustered dwarf birch, unable, it seemed, to put a foot wrong. The forest verge was close now, a shimmering, moving wall of stunning complexity.

Pawli paused. The trees were lapped in an intricacy of soft green light that pulsed rhythmically. He could sense their yearning towards the sun, the way they tethered earth and sky together, root and branch, a great crowd of ponderous beings, limb and leaf turning in a slow, wondrous dance.

Yet he could also see them as he had been wont to, gnarly trunk and rough bark and branch. In fact, he realised, it must be just hereabouts that he had left his iron blade behind. It seemed a hundred years ago since he had climbed up here in the rain, blind-deaf to the world's greater depths, uncertain and confused. The remembrance of it made him laugh, almost. He was no longer that boy.

The sword in his hand felt heavy. The wire binding on the scabbard was warm under his palm, and he sensed the great hidden strength of the thing. The hilt beckoned. He drew it.

Such a terrible, scalding surge of raw strength filled him that it was like boiling water coursing through his veins. His vision exploded and then went black. He hurled the thing from him.

He found himself on his knees, then, sight returning in painful jags of light, sick and shaken. How had Elinor ever wielded such an awful object? The brute shock of it . . . The sword had landed point-down in the sod, he saw, blinking his vision into focus. The dragon hilt glowed like a torch and the ruby eyes flashed. It was . . . *alive* in some unnatural way.

He did not want to ever touch it again, but the naked blade shone like a beacon. Leaving it here like this would be most dangerous, for it was not a thing that liked to be alone, he sensed. It *needed* to be in human hands and, sooner or later, somebody would be drawn to it.

He got up and went to it, forcing himself. Reaching towards the hilt, his hand shook. His whole self did.

The shock of it in his hold was no less great, only less unexpected. He managed to thrust the white-shining length of the blade back into the sheath and then collapsed, vomiting up the little food he had eaten.

The sword lay inert in the grass, hooded. Safe. Or, rather, safe as such a fell thing could ever be. It ought never to have been made. Pawli got to his hands and knees. He felt sick. The glowing green of the turf under him was bright enough to hurt his eyes. He turned his head away and . . . leaned against the rough bark of a pine, trying to catch his breath.

Dimness all about him, whispering leaves. He was in the forest! Behind, he could see light streaming in from the verge. How had he got here? Another one of those moments of blankness . . . Looking down, he saw that he gripped the sheathed sword in his hand. In a spasm of repulsion, he flung it away, sending it tipping through the tree-tangled air back into the light behind him.

Anger lanced through him. *Get it back,* a voice said, or seemed to say. But he could not – would not – touch the thing again. It was not for him. He felt that with an absolute, blood-deep certainty.

He was quivering with anger, his fists clenched painfully.

He must have a weapon.

Pushing himself away from the tree, he staggered along, looking for familiar landmarks, knowing it could not be far from here . . . Until he spied the tree he needed and reached into the cradle of its roots to lift out his own iron sword. Here was a weapon, dangerous-heavy, with a sort of soul to it, as Bryn had once said, but more wholesome. Pawli could see the soft glow of it, feel the memory the iron held of blow and blood and grim exaltation.

The anger was dying in him, but the pull grew stronger. He had a weapon now, a lesser one, to be sure, but one he could wield without peril to himself. So be it. Let that which had come into the world beware!

Quickly, he leaped away through the trees.

XVI

Elinor blinked her eyes and found she was flat on her back. It was a pure thrill to have eyes once more, and a back to be flat on. They had returned! She tried to lift herself up on one elbow, but it was too hard, her arm too weak, or she too heavy. She stared fuzzily about her.

Dim light, silence. She let out a breath. Where was Moreena?

Slowly she rolled over on her hip. She felt weak as a new-born kitten. Even such little effort as she had just made had her heart thumping. She tied to swallow, but her tongue and throat were so dry and swollen she could not. Water . . . she needed water. But there was no water in the Otherwhere, was there?

Blinking, she tried to make sense of her surroundings. On her left, a smooth cliff-face reared up like a wall, its top lost in the dim nothing of the starless Otherwhere sky. That did not make sense. She ought to be on the stony tableland where she had left Moreena. She recalled no such cliff as this.

Closer to hand, laid out on a queer-looking rise of rectangular rock, she could make out a dark, still form. Brynmaur. Unmoving as any log. And beyond him, but close still, there was . . . a shaft of hard brightness.

Elinor froze. She shifted position and, after much effort, raised herself partway up, her heart beating painfully with a sudden excitement. It was not the eerie, directionless radiance of the Otherwhere. This was sunlight shafting in through a half-open door, and what she had first taken for a cliff face was . . . a wall.

Brynmaur's cabin.

She felt quickly at her left hand, feeling the pad of hard scar tissue that marked the severed nub where her little finger had once been. They were returned to their own world!

But with this realisation, a sudden sober disappointment filled her like a welling-up of chill water. What of Moreena? And poor Pawli? They were not *supposed* to have returned here, she and Brynmaur. Moreena's 'draw line', it must be, working most powerfully. Brynmaur must have been focusing on his home, and the pack creatures, using that pathway, had . . . *ejected* them here. 'There is always the element of the unexpected,' she remembered Moreena saying. 'And what is drawn to you may help, but also may be not what you looked for.'

She had certainly not looked to find herself lying on the floor in Brynmaur's mountain cabin.

Elation and dismay filled her at once. It felt *good* to breathe normal air again, to see new sunlight slanting down through the windows. But she ached in every joint and muscle, and her mouth was a dry torment. And what of Moreena and Pawli?

Pawli . . .

Was he, too, returned here?

She lifted her head, peered about the cabin, but could see only Brynmaur. It was hard to move. Looking down at herself, she discovered that she was half-wrapped in a damp blanket. She tried to disentangle herself, but the sight of her own hands froze her. They were mere skin and sinew and knobbly bone, with the blue veins showing clear. What had happened to her? Her arms, too, were stick-thin skinny. She tried desperately to swallow, to bring some saliva into her parched mouth – which was a growing agony now – but it was no use. She needed water. And the only water she could think of would be in the barrel outside the door.

She tried to unroll herself from the blanket and fell

heavily on her face, so hard her vision swam with bright specks. It took her a long few moments to realise what had happened: she had fallen out of Pawli's bed, where she had been when she began her travel to the Otherwhere.

It was hard to get proper breath even, so infirm did she feel. Forcing herself up on one arm, she reached back towards the bed where she – how had Moreena put it? Where her 'flesh body' had been lying. Under the blanket there, where she had tucked it carefully away, lay her sword. She had no way of knowing how long their Otherwhere sojourn had lasted, but judging by the debilitating weakness that gripped her, it must have been many days. Just let her get the dragon hilt of the sword in her hand and draw it, and all her feebleness would be driven out by the blade's wondrous strength, and she would be able to . . .

It was gone.

She could not believe it. It *had* to be there.

But it was not. Elinor lapsed to the floor with a sob. What had happened to her precious blade? Thieves? Lifting her head, she surveyed the cabin's interior. There was no sign of intruders, nothing vandalised. There lay Brynmaur in his bed, as she and Pawli had placed him before they began their Otherwhere voyage. And there, in a tangled heap on the floor, lay Brynmaur's starweed paraphernalia and the blanket Pawli must have wrapped himself in when he undertook his journey.

So he *had* made it back! Was he escaped from Khurdis/ Tancred, then? Clearly, he had revived here before she and Brynmaur. 'Pawli?' she called, or tried to, for her voice was so hoarse that the word came out as no more than a croak. She swallowed as best she could, tried again: 'Paw . . . *Pawli!*'

No answer.

Where had he gone?

For help, maybe? But if so, he surely would have left some sign for them. He might not be able to write, but there were other ways – a scrawled image, food left out, water waiting and ready.

But there was nothing. Which left . . . what?

She did not like the answer that came to mind. 'He will make me a *most* useful tool,' Khurdis/Tancred had boasted to her about Pawli. Did Khurdis/Tancred have the where-withal, then, to bend poor Pawli's mind, to send him back here to their own world to steal Elinor's blade and then bring it along to the Tower? Which was, surely, where Khurdis/Tancred was laired.

The very thought of it made her sick. The white-bladed sword in the hands of a man such as Khurdis/Tancred could do *terrible* things.

She ached to feel the solid heft of its bronze hilt, to have the blade's strength flow into her like a tide, to have it safe and secure with her. But it was taken. What was she to do, now?

Not lie here paralysed with dismay, anyway, she told herself. And maybe she had jumped to the wrong conclu-sion about Pawli. There were, surely, other possible explanations. She pushed up on her elbows, took a grip on herself. Whatever might or might not have happened, at this instant there was only the one simple choice for her: live or die; get to water and drink – or not. She began to drag herself across the floor, for she lacked the strength even to crawl.

The door was swung inwards, half-open, but she some-how managed to fall inadvertently against it and slam it shut. The iron latch closed with a *snick*. She reached up to the handle and wrestled awkwardly with it in the cabin's closed-door dimness. Grunting with the effort it took, she dragged herself up to her knees . . .

. . . and came back to herself with her face squashed into the chill dirt floor. There was nothing for it but to try again, and again, her hand flailing weakly until, at last, she managed to get the stubborn thing open and fall out the threshold. From there, it took every last shred of strength

201

and will she had to drag herself to the water barrel. Hauling herself shakily to her feet, she grabbed the dipper from its hook – thank the Powers it was still there – and reached into the water.

The wonderful wet coolth of her first swallow sent her head spinning. It was the finest thing in the world, that water. She took another drink, luxuriating in it, feeling the dry flesh of her mouth suck it in greedily, her throat open and soothe, her whole self expand like a parched plant in a rain shower.

She let out a long, heartfelt breath of relief and keeled over.

Elinor returned to awareness with warm sunlight pouring down upon her. Off in the distance somewhere, a lone bird was singing: *tee wee hoo! tee wee hoo!* A most beautiful sound.

With a grunt, she tried to roll over and get up, but she could not, so weak were her limbs. She fell back, her heart labouring, trying to gather her strength.

With great effort, she retrieved the dipper – it had fallen against the cabin's wall when she fainted – and managed to get another drink. The water seemed to fill her like ballast, settling her into the world more firmly. Her breathing eased. She took a few more sips, but no more, for too much water too quickly now would only make her sick, she knew.

Filling the dipper, she tottered carefully back into the cabin. It was dim and close-feeling inside, and it smelled of old decays, like a once-used cave now gone to rot. Brynmaur lay unmoving. She went over to him, holding the full dipper with utmost care. 'Brynmaur,' she said, kneeling next to where he lay in the bed. Her voice was still so hoarse she had to try several times to get the word clear. 'Brynmaur!'

For a bad few moments, she thought she was too late and that all had been for nothing – for he truly looked dead. But she persisted, dribbling some of the water onto his face, calling his name.

His eyelids fluttered a little.

'Brynmaur!'

He blinked, sighed, moved weakly.

She leaned over him, trying to lift his head with one shaking hand. 'Here, drink some of this.' Awkwardly, she put the dipper to his lips.

He spilled more than he drank, but even that much was enough to revive him a little. 'Wha . . .' He coughed, swallowed, licked some of the spilled water from his bearded lips. His hair and beard, which had been dark brown laced with grey, were now gone almost entirely white – Elinor had heard of such things happening after a great shock, but had never actually witnessed such. It made him seem an old, old man.

'Where am I?' His voice was hardly more than a gasp.

'Home,' Elinor replied. 'In your cabin.'

He looked around blearily. 'How . . .' But then he slumped back, his eyes rolling in their sockets, and went limp.

'Brynmaur!' Elinor cried. 'No!'

But he was still breathing.

She let herself down on the floor next to his bed, too weak to move further for the moment, her head spinning. The ground came up and enveloped her, and she fell away into darkness.

'Eat,' Elinor said, offering Brynmaur a bowl of steaming porridge oats. The very aroma of it near made her faint, it was so good. 'Here!' she said, thrusting the bowl at him impatiently, for her own bowl lay waiting and she felt empty as a dried gourd.

Perched on the edge of his bed, ratty blanket draped about his shoulders, Brynmaur merely stared at her.

'You've got to eat,' she said.

He looked like a scarecrow, rumply-tangled and dirty.

His white hair and beard were a tangled rat's nest which he had not bothered to try to straighten out. His skin seemed to have gone almost translucent; his fingers were all knobby bone and small blue veins, his face so gaunt that she could see the angular structure of his skull underneath. The skin under his eyes hung in little puffy folds and his gaze was wide and staring.

'Eat,' she urged him again. 'You've got to gain your strength back.'

He shrugged, looked away from her.

Elinor felt a flash of irritation. All the effort she had put into making this porridge, rooting about in the cabin to find the makings, burning her fingers on the fire – her limbs were so weak that she was clumsy and unreliable in even the simplest of tasks – nearly spilling the lot of it onto the dirt floor when ladling it out . . .

'Here!' she snapped, grabbing him by the shoulder and hauling him round, exasperation lending strength to her grip. '*Eat!*' She thrust a spoonful of hot porridge into his mouth before he could do anything to prevent it.

He spluttered and gagged, spitting half of it out onto the dirt floor, trying to grab up his blanket which had slipped from his shoulders.

'Eat,' Elinor insisted, aiming another spoonful at him.

'Lea . . . leave me alone!' he said hoarsely.

'You're going to eat,' she replied, 'even if I have to feed you like a baby.' She leaned forward, porridge-heaped spoon out threateningly.

He made to fend her off, but he was too weak.

'Eat!' she ordered, forcing the laden spoon into his mouth.

This time he swallowed most of it, and then sat hunched in upon himself, arms wrapping the blanket tight across his bony chest, scowling. He opened his mouth to say something.

She filled it with porridge.

It was the exasperation in her that made her treat him

so, but it was also the only way she could think of to prod him back into life. He had spent the whole of his waking time so far with his mouth tight shut and his eyes too far open, staring blankly, like a man who had seen too much, or lost too much. It was a look she had seen before in her life. Folk died, sometimes, who looked like that – too stricken to go on.

'Eat,' she insisted, more gently now. 'You need the strength.'

He looked at the bowl, which was still steaming slightly, licked his bearded lips where some little gobs of the force-fed porridge had stuck. She could see the struggle in him – part of him wishing only to shrivel up, part of him hungry and yearning still for life – and for a little it was hard to say what he would do.

Natural hunger won, finally, and he took the bowl from her in shaking hands.

'Good,' she said with satisfaction, watching him put the first spoonful weakly into his mouth. Chances were she would not lose him now.

Turning, she went for her own bowl. The warmth of it in her hand was a comfort, and the taste of the porridge, rich and nutty and delicious, was enough to make her a little weak in the knees, so that she had to sit down quickly.

Brynmaur was scooping up his porridge with a will now, and she did the same, feeling the good strength of it fill her with every chew and swallow.

XVII

Pawli stood upon a bare hillside crest. All about him was open air and shimmering sky and the great hulks of the peaks. He could sense, faintly, the slow-droning beat of their stony being. The living world itself *kerrroomed* so that his flesh vibrated with it, as if he were some liquid vessel quivering to the undertones of a deep-distant music.

He was uncertain how he had got here. His travelling pack was gone and he stood now with nothing but the clothes on his back and the scabbarded iron broadsword in his hand. The past days were a dream filled with disturbing images: a long, tree-choked slope with strange things moving across it; the visage of some foul beast, needle-sharp spines protruding along its back, slavering at him; a flock of insectile predators in the tree tops – kin to the dread creature he had seen in the *other* wood.

And in the distance before him now, tall and dark and most, most solid, like a great stake set deep into the earth to hold the world in place . . . The *Tower*.

Gazing at it, he experienced a moment of disorienting double-vision: the Tower a stone pinnacle thrusting into the sky, but at the same time a well into which all the world was draining, swirling round and round like water in a whirlpool. The motion of it made him sickly dizzy. He looked away, rubbing at his eyes and . . .

. . . steadied himself with one hand on a moss-slick boulder, for the ground hereabouts was rocky and uneven, and he had to be careful lest he take a hard tumble.

Another of those sudden dislocations. Pawli felt like a creature born along by a murky river, now bobbing on the surface, now tumbled down into the depths, blind and unaware.

The Tower was close now, dark and imposing and far taller than he had expected. Flying creatures circled it. Faintly, he heard them cry, a thin keening. They did not look like any wholesome beasts he had ever seen. He felt a thrust of pure panic go through him. What was he doing here? What was *wrong* with him that he could not keep his mind clear for more than a little while at a time?

His feet began to move of their own accord, it seemed, bringing him in. He struggled to hold back, to fling himself to the ground; he beat at his traitorous legs with the sheathed sword. All to no avail.

The Tower reared before him hugely. A portal opened. Darkness like a flood . . .

XVIII

'Where's Pawli?' Brynmaur asked in a voice hardly more than a hoarse whisper. He was lying on his back on his bed, staring up at the ceiling.

'Gone,' Elinor replied.

'Gone where?'

'Left us.' Elinor was on Pawli's bed, half-dozing. She pushed herself up and let her legs down over the edge so that she was sitting with her feet on the cabin's dirt floor. 'He returned here before us, revived himself, took some supplies, I'd guess, and my blade, and left.'

'Returned from *where*?'

'From the . . . the Otherwhere.'

Brynmaur rolled stiffly over, frowning at her, then struggled up on his bed to sit facing her. 'You brought him *there*?'

'It wasn't any choice of mine,' Elinor said.

'You should have stopped him!'

'How? He came after me of his own accord, after I'd already made the . . . the transition.'

Brynmaur had his head in his hands. 'Sending Pawli there as he is, unshielded and unarmed . . . he'd be like a minnow dropped in a deep pond, breathing all that strange water into himself, prey to anything that might hunger for him. How *could* you let such a thing happen?'

'I didn't *let* it happen!' Elinor snapped.

Brynmaur lurched unsteadily to his feet. 'Pawli's made the transition back already, you say?'

Elinor nodded. 'Recovered and left, taking my blade with him.'

'Why would he . . .' Brynmaur rubbed at his eyes with the heels of his hands, shook himself. 'No. Never mind. There's no telling what phantasms might have hold of the poor lad's thinking. It's Khurdis's fault, all this. It was he who trapped me in the Otherwhere, though how he managed it, I have no notion. I would never have thought him able. He's got to be dealt with, that Khurdis Black-eye . . . I must go after him.'

He did not look capable of going after anybody. 'Brynmaur,' Elinor began, 'I don't think you ought . . .'

He waved her off irritably and headed out the door, weaving like a drunkard.

'Brynmaur!' Elinor called. She caught up with him outside. He was sprawled on the weathered wooden porch, panting as if he had just run a fast race. She felt little better herself. 'It wasn't just . . . Khurdis,' she said.

Brynmaur squinted at her. 'He had help? What manner of help? And just how do *you* know anything about it?'

'I met him.'

'Khurdis?'

Elinor nodded. 'In the Otherwhere.'

'There's too much here I don't understand,' Brynmaur said. He ran a trembling hand through his tangled white hair. 'My mind is still a bit addled. What's going *on*, girl? However did you manage to follow me into the Other-where?'

'I . . . we used the starweed and the *talanyr*. I found your little book.'

Brynmaur scowled at her. 'You had *no* right to—'

'To save your life?' Elinor said before she could stop herself.

Brynmaur stiffened, then let out a long, sighing breath. 'How did you come to me in that . . . *place* where I was imprisoned? And what has Khurdis become – or what manner of help has he enlisted – that he is capable of doing what he has?'

Elinor sat down beside him. 'Are you familiar with the tales of the older days?' she said by way of beginning.

Brynmaur nodded. 'But what has that got to do with—'

'Do you know the story of the War of the Lords Veil?'

Brynmaur thought for a moment. 'I recall a little. They were the cause of the last great struggle that brought ruin to the southern lands. Idiots! What were they thinking? They tore everything apart with their violent, stupid aspirations for supremacy.'

'Have you ever heard of a Seer named Tancred?'

Brynmaur frowned. 'I think . . . Wasn't he Seer to the Lords Veil? If I remember aright, he was one of the most puissant of the ancient Seers. The Lords Veil almost triumphed indeed, with his arcane aid. All very interesting, no doubt, but surely we have more pressing matters at hand than ancient history?'

Elinor swallowed. Hearing Brynmaur confirm everything so matter-of-factly brought it all home with unexpected force. 'It seems that ancient history walks amongst us again. After we sent him packing, Khurdis Blackeye did a desperate thing.' Elinor explained what had happened, as the revivified Tancred had told it to her. When she had finished, Brynmaur went silent, frowning.

'This tower explains much,' he said finally. 'I felt certain Khurdis had gained access to *something*. I just never knew what. But Tancred the Seer . . . Are you *sure*, girl? The Otherwhere is a most disorienting place. Perhaps you . . . well, not *imagined* exactly, but misunderstood? Perhaps Khurdis misrepresented himself to you somehow?'

Elinor snorted. 'There's no mistake. I've seen enough strange things in my time, and I talked with this Tancred long enough.'

Brynmaur went silent again for a little, then said, 'I must still go after him. More than ever now.'

'*We* must go after him,' Elinor said.

He looked at her.

'Pawli has my blade.'

Brynmaur frowned. 'I don't need your help.'

Elinor almost laughed aloud. 'You need all the help you can get. Look at you! You've hardly the strength to stand.'

'Don't presume to know me, girl. Nor what I can and cannot do.'

'I know this much, anyway: Pawli's become a . . . a *tool*. He's been taken by Khurdis/Tancred and turned. It's the only answer that makes sense. And he's got my blade and is on his way to that Tower, most like. In the hands of a Seer such as this Tancred, the white-bladed sword is a terrible danger. He boasted that he knew more of it than I. There's no telling what he might be able to do with it.

'You need me, Brynmaur. I know that blade like none other. Working together, we can retrieve it, save Pawli, bring Khurdis/Tancred down. It's the best, most sensible way. Surely you see that?'

But Brynmaur shook his head. 'The likes of *you* have nothing to offer that I need.'

'Oh yes?' Elinor said, stung. 'And just what is the likes of me?'

'Like that Nerys Ironblade. Maddened redjack hornets, the lot of you, armed with your stings, buzzing about trying to undo each other and everything else in the world that you can.'

'That's so *unfair*!' Elinor hissed. 'You can't . . . you have no idea—'

'I have *every* idea! I've seen you work, remember? You *like* what you do. I saw the smile on your face as you backed that poor bandit down and killed him. You were *playing* with him, like a cat with a hapless mouse. And you were so eager to cut Khurdis down I had to physically hold you back. And then you very nearly went for *me*!'

Elinor took a breath, bit her lip. She wanted to slap him. The man understood *nothing*!

'There is no place for ignorant violence in what I must do,' Brynmaur went on. 'I go alone.'

'I will not walk away and leave my blade.'

'Best thing you could ever do, girl. A peril to your soul, that fell thing.'

Elinor opened her mouth for a sharp retort, but stopped. He saw clear enough, in a way. The white blade *did* affect one's spirit. She knew that. She had seen it seduce men with the uncanny strength it gave, enticing them to their own bloody ruin. But it had never corrupted her in that way . . . or, never very much, not enough to make the final difference. She had wielded it without ever letting it take her completely. And she had wielded it in causes that helped innocent folk.

Or she *thought* she had . . .

Did this Brynmaur see clearly something she had missed in herself? She had *smiled*, he said, as she had killed that Nerys Ironblade. She had no recollection of that.

'Abandon that foul sword of yours, girl,' Brynmaur was saying. His haggard face was grim and crooked with distaste. 'Look what it's brought you to! Rags and misery and crass dissembling. Go back to whatever home you have and try to put together a proper life for yourself.'

'Oh *yes*?' Elinor replied. 'And you even know my life better than I do!' She glared at him. 'For your information, there *is* no home for me to return to. You see me as I am, with all I own in the world.'

'Then I feel sorry for you, girl.'

Elinor bridled. '*Sorry* for me? *You?*' She laughed bitterly. 'You're the one *I* ought to be feeling sorry for. A sad, frightened man, so scared of what the world holds, and of what he is – or may be – that he falls into a drug-induced retreat.'

'You understand nothing!' Brynmaur all but shouted. 'You accuse me of knowing nothing of your life. Well, you know *absolutely nothing* of mine!'

'I know enough. It was clear to see the day I arrived here.'

'Oh, aye?'

'I saw the way poor Pawli was living, the way you neglected him, the way—'

'You leave Pawli out of this. It's *you* who were the ruin of Pawli, not I!'

'Me?' Elinor gasped. '*Me?*'

'You were the one who led him into the Otherwhere so that he could fall into the clutches of this Tancred. If you had just left well enough alone . . .'

'You'd be dead now!'

'And as for my starweed,' Brynmaur went on, ignoring her interruption as he staggered to his feet, glaring, 'you know nothing, less than nothing about its true nature. I never used it as a . . . as a *retreat*! It was a bridge, a doorway, an entrance into—'

'I know all about it,' Elinor said. 'Into the Otherwhere, where you met Moreena. Dress it up as you wish, it's still a retreat, a running away, a . . .' But Brynmaur was looking at her so strangely, she went silent.

'How do you know of Moreena?' he said in a cracked voice.

'I . . . I met her in the Otherwhere.'

Brynmaur stared at her, sat back – fell, more like – onto the porch. 'But she . . .'

Elinor's head had begun to hurt, a dull throb at the back of her eyeballs. 'She came to me in the Otherwhere, this Moreena of yours. While you were there, limp as a corpse.'

'How could you . . .' Brynmaur faltered, took a ragged breath. 'How did she . . . *look*?'

'She came to me and I—'

'No!' He turned from her. 'I cannot talk of this!'

'But she . . .'

With an inarticulate groan, Brynmaur launched himself at the cabin's door. He was so awkward-weak that he smacked into the doorjamb, taking a hard fall that spilled him across the porch.

Elinor went to him, but he pushed her away. Grunting, he dragged himself against the cabin wall and propped his back against it, his legs splayed out before him. He was white-faced and shaking and would not look at her.

'I'll get you water,' Elinor said, not knowing what else to do. She went to the barrel for a dipper-full, feeling a little sick with guilt. She ought never to have mentioned Moreena so soon to him, or, at the very least, not so abruptly. He was still too shaky, in body, mind and heart. But he got under her skin, this Brynmaur. He could be such an infuriating man.

Pushing aside his attempts to fend her off, she knelt and fed him water in little sips.

When the dipper was empty, he grabbed her hand with sinewy strength. She braced herself, expecting a thrust or a hard twist or something equally unfriendly. But he merely gripped hold of her, locking his gaze with hers. His green eyes had a surprising depth to them. 'I am not . . .' He lost his voice, swallowed, tried again. 'I'm not usually as churlish as this. Past events have been . . . hard. Forgive me.'

Elinor blinked, taken aback.

'You are a disturbance,' he went on. 'Not the sort of person I would choose to have around.'

'Thank you *very* much,' Elinor returned coldly.

He held up a bony hand in a gesture of peace. 'I am what I am, girl. What I'm trying to say is . . .' He grunted, shifted position against the cabin wall. 'We . . . we owe you, I and Pawli both. Thank you for . . . everything.'

All the combativeness had gone out of him, and Elinor could not bring herself to refuse such an open apology. Brynmaur had suffered; it was plain to see in the lines of his face and the cast of his eyes. Suffering made folk act in rough ways, sometimes. What it must have been like for him to witness his Moreena metamorphose into something insectile and horrid, she could not imagine. And, as a Curer, he could naturally be expected to have no high opinion of a weapon like her sword, or of its wielder. She wondered if she would ever know the full story of his life, of what had driven him to be the man she saw before her now – this odd mix of force and weakness, prejudice and understanding, determination and despair.

'Come on,' Elinor said, smiling tiredly at him. 'Let's go back inside and see if we can't get a little more food into us.' She stood up, her knees creaking, and reached a hand to him.

Brynmaur let her bring him to his feet. Shoulder to shoulder, each needing the support, they limped back into the cabin together.

XIX

'I'm going alone,' Brynmaur said. 'I don't need you.'

'Need me or not,' Elinor replied, 'I'm going with you. I walk with you, or I walk along behind you. Take your choice.'

Brynmaur scowled at her. 'You're the pig-headedest, most stubborn person I've ever . . .'

'Shall we go?' Elinor said.

He stomped out the door.

Elinor lifted up her rucksack, packed with what travel food they had been able to muster, blanket roll, water flask, and went after.

'Make sure to latch the door properly,' Brynmaur told her.

She did, biting back a quick retort. He had already turned his back on her and set off, traipsing across the turf and on through the dwarf birch. She hurried after.

They walked downslope, going slow. The morning was only just begun, and Elinor found herself shivering. Summer had not truly arrived yet here in the high country, and the air had a bite to it. And, she suddenly realised, she had forgotten her travel-cap back in the cabin . . . She had had that little cap for the better part of a year now. Comfortable as could be, it was, and just the sort of thing to keep the morning draught from her scalp. She glanced back at the cabin, some considerable distance behind them now, for all the slowness of their pace. Too late to go back, what with Brynmaur pressing on as he was. She cursed herself for an empty-headed fool and kept walking, shivering and grouchy and stiff-limbed.

As she hiked along, however, the chills slowly left her and her stiff legs began to unlock. Brynmaur, too, looked like he was walking a little easier. Just let them have a quiet time of it, Elinor wished, until this first day was through. At the rate they were moving, they would never make it to Woburn village before sunfall. Which might not be an entirely bad idea. A night in the open would be a bit uncomfortable, but it would give them one more day to gain strength before they had to face . . . whatever it was they had to face.

Days and days had passed since they had first revived, but they were still far from gaining all their old strength back. Brynmaur walked like an old man, shoulder bowed under the weight of his little travel bag.

He *looked* like an old man, with his white hair and beard, both long and unkempt. And he was so skinny now, it seemed the first good wind would pick him up and blow him away. Mind you, Elinor had to admit to herself, she probably looked little better. Her hair, at least, had not turned white as his had (she had checked), but she was as skinny as he, nearly, her clothes hanging on her baggily, and little stronger. Her knees ached as she walked, her back did, and the old scar along her thigh throbbed – and they had only just begun.

A fine pair of champions, she thought glumly, marching off to contend with one of the great, puissant ancients revived into the world.

As they drew closer to the forest, Elinor could hear the soft murmuring leaves in the morning breeze. A nice sound, that. But the way the forest began, the trees forming a kind of green-black wall, put her in mind of the dark wood in the Otherwhere. She shuddered, not liking to recall it too clearly. At least, whatever might lie ahead for them now, they would not have to face the bizarre creatures they had encountered in that *other* place. This was a normal, natural forest they were approaching, without any outlandish, deadly residents.

In the turf at the trees' verge, something glittered in the morning sun.

'What's that?' Elinor asked.

Brynmaur squinted ahead. 'I don't know.'

They approached it carefully, having no especial reason to be suspicious, but also having no reason not to be.

It was half-sticking up out of the sod, the rest obscured by the grass: brassy-golden dragon's head, small, red-glinting ruby eyes.

Elinor rushed forwards, stumbling in her haste.

It was the most wonderful thing in the world to grip the hilt of it again and feel the *thrumm* of the strength it lent her as she drew it from the sheath. It was intact and unblemished and . . . *perfect*! All her weakness fell away from her and she turned to Brynmaur – grinning like a maniac, she knew, but she could not help herself – and flashed the sword at him, the white-shining blade of it making graceful, radiant arcs.

He flinched away, tripped and fell sprawling.

Elinor laughed, brandishing her blade, feeling the wonderful strength of it thrill through her limbs, her body, her self.

But Brynmaur, on his back, his travel bag snagged awkwardly about his shoulder, was staring up at her with a distaste so clear on his face that it brought her up short. Reluctantly, a little sheepishly, she re-sheathed the blade. The strength seeped out of her and she gasped, staggering a little before she could get her balance back.

'Happy, now?' Brynmaur enquired scathingly. He struggled back to his feet, wiping grass strands and dirt from himself. Without another word, he turned from her and started plodding away.

'Brynmaur!' she called after him.

He ignored her, stepped in amongst the first of the trees and disappeared.

Cursing to herself, Elinor hastened in his wake, tripping and stumbling though the trees. It took real effort to catch him up, for she had to cast about at first, walking two or three paces to each of his, before she found him. All the while, her hand was itching to draw the blade – that would give her all the strength she needed. She could outpace him easily enough then, trounce him properly for leading her on like this, irritating, ungracious, ungrateful man that he was.

But she did not draw the blade. When she finally did catch Brynmaur up, she was panting so hard she could hardly gasp the words. 'Sto— stop for a . . . a moment, will you? Wha— what's the *matter* wi—ith you? *Stop*!'

He did, finally, panting only a little less than she. 'Go away!' he said. 'You have your blade. That's what you wanted, isn't it?'

'And that is . . . is *all* I wa— wanted, do you suppose?' She was stung by his ingratitude. 'What's wrong with you?' she demanded. 'After all I've done for you, after all we've been through together these past days . . . What do you have *against* me?'

Brynmaur crossed his arms. 'I don't want you or that . . . that *thing* coming along with me. It ought never to have been made, that blade. It's . . . *foul*.'

Elinor opened her mouth for an angry denial, but the words never came. In her guts she knew him to be right – or partially right, anyway, for the blade *was* a fell object, and too powerful. But she knew how to use it properly, had learned to her cost how not to let it dominate her. It was in its sheath now, was it not? And there was such a thing as making too much of such dangers. Did he think her some silly *child*, helpless to resist the dark allure of it?

'Go home,' Brynmaur said tiredly. 'I have things I must do.'

'I have no home to go to,' Elinor snapped back. 'You know that.'

'Then travel on until you find one. Only stay away from me!' Brynmaur passed a hand wearily over his face. 'Look, girl, we're been through all this. I thank you for all you have done, for me and for Pawli both. But I truly, *truly* do not want you and that blade of yours along with me. I have my own ways of facing a man like this Khurdis Blackeye.'

'Khurdis and Tancred.'

'Whatever,' Brynmaur said irritably. 'I have my ways. You would only be a liability.'

Elinor scowled at him. 'What? You expect me just to . . . to stumble about indiscriminately lopping limbs off, then?'

'Something like that, yes,' Brynmar answered. 'You refuse to understand. There is no place in what lies ahead for ignorant violence. You stink too much of blood. For your own sake, girl, go back.'

'Don't call me *girl*!'

Brynmaur shrugged. 'Goodbye. Fare you well. I must away.'

'Brynmaur!' Elinor snapped. 'You need me and my blade. You know you do. Look at you! You're headed off to who knows where, to face the Powers alone know what. You're skinny as an old scarecrow and still weak. And you haven't any sort of weapon at all, aside from a little paring knife. And a fat lot of good *that* will do you!'

'You understand nothing, girl,' he said in reply.

'Don't call me . . .'

But he had turned his back upon her and, without another word, trudged off through the trees.

Elinor glared after him. *Ingrate!* she thought. She took a step after him, another . . . then stopped. What was the use? The man did not want her along. He had made that *abundantly* clear. Let him face what lay ahead alone, then. He was headed straight for disaster, and it served him right. Pig-headed, unthinking fool! He had been so blinded by his own high-and-mighty prejudices that he had not even thought to question how her sword had come to be here in the first place.

She looked down at the sheathed blade in her hands. It made no sense, really, finding it where she had. Why in the world would Pawli just abandon it like that after taking it?

With a sigh, she sat down where she was, her back against a pine bole. The weight of the sword was good, like an anchor. What did it matter why it had been lying where it had? The only thing of importance was that it was back in her hands once again, and not in that Tancred's. She shivered, thinking on what might have happened if he *had* got his hands on it.

She drew the blade, relishing the familiar thrill of the hilt against her palm. Maybe the sword had somehow . . . abandoned Pawli. She smiled, looking down upon it.

But the smile did not last. Tancred had claimed that she knew less about it than she thought. It rankled, that remark. What did he know about it? She had *earned* the right to carry this blade, had learned the power of it the hard way, through grief and blood and loss. She felt the *thrumm* of the unnatural strength it lent her, coursing through flesh and sinew and bone. Brynmaur called it a foul thing, but it was not, or not simply that. The thrilling strength of it was blackly seductive and could lead one on to foul deeds. She had seen it happen. But it could also allow one to perform marvellous feats.

It had made her and marred her, this shining blade. With it in her hold, she became something far beyond ordinary folk. But behind her were too many dead, foe and friend alike, and she lived her life now without companions, swayed by Powers she could not comprehend. More than once she had nearly flung the sword away. But it was grown too much a part of her. She was wedded to it, and knew its foibles as intimately as any wife knew her husband's.

Abandon it, Brynmaur had told her. But she could not.

She made a fast slash and feint, going into the attack sequence Master Karasyn had taught her as the Crane Dance. It felt good to execute the familiar steps, feeling her limbs move quick and sure. She ended with a final flourish and then sheathed the blade. It was never healthy to keep it free too long; the fight-strength of it tended to curdle in one's limbs and belly if it was not employed in real combat.

The sword-strength gone from her, she collapsed on the turf, panting.

Off in the distance somewhere a bird twittered softly in the trees. The sounds of Brynmaur's passage had long since dwindled away to nothing. She was all alone.

She had been alone too much in her life, she thought.

Damn that Brynmaur for a blind fool! He was so filled with self-righteous precepts. Well, upon his own head be the calamity he was surely going to bring about.

She could walk away easily enough now. She had walked a lot in her life, especially the past year or so. Her feet knew the feel of the road. Let this be just another episode in her past, then. Just another memory. She and her 'foul' weapon would vanish from Brynmaur's life – and good riddance to him.

But the fool would walk right up to that Tancred like a sheep to the slaughter. She could just see him doing it, full of that odd, blind confidence he had in himself at times, despite everything. A deep Curer and a man of knowledge he might be, and with hidden strengths, but she had met this Tancred. She *knew*.

And Khurdis/Tancred would make trouble – serious trouble – for this whole area for years to come. More than this area, perhaps. She had witnessed the sort of damage such a man could wreak, arrogant as he was. Iryn Jagga had been one such, him and his Ancient Brotherhood of the Light: brutal and blindly self-righteous men who, under his leadership, had dragged their part of the world down into bloody chaos in pursuit of Iryn Jagga's self-aggrandising ambitions. This Khurdis/Tancred was like to be just such a man, filled with huge ambition and brooking no resistance to his will – and having the Powers alone knew what arcane strengths.

It would not do to let such a man ride roughshod and unchecked over this highland country. Besides, she owed that Tancred, for what he had done to her.

But beyond all that, nothing in her life was altogether coincidental anymore, and she had been channelled here to this mountainous hinterland by Powers obscure – of that, she felt certain. She had sensed faintly the flow that led her to that first meeting with Pawli and all that had followed, could sense it now if she concentrated, like a shadow-current running subtle and deep. Faint it might be, but the direction was still clear enough: towards Tancred in his tower haven.

Elinor thought of the life she had once envisioned for herself back in Long Harbour: she and Annocky – beautiful, faithless Annocky – how she had imagined the two of them would be, mellowed by the years, sitting upon the verandah of their own little house by the Ferth's shore across from the city, watching the sun set, with their growing children about them, perhaps.

The young girl in her who had harboured such simple, small and homey dreams was long since gone, burnt away by hard events. And now . . . Who was she now? What dreams ought she to have for her future? She did not truly know. She looked at the sword, glinting bronze dragon hilt with its small-bright ruby eyes, crimson leather scabbard concealing the pure shine of the razor-edged blade.

Brynmaur had told her to travel onwards till she found a home. But she did not think there would be any home for her. She was too changed.

Which left her with only the one path to follow.

Elinor levered herself to her feet. Brynmaur could be as blind-ornery as he liked, could order her away and refuse her company, but he could not, finally, force her to abandon either him or the task that lay ahead.

But it galled her, sneaking along after him like this, as if she were some thief rather than the one person most likely to be able to salvage events here.

How ever did things get to such a pass?

XX

Elinor crept down through the pines, slow and careful as could be, for something was desperately wrong here, that was plain.

No sign of Brynmaur had she found. Despite her best efforts, she had lost his trail in the trees and ended up spending a cold night alone in the forest. It had rained in the dark time just before dawn, a heavy, icy shower that chilled her to the bone. Now, shivering still despite that the morning sun was come, stiff and sore in her joints from the wet night, her scarred leg throbbing painfully (it was always a misery in the morning after long walking, especially in the wet), she was drawing nigh to Woburn. She had yet to see any sign of Brynmaur's passage ahead of her, but she reckoned he would go by way of the village. At the very least, she had figured on getting word from the Woburners about him.

But something was wrong. From where she crouched on the crest of a stone ridge, she ought to be able to see chimney smoke. There should be folk in the little terraced fields she could make out away to her left. There ought to be the sound of human voices in the distance. There was only silence.

For a long while, she stayed where she was, unmoving, uneasy. She could see no sign of anything down there, living or dead. Even the forest birds appeared to have forsaken the area.

Shivering, she cast about until she found the same winding hunters' track that she and Brynmaur and Pawli and the rest had taken on their first trip down to Woburn

Village to face Khurdis and his hired bandits. If Brynmaur – or anybody else – had preceded her along this track yesterday, the rain had washed any footprints away. And since the rain, nothing. Slowly she padded onwards, working her way through the trees parallel to the trackway so as not to leave any betraying prints of her own, feeling mortally the weakness in her limbs.

She did not unsheathe the sword, needy though she was for its strength. It was stealth now that she wanted, and the shining radiance of the naked blade would only give her away in the early-morn dimness here under the pines. But she kept one hand on the dragon hilt, the scabbard in the other, ready to draw in a breath if the need arose.

Nothing stirred in the forest that she could see and, eventually, she came upon the village clearing. Standing under the tree-shadow, she looked out at the remains of the houses Nerys Ironblade and his thugs had burnt at the village's verge. Their broken structures were wet from the rain and she could smell the soggy charredness of them. Nothing moved. Nothing, it seemed, had changed since last she had been here. Nobody had begun to rebuild.

Silence hung over everything like a stifling blanket. It reminded her of the heavy silence of the Otherwhere, and she shuddered.

Her heart was thumping. There was that in the air that made her skin crawl. But what? *What?*

Onwards she continued, past the upthrust, charred timbers of the burnt houses. Woburn lay dead quiet. Not the slightest thing moved. The houses in the village centre seemed entirely undamaged, save that, on the nearest, the front door hung open and out of kilter, one hinge ripped from the frame. Elinor sidled warily over, the white blade out now, feeling the welcome strength of it fill her. Holding it before her, she stepped past the half-open door and into the house.

The first thing to hit her was the smell. Something – or some*one* – had died in here.

Silence.

She shivered, peering about. She had entered into a front room. On her right was a doorway through into another room. A staircase rose at the back. To the left stood a fireplace, empty and cold. Three wooden chairs were scattered about it, two of them upturned. Blood, black-dark and congealed, stained the plank flooring. Elinor gagged. The sweet-sick stink of death filled the room like a fog.

She went forwards slowly, looking this way and that. In the dark stickiness of the blood near the chairs, she could make out a fresh skid mark. A couple of footprints showed a little distance away, faintly outlined. Brynmaur? She was not certain, but she reckoned so. The prints led back towards the stairs. She headed that same way, searching the house as she went. There was no sign of any dead thing yet, neither in this front room nor in the one that abutted it. Upstairs, perhaps?

Standing at the foot of the stairs, gripping the sword's hilt hard, she surveyed what lay ahead. There was a thick, carved newel post supporting the balustrade that went upwards with the stairs. The crest of the post had been gouged, as if someone with an iron pick, or a sharp sickle, had struck at it: a long, deep gash in the wood, showing white against the dark patina the years had left on the rest of the post.

There was nothing to hold a print on the steps themselves, nothing to show if Brynmaur – or anybody else, for that matter – had come this way or not. The panelled wall against which the steps rose had also been gashed, however, and some of the risers of the steps, too, leaving pale scars. At the top of the stairs she could make out the soft, insistent *buzzz* of flies . . . and a black stain of more congealed blood.

Elinor took a breath and went up, one stair at a time.

A little ways along the landing beyond the top of the steps, she found the first one. A small girl, it was, covered

227

in a swarm of busy black flies, her belly torn open and her insides strung out across the floor like so much dirty washing. Elinor gagged and looked away. She eased past, trying not to step on the poor girl's remains spread out across her path, the flies *zinging* up in a loud, startled cloud about her. There was no clear sign whether Brynmaur had come this way. She hoped that he had not.

A door stood half ajar just ahead, leading into a room. Edging it further open with an elbow, Elinor peered inside, her heart banging.

Empty.

She took a shallow breath, taking the air in through her mouth to try to avoid the death-stink in the air, and went on to the next door, which was closed. Lifting the latch, she opened it slowly . . . onto yet another empty, silent room.

Which left a third, and last, door at the far end of the landing. This one, too, was shut. She lifted the latch, eased the door open with a little *hreeek* of old hinges, and heard the *buzzing* of the flies again. Inside were three . . . no, four bodies. Elinor looked away, her belly heaving. They had been so torn up it was difficult to tell.

She forced herself to look back. A man – it seemed to be a man – lay sprawled half off a bed. His head lay nearly torn from the rest of him, attached by a string of sinew. His mouth was agape in a frozen scream of agony. There was a dried splash of blood all across one wall, and the floor was sticky-thick with it. Torn limbs and clothing, a clutching, dead hand reaching, a length of splintered white bone thrusting up through ripped flesh, the flies *buzzing*, *buzzing* busily, hungrily . . .

It was too much. Elinor backed hastily away and was wretchedly sick. She had seen more than a little death in her day, but nothing quite so awful as *this*.

Wiping her mouth and spitting out the last speckles of vomit, she stumbled down the stairs and outside into the clean air. She was panting like a hound, her stomach still heaving in dry spasms. What manner of men would be capable of such fearsome brutality? she asked herself with a shudder. What had *happened* here? She glanced about. Was the whole of the village so massacred, then?

Not wanting to, she headed towards the next house.

Here, the door was closed, and still intact. She tried the latch gingerly. The door opened with scarce a sound. Inside, there was silence – and the same carnal stink as the first house she had visited. Swallowing, she forced herself to go in and investigate.

Once again, the house's inhabitants had been flung into a single room, the poor souls slashed and brutalised. What must it have been like in here? Shrieking and wailing and blood everywhere . . . It did not bear thinking on. Quick as she might, she got out into the fresh air again before her belly cramped into another spasm of retching.

Which left five – no, six – more houses to check on.

Haltingly, she checked each one. Two were empty. Perhaps the inhabitants had fled to safety. The rest were all filled with the dead – children, men, women, infants – each pitiful lot piled in a mutilated tangle in a single room.

She was left shaking and sick to her very bones.

Perhaps as much as two days old, she reckoned, from the state of the bodies. No more, certainly. Perhaps only a day. And no sign as to who might have been the killers – save for one bewilderingly queer track. Twice, she had spotted what she took to be more of Brynmaur's prints. How had he born up under this horror? But in the last house, in a back corner near a closet, she had seen something in the dried blood there that had made her heart stop for an instant. Like a huge bird's track, it had been, three toes in front, with a long 'thumb' behind, all clawed (she remembered the gouges on the stairs in the first house), and larger than any man's footprint. The shape of it put her in mind of Moreena's unhuman, three-taloned hands.

Elinor shivered, staring about her uneasily. What was going on in the world?

And where, by all the Powers, had Brynmaur got to?

Whoever – or whatever – had done this terrible thing here was still on the loose somewhere. Quite some number of them, too, in all likelihood. It would take more than one or two men – or creatures – to do what had been done to the poor Woburners. Elinor regarded the green-dark wall of the forest pines on the village's periphery uneasily. She was completely exposed here, out in the open in the village clearing. Things could be spying on her from under the trees at this very moment. A long, twitchy shiver went through her, and she felt the short hairs at the base of her skull prickle.

But common sense told her that if she were actively in danger here, something would already have happened. Woburn Village had a deserted feel to it. There were none hereabouts save the dead.

Which left her safe for the moment, perhaps. But what about Brynmaur? There was certainly no sign of him here. He had gone on, it seemed, headed away towards the Tower, most like. Elinor shook her head. Some dreadful thing was loose in the forest, and he – blind fool that he was – had marched straight off on the task he had set himself, him and his ridiculous self-confidence and his stupid little paring knife.

She only hoped she would be able to find him before something else did.

The inhabitants of the two empty houses in Woburn had not escaped.

Elinor stood looking on what she had found, trying to keep her stomach from spasming yet again. She had come a little ways off into the forest, drawn by the dirty scent of burnt wood – and other things. Before her, there was an old, dead firepit. It had been large, twice the length of a man, perhaps, and carefully banked. Nothing but black charcoal now, soaked from the night's rain. And burnt bones. She could see a spray of what looked like half-charred vertebrae lying across the edge of the firepit, and, a little ways further off, a blackened human skull, split open like a gourd and cast away carelessly onto the forest floor.

She shuddered. The poor souls had been eaten.

Cooked over an open fire and *eaten*.

She turned her back, unable to look further. There had been nothing she had been able to do for the dead back in the village – there had been simply too many for her, alone as she was, to even contemplate burying them. Here, too, there was nothing she could do. Bones were scattered about haphazardly. She looked down at the sad, broken skull. Was this somebody she had met? Stroud the Smith, perhaps? Or old Tomae, Head of the village? And if it was . . . where did the rest of him lie? It was impossible to tell.

Elinor felt tears sting her eyes. Gone, the lot of them, their souls sent shrieking into the Shadowlands of the dead. What had these poor innocent villagers ever done to deserve such a brutal fate?

There was only one thing she could think to do for them. Lifting her head, she took a steadying breath, and began to recite the death litany, slowly, softly, for all of them, those here strewn about before her, those back in the houses: 'A scathless journey in the darkness, friends. A scathless journey and fruitful ends. Gone from the world of living ken. Into the Shadowlands . . . to begin again.'

She looked at the charred mess before her, still feeling she ought to do something. It was all too horrible. 'May your next lives be better than this,' she said softly, wishing with all her heart that it be so.

At the far edge of the firepit, there was a trampled area, and tracks leading away off through the trees. She went over to investigate. The soft carpet of brown pine needles left little in the way of detail for her to read: the water from last night's rain had blurred things, and she was far from being the world's greatest tracker, but it was clear that a fair number had passed this way. There were gouges on some of the pine trunks, like the gouges she had seen in the Woburn house, as if somebody had swiped at the tree bole with a sickle – or a great claw. And if she bent close to the scuff marks in the needles, she could just detect a lingering, faint odour, acidic and sour, not quite like anything she had ever smelled.

There was nothing to tell her definitively what manner of beings had made these blurry tracks, but she shivered, looking at the white slashes in the pine bark, that faint, strange scent in her nostrils. In her heart, she felt a sickening certainty that whatever had passed this way was not human. It made no sense, but the certainty would not leave her. This Tancred, maybe, had done something, brought something into the world. They had been days and days, she and Brynmaur, recovering. Who knew what such a man as Tancred, one of the ancient and most puissant Seers, might or might not be capable of?

She remembered her thought upon first entering the forest up by Brynmaur's cabin: how these woods, at least, would not harbour outlandish, deadly creatures. Almost, she laughed – to be so entirely, naïvely wrong.

But whatever these eaters of human flesh might be, she felt a blind, hard rage rise in her, looking upon the foul and brutal thing they had done here. The air still held a sickening tang of charred meat, and the poor, blackened bones of the Woburners seemed to call out for vengeance.

Turning, she headed off through the woods, following the tracks, grief-stricken and sickened and furious. She gripped the sword's dragon-hilt tight, the blade sheathed but ready. Just let her find them, whatever they were, and they would rue their actions. Oh *yes* . . .

But the straightforward, bloody vengeance she had hoped for was not to be.

The tracks went on, clear as clear, for perhaps twenty paces, the needle carpet torn up and bruised. And then they simply . . . vanished.

Elinor stood staring about her, bewildered. What could explain it? Here were the marks of their passage, the ground showing as a dark smear where the brown needle-covering had been torn up, a small branch broken, showing white, a blurry impression of a three-toed, taloned 'foot'. And then . . . nothing. Bare brown needles between the trees, as smooth as a pond on a still day.

It made no sense! She stood there frozen, gripping her sheathed sword, her heart banging. What manner of creatures could they be to just disappear off into thin air like this? She shivered, felt the skin along her back prickle.

Where were they gone?

The answer, when she saw it, proved deceptively simple. Several trees here had been gouged, just like those back at the firepit. Stepping over to examine one set of gouges more closely, she realised that they went up the tree, as if their maker had been a great cat, clawing his way aloft.

Up the tree . . .

She remembered the agile surety with which Moreena had moved in the trees of the Otherwhere. There was no especial reason to conclude that these creatures were identical to Moreena, but, whatever they were, they certainly appeared to have taken to the trees in a manner similar to hers. Elinor could read it clearly now. The tracks filtered off towards several large pines, each of which was scarred by the passage of . . . of whatever they were, as they ascended.

Not – definitely not – human.

Elinor backed away involuntarily. Were they still up there? The mountain pines in this part of the forest were big trees, standing a good twenty or thirty paces or more tall, the greatest of them, and thick around as two stout men standing back to back. The trunks of them went up, bare of branches, knobbly and sticky-barked, for perhaps twice a man's height, after which they sprouted limbs in every direction. The interwoven tapestry of their branches formed a complex canopy, dimming the sunlight – and

233

offering, for those who could use it, a webbed pathway leading anywhere at all through the forest.

Elinor shivered, peering up into the trees, listening hard as she could. Save for the softest sighing of the breeze, there was only silence. Not a fly buzzed. Not a bird chirruped. Not a squirrel flitted. Nothing . . .

The natural forest creatures *knew*.

She turned and hurried away quickly. Somehow she had to find Brynmaur. Before it was too late.

But finding him was easier thought than effected.

She had a less-than-certain notion as to the exact whereabouts of the Tower to which he was, surely, headed. He could be anywhere in the wood ahead of her. Anywhere at all . . .

Damn the man for a pig-headed fool! If he had only listened to her, none of this would be happening. Perhaps he lay dead already, innocent as he would be to the uncanny dangers that now walked – and climbed – the wood. Perhaps – she did not like to even think of it – he had become some fell creature's food.

No. She refused to believe that. She stopped, took a steadying breath, gripped the hilt of the sword more securely. If he had come through Woburn and out as she had, he most likely had spotted the firepit too. Or, at the very least, he would take warning from the terrible events in the village. If she had understood what had happened, so too would he, surely. Bull-headed and blind to some things Brynmaur might be, but he was no witling. Perhaps he had even turned back.

But she did not think so. He was too rigidly determined.

So she began to hunt for his tracks, leading from Woburn, or the firepit, or anywhere in the area.

It took a long, wearisome while before she found anything, and then it was not so very much: a small series of scuff marks and a single, clear print of a booted foot in the exposed dirt near a pine root. It had been made since the rain, and so did not likely belong to any village survivor – if there were any such. As far as she could make out, the track led in what she reckoned was the right direction.

She followed, most carefully.

XXI

Elinor made a slow progress of tracking Brynmaur (glancing round her shoulder all the while, lest some creature were creeping upon her from the trees). The faint boot-track she had begun with soon petered out to nothing, leaving her with no option but to continue on blindly in the direction in which she reckoned the Tower lay.

Onwards she went, casting about fruitlessly in hopes of some sort of clear spoor, till the daylight began to wane. She halted then, achy-weary, and made what camp she could, chewing on a stale journey cake and a bit of dried meat, sipping water from her flask, tucking herself away against the root-cup of an old pine, quiet and unobtrusive in the forest as she could be.

A cold, uneasy night it was, scrunched up there against the unyielding and knobbly roots of the pine, her sleep haunted by the terrible things she had witnessed. Dawn could not come any too quick, and she spent the tag end of the darkness wide awake, hunched in a shivering ball against the dead-of-night cold, ready to move the instant she could see clearly enough to walk.

With the forest just greying into day, she set off, heading down a long slope that took her in what she reckoned was the right direction, but slowly, with eyes open and alert, scanning the trees above her as well as all about. She was clumsy-stiff from her uneasy sleep, and the night-chill clung to her bones. Her scarred leg throbbed and she rubbed at it as she walked.

After a little while, she heard the soft gurgling of a stream and turned towards it, for her water flask was low.

A dawn mist obscured everything hereabouts; she went most carefully.

Finding the stream, she stood for long moments, looking, listening. But all was still, and she knelt to drink, the water icy-cold and tasting of rock, and then to refill her flask. As she knelt there, water bubbling down the neck of the flask, her eyes wandered along the stream's earthy verge.

She froze. Two tracks there were, too clear to be mistaken. Quickly she stoppered the flask and stowed it. The light was still so dim, and the dawn mist thick enough, that she had to squat close over the tracks to see them in proper detail. One print was that of a man's booted foot. Brynmaur's, she hoped. The other . . .

She did not know what the other might belong to. It was bigger than a man's print, large as the track of a great bear. But this was no bear's track – she knew very well what a bear's paw print looked like. This resembled nothing she had ever seen. The creatures that had destroyed Woburn had left a three-toed bird track. This was altogether different, elongated like a man's, with a round heel and recognisable toes. But those toes were clearly taloned.

Elinor shivered. How many sorts of outlandish creatures were haunting these woods?

Both tracks were fresh. She got to her feet, glancing about uneasily. But no creature stirred in the misty dawn forest so far as she could tell. All was still quiet as could be.

Gauging the direction in which the human footprint seemed to lead, she turned and walked along the stream's verge, leaped across it where it narrowed, and found, to her satisfaction, another print on the far side headed in the direction she would have expected. Brynmaur – at least she presumed it was him, for who else would be wandering these woods? – was ahead of her, then. But was anything else?

She settled her rucksack more securely. Unhooking the

sword from her belt, she gripped the scabbard in her left hand (feeling a little vestigial spasm of pain from the severed joint of her little finger), and the dragon-hilt in the right. No point in drawing the blade yet; its radiance would just betray her. She moved onwards carefully. Day might have begun, but the air was still brisk with night-chill, the sun not yet risen above the peaks eastwards, the forest shadow-shrouded and mist-hid and unpredictable.

Elinor froze in mid-step. Off to her left, very soft, she heard a small sound: *rinch rinch* . . . pause, *rinch*. Something moving stealthily.

Where was Brynmaur? How far ahead of her? Damn the man! That boot print by the stream had seemed very fresh. Had she and Brynmaur spent the night within a few hundred paces of each other, all unknowing?

Rinch . . .

What was it? Elinor peered through the mist-wrapped trees, trying to make out something, anything. But the mist was too thick, the light too dim. She stepped forwards warily. If the outlandish creature out there was anything like the three-toed, taloned killers, it would be ferociously dangerous. The only sensible action here was to rid the woods of it quick as could be, before it could pose a threat to Brynmaur or her – or anybody else, for that matter.

She wished fervently that Brynmaur were not wandering about out here somewhere by himself, blind and foolish.

The *rinching* sound came again, fainter now, as if the thing were moving away. She did not know if that was a good sign or not. It might have picked up Brynmaur's spoor and be tracking him. She padded on, stepping carefully over roots and around tree boles, her feet making no sound on the damp-soft, brown needle-carpet. Her heart was thumping well and proper now, and the hairs on her scalp prickled uncomfortably. She took a firmer grip on the sword's hilt, jiggled it in the sheath to make sure it would come free at the slightest pull.

The ground began to fall away before her and she found herself descending a steepish slope, slipping from tree to tree warily. Ahead, she made out scuff marks on the brown-needle carpet and went to one knee to examine them. It was hard to make much out – the needles did not take anything like the impression bare earth would have – but it seemed to be the same sort of humanesque, taloned-toed track she had seen back at the stream. Bear-size and most, most odd. She was far from being an expert at such matters, but she had learned by watching Gyver at it – Gyver, who could track a flea over stony ground – and she thought that the creature that had left this scuff mark had been moving on two legs, rather than four. The thought of Gyver brought with it an abrupt, sharp gust of memory: his wiry, furred body, the way his nose would crinkle when he was surprised, the way he . . .

She pushed it away from her as too painful, too sudden, too inappropriate. She had to focus on the here and now, not sink into a maze of old memory.

Folk died, doing that.

On the trunk of a pine near her, she saw a raw white scar, as if the creature, leaning against the tree bole, had inadvertently torn it with a talon or a claw – different from the gouges made by the creatures that had murdered the Woburners.

That tree-scar was up above the level of her head. Whatever had left it was *big*. Elinor swallowed. It was not her idea of a pleasant morning, this: wandering blindly through a mist-shrouded forest, Brynmaur missing, some sharp-clawed, huge . . . *thing* out there.

But there was nothing for it save to press on.

Softly, she continued downslope, eyes and ears sharp. Ahead, she began to hear the faint *chinkle* of falling water. The long corpse of an ancient, downed pine lay before her, rotted and green and layered with rows of white-orange fungi. Using this as cover, she half-crept along it until she could peer past what was left of its roots – an upthrust clump of twisted limbs – and catch a first glimpse of the water that lay ahead and below.

It was a small lake, still and quiet. Behind it rose a steep slope, dark-forested. Mist hovered upon the surface of the water in soft, thick swirls. The first of the true morning light was beginning to show above the dark slope behind now, lighting the mist a pale, glowing yellow. There was no indication of Brynmaur anywhere, nor of any living creature. The only sounds were the soft *chinkle* of a little waterfall at the lake's far verge, the falling water she had heard, and the quiet sighing of the morning breeze in the pines.

Slowly Elinor stepped from behind the downed pine and slipped forwards. There were more scuff marks on the needle carpet ahead, leading to the lake's shore. She followed them, keeping wary watch. The tracks led right into the water.

Wonderful, she thought. It could be anywhere now. She felt her belly crawl. It might be watching her this very instant from cover somewhere. What was it thinking? Was it a mindful creature at all? Clearly the three-toed killers were such, appallingly vicious though they might be. This creature might be like them, or merely some slavering, mindless predator. She did not know which would be preferable.

Damn Brynmaur for a complete ass! Where *was* he? Relinquishing the sword's hilt for a moment, she wiped her palm on her thigh. Then, sword in hand again, she crept onwards along the lake's verge. The trees came down to the waterline all about, so she was still moving through them, zagging closer to, or further from, the water as she wove her way along.

Hissk . . .

Elinor froze in mid-step. Again, she heard it.

Hissk . . .

A soft, almost serpent-like sound, only just audible over the voice of the waterfall. Like breath being sucked across sharp teeth, perhaps. She shivered at the image and gripped the sword tighter, though keeping it sheathed still – for what little advantage that might give her. It was difficult to tell how far the sound had travelled. The morning was so still, the creature might be very near, or quite far. The sound had come from the direction she was headed, though. She continued on, nervously alert.

Around the next clump of trees, she came upon a sudden cliff face cutting across her path. Thrice her own height, it reared up like a wall, green and slick with moss, stretching from the lakeshore into the woods as far as she could see. There would be no easy way over it, or around it, if she were to go deeper into the trees. Which left . . . the lake?

That seemed her best bet. Wade out softly into the water – if it proved not too deep – and circumvent the cliff that way. Slipping to the shoreline, she peered about. All was still and quiet. And she seemed to be in luck, for there was a line of half-submerged stones here which she could use, their backs showing above the waterline like a clan of turtles frozen in the middle of a migration.

The first stepping-stone lay a few paces out. Slipping her boots off, she hung them on her rucksack, and waded carefully into the water, feeling for purchase with her bare feet. The water felt cold as ice, but it was no more than mid-shin deep here, and she got to the first rock easily enough. From there to the next stone was a simple step, and to the next. After that, she had to put one foot in the water again – it was still shallow – and then the other before reaching the next stone in line.

Ahead of her sat an upthrust of naked rock, the raw bones of the world pushed up at the water's edge in a stony jumble. She headed for that, moving along the line of stepping-stones, having passed the cliff now. Only a few more steps and she would be there. Then she could . . .

The rock, suddenly, had something on it.

At first, it seemed nothing more than a dark lump,

almost a silhouette. But it had teeth – she could make that out clear enough. And it was big. Elinor gripped the sword's hilt, frozen, uncertain.

She heard the *hissking* sound of breath again, and then the thing growled, soft and deep and menacing, and raised itself up.

The sheer ugliness of it made Elinor shudder involuntarily. Though oddly man-like in general outline, it was lizardish and hairless and bony as an old carcass, with thin, sharp spines protruding down the length of its back and flaring out from its arms. And it was big. Twice the size of any man, yet queerly man-like in general outline.

Elinor shucked her rucksack and boots and drew the white blade in a quick flash. The bright shimmer made the creature on the rock start back, then growl the louder.

What now? she thought uneasily. Her position was far from enviable. It seemed a wild, unmindful, ferocious thing she faced. It had the advantage of height, and she was balanced precariously upon a pair of slippy rocks. One misstep and she would go down – easy prey.

The creature was shifting about where it perched on the rock, glaring at her out of small, reddish eyes. It raised a taloned paw at her and growled louder. Very like a human hand, that paw was, with knobbly-jointed fingers, each equipped with a long, sharp talon. It looked most dangerous.

Elinor took a defensive stance and stood unmoving. She could hear it growling still, a steady, subdued sound. Its fangs were long as her fingers nearly, and needle-sharp. She could see a string of saliva dribble from its almost lipless mouth. Her heart was thumping hard. She wanted to move, to flee, to attack – anything but stand here frozen like this, waiting . . .

The creature lifted itself, came slipping forwards menacingly over the crest of the jumbled stone upthrust, moving with the slow surety of a stalking cat, one sharp-taloned hand reaching out and downwards across the rock.

Elinor tensed.

It roared suddenly, a great, ear-hurting barrage of sound that echoed off the little lake's forested slopes and seemed to be coming at her from all sides.

She tensed for the leap, her hands shaking with fright-fight, ready to take the creature through the belly if she could, letting the razor edge of the white blade rip it open – the surest way she could think to immobilise it.

But the rush she expected never came.

It growled and roared, shaking its strange, deadly-looking hand-paws at her. But it made no move to attack.

Elinor stood as she was, uncertain. Was it defying her? Challenging her? Could she take it if she were to rush it now? Could she leap, without slipping, up onto the rock upon which it crouched? She felt her pulse speed, felt the sword-strength thrill her bones. She could not let such a fearsome, uncanny, dangerous thing run free in the forest. No telling what disasters it might accomplish. Perhaps she could entice it down.

There had to be some way to kill it.

But the thought of Brynmaur came to her suddenly, and his sneering dismissal of her and her blade. 'You *like* the killing,' he had said in accusation. Elinor shivered. Not true, that. Never true.

Slowly she lowered her blade. The creature growled. They looked at each other. What was it thinking? she wondered, gazing into its reddish, utterly unhuman eyes. Was it mindful in any way she could recognise? She had had more than enough experience with humanimals – those wondrously strange beings with furred or feathered bodies and human spirits – to know that mindfulness did not always abide in human shape. And that ferocity was not limited to unmindful beasts.

Where had it come from, this ugly, queer creature? What *was* it?

She had no idea. But the sight of it . . . moved her

somehow. The creature was all teeth and snarl and bony, lizardy queerness – a monstrosity. But Moreena had been just as monstrous-seeming. Appearances could be most deceptive.

'I . . . I mean you no harm,' she said, lowering her blade till the tip near touched the water. It was foolishness, perhaps, but she suddenly had a strong sense that this creature was more afraid of her than anything else. It had the feel of some mortally confused, stranded thing.

Stranded . . .

She remembered her talk with Moreena about how there were many strange worlds. Was this Tancred, through his arcane knowledge, somehow bringing in inhabitants from those other places?

She did not know. But this creature before her was clearly no natural denizen of her world. An outcast from its proper home – frightened and confused?

'I mean you no harm,' she repeated. She did not know if it could understand anything she said. Most unlikely that it could. But one never knew. If her feeling about this was right . . . 'We have a common enemy, you and I,' she said. 'He who brought you here against your will.'

It had stopped growling now and cocked its bony head to one side in a gesture surprisingly like a dog's. There was no sudden enlightenment to be read on its ugly features, however. Elinor sighed. Too much to expect, then. But perhaps it might still be able to pick up her intention?

'Go,' she said to it. 'I wish you no harm. Go your own way. I too have been a castaway.'

It stared at her.

'Go.'

Slowly it turned, keeping her in sight over its shoulder, and then disappeared with a rush behind the rock. Elinor heard a low grunt and a splash, the thumping of great feet . . . and then silence.

She took a steadying breath, another. Perhaps she had just committed an unconscionably stupid act by letting it go. Now it was free to wander the woods, to do whatever mischief it would. But she could not bring herself to regret what she had done. She felt an instinctive sympathy for it, poor castaway that it was. And, quite suddenly, she felt about her action a kind of . . . *momentum* that was familiar.

Like taking the first few steps down a long hillside, feeling the slope pull at her: it was the coming clear of the subtle current that had carried her into these mountains.

But it did not stop there. She felt a convulsion go through her, belly and bones, and through the bones of the world, with force enough to take her breath away. Powers were being vexed into motion. The Seer Tancred's doing, somehow. She felt sure of it. What manner of man was he that he could move the world to such a depth of unease as this?

Shivering, Elinor retrieved her drowned rucksack and boots, sheathed the white blade and waded unsteadily back ashore. Not since Sofala and the final, bloody destruction of Iryn Jagga's Ancient Brotherhood had she experienced anything quite so gut-wrenchingly intense as this.

The feel of it brought on a rush of memory . . . old Mamma Kieran back in Long Harbour, wise as the moon; the crumbling magnificence of Minmi City; mad Lord Mattingly, who had first gifted her with the white blade – in return for his own death; fat old, wise old Tildie, and the small blue birds she cherished that were the first humanimals, the first mindful, non-human creatures, that Elinor had ever seen; Master Karasyn, who had taught her blade work; the poor folk of Margie Farm, who had given her refuge and died for it in flames; the great, sombre stone hulk of Sofala, home of the Ancient Brotherhood of the Light, and of Iryn Jagga, whose ambitions had brought about such bloodshed as had not been seen since the days of the warring ancients; Scrunch the humanimal bear, and Spandel the little Lamure, Otys the crow and the other humanimals whose fates had been interwoven with her own for a time; the Lady, that strange, almost-being of the humanimals, neither quite one thing nor another; Ziftkin, the songster, with his uncanny flute; the great, violent destruction of the Brotherhood in Sofala; Gyver, poor, lovely, furred Gyver, dead and gone, like so much else . . .

It rolled over her like a tide, and she stood by the verge of the little lake, tears flooding her eyes for the pity and wonder of it all. That her life could be so . . . she did not even know what word to use.

And now she felt herself to be once again on the cusp. *Axle*, she had been named. And *fulcrum*. One through whom the Powers worked, a channel through which they could modulate and flow in the eternal great dance that balanced the world. It made her special, but all too often it left her feeling like some small creature tumbled by currents too deep for it; and it had brought her too much of grief, left her stranded on too many strange shores, with too many dead behind her.

But railing against it, she had learned, availed her not at all.

She put her wet boots back on, laced them up, took a few experimental, squishy steps. They would have to dry as she walked – uncomfortable, but not the first time she had had to endure such. Settling her rucksack and shifting the sword to a more comfortable position on her belt, she took a long, focusing breath. She found her vision was still prismed by tears and she shook her head, blinking them away impatiently, and wiped her nose.

She turned then, and headed slowly off through the trees, leaving the lake behind, feeling the shudder and stress of the world's deep shifting all about her. Let events unfold as they would. It was beyond her to prevent it. She only hoped it did not lead to too much grief.

XXII

No longer did she have to track Brynmaur laboriously through the forest. She could *feel* the way. For that was the manner of it at times like this: she followed the world's hidden contour, and . . . things happened.

Padding on through the trees towards the cooling end of the afternoon, she caught the scent of wood smoke and followed it till, finally, she was able to sight Brynmaur ahead, squatting by a little fire, boiling water in a metal cup.

'You!' he cried, springing to his feet as she drew near.

Elinor stomped his small fire out unceremoniously.

'What do you think you're doing?' he spluttered.

'These woods are far too dangerous for fires.' *Fool!* she felt like adding, but did not.

He glared at her. 'What are you *doing* here? How did you find me?'

She shrugged, not wishing – not quite knowing how – to tell him.

'You . . .' He stared at her till she began to get an uncomfortable prickling sensation in the pit of her belly. 'You are become . . .' He let out a ragged breath, ran a hand through his tangled white hair. 'I see.'

'See . . . what?'

'You are one of those who . . .' He sat down with a soft *kerwump* on the pine needle carpet and did not finish the sentence.

'What?' she demanded a little nervously. There was no telling what, exactly, a man like this Brynmaur might be capable of perceiving. 'What do you see in me?'

He looked up at her, clearly shaken. 'Nothing I ever expected to see in the likes of *you*.'

'Meaning what?' She did not know whether to feel vindicated or anxious.

'You are a gudgeon. Clear as clear.'

'A *what*?'

Brynmaur stared at her, then shook his head. She felt as if she were some questionable object he had suddenly discovered. She did not like the feeling.

'When I was just coming into my manhood,' he said, 'I apprenticed myself to Mortis the Smith, Stroud's father. Before I followed the Curer's path.'

'What are you talking about?' Elinor demanded. 'What does this have to do with . . .'

Brynmaur held up a hand. 'Wait. It will come.'

Elinor frowned.

'Smiths make many things,' he continued. 'Ploughs and blades and such, but also smaller, more complex items. Like hinges, for instance.'

Elinor had begun to fidget. While she stood here listening to him prattle on, anything might be skulking about in the trees near them. 'Listen,' she said, 'all this reminiscing may be most fascinating, but we have to—'

'No. *You* listen.' He got to his feet, dusted his hands of clingy brown pine needles. 'A good hinge is a demanding piece of work. One has to get the proportions just right. And the part that counts most is the tubular section into which the pin fits in order to make the joint. It's like curled fingers, see?' He folded the fingers of one hand to make a sort of tube. 'And they hold the pin just so.' He slipped the index finger of his other hand into the tube his folded fingers made. 'Without that being right, the hinge works not at all. No movement, no joint, no connection, no balance between the parts.'

'Brynmaur!' Elinor interrupted. This rambling did not bode well. He had undergone too much, perhaps, and his mind was beginning to loosen under the stress of it all.

'We've got to get away from here. Now! Who knows what that silly fire of yours will have drawn? Come on, now. We must—'

'You asked me a question, girl. I'm giving you an answer.'

'What question?'

'That section of the hinge that holds the pin, that holds the balance between the parts . . . It is named the gudgeon.'

She looked at him, uncomprehending.

He smiled then, a little slice of ivory-yellow teeth between his white-bearded lips, there and gone. 'It is my own private term for it. You're a gudgeon, girl. A point of balance between. You are one of those through whom the Powers work.'

Elinor stared at him. How had he seen so clear, so quick?

'I don't know how I missed seeing it in you before this,' he said, shaking his head. 'It explains much. You have my . . . sympathies, girl.'

Elinor was stung. 'It's not your sympathy I need. It's your co-operation. There are *things* loosed in this wood. Dangerous things. What were you thinking, lighting a fire like that?'

Brynmaur shrugged. 'I needed tea.'

Almost, Elinor laughed. 'Do you have *any* idea of what walks these woods now?'

He frowned. 'The world is . . . rent by something most strange. But I've seen nothing untoward.'

'But, surely, what you witnessed in Woburn must have warned you?'

'I haven't been near Woburn.'

Elinor stared at him. 'Of *course* you were at Woburn! I saw your footprints there.'

'Somebody else's, perhaps. Not mine. I've been alone in the woods these three days. Woburn was out of my path, and I've been pushing on as fast as could be.'

Elinor paused, trying to digest this. Who had been in the village, then? Some lone survivor? She looked at Brynmaur. 'You truly have no notion as to what's been happening?'

'Something's seriously amiss. I can sense *that* clear enough. It's that Tancred, rupturing the world's fabric as such men will. He's like a rock heaved into a still pool, that one. I can feel the disturbance he causes rippling through things. Meddler that he is.' Brynmaur ran a hand through the dirty white tangle of his hair, looked about him. 'But as I keep telling you, girl, I've not actually seen anything untoward yet. I have no notion as to what the man might be doing to create the disturbance he has.'

Elinor let out a breath. Brynmaur had luck, she had to hand him that. Or . . . could it be something else? Perhaps a man like him had . . . protection?

'What is it?' Brynmaur asked her. 'What have you seen in the woods?'

She told him then of what she had witnessed at Woburn, of the gruesome firepit, and of the creature she had faced at the lake.

After she had finished, Brynmaur stood silent for a long while, tugging jerkily at his white beard, his face tight, eyes screwed shut.

'Well?' she demanded of him.

He blinked, looked at her, shook his head sadly. 'The poor souls. First Khurdis and that violent-stupid lot of bandits, and now this . . .'

Brynmaur let out a long, tired breath. 'I reckon you've got the right of it, though. This Tancred has somehow managed to open a bridge between the worlds. By all accounts, it was not so uncommon in the olden days. It's the only explanation that makes sense. If "sense" be the right word. There must be resources in the Tower that he has somehow made use of. And quick, too. But the man's *mad*! Whatever does he think he's doing, bringing such

250

creatures into our world? Nothing but disaster comes of such, as you have seen. Such stranded creatures are frightened and furious and altogether unpredictable.'

'Have you had experience with such before, then?' Elinor asked uncertainly. She was beginning to lose the conviction of her previous, dismissive judgements of Brynmaur. There were who knew what hidden depths to the man beneath his less-than-inspiring exterior.

Brynmaur shook his head. 'I've only read old accounts. I didn't think there were any living persons left with the knowledge to accomplish such a thing.'

'This Tancred is no ordinary living person.'

Brynmaur sighed. 'Too true, that. And filled with who knows what mad ambitions. We must stop him before he has a chance to do anything irreparable.'

'We?' said Elinor. 'Is it "we" suddenly, then?' She could not quite keep the sarcastic edge from her voice. 'You reckon you'd like my help now, do you, with monstrous, violent creatures roaming freely hereabouts?'

Brynmaur gestured at her impatiently. 'You're a gudgeon, girl. You're here because of some need, some deeper balancing of the world. It isn't *my* choice.'

'How can you be so certain of who or what I am?' Elinor demanded. 'You don't really know me. You might be mistaken. When we parted, you were glad enough to see the back of me.'

'I know you now, girl.'

'Don't call me *girl*,' Elinor said sharply. 'I hate it when folk call me that. I'm nobody's *girl*.'

Brynmaur paused, nodded. 'As you will.' He reached to the ground where his small travel bag lay and lifted it up. 'Shall we go, then?'

Elinor looked at him.

'Come on. It's no short walk to this Tower. The quicker we start, the sooner we arrive.'

Almost, Elinor laughed in his face. He was still a bit tottery on his feet, frail-looking and pale, and thin as any rake – and yet he spoke with that ridiculous confidence of his.

'Well . . . come *on*,' he repeated. Picking up the tin cup in which he had been trying to boil up water for tea, he started to walk off.

Elinor stood where she was, staring at him. Just like that. All his prejudice against her seemed to have evaporated on the instant. Now they were to be allies together.

'Come *along*,' he called back. 'Now isn't the time to dawdle.'

Elinor stayed where she was. 'I'm just expected to . . . to forget all the hard things you've said to me and tag along behind you now like some eager puppy? Is that the way you think things will work?' It was petty of her, she knew, to make herself obstructive like this. But she could not help it. The man rankled her so.

Brynmaur looked back at her and frowned. 'It's neither my choice nor yours, girl. I don't like you any more now than I did the last time I saw you, but we must go where the world pushes us.'

'Don't call me—'

'Yes, yes,' he said impatiently, waving her to silence. 'Now come along.'

'You—' she began, then bit her tongue. Whether she liked it or not, he did have the right of it. She could feel the subtle momentum here. She would go where she must, with whom she must, as would he.

Brynmaur was urging her on impatiently.

She gathered herself and went after.

They left the remains of Brynmaur's betraying fire behind as quick as they could and pushed steadily on. Elinor kept watch on their backtrail, but there was no sign of any pursuers. By so much, then, were they in luck – or on the right path, at any rate, for when things went like this and the world was in flux, luck was an uncertain notion.

By midday, it had begun to rain, a steady, chill drizzle.

Neither of them had rain cloaks, and they were soon soaked and shivering miserably.

'Best look for some shelter till it passes,' Elinor suggested. Her hair was plastered coldly to her scalp and she pined for her forgotten travel-cap.

Brynmaur shook his head. 'Looks like it's set to rain for the rest of the afternoon. Best we keep pressing on.'

'Look at you!' she said by way of reply. 'You're shivering so hard you can barely walk.' It was true. He had his arms wrapped about his thin chest and was shaking like a leaf in the rain. 'And I'm in not much better shape. Best we find what warmth we can and rest, and eat a little, perhaps. Who knows what the next days may bring?'

'Exactly,' Brynmaur returned. 'Who knows what may be happening. The world is reeling. Who knows what this Tancred might be up to? Every moment we hesitate gives him that much longer to mould events to his will. Best we get along as fast as we can, whether we like the idea or . . .'

But he never finished the sentence.

They had been trudging along a ridge, forest on all sides, working their way slowly upslope. Now, suddenly, the trees fell away to their left and they had a view of a rolling valley with a river winding through it like a great, silver-grey snake. The rain made distances hazy, but they could see the slope on the far side of the river clearly enough. Where the dark cover of the trees parted, an expanse of rolling meadow showed there. And on that meadow . . .

'What is it?' Elinor hissed.

Dark shapes moved about, like a pack of wolves. But they were definitely not wolves. Bears, perhaps? It was hard to judge size reliably at this distance, but the creatures certainly looked massive enough to be mountain bears. They moved all wrong, though, with a shambling, rocking motion quite unlike anything Elinor had ever seen. And they walked on two legs rather than four – on legs that seemed queerly too long.

'I've never seen anything like *that* in these mountains,' Brynmaur said.

Elinor shivered. Could this be part of the . . . the pack that had murdered and eaten the Woburners? But she could not imagine the creatures below climbing agilely through the trees. They did not look at all like they were built for such, with their too-long hind legs, their peculiar rocking gait, the heaviness of their bodies. But they did not resemble the creature she had encountered at the lake, either. A different sort entirely, then. How many such monstrosities had this Tancred brought into the world?

'The man's mad!' Brynmaur hissed, 'to do such a thing.'

Elinor agreed wholeheartedly. It made her belly twist to see the queer way these creatures moved. 'Quick,' she said, 'let's away from here before they have a chance to spot us.'

'They'll never see us up here in this rain,' Brynmaur returned. 'And they're on the far side of the river, anyhow. Even if they were to spot us, we'd be long gone from here before they could turn up.' He was crouched down now, shoulder propped against a pine bole, squinting into the rainy distance, rapt with fascination. 'Just look at the way they move.'

'How do we know what such creatures can or cannot see?' Elinor demanded of him. 'They might have eagle's sight for all we know. And be faster than any animals we're familiar with. I've seen what some of these Otherland creatures are capable of doing. Let's away from here.'

'Look!' Brynmaur said, pointing.

There was a sudden commotion on the far slope. Something leaped out of the dark edge of the trees and into the grassy meadow. For an instant, Elinor thought it was another of the outlandish creatures. But no. It was a mountain elk, a bull, tall and broad-antlered, running and leaping in great, frantic, graceful bounds.

Through the steady, soft drumming of the rain, Elinor could hear him bellow. And then there was another sound, a sort of harsh screeching that grated on her ears. From the forest behind the elk two of the outland creatures came streaking. Their hind legs, upon which they ran, seemed hugely long, scything through the grass like stilts. It was an ungainly, almost comical motion, but deceptively fast. The elk, for all its grace and speed of movement, was caught up almost immediately.

The creatures they had seen on the meadow angled towards it while those behind caught up. They all met in a single, bellowing, shrieking, writhing mass. Elinor distinctly heard the distant *kerrump* of the impact, it was so terrific. The elk went down screaming. There was a gush of liquid red, and then only a squirming, violent struggle as the pack – a true hunting pack it was, evidently – tore the poor elk into quivering bits and consumed it.

Brynmaur pushed himself away from the tree and stood up shakily. 'You're right,' he said in a cracked voice. 'Let's away from here quick as can be.'

They skittered down through the rain-soaked trees, putting the ridge they had come up along between them and the hunting pack back in the valley.

At first they made good time, for the going was easy enough, with smooth, needle-carpeted ground and no undergrowth under the big trees. With more than a little relief, they were able to put the ridge well behind them. The cold drizzle began to let up after a while and their spirits rose with the prospect of the otherland hunters left well behind and a rainless night ahead to look forward to.

As they continued onwards, however, the ground began to be marked by stony outcrops, sharp-edged and mossy-backed and unpredictably slippery underfoot, and their progress slowed. Rounding a little knoll, Brynmaur skidded and went down heavily, gasping. Elinor helped him to his feet, worried. He was wet and pale and shivery, his skin cold to the touch. It was all too easy to take a fever, force-marching in weather like this. And Brynmaur had been far from strong at the outset. He stood now leaning against her for support, panting like an old hound, his white hair hanging long and limp like string, the tangled strands of it dripping wet.

'Come on,' she urged him. 'We've got to find shelter of some sort and lay up for a bit. You need some food in you and warmth, if we can manage it.'

He shook his head. 'No, I . . .'

But she would brook no refusal from him. Instead of arguing fruitlessly, she simply dragged him along.

Across a ridge of wet-moss stone she went, casting about for some sort of shelter, and thence through a little cut and onto a gradually upwards slanting slope. Broken branches were littered everywhere here, as if a gang of men had been working up in the trees above them, clearing out the dead wood and chucking it earthwards.

Elinor glanced up uneasily, but she could make out nothing untoward. She stopped, Brynmaur leaning against her, and stood listening. The woods were silent.

'What is it?' Brynmaur demanded in a whisper, looking about uneasily.

Elinor shrugged. 'Nothing, I think. It's just . . .'

She had been casting about through the trees as she spoke, and now, suddenly, she caught the faintest of little movements. Her heart lurched. 'Quick!' she hissed at Brynmaur, 'over here.' She dragged him by the arm towards the closest thing to a clearing she could find, a little wider space between the trees where a large slab of moss-flecked, grey rock humped up above the needly earth, like the great grey back of some subterranean beast come up for air.

'What is it?' Brynmaur demanded as she hauled him across onto the moss-slippery surface of the rock.

Elinor made no reply. She shucked her rucksack and gripped the bronze hilt of her blade, ready to draw.

'What *is* it?' Brynmaur repeated, looking every which way.

Elinor had it spotted now. Up in a tree off to their right some fifteen paces or so – a tangle of knobbly limbs. If she had not seen Moreena in that Otherwhere wood, she probably would never have recognised the uncertain, only partially glimpsed shape before them now for what it was. 'Look!' she hissed in Brynmaur's ear, pointing.

He squinted along the direction of her arm, but shook his head.

'Like a tangle of branches. There!'

'Are you sure, girl? I can't see . . .'

But then it moved, and he let out a surprised little 'Huh!'

Down it came, climbing with the same grasshoppery sort of motion that she had seen in Moreena. Its skin was a mottled grey-brown that blended so well with the tree down which it was creeping that at first it was hard to make out the form of it clearly.

Then Elinor spotted a bony, three-fingered hand, the fingers tipped with sharp talons that showed pale and wicked against the darker bark of the tree's bole. Partway out of the tree now, it clung there like some great insect, head down, peering at her around the edge of the trunk. Its skull seemed all bone, full of vents and spiky knobs, covered by hairless skin. The nose was a mere slit, the mouth a long, tapering muzzle ending in thin white lips past which the needle points of ivory-yellow fangs protruded. Its eyes were round and large, where human eyes would be, but set in sockets of jagged bone.

Elinor shuddered, looking upon it. Moreena's eyes had been red and entirely unhuman. This creature's, too, had nothing of humanness to them, but they were so black they appeared more as gleaming holes in its bony skull than actual eyes. There was nothing at all to be read in them.

With a sudden, agile leap, it was upon the ground and stalking towards them with a slow, insectile grace, on legs that were all bone and sinew and bent in odd angles. Its feet were three-toed, spurred with pale, sharp talons.

Elinor drew her blade, her heart thumping. With no trees close above them, it had no way to come at her and Brynmaur except along the ground, and it appeared less agile on the ground than aloft – by so much, anyway, did circumstances seem in their favour, then.

It halted some five paces or so before her, standing slightly hunched, queer legs flexed, regarding her and Brynmaur silently.

This must surely be a member of the pack that had murdered the poor Woburners. Everything about it pointed to that. But there seemed to be just this one, alone. What of the rest? Look as she might, she could see no sign of any others. Was this a lone scout of some sort, then? A hunter?

Elinor stared at it, her skin crawling. It was such an alien-looking thing, an unwholesome mixing of insect and predatory beast. What was going on behind those soulless-seeming black-gleaming eyes? Was it truly a mindful creature? But it had to be, did it not? Mindless beasts did not construct firepits upon which to roast their kills. Yet there was no evidence about it of clothing, or tools or weapons or supplies, or of anything that would mark the creature as more than a simple beast. Most utterly strange . . .

Seeing it so close like this, she grew more certain that it was of the same type of creature as Moreena. And despite its disturbing and menacing appearance, it had made no truly aggressive move as of yet. She remembered seeing Moreena in the *other* wood for the first time, standing unmoving as this creature was, threatening only in her appearance, not her actions.

The Fey-bone at Elinor's breast hung inert. It had not, she realised, responded to any of the creatures she had crossed paths with. She did not understand why. It had certainly reacted strongly to Moreena. Yet here was one of Moreena's kind – or something that seemed so – and the amulet remained entirely quiescent.

But she *had* been able to communicate with Moreena. After her experience back at the little lake, it seemed worth the attempt here.

Elinor slid the white blade back into its scabbard and raised both her hands, palms out, as a gesture of good will. 'We mean you no harm,' she said quietly. She did not expect it would understand her words, but perhaps the intent of them would be clear enough.

The creature stood without moving, regarding her with its black, inhuman eyes.

'I have met . . . one of your kind,' Elinor went on. 'We . . . talked. There is no need for enmity between us, you and I.'

Still it made no move, merely continued staring, silent.

Brynmaur, meanwhile, had begun moaning softly under his breath. Putting a hand to him, Elinor felt him tremble. What must the poor man be feeling, faced as he was like this with the very embodiment of his lost lover – an embodiment out of terrible nightmare brought to life in the world before him? 'It's all right,' she said, trying to sound reassuring, though she felt far from secure.

He fell to his knees, face buried in his hands, moaning.

'Brynmaur,' Elinor said concernedly. 'You've got to—'

Without any warning at all, the creature was suddenly upon them in a great leap that was beyond anything human. Hissing like a serpent, it went for Elinor with one of its taloned hands, so fearsomely quick that even the uncanny strength and agility the sword lent her was nearly not enough. Only barely was she able to ward off that deadly lunge, which would have ripped her belly open like some over-ripe fruit, spilling her insides wetly across the forest floor. Whipping the white blade out and striking in one desperate motion, she felt the razor edge of it grate against something surprisingly hard, then bite through flesh and sinew.

The creature shrieked, a high, keening, painful sound, and tumbled back, leaving behind a single, twitching finger and a splash-trail of pale green liquid that had to be blood.

Hissing and spitting like a great cat, the creature shook its head, put the truncated finger to its mouth, and lapped at its own green blood with a thin white tongue. There was an acrid, unpleasant odour in the air, like burnt metal and rotted flowers combined. Elinor stepped forwards with slow wariness.

There seemed to be just this one, alone. What about the rest? Look as she might, she could see no sign of any others. She had to make sure it never returned to the rest of its kind.

It came for her, its wickedly taloned hands stretched out menacingly, the mutilated finger still oozing green blood. Its movements were not like any creature's Elinor had ever seen – not even like Moreena's. There was the same insectile grace that Moreena had shown, to be sure, but this creature's limbs were articulated in some subtle way that was altogether bizarre. Its spiky knees seemed to bend in unexpected directions, giving its gait at once an insectile jerkiness and queer fluidity. She could hear the soft *kreek* of its joints as it moved.

There was no speedy rush this time. It came at her slow and wary, hissing.

Elinor took up the Double Tree defensive posture, the sword held in a two-handed grip, feet just so, waiting.

They circled each other like fighting cats. The creature feinted, a fast swipe with its uninjured hand. Elinor blocked with her blade and it only just managed to skip back and keep the hand intact.

Back to circling again.

She had to do something, and quick. If more of its kind should appear, she would be in dead trouble. One alone she might handle, the pack, never.

She moved then in an attack sequence Master Karasyn had named the Rolling Wheel, a quick series of short, hard, overhand strokes, her feet dancing through the familiar motions in perfect sequence. The creature backed away, flinching from the bright arcs the white blade made, hissing.

She pressed hard, but it faded away from her blade with uncanny agility and, try as she might, she could not get within striking distance. And once, when she overstepped herself a fraction – her limbs were still a little shaky-weak, even with the sword's strength thrilling through them – it came within a hair of sinking two taloned fingers in her throat.

Standing away from her, it suddenly threw back its head and let loose a long, wailing howl.

Which had to be a call to its kin.

Elinor rushed it, driving it back. But it skipped away easily enough. It made no attempt to attack her now, seemingly content with merely keeping her occupied – which did not bode well at all. She lunged, danced back, lunged again, whirled and ducked and thrust, feeling a cold desperation well up in her, but all to no avail.

And then, from behind her, she heard a dull *thunk*. The creature's head snapped forwards. She chanced a flashing glance behind, saw Brynmaur standing, a clutch of stones in his hands, a couple at his feet where he had fumbled them.

He hurled one at the creature, which ducked it easily enough. Then another, and a third. They did no damage at all, but the distraction of it proved enough, in the end. Elinor leaped in, the white blade up in a desperate-fast, deadly thrust, taking the creature through its bony chest, in and out and back again almost before it knew what had happened.

It stood there, needle-fanged mouth agape. Even with the utter unhumanness of its features, she could read the shock on its face. Green fluid welled up out of the puncture in its breast. It put its uninjured hand there, staring, then half-fell, struggled up again, staggering about on its queerly jointed legs.

Elinor moved in quickly, finishing it with a hard strike to the neck, uncertain what sort of internal organs it might or might not have, but reckoning no living creature could survive having its throat severed. The razor edge of the white blade all but took the thing's head clean off. Green blood pumped in a gush and it collapsed, thrashing jerkily.

And then half-rose, struggling.

Elinor stood facing it, shaking, the sword gripped tight in her hands. The way it twitched and twisted and struggled blindly to gain its feet, she had a sudden, horror-filled vision of it rushing at her, taloned hands out, like a huge, nightmare version of some barnyard fowl scuttling about after being beheaded on autumn Slaughter Day.

But it settled, finally, collapsing in hard spasms until it lay stiff and still.

Elinor stood, blinking sweat out of her eyes, her breast heaving, sick and shaken. The thing lay there like some sort of horrible manikin, limbs splayed out at strange angles, its head attached by no more than a few shreds of sinew and skin, the needle-fang mouth agape, white tongue lolling. The image of one of the poor dead back in Woburn came suddenly to her: the man amongst the first group she had found, the one whose head had been severed from his torso in almost the same way as this. She felt a certain satisfaction in the justice of it. But her hands were quivering uncontrollably.

Brynmaur came staggering up to stand beside her.

'Tha . . . thank you,' she said, swallowing.

He stood staring down at the strange corpse, wordless.

'Come along,' she urged after a moment. There was a glutinous lacery of the creature's blood on her blade and she began to wipe it clean with a handful of moss she tore up. The green liquid was sticky as honey, almost, and the acrid odour she had noticed before was so strong about it, it made her belly heave. Her hands were no steadier yet, and she made an awkward job of it.

'We need to be away from here quick as can be,' she

262

said, looking at Brynmaur. 'That was a cry to the rest of its kind that it made, for certain sure.'

Brynmaur nodded, but stayed as he was, white-faced and staring.

'Brynmaur!' she hissed at him. Her blade was cleansed now, though it had taken some considerable effort, and she sheathed it. The strength of it ebbed from her and she sagged, feeling suddenly sick and exhausted, her heart labouring. Putting a hand to Brynmaur's shoulder, she tugged at him. 'Come along.'

He shrugged her off. 'Give me a moment for this.'

'We may not have a moment!'

'I need . . .' He stopped, swallowed. 'You don't understand. This . . . thing is so like . . . so very nearly.' He gulped, rubbed at his eyes. 'It's *her*. And yet . . . not. And she . . .'

He turned to Elinor. 'It was *him*, wasn't it, that Tancred, who . . . who stripped the veil of seeming away from my Moreena and showed her to me like . . . like *this*?'

Elinor nodded. 'So she told me.'

'So she . . .' Brynmaur put a hand to his head. 'I don't . . .' What little colour was left in his face drained all away and, for a moment, Elinor really thought he was going to faint dead away. But he pulled himself together. 'That Tancred is going to rue the day he ever . . .' The words dwindled and he stood, shivering.

'Come on,' Elinor urged. She reached up her rucksack and settled it on her back. Her hands were still trembling in little spasms and she fisted them together. She took a last look at the grotesque, dead creature before her, then turned from it, shuddering. 'Let's away from here.'

Brynmaur nodded weary agreement, and off they hastened.

XXIII

Elinor led the way, searching for hard ground over which to move, so as to leave as little spoor as possible. She did not know what was likely to happen if – once, she reckoned – the rest of the pack discovered the creature she had killed. Could these outlandish things track them through the forest? She did not know, but she saw no point in taking chances.

Stumbling onto a stream, she took advantage of it and dragged Brynmaur in, wading along through knee-deep water, getting both her and his boots thoroughly soaked, but leaving no spoor at all behind – what with all the rain, their boots were pretty much waterlogged anyhow.

She brought them out, finally, at a bend where a slab of naked rock came down into the water. The only clear track they would leave behind them here would be their wet footprints, but on a day like this, with rain still in the air and everything damp, those would soon meld with the rock face into invisibility.

Brynmaur was gasping.

'I reckon we can take a rest here,' she said. She was panting herself, her heart labouring. 'But further along, in amongst the trees over there, where there's shelter.'

He nodded wordlessly.

Together they slipped along through a brace of old pines and found a little concealing nook. Brynmaur all but fell to the ground, his head lolling.

Elinor knelt next to him, unhooked her water flask, and offered it. 'Here,' she said. 'Drink.'

He did, in desperate gulps, his hands unsteady where

they held the flask. For all their splashing through the stream, neither had had a moment to stop and drink.

Brynmaur handed the flask back. Elinor drank, a sip at first, then more greedily, feeling the blessed coolth of the water soothe her throat. She had not realised how thirsty she was until the liquid filled her mouth. Her hands, as they gripped the flask, were quivering still, but less than before.

'What now?' Brynmaur asked in a hoarse whisper. 'Will the pack come after us, do you think? Will they be able to track us?'

Elinor shrugged. 'Who knows what such creatures may or may not be able to do. What of you? If they come after us, can you . . . is there anything you can do to . . . aid us in this?'

He looked at her, puzzled.

'Do you have any . . . is there . . .' She did not know how to word what she wanted to ask. 'Do you have some . . . *power* or other that might aid us in this?'

He looked at her and laughed weakly.

'This is no joke!' she chided him, aggrieved. 'These creatures are deadly dangerous.'

'I know,' he said, but there was still the echo of the laugh in him.

'What's so funny?' she demanded acidly.

He shook his head. 'Not . . . funny. What were you expecting of me, girl? That I wave my hands and chant a few special words and that we would grow invisible, you and I, and fly through the air to our destination?'

'No,' she said, stung. 'Of course not. But you . . . you keep acting like you have these hidden strengths. I thought perhaps you might be able to . . .'

He shook his head. 'You do not understand. I am no mage out of some child's wonder tale. I have the *sight*, yes. And I can do some things beyond the abilities of ungifted men . . . within limits. But I am too-ordinary mortal flesh, and no wonder worker.'

Elinor bit her lip.

'Don't look so distraught, girl. The way—'

'Don't call me *girl*!' Elinor snapped. 'I've told you that.'

Brynmaur nodded. 'My apologies. Old habits die hard, I'm afraid.' He put a hand out to her arm. 'I would have died this day but for you. I thank you for that. What you did with that blade of yours was . . . impressive.'

'So it's praise now, is it, for me and my wicked blade?' It was Elinor's turn to laugh. She could not help but feel a certain satisfaction. Having a dig at him for all his past condescending dismissals was just too good to pass up.

He scowled at her. 'I only . . .'

'The white blade *does* have its uses now and again, foul though it may be. As do I.'

'You have the grace of a barn rat,' he snapped, turning from her. 'I was trying to make amends and thank you, was all.'

The dark little triumph that had lit her went all to ashes in an instant. 'Brynmaur,' she said softly. 'I didn't . . .' She bit her lip, took a breath. 'You've *hurt* me with your dismissals and hard words. How can you expect me to be anything but angry?'

She had not intended to say any such intimately betraying thing. The words just seemed to tumble out of her mouth of their own accord. She looked away from him, embarrassed, and began to prod at her soaked boots, wishing she had the luxury to take them off and dry them properly over a fire.

After a little, Brynmaur put a hand to her arm. 'I have been too hard on you,' he said, 'not knowing what you are . . . or what you must have endured, being such.'

She glanced at him. His face was earnest and open, his eyes searching hers. For a moment, they looked into each other, defenceless.

Quickly, she turned away, shivering and self-conscious and uneasy.

'Peace,' he said softly. 'There is no further need for hard feeling between us.'

'Am I just to forget all you have said, then? Just like that?'

He bristled momentarily, his eyes flashing, then subsided. 'I deserve that, I suppose. I have been overhasty and callous.' He looked at her with the same open earnestness he had shown before. 'Forgive me.'

She felt a little hard knot in her belly still, but there was no gainsaying him like this, humble and sincere and truthful. She shrugged ruefully. 'How can I refuse you?'

He smiled, a small, weary stretch of his white-bearded lips. 'Good.'

She smiled back, tentatively. 'Thank you,' she said, 'for . . . for what you did with the rocks back there. Without it . . . well, I doubt we'd be sitting here arguing now.'

'You're entirely welcome.' He put a hand on her arm again. 'I reckon, now, that we—'

From the woods along their backtrail there came a sudden screeching wail, made faint by distance, but still clear for all that – the same sort of cry made by the creature Elinor had killed.

'Them!' she said.

Brynmaur nodded. 'They have discovered the body, I would guess. We have not come far enough.'

'Come on,' Elinor said. 'Let's away from here. There's still a chance they may not be able to track us – or may not want to.'

'Fast as we can,' he agreed.

They set off together, still trying to keep to the hard ground, but too intent on speed now to be overly precautious.

The stream they had waded along flowed through a narrow defile, and now they had to toil their way up the upslope side of it, hauling themselves along from tree to tree, sweating and straining and pushing themselves to the limit of their strength, their soaked boots squishing at every step. Brynmaur was soon gasping and shaky.

Elinor reached to aid him round a particular tricky spot and he took her hand and let her haul him up. But when she put an arm under his shoulder later to help urge him along, he fended her away. 'I'm not that weak yet,' he panted.

She let him have his way.

Onwards and up they struggled till, at last, they reached the crest of the slope. Once there, they stopped for a breather. Brynmaur stood, hands on his thighs, thin chest heaving. Elinor was in only slightly better shape. She could feel her heart thumping madly. She caught Brynmaur's eye and smiled. 'It's worth it, though. I reckon we left them well behind with that mad climb of ours.'

He nodded, too out of breath to speak.

The rain began again then, a light, chill curtain drawn down over the trees. Elinor shivered. She was slick with sweat, and cooling fast now that they were standing about, and the rain felt like ice. 'Come on,' she urged. 'We need to keep moving or we'll get well and truly chilled.'

Brynmaur nodded, but without enthusiasm. 'I reckon your first suggestion was a good one after all.'

Elinor raised an eyebrow at him quizzically.

'About finding some manner of shelter, and warmth and food. I could use that about now.'

'Me too.' Elinor sighed. There would be no chance of that for a long while yet; they had to put distance between themselves and what lay behind. She turned and gestured. 'Can you get us to this Tower?'

Brynmaur nodded. 'It ought to be northwards of us.' He looked about, getting his bearings. 'Along this ridgeway for a bit, then down and across in that direction. Then onwards and beyond and up into the Heights proper.'

The direction he indicated agreed with Elinor's own sense of things, with the way the world pulled on her.

After the flare-up this morning, the Powers had settled. But she could still feel the subtle tide clear enough. Turning her collar up against the cold, prying little fingers of the rain – and still missing her forgotten travel-cap – she set off with Brynmaur along the crest of the slope they had just toiled up.

The woods about were silent save for the soft, wet sounds of their own passage and the steady *shooshing* of the rain. There had been no repeat of the outlandish wail that had sounded on their backtrail. The going was good, and they made reasonable time, despite their weariness. Brynmaur actually seemed to be getting his wind back.

'How far is this Tower, then?' Elinor asked as they took a little breather, sheltering under the canopy of a broad pine.

Brynmaur shrugged. 'A ways, yet.'

'A far ways or a not-so-far ways?'

Again, Brynmaur shrugged. He was shivering, arms wrapped about himself. Reaching round awkwardly into his travel bag, he worried a little piece of dried goat's meat out and began to suck on it, still keeping his arms wrapped tight about him.

'How long,' Elinor persisted, 'till we see this Tower? A day? Two?'

'Mumff . . .' Brynmaur said.

'What?'

He swallowed. 'I'm not sure.'

'But you have been this way before. You *do* know where it is, right?'

He sucked on the goat's meat some more, then nodded. 'I do know where it is. Or where it ought to be, at least.'

Elinor sighed. ' "Ought to be"? That's not terribly reassuring, Brynmaur.'

He turned on her. 'I've never been to where this Tower is, but I know where it's got to be. All right?'

Elinor opened her mouth, closed it.

'This is my country, girl. I may not have been to the

particular spot where we need to get, but I *know* this part of the world. I'll get us there, never you fear.'

'Don't call me *girl*.'

Brynmaur sighed. 'Yes . . . Right.' He sucked some more on his meat. 'You're too sensitive by half.'

Elinor said nothing.

'Let's get along, then. The rain seems to have slackened a little.'

Emerging from under the cover of the pine, they set off once again. The afternoon was getting on now, and Elinor truly wished they could just hole up at the next likely place. Her scarred leg was aching and she was beginning to be utterly fed up with this traipsing around trees and over humped rocks and soggy hollows. A pathway would be nice. Or, better yet, a road. A nice clear, easy-walking road.

Might as well wish for a nice dry cabin while she was at it, with a dancing fire and a savoury stew on the hearth . . .

From behind them, the wailing cry they had heard earlier came again, several voices this time instead of just one. And closer.

Elinor looked at Brynmaur uncertainly. Before she could say a word, the cry sounded once more, louder, with a frenetic note to it now.

'Sounds like a hunting cry,' Brynmaur said bleakly.

They turned and ran flat out, angling down a shallow slope ahead of them, taking the path of least resistance, skidding on the rain-slicked ground, clutching at low branches for support when they could.

At the foot of the slope down which they had dashed, they hunkered down behind a fallen pine and looked back. They must have come a good two or three hundred paces, slantwise across the slope, and the crest where they had begun was some distance above and behind them. But they could clearly see movement up there, insectile figures casting about like so many nightmare hounds on the trail. The air was filled with their inhuman, shrieking wails.

'However did they track us?' Elinor whispered. But it did not matter. The creatures were up there, and any moment now they would find her and Brynmaur's spoor and come streaming down the slope. 'Come on,' she whispered, and the two of them slipped away, then took off running, hard as they could.

Along the edge of a stretch of more open, stony ground they went, then through into a dark thickness of crowded pines. Elinor felt her heart straining as she ducked under and through the tangled, needly branches. Her thighs burned with the effort of their flight, and she was growing weary-clumsy. She was too weak still, to cope with this. She needed the sword's lent strength. But to draw it now would be to light a beacon for their pursuers.

Suddenly the ground fell away abruptly and they stumbled, teetering on the edge of a sharp ravine that opened before them as if the earth had suddenly split itself apart under their very feet. Their flight carried them irretrievably over the brink, and they went hurtling down in a desperate plunge through a tangle of dead branches and leaf mould and loose stones, leaping and skidding, trees whipping past, down through a more open section, spinning round the side of a grey-white, moss-draped stack of rock as large as a house, plunging through more trees . . .

Almost to the end of the slope they made it, before Brynmaur lost his footing and tumbled on his face with a little cry – but the momentum of their rush kept him shooting on, rolling like a sack, till he smacked up against a mass of moss-buffered rock at the ravine's bottom. Elinor fell to her knees beside him, gasping for breath, her heart hammering so fast she thought it was going to jump right up her throat.

'Brynmaur,' she gasped. 'Are you . . .'

'I'm all right,' he replied. 'I think.' He sat up weakly, groaning, and ran a hand over his legs, his ribs, his head. He was breathing in great, wheezing pants, his thin chest heaving. 'Feels like . . . like somebody's been at me with a . . . a hammer.'

Elinor rubbed at her elbow. She had smacked it against something and it hurt – just as Brynmaur said: as if somebody had hit her with a hammer. She struggled to her feet, feeling her knees weak as jelly, her heart still thumping crazily. She was breathing almost as hard as Brynmaur, and she laboured to get air.

Along the ravine down which they had plunged, there was no slightest sign of pursuit. The rain had stopped again and the woods above them were silent now except for the soft, wet sound of dripping water.

Elinor let go a weak little laugh and gestured. 'Look.'

The ravine slope was steep and thick with trees and jagged outcroppings of the grey-white, mossy stone. It was incredible that they had come down that at the speed they had with so little hurt.

Brynmaur merely shook his head and leaned back weakly. His face was drained of all colour and he was shaking. 'What . . . now?'

Elinor shrugged. 'With any luck, we've lost them. At least for a little. Maybe now we'll have time to—'

But at that moment, the hunters' wailing sounded once again, eager and wild.

'So much for luck,' Brynmaur breathed.

Rubbing her hurting elbow, Elinor looked about, trying to orient herself. She and Brynmaur were in a kind of cut, she saw, a mass of tumbled rock to their left, a thick clump of pines to their right. Neither direction looked especially promising. She turned her back on the slope in hopes of finding something better – only to see that they were squatting at the base of a sheer cliff face. Somehow, in the mad scramble of their plunge down here, she had been blind to it. Five times a man's height, it looked to be, a ragged wall of splintered rock and grey-green moss, with stunted little bushes sprouting here and there along its face.

Seeing the direction of her gaze, Brynmaur craned his head about for a look. 'Wonderful!' he said after a moment. 'Just wonderful. What do we do *now*, then?'

From the ravine above them came again the wailing cry of the hunters.

Elinor stepped back a bit for a better view. The cliff face was steep as any wall, but it was pitted and split and cracked. 'Looks climbable,' she said

'For you, maybe.'

She went to him and reached a hand under his armpit. 'Come on. Those hunters won't be long in getting here.'

Brynmaur shrugged her off, staying hunkered down where he was. 'You go.'

Elinor stared at him.

'Go!' he said. 'You're right. Those hunters will be here any moment. No point in both of us feeding them. Go, girl. Get to the Tower. Do what you can. *Go!*'

Elinor only shook her head. 'Don't be stupid. I'm not abandoning you.'

'Then what are you going to do? Sprout wings and fly me up to the top of that cliff?'

'No. Of course not. I . . .'

'What, then?' Brynmaur let out an exhausted breath. 'I haven't the strength. That's the bare truth of it. There's no possible way I can manage that climb.'

The hunting cry sounded again, louder, with a frenetic ring to it now, like the sound of a pack of wild dogs just before they flushed their quarry.

Elinor looked about desperately.

'Save yourself, girl. There's no escape for me.'

'Yes there is.' She put a hand to the bronze hilt of her sword.

Brynmaur looked at her bleakly. 'Aye. There's that. Perhaps you have the right of it, then. Better to end it quick than have those *things* tear me apart.'

'Don't be stupid,' she said. 'Now listen to me. You take the blade—'

'No,' Brynmaur said hastily. '*No!*'

'You *take* it!' she insisted.

'No. I will not. What sort of crazy-mad plan is this you're trying to hatch? I have no idea how to wield such a weapon. And even if I did, I would not. Save yourself, girl, and stop trying to—'

'Listen to me,' Elinor said. 'Just *listen*, can't you? I don't want you to wield the sword. Take it in hand, is all. The white blade gives *strength* to whoever holds it. With it in hand, you'd be able to make the climb.'

Brynmaur stared at her.

'It's the only way.' She drew the blade, feeling the rush of sword-strength fill her. 'Here! Take it. Quick!'

'No! I will not. I cannot.'

The hunting cry came again, louder and closer.

Brynmaur shuddered.

'Take it!'

He shook his head. 'No. I will not leave you here alone to face them, unarmed and defenceless.'

'Take it!' Elinor hissed. 'I won't be here alone and defenceless if you're quick enough. Take it and climb the cliff and throw the blade back down for me so I can follow after.'

Brynmaur blinked, opened his mouth.

'Don't argue! Take the blade and go. Quickly! Every instant we waste disputing this gives those creatures a better chance to catch me here. If you're quick enough we'll both be up that cliff before they reach us.' She held the sword out for him, hilt first, holding it by the tangs so as not to slice herself on the razor edge. 'Take it and *go!*'

Brynmaur hesitated for a moment longer, then reached up from where he still crouched and took the hilt gingerly. His eyes opened very wide and he shuddered.

'*Go!*' Elinor urged.

He got to his feet in one quick motion, moving with the easy grace the sword always gave.

'*Go!*' she repeated.

He went then, scrambling up over the rocky outcrop he had been leaning against and thence up to the cliff face. For a moment he hesitated, then began to climb, awkward because of the sword in his hand, but moving fast nevertheless, slipping from crack to crack, hauling himself one-handedly up using the roots of the stunted bushes that dotted the rock face.

Elinor watched him and let out a long, relieved breath. Being what he was, she had not been entirely sure how Brynmaur might react to the blade's reality. She shivered. It had been no easy thing to hand it over to him like that. He would never know . . .

The hunters' wail sounded again, getting closer. Distantly, she could hear the first faint sounds of their progress through the trees. Brynmaur was moving well, but he was still no more than halfway ascended. She looked about. There was precious little in the way of anything she could use to defend herself. Throw a few stones, perhaps. The idea was ludicrous – lobbing little chips of rock against such creatures as hunted her. But there was nothing else. And if the worst should come to pass, she was not going to stand here entirely defenceless as they overwhelmed her.

There were plenty of loose stones about – droppings from the splintered cliff above. Quickly, she gathered up a double handful and laid them out beside her on the mossy shelf of a boulder. She could clearly hear the sounds of pursuit in the ravine woods now.

Craning about, she saw that Brynmaur was no more than three-quarters of the way up at best.

The first of the creatures appeared, up in one of the pines, skittering head-down round the bole like a squirrel – but a squirrel out of nightmare. Seeing her, it let out a long, exultant screech and leaped to the ground. Three others came after in quick succession, one from out of the trees, two along the ground, leaping with the queer, insectile speed they had.

Elinor stood facing them as best she could, sick with fight-fright, her back to the mossy stone Brynmaur had crouched against, a little rock clutched in each hand. She glanced up and behind her. Brynmaur still had a ways to go. So much for her great plan . . .

The first of the creatures was almost upon her now, its black inhuman eyes gleaming with a horrible, predatory glee. She let go with a rock and scored a lucky hit, smacking the thing in the face. It stopped with a hiss and fell to its knees, spitting blood and needle-teeth.

She grabbed up more rocks. The others were coming fast. She cast a desperate glance upwards. The cliff face was empty. Brynmaur had made it to safety, She felt a quick surge of satisfaction – and then her heart faltered. The white blade was seductive. She had seen too many men fall under the spell of what it offered. Despite all his grand talk, Brynmaur would be prey to the sword's temptation just as any other man might.

She could just imagine him standing up there on the cliff top, the blade in his grip, the uncanny strength of it pouring through his limbs. He would feel himself unbeatable. He would look down upon her and smile and think only of himself and how he would be the grand saviour of the world, and of how he would bring Tancred down . . . and he would turn and walk off, intent, the sword's power thrilling through him, and leave her to the bloody ministrations of these otherland creatures.

Elinor swallowed. She had doomed herself by handing the blade to him.

The nightmare pack was drawn close now, poised and ready. The air was thick with the unpleasant, acrid scent of them. She gripped her little rocks, shuddering, her pulse jumping, and made ready to fight them as best she might.

Then, 'Here!' she heard from above.

Like an arc of light, the sword came down, spinning and shining and whirling, to thump into the ground midway between Elinor and her attackers.

For a frozen moment, they all stood still. Then Elinor dived forwards and closed her fingers round the bronze dragon hilt. The sword-strength filled her. She rolled to her feet before any of the creatures could prevent it, scuttled back to the cliff face, and took up the Double Tree defensive posture there, her back to the rise of stone.

The pack closed upon her, the creatures darting in and out on their queerly jointed legs, hissing and wailing. She stayed still, ready, refusing to be drawn. They were close all about her, and she felt her nose sting with the outland odour of them. One rushed her, and she nearly committed herself too soon. But the thing whirled and skipped back and she held her stance, ready. And then another lost patience – if she could attribute human motives to such creatures – and went for her, raking at her belly with one of its long-taloned hands in a quick, vicious swipe.

But not quick enough. She took the hand from the arm in one clean slash and came back to the Double Tree stance, all in a breath. Blood spurted from the stump of the creature's arm, green as new spring leaves.

The creature spun about, howling, sending a spray of viscous green blood across Elinor's thighs, soaking her with the acrid smell of it. On the ground, the severed hand clutched spasmodically at nothing. The others let out a great howling, like a pack of demon-wolves gone mad. Elinor shuddered and held her position. There was little else for her to do. The cliff reared itself behind her, but there was no way she could turn her back upon the hunters. And it would only be a matter of time, surely, before they flung themselves upon her in a mass. One she could take, two, even – but not all at once. One concerted rush and she was finished.

This was not the fate she had envisioned, torn to shreds by these horrible otherworld creatures in a nameless bit of mountain forest. So much for any role she might have been able to play in the bringing-down of Tancred/

Khurdis. So much for the subtle slope along which she and Brynmaur had been pulled. For that, too, was the way of things. Being a . . . a gudgeon, as Brynmaur termed it, meant one might be guided – in some manner, anyway – but it was no guarantee of safety.

The creature she had maimed was on its knees now, reeling weakly. It held the stump of its arm against its chest, squeezing it with the other hand, but the green blood still gushed, soaking it and the ground round it. The rest were gathering close. And more began to appear out of the trees, shrieking and crying.

One of them went to the wounded creature, yanked its head back, and ripped its throat out with a taloned finger. Then it reared up and flung itself straight at Elinor.

She took it in the face with the tip of the sword, slicing upwards in a move Master Karasyn had named the Updraught. The white blade split the creature's face like splitting a hard-shelled melon, and it fell to the ground, welling green blood and grey matter and writhing.

The rest let up a great howl.

Here it comes, she thought.

But as they drew in, one of them abruptly fell away to the ground, clutching at its arm. Then another crumpled, and a third stumbled away, hissing in pain.

A hail of stones from above, it was, small ones and large, plummeting down upon the creatures.

'Hurry, girl!' Brynmaur cried from the cliff top. 'Climb!'

Elinor whirled and leaped for the cliff face. Behind her, she heard shrieks and hissing. Clutching at one of the stunted cliff-bushes, she hauled herself up one-handedly, dug her toes into a crack for support, then jammed the sword's bronze pommel into a hollow pocket and clambered higher, scrambling like a fly on a wall, fast as fast could be.

From below, she heard the *scrut scrut* of talons on rock. Glancing down, she saw three of the creatures clambering after her, much faster than she, making light work of the climb, their claws providing far better purchase on the rain-slicked stone than her bare hands and booted feet.

There was, she realised, no possible way she could make the top before they caught her.

Looking about desperately, she spotted a little ledge – a sort of ledge, anyway – that offered a better hold than where she was at the moment. Her shoulders and upper arms burning with the exertion of the climb, she scrambled across, hooked her left arm onto the ledge – banging her sore elbow in the process – and found a crack into which she could wedge one heel. It was the best she could do.

The three pursuing creatures were almost upon her now. The rest had stayed behind at the cliff's base. She could see them staring up at her hungrily, their black, inhuman eyes like so many dark-burning coals in their faces.

She gripped the sword, tried to feel her balance on the rain-slicked rock, waited.

The first one, needle-teeth gleaming wetly, reached up a taloned hand for her, and she shifted balance, trying to bring her feet up and her torso down and sideways for a slashing stroke at it.

A rock the size of her head came hurtling down and took the creature in the face, sending it plummeting downwards, heels over head, shrieking.

The next one tried to come at her sideways along the cliff face rather than from below. She kept it back with her sword, but it would have been only a matter of time before the third came upon her from behind – except that another rock took it, and it, too, fell tumbling and shrieking to the ground.

She swung herself sideways in a reckless move, nearly yanking her shoulder out of joint, and caught the last creature before it knew it, setting the white blade's razor point into its hip and twisting so that it reared up from the stone face in sudden agony and fell away, scrabbling

279

desperately. This time, she heard the bone-breaking *kwump* as it smacked into the rocky ground below.

'Hurry, girl!' Brynmaur urged from above.

Elinor swung herself up as fast as she could, awkward with the sword still in hand, scrambling and grunting and gasping, till, at last, she felt Brynmaur's hands reaching to help her over the lip.

On her back, she lay gasping on wet sod. She could feel her thighs sticky-wet still with the green blood that had been splashed across her. The smell of it made her gag. Even with the sword's lent strength, she felt her muscles quiver painfully and her pulse raced. She felt utterly spent.

But 'Up, girl!' Brynmaur hissed. 'They come.'

She rolled to her knees and peered down over the cliff top. A good six or seven of the creatures were climbing now, skittering like so many huge insects up the stone wall, hissing and wailing and coming fast.

'Gather more rocks,' Brynmaur said, gesturing one-handedly at a mass of decaying stone amongst the turf some paces way. 'Quick as you can!'

Elinor nodded and struggled to her feet. Stumbling over, she found there was stone aplenty, lying in a tumbled, weather-split heap. But she needed two hands to carry it, and when she sheathed the sword she nearly fell over with very weariness. But there was no time. She shook herself, took a breath, and forced herself to go on, heaving up as many of the rain-soaked chunks of rock as she could in one armful and staggering back with them to Brynmaur who stood on the cliff edge launching stones downwards, grumbling and muttering breathlessly to himself. Only two or three bits lay beside him now on the ground.

'More, more!' he gasped. 'Quick as you can!'

She dropped her load and went back, splitting a finger-nail on the unyielding rock in her haste, carting three full armloads as fast as she possibly could. From the last load, she grabbed up a hunk the size and shape of her foot and went to the cliff's edge with it. Only four of the six climbers were left now, but they were getting close. She let fly violently with her rock and missed. Cursing under her breath, she grabbed up another with desperate haste. This one was smaller, and she aimed more carefully, catching one of the climbers a glancing blow across the shoulder. The creature halted momentarily, hissing in fury, but kept its hold on the cliff face.

At her side, Brynmaur flung a hunk of stone the size of a double fist, his arm windmilling, sending it hurtling down. It struck the same creature Elinor had been aiming at, landing solidly against its knobbly skull with an audible *krunk*. The creature toppled and was gone, without a sound.

Which left two . . . no, three more still climbing.

She and Brynmaur let loose a veritable storm of thrown stones then, till only one of the climbers remained. But in a final burst of unexpected speed, that one scrabbled the remaining distance and was upon them before they knew it. Brynmaur flung a stone at it, which it batted away one-handedly. By then, though, Elinor had time to draw the white blade. She took the creature in the belly with a desperate thrust and sent it toppling backwards over the cliff top, screaming.

The cliff face was clear. The creatures howled and shrieked down below, but none appeared willing to venture the climb upwards.

'What now?' Brynmaur panted. 'If we leave here, they'll be up after us as soon as they see us gone.'

Elinor thought him most likely right. 'So we wait.' She picked up a stone and flung it at the gathering of creatures below, sending them skittering away. 'At least we can clear them from the cliff face.'

Brynmaur nodded and set to work with a will. Elinor fetched more rock, and the two of them sent chunks of stone sailing out, one after another, till the band of creatures below retreated back under the cover of the trees and disappeared. Even then, they sent a few shots, far as they could, out into the maze of the trees themselves, and were rewarded with at least one cry of pain.

But the creatures had enough cover now to shield them. The pines along the ravine slope grew nearly as tall as the cliff itself. Elinor spotted a dark form sneaking through the branches and hurled a stone. The creature slipped away, unharmed.

Silence now, save for the soft, damp whisperings of the trees, and nothing to be seen but the sprawled forms of the dead at the cliff's foot.

Elinor knelt, grabbed up several handfuls of the ragged grass that grew here at the cliff top, and began scrubbing at the sticky blood on the thighs of her pants.

'What now?' Brynmaur asked, stepping back from the brink. He ran a hand wearily across his face, then slumped down on the turf, 'How long do you reckon they'll stay hidden in those trees?'

Elinor shrugged. She dug up a fistful of dirt and rubbed it into her trousers, obscuring what remained of the green bloodstain. Standing up, she went to the edge and peered about. The cliff went on far as she could see in either direction. 'If I were them, I'd move off and try to climb the cliff some distance away, where we can't see them.'

Brynmaur got unsteadily to his feet and leaned over the brink, peering uneasily in both directions along the cliff face.

'Or wait till dark,' Elinor continued. Then, 'Come away from the brink, Brynmaur.' He looked far too shaky on his feet to be standing so close to the drop.

Brynmaur backed away from the cliff top and sat down again, landing with an awkward *krump* on the sod. 'We'd never see them in the dark.'

Elinor nodded. It was not a pleasant thought. And they could not simply flee from here. Though the forest was silent now, Elinor was sure that, from their hidden vantage point up in the trees, the creatures would know the instant they turned to run, and come racing up the cliff face after them.

'A right mess we're landed in,' Brynmaur said, with no enthusiasm.

Elinor reached up a couple of fist-sized stone chunks and lobbed them into the trees, just for good measure. 'There has to be some way . . .'

Below, there was sudden movement. Elinor grabbed up more stone.

Brynmaur scuttled hastily over to his own supply of rocks. 'What is it?'

'I don't . . .' Elinor began. She had expected another rush at the cliff. But no such thing happened. Instead, several creatures came out of the clump of pines on the side of the rock Brynmaur had originally taken shelter against. They were larger than those that had been hunting her and Brynmaur, and they moved in an entirely different way, loping along on stilt-like legs.

'It's the ones we saw before,' Brynmaur said. 'Those that killed the elk. They must have been drawn here by all the commotion.'

As Elinor watched, the pack in its entirety came out of the cover of the trees and began to worry at the carcasses of those whom Elinor and Brynmaur had slain. From the trees a shriek went up and the hunters leaped out. Bloody chaos ensued.

'Now's our chance,' Elinor said.

Brynmaur sighed wearily and nodded. 'As you say. But I don't much fancy another run like the last one.'

'Nor I,' Elinor agreed.

Ten or twelve paces behind them, the turf that carpeted the brink of the cliff top gave way to the inevitable pines. Having precious little in the way of alternatives, they turned, plunged in amongst the trees, and ran for all they were worth.

XXIV

They found a little cave partway up a steep, rocky slope just as darkness was drawing in.

'Is it safe to stop for the night, do you think?' Brynmaur asked, hoarse-voiced. He was leaned against a tree bole, shaking, his face grey with fatigue.

'Safe or not,' Elinor replied, 'neither of us has the strength to go much further.'

He nodded wearily.

Elinor gazed up at the dark slash of the cave mouth on the slope above them. Such places often had wild inhabitants. She hoped it was not the home of one of the great mountain bears. 'I'll go see if it's empty,' she said.

Brynmaur made no reply, save to nod once more. He slumped down weakly against the roots of the tree.

Elinor clambered up the slope most carefully, trying to make as little noise as possible. It did not seem an especially large cave, though, and she reckoned on meeting nothing more formidable than a fox or perhaps a mountain puma, neither of which would stand up to a determined human person.

At the cave mouth, she stood sniffing, trying to peer inside. There was an old musty smell here, but none of the sharp scent of living animal. Empty, then. As long as her nose did not betray her. The cave mouth was a low, slanting aperture set in an overhang of grey-green rock. To go in, Elinor had to squat down almost on her knees. She drew the sword, welcoming its strength. With it held before her so that the shining blade acted as a sort of torch, she duck-walked her way gingerly inside.

By the white blade's glow she saw that the ceiling opened up a bit, though not enough for her to stand. The musty odour was stronger here, but there was no sign of any inhabitant. The space before her went inwards in a kind of dog-leg, the cavern going straight back for perhaps three paces, then veering leftwards. She crept on and peered round the bend. A pile of bones lay in the back. But they were old and crumbled, and what manner of creature had left them, she could not tell. There was nothing else.

Back outside, she motioned down to Brynmaur, who waved listlessly back. She did not want to call out to him – she no longer trusted these woods even the slightest bit – so she gestured him up.

He struggled as best he could, but she had to all but carry him bodily up the last of the slope before they were finally settled inside the safety of the cave. He lay gasping and white. She bent over him worriedly. 'Are you . . . all right?' It was a foolish question. Of course he was not all right.

'Here,' she said, offering him her water flask. 'Drink.'

She had to lift his head for him to do so, but the water seemed to revive him and he sat up stiffly.

'I'm getting old,' he grumbled.

'You ought to have looked after yourself better,' Elinor returned. 'Pawli told me you hardly ever ate. All your time was spent with the starweed.'

'Pawli . . .' Brynmaur echoed slowly. 'Where he is now, I wonder? And doing what?'

Elinor had no answer. She reached into her rucksack and brought out a couple of stale journey cakes. 'Here.'

They ate in silence for a while, alternately munching on the chewsome cakes and sipping water.

Elinor had sheathed her sword. Without its blade-radiance, the cave was illumined only by a dim half-light that seeped in from the low entrance. To keep holding and then relinquishing the white blade as she had been doing was no simple matter. It *wanted* her flinging herself about, leaping and thrusting and sweeping the shining length of it in quick, deadly arcs. She could feel it agitating in its scabbard at her side and had to stop her hand from sidling over towards the hilt.

'I'd give a lot for a fire,' Brynmaur said, shivering in fits.

It was chilly here in the cave, and though it was dry, they were not. Elinor could feel her toes still squishing about in her water-sogged boots, and her clothing, though it had dried some with the travelling, was still uncomfortably clammy. Brynmaur was in no better shape. A bit of a fire would make all the difference. But it was out of the question. They would just have to make do as best they could. Reaching her sleeping blanket out of her rucksack, she offered it to Brynmaur, wrapping it round his shoulders. 'Here. This'll help.'

'Thank you,' he said softly.

They sat in silence for a while more, finishing the last of their journey cakes and a couple of slivers of dried goat's meat.

'I could eat three or four more of those cakes,' Brynmaur said.

'Only six left,' Elinor said. 'It's eat them now or save them till later. What do you think?'

Brynmaur shrugged. 'I think I need the strength now.'

They ate another cake each.

'Thank you for . . . for returning the sword,' Elinor said finally. She had been trying to think how to broach the subject. 'There's many a man would have kept it for himself.'

Brynmaur snorted. 'Keep *that*? Do you think me mad? I told you I wanted nothing to do with the cursed thing.'

'So you *said*,' Elinor replied.

He looked at her.

'Well . . . the white blade can be seductive.'

'And you reckoned . . .' Brynmaur sat up more straightly. 'You reckoned I was going to just take the thing and walk off, my head filled with grand, violent ambitions, is that it? And leave you there to the mercies of those Otherwhere creatures?' He grimaced. 'You don't know me at all, then.'

'I . . . Few indeed are the men who have returned that blade to me willingly once they have held it in their hands and felt the strength of it thrill them.'

Brynmaur leaned forwards. 'I am a man with many weaknesses, Elinor. But I am not stupid. You have my sympathy and my . . . respect. Such a blade as you carry is no light burden. It is a cursed thing, and nothing I want any part of.'

Elinor let out a relieved breath – though she felt the sting of that 'cursed'. 'I . . .' She did not know quite what to say.

Brynmaur reached a hand to her awkwardly. 'It was no simple act, handing it to me. I thank you. Once again, I owe you my life.'

'And I owe you mine.'

He was such a strange man, Elinor thought. There had been times when she would just as happily strangled him as said hallo. And yet . . .

'Sleep, that's what I need,' he said, his mouth opening in a great, jaw-cracking yawn. 'Blessed sleep.'

Elinor nodded. She could feel her own weariness settling over her like a weight of sand. They ought really to set a watch, she knew, turn and turn about through the night. But Brynmaur was too exhausted, and she could not stand watch the whole night alone and still be able to travel tomorrow. And, besides, this cave seemed hidden well enough away, and there had been no sign of anything at all along their backtrail.

She tried to feel how this fit with the subtle tide that underlay their journey. It was never simple, this feeling into the pattern of things, but she could sense no misgiving in her bones, no uncertainty. They would trust to luck, then, or the slope of the world along which they travelled, to keep them safe this night – unconscionable risk, some might say, but she had learned to trust the way the world's currents moved.

Brynmaur had shrugged out of the blanket she had lent him and was holding it out to her. 'Here. I've got my own.'

But his sleeping blanket, when he produced it from his battered travel bag, proved to be threadbare and thin, with a line of rents all down one side. Elinor laughed, seeing it.

'What?' he said, bristling a little.

'That's a pitiful thing.'

'It's kept me warm enough so far,' he insisted.

'But now you're wet and chilled.' She offered her blanket back to him. 'Here.'

'And you? You're dry as could be and toasty-warm, I suppose.'

He was right. They both needed as much warmth as they could get. 'Only one thing for it,' Elinor said. She swallowed, looked at him, looked away. 'Best we sleep together then. For the warmth.'

Brynmaur blinked. 'For the warmth. Yes. Sensible notion.'

They settled towards the back end of the cave, where the dirt of the floor was a little softer and they were away from the draughty entrance. Elinor's rucksack and Brynmaur's travel bag made decent enough, if lumpy, pillows, and they curled together, both blankets wrapped about them.

Brynmaur had lain with his back pressed to her, and Elinor's arms were trapped awkwardly against her belly. For comfort's sake, she ended up putting one arm about him. He sighed and pushed his angular hip closer in to her. His ribs rose and fell softly, and she could feel the bones clearly under her hand. There could not be a scrap of excess flesh to him. He was still shivering a little, but that ceased after a while. Under the twin blankets, it grew soothingly warm.

''Night,' he murmured.

'Good night,' she replied.

He fell into exhausted sleep then, his breathing settling,

the tension in him letting go. It was pleasant to lie here in the growing dark feeling the rhythm of his breathing. It had been a long, long while since she had felt this simple warmth of touch.

But though she lay comfortable, and though her limbs ached with weariness, she could not manage to drift off. She felt like a cork bobbing on the surface of a lake. No matter how hard she tried, she simply could not sink down into proper sleep. She kept seeing images of the dead at Woburn, of that needle-fanged pack of creatures like Moreena, of Moreena herself, stranded back in that Otherwhere, who could have no notion of where they were or what might be happening.

She knew better than to fall prey to this. Sleep and food were the two most basic requirements when one had to travel under adversity. She had long ago learned that one took as much of both as was possible, whenever possible. To lie here tossing and turning was a useless waste of energy.

Stop thinking, she told herself. *Just stop it!*

It ought to have worked. She had learned to focus on the present moment; there were too many regrets and pains in her past to bear dwelling on. But the thoughts and images kept swirling through her mind.

And then, as she lay there, sleepless and frustrated, her little finger started to itch. It happened, sometimes. The finger itself might be long gone, but there was still a phantom there, and that phantom grew a torment sometimes – with no possible way to scratch it.

Elinor shifted and twitched, trying not to disturb Brynmaur, hoping her mind might somehow settle, the itch go away. But it was no use. Sighing, she raised herself carefully up on her elbows. She could hear Brynmaur breathing steadily still, and envied him most profoundly. Moving with slow care, she slipped from under the warmth of the blankets. Then, quietly as could be, she made her way through the dark cave and out into the night.

Outside, the air was cold as ice, but invigorating for all that. She took a breath, another, shivering, but glad of the clearing shock of it. She rubbed at her scarred leg, which was achy-stiff, and then shook her maimed hand vigorously in the air – a trick that sometimes cleared it of its phantom itch. It worked, though not perfectly.

Overhead, the sky was cloudless. There was no moon, and the stars glimmered and twinkled in their innumerable hosts, a great, blazing cascade flung against the deep black dome of the sky. As she looked, head craned back for a better view, there was the sudden streak of a shooting star, there and gone again. So bright, so quick. Where had it come from? Where gone? Elinor felt a little shudder go through her. The world was more than a little mysterious, even at the best of times.

She thought of what she had learned in the Otherwhere: world after world after world, all strung out like beads on a string, perhaps, or like reflections of each other, on and on and on . . . and each more strange than the last. It made her belly quiver, thinking on it.

And then, standing there, she heard a faint cry, like a hawk's screech, almost, yet not. Diminished by distance, it was, but Elinor felt certain it was not the cry of any natural creature of these woods and slopes. What, then? A cold shudder went up her spine. It was not quite like any sound she had heard from the outlandish creatures she had so far encountered.

She scrutinised the surrounding country as best she could in the darkness, but could make nothing out. Which did not mean that there was not some otherland creature nearby this very instant. She had left the sword behind her in the cave and cursed herself now for a fool.

She turned, most slowly, intending to creep carefully back into the cavern and take the sword up and alert Brynmaur.

With heart-stopping suddenness, the cry sounded again, clearer and closer.

From overhead.

She looked quickly up and there, silhouetted against the multiform glow of the stars, she saw . . .

She was not sure what it was. Huge, perhaps, and flying high. Or perhaps not so huge, and lower. She could not tell. A soaring black shape. Long wings, the trailing edges scalloped like those of a bat's. But this was clearly no bat. It flew with the strong, oaring wing motion of a hunting eagle, but its head was long and snake-like.

And then it was gone, swallowed by the night's dark.

No eagle, that. No winged creature such as she had ever known. Elinor shuddered. What mad scheme did this Tancred harbour, that he had brought such an array of terrible creatures into the world?

She slipped into the cave, retrieved her blade, and came back out again. For a long while she stood there, shivering, the sheathed sword gripped tight, eyes and ears alert. But there was no further sign of the uncanny bat-creature, or anything else, and the world stayed quiet.

Eventually, the night's cold drove her back inside.

Brynmaur was warm under the blankets. She tried to stop the shivers than gripped her, but with limited success. He grunted, rolled over in his sleep and put his arm around her, gathering her in close. It was an intimate gesture, one he surely would never have made if awake. But it was welcome, for he radiated slumberous warmth like a stove. She snuggled against him, feeling her shivers gradually subside, and closed her eyes. The phantom itch in her missing finger was still there, but only faintly. It was not enough, now, to prevent sleep from taking her, and she felt herself slipping away finally into soothing darkness . . .

. . . to be awakened by a wild shout and a painful stab in her ribs.

She jerked herself up, thrashing about, groping for where she had laid the sword. The shouting had stopped, to be replaced by a sort of gasping sob. She was on her knees now; her flailing hand found the sword and she whipped it out, spilling pale radiance everywhere. She stared about, her heart thumping, aquiver with sword-strength.

The cave was empty save for her and Brynmaur.

Who sat rocking back and forth, curled in a tight, foetal coil against the cave wall, moaning and gasping.

'Brynmaur!' she cried. 'What is it?'

He made no reply. She reached a hand to him, but he shuddered away from her touch. She knelt next to him. 'Brynmaur . . . *Brynmaur!*'

Still no response.

Sheathing the white blade, ignoring the sudden wash of weariness that went through her, she leaned over and put her arms about him. He struggled to break away from her, but she persisted, holding him as if he were some delirious child beset by a high fever.

'No!' he hissed. and then, 'No! I cannot. I . . .' Then he let out a long, moaning cry.

'Brynmaur!' Grey daylight was spilling in from the cave mouth, and Elinor could see his eyes were screwed tight shut, his mouth drawn in a thin line of pain.

'*Brynmaur!*'

He shuddered, blinked.

She gripped him hard, willing him back from wherever he might be. 'Brynmaur . . .'

His muscles alternately locked stiff as iron and then went like jelly. She heard his teeth rattle together like thrown stones. Then he surged up abruptly and smacked her just above her left eye with a hard elbow, spilling her from him. Her vision filled with shooting stars for a moment, and she was helpless.

When she recovered, he was sitting propped against the cave wall, head in his hands, panting.

'Brynmaur?' she asked hesitantly.

He raised his head and looked at her, his face haggard and white.

'What was it?' she asked.

He stared at her for long heartbeats, silent. Then, in a voice hardly audible at all, he whispered, 'One of them.'

'One of who?'

'*Them!*'

Elinor drew closer to him, put a hand on his arm tentatively. He flinched, but did not pull back. 'Brynmaur, I don't . . .' she began, but then it hit her. 'Do you mean the . . . the Otherwhere hunters who have been after us?'

He looked at her, looked away, nodded.

'It was a dream, Brynmaur. Just a dream.'

He shook his head. 'No ordinary dream. It was . . . one of them, come hunting me in the dreamscape.'

'But however could they—'

'I don't know . . . I don't *know*.' Brynmaur shuddered. 'I . . . It was no ordinary dream.' He ran a shaky hand through his tangled hair. His face was sweat-slicked and pale and he was shivering so that his teeth were chattering.

Elinor felt a cold shiver go through her. If what he said was indeed so, it bespoke a kind of predatory tenacity beyond anything she had ever imagined.

But they had had a hard, hard time of it this past day. Perhaps it *was* just a dream, an ordinary nightmare, despite Brynmaur's protestations to the contrary. Any man might dream such after what he had experienced. And he had been smoking that starweed for so long – and then suddenly stopped, cold. Would such an abrupt stoppage not affect a man's mind?

'Don't look at me like that!' Brynmaur snapped suddenly, pulling away from her.

'Like what?' Elinor responded, confused.

'You have that accusing look on you again.'

'What accusing look?'

'You look at me like that all too often, like I'm some clumsy farm lad who doesn't quite measure up.'

'No . . . I never—'

He silenced her with a sudden, sharp gesture of his

hands. 'You should see to your own life, girl, before judging others. Just leave me be.'

'Fine,' Elinor said, stung.

Turning from him, she reached for her water flask and took a drink. 'Best we get started, then,' she said flatly after a little. 'Day's all but here.'

Brynmaur made no response.

'Did you hear me?'

He shrugged.

Elinor felt a stab of irritation go through her. Then worry. What if this dream experience of his proved to have been too much for him? What if it had unnerved him completely? Could she continue on with him like this? Could she go on alone? 'Brynmaur?' she said more softly.

'I hear you,' he replied. 'I'll be ready in a few moments. I just need a little time, is all. To gather myself. Do you have any difficulty with that?'

'No,' she said quickly. 'Of course not.'

'Good,' he answered. 'I'll see you outside, then.'

Elinor hesitated, looking at him, trying to will him to turn and face her. But he would not. There was little for her to do save as he asked. Sighing, she packed up her gear, such as it was, and headed outside.

XXV

They headed off slowly, away from the cave, keeping in the general direction they had been following all along, and that Elinor still felt as a subtle tug upon her.

She was stiff and sore, her scarred leg an annoying ache that nagged each step. She glanced at Brynmaur whenever their travel permitted, but he kept his gaze resolutely turned from hers. He moved like an old man this morning, as if all his joints pained him.

After a time walking, they came to a little tumbling stream and stopped for a breather.

Elinor knelt down stiffly, dipped her flask and took a long drink of the frigid water. She rubbed at her leg, which still ached, but much less now that she had been able to walk some of the stiffness out. Her belly grumbled and she reached out one of the remaining journey cakes from her rucksack. She broke it open and offered half to Brynmaur, for neither of them had eaten anything yet this day.

He ignored her, staring off into the trees.

'We can't go on like this,' she said irritably.

He looked at her slantwise, his eye flashing anger.

'Brynmaur,' she said. 'Talk to me!'

He sighed. 'I . . .'

There was a sudden sound off amongst the trees, distant but clear: a *thunk*, as if somebody had struck one of the pines with a hammer.

And again: *thunk . . . thunk*.

'What is it?' Elinor whispered.

Brynmaur frowned. 'Certainly not natural. The sort of sound made by men, I'd say. Or . . . something.'

'Best we move off in the opposite direction, then.' Elinor stuffed the broken journey cake back into her rucksack. 'Fast as we can.'

He nodded and they set off, quiet and quick.

But luck was not with them, or there was something else that was come into play.

They made the best speed they could, and the *thunking* noise dwindled. But coming through a more open, stony patch, pushing on a little recklessly perhaps in their effort to leave whatever was behind them well and truly behind, they saw sudden movement ahead.

Elinor froze. The forest was changed here: by some combination of soil or weather, or of height, perhaps (for they had been steadily ascending), the usual pines were replaced by a stand of mountain birches, smaller and far slimmer than the pines, their limbs clothed in a bright green lacery of new leaves.

At first, Elinor was almost able to convince herself that it was no more than a high-slope deer, or puma, perhaps, in the birch stand ahead of them. But it moved with more noise than any forest beast ought.

Which left . . . what?

'Is it one of *them*, do you reckon?' Brynmaur asked uneasily.

They were crouched for cover behind the last of the old pines, peering out at the birches on the far verge of the more open space before them. In one spot, the green-lace limbs were shivering as if a strong breeze blew through them. But there was no such breeze.

Elinor watched closely, her right hand gripping the hilt of her blade, ready.

But what appeared, finally, was no needle-fanged, insectile creature, no stilt-legged hunter, no great lizardish beast. It was . . .

A man.

He came out of cover cautiously to stand peering about.

He was ragged and dirty, his clothes showing the rents of hard travel. A long knife was thrust through his belt, and he carried a battered-looking longbow in his hand, an arrow nocked to the string.

After a moment, he put two fingers to his lips and blew a lilting, clumsy-imitation bird call.

More men appeared, moving apprehensively. There were a dozen or so of them, perhaps, ragged and desperate-looking, armed with staffs and clubs and knives. One of them had a long-handled axe which he gripped tight in both hands. Only the first one carried a bow.

'Who are they?' Elinor whispered in Brynmaur's ear.

'Let's find out,' he said by way of reply and stood up so as to be in sudden, full view of the gathered men.

Elinor tried to prevent it, but she was too late. Which left her precious little option but to stand up beside him, fuming quietly at such foolish risk-taking.

The men startled like a flock of nervous fowl, spilling back from Brynmaur and Elinor's sudden appearance.

The bowman was the first to recover himself. He raised and sighted at them, his hands quivering. 'Why . . . who are you?' he demanded. 'What are you doing here?'

The rest stared at Elinor and Brynmaur as if the two might suddenly sprout wings and fly at them.

'We could ask the same of you,' Elinor replied. She had one hand on her sword's hilt, just in case, but kept the blade sheathed.

The bowman eyed her suspiciously. 'I am Kory, out of Minth's Steading, just by the village of Stobbal. Or what *used* to be the village of Stobbal. These others here are from . . . various places.' He gestured with the nocked arrow and bow. 'And you?'

'They're just like the rest of us Kory,' one of the other men put in. 'Wandering these woods alone and unsure. Can't you see? Put that bow of yours down. What's the point? They're no threat to us.'

'Oh yes?' Kory replied. 'And you have the *sight* now, do

you, Munch? You can see under the surface of things to the hidden truth of all?'

'Oh, let be,' another man called out. 'Munch has the right of it. These two are no threat. Anybody with half an eye can see that.' The man who had spoken came out of the group and walked towards Elinor and Brynmaur. He was balding and thin, with a long face, creased and lined and very dirty. There were dark smudges of exhaustion under his eyes and he had a staring look to him. He gestured at Brynmaur. 'This lad here your son, then?'

Brynmaur blinked. Elinor kicked him smartly on the ankle. She did not trust this rag-tag group at all, and was of no mind to contradict them in anything. 'Aye,' she said quickly. 'You guessed it aright.'

'The Powers have smiled upon you,' the man said to Brynmaur. '*My* son was killed eight days ago.'

'I . . . I am sorry,' Brynmaur replied. 'What happened?'

'It was them beasts.'

'Which . . . beasts?' Elinor asked.

Another man was come up by now, pushing his way past the bowman, who still stood regarding them suspiciously, arrow nocked to the string. The man who came up was panting, red-faced, glancing about as if he expected some demon to launch itself upon him from the trees at any instant. 'The very world is coming apart at the seams,' he gasped. 'Can't you see it? Are you blind? Monstrous beasts are loosed upon us!'

'We know,' Brynmaur said calmly.

'They killed my family and . . . and *ate* them!' another of the raggedy men put in from where the most of them still bunched together.

'Everything's destroyed and taken,' the bald man who had first come up to them said.

'One of them great bat-winged things took my sister's son,' a man spoke up from the group. 'Plucked him from the grass before the front door like a hawk plucking up a field mouse. I was just standing there, sipping a cup of mint tea. I thought I was going mad when I . . .'

'Shut up, Barth,' the bowman snapped. 'We all know that story.'

'Best you all turn about and head down into the lowlands,' Brynmaur suggested to them. 'Follow the Keel Track out if you can. That'll take you to safety.'

'Haven't you been listening?' the red-faced man demanded fiercely. 'Don't you *know*? The whole of the Three Valleys is destroyed. And beyond . . . The wide world itself is coming apart. The very Powers themselves are thrown down.'

Brynmaur shook his head. 'No. This is . . .'

'How can you deny it? The woods are full of monsters!'

'Listen to me,' Brynmaur tried.

But they were not interested. 'There's only one hope left,' the red-faced man declared. 'Only Lord Jossa.'

'Who?' Elinor said.

'Lord Jossa,' the bowman replied, eyeing them in no friendly manner. 'You have not heard of him, then?'

Both Elinor and Brynmaur shook their heads.

'Where have you been?' the red-faced man asked. 'Lord Jossa has risen in this terrible time to become our salvation. He is stronger than any ordinary man, faster, armed with a great, red-bladed sword . . .'

Elinor stared at the man. 'What are you talking about?'

'Lord Jossa is our only salvation, him and his great blade.'

'What makes you think such a person even exists?'

'His name is on every man's lips,' the red-faced man responded. 'How could that be if the man himself does not exist? He is up here in the mountains, in a hidden Keep. He has called every man to him. We go now to offer our services, to help return the world to its proper form.'

'How do you know the location of this "hidden" Keep, then?' Elinor demanded. 'Or even if it really exists?' It all sounded crazy to her, the fantasies of men who had been driven past the breaking point by bloody violence and tragedy.

'It's here up in the wild mountains,' one of the men in the group answered eagerly. 'Word has got about. Lord Jossa calls in all those of us who have survived the slaughter. We will find his hidden stronghold.'

'There is food aplenty there,' the red-faced man announced. 'And weapons for all.'

'And with him and his great red-glowing blade to lead us,' another put in eagerly, 'we will drive these abominations from our land!'

A little ragged cheer went up at this.

A young man stepped out of the group, limping, his head wrapped in a clotted bit of bandage. 'Yo— you . . .' he started haltingly. He stared at Elinor and Brynmaur, a sudden look of hope upon his battered features. 'You're not . . . not *from* Lord Jossa, are you? Sent to lead us to his hidden Keep in the heights?'

A shiver of excitement went through the clustered men.

'No,' Elinor said. 'No. Of course not. We're just as you. Wandering these woods alone.'

'Join us, then,' the bald man invited. 'We need every man's help. These monstrous beasts that have been sent amongst us must be destroyed. We must drive them back from whence they came. And we must destroy him who is responsible for shattering our lives like this.'

'You mean . . .' Elinor wondered how they could know any of this. Tancred had only been in the world such a short time.

'Aye,' the bald man agreed. 'We must destroy this evil Brynmaur Somnar.'

Elinor tried to keep her composure. Out of the corner of her eye, she could see Brynmaur start.

'For years now we've been hearing dark rumours about him,' the bald man went on. 'You must have heard them.'

'Him it was who was responsible for that terrible

300

epidemic of lung sickness,' the young man with the bandaged head said. 'I wasn't but a babe.'

'Back in the year of the hard spring it was,' the bald man added. 'Remember?'

'Aye,' Brynmaur said flatly. 'I remember.'

'A dark sorcerer, that Brynmaur is, needing blood and pain for his unwholesome magicks.'

'How . . . how do you know all this?' Elinor asked.

'*Everybody* knows,' the red-faced man responded. 'Brynmaur Somnar has been working his black and wicked spells for years. And now he has this new ally he has summoned up from whatever fell nether world he has called her from – this Ellnor Witchblade.'

Elinor felt her belly twist. 'Who?'

'Ellnor Witchblade,' the red-faced man answered. 'Her of the terrible blade of ice that sucks the soul from a man soon as it touches him.' He shivered, as if a cold wind had suddenly put teeth to him.

'We go to Lord Jossa,' the bowman said then. He still had not loosened the nocked arrow. 'Will you join with us?'

Elinor glanced at Brynmaur. 'I . . . we have our own path to follow, and—'

'There are reasons why you would not wish to go to Lord Jossa, then?' the bowman demanded.

Elinor shrugged. 'I . . .'

'Let them go their own way, Kory,' the bald man put in. 'It's their own choice what they do. They're lucky enough to have kept together, father and son. Let them be if they don't want any more of the fight.'

'Aye,' somebody else agreed. 'Let them go their way, if they wish.'

'I think not,' Kory said, his eyes narrowing. 'Look at the blade this lad carries.' He scowled at Elinor. 'Where did you get such a weapon?'

She did not know what to reply.

'The Witchblade is gold and crimson, they say,' a man piped from the group.

'Who *are* you?' the bowman demanded.

'It's him!' one of the men said in cracked voice.

'Can't be,' the bald man said. 'I've *seen* Brynmaur Somnar. His hair isn't white.'

'Fool!' the bowman chided. 'A black sorcerer can look any way he wishes.'

Elinor took a small, slow step towards them, both her hands up in a gesture of good will. 'I don't . . .' she began.

Without warning, the bowman drew and let fire at her.

Only barely was she able to draw the white blade and deflect the arrow, sending it *krumping* softly into a tree behind her.

The men stared.

'*Witchblade* . . .' somebody gasped.

The bowman was nocking another arrow with shaking hands.

'Do not try it, man,' Elinor warned him. She felt the surging strength of the sword fill her and flashed the blade in a quick, bright arc about her head. 'You cannot harm me with such a weapon.'

He stared at her, white-faced, frozen in mid-motion with an arrow halfway to the string. Those who had drawn close to Elinor and Brynmaur scrambled hastily back to the safety of the group. She moved towards them, stepping like a cat, the blade weaving a little sharp pattern in the air before her. It would be an easy matter to disperse such men as these.

'Put it away!' Brynmaur hissed, suddenly at her side.

She glanced at him, surprised.

'Sheath it! I will *not* have innocent blood spilt here.'

There was a fierceness to him she had never seen before. His eyes were like a hawk's, bright and unblinking and brooking no dispute.

'Do it!' he ordered.

Against all her better judgement – and against the surge of the sword, which wanted movement and the hard, bright shock of conflict – she found herself sliding the white blade slowly back into the scabbard.

The gathered men stared at her. The bowman started to nock another arrow. The man with the long-handled axe stepped forwards, his face screwed up with fright and rage.

Elinor's hand clutched the sword's hilt. It was the height of madness, what Brynmaur would have her do. Innocent or not, these men would have *their* blood if she did not keep them back. But she felt Brynmaur's hand upon her arm now, in a grip of surprising strength. 'Do not move,' he said in a fierce whisper. 'No matter what. Do not move! Is that clear?'

She looked at him. He was unwavering. 'Clear,' she said after a last moment's hesitation.

But it was craziness. The bowman had the arrow nocked and drawn by now, was sighting at her . . .

She felt a shudder of something unaccountably strange, as if an invisible whirlwind had suddenly risen up through her. A look of utter consternation came over the bowman. He blinked, stared first this way, then that.

'Where did they *go*?' the red-faced man demanded in a high-pitched, quavery voice.

Elinor stood stock still, remembering Brynmaur's insistence, but not understanding any of this.

The men before her were rushing about now, shouting and crying to each other hysterically, as if they had all gone abruptly mad.

'Don't move,' she heard Brynmaur whisper in her ear.

The man with the axe rushed past them, nearly smacking into Elinor's shoulder. His eyes flicked here and there in desperate search, but he never noticed them.

'This way!' somebody shouted. 'They must have gone by here.' The men streamed off in a discordant mass, shouting and muttering and looking about over their shoulders all the while.

Brynmaur kept still for long moments, till the sound of

the men had dwindled into nothing. Then he let out a long breath and collapsed to his knees.

Turning, Elinor saw that he was pale as a mushroom, his face slicked with cold sweat.

'Here,' she said quickly, and offered him her water flask. It was all she could think to do. Kneeling next to him, she steadied the flask in his hands while he drank.

The water seemed to help. 'What did you do?' she demanded of him once he seemed a little recovered. 'It was like we were . . . *invisible*. Did you . . .?'

He shook his head. 'Nothing quite so dramatic as all that. I merely turned their sight from us. We were plain for anyone to see – save that none of them actually ever *looked* at us.'

Elinor swallowed. Her belly felt like somebody had tied it in a knot. 'It would have been *most* useful if those creatures hunting us yesterday had been unable to see us. I asked you, but you denied having any such special abilities, if you remember.'

Brynmaur shrugged uncomfortably. 'I am not sure I could explain it to you. It came out of the stress of the moment, somehow, what I just have done.' He ran a hand shakily over his face, struggled back up to his feet. 'I've never done anything quite like it before. Truly. Those otherland creatures were utterly alien to me. There was nothing I could do. But these men . . . they were out of the Three Valleys, all of them. I know exactly what manner of men they are. It just . . . came to me how I could turn their eyes from us. There was blood going to be spilled. I could sense it sure, and I was not about to let the poor souls be hurt by you. Not after . . . after all that's already happened to them'

Elinor stared at him. 'You're full of surprises,' she said, finally.

He smiled a thin smile. 'I'll take that as a compliment then, shall I?'

She snorted. 'What do we do now, then? You heard

what those men were spouting. Lord Jossa the saviour. Brynmaur Somnar the wicked sorcerer and his evil ally Ellnor Witchblade. Wherever did they get such nonsense? If it's as widespread as they claim it is, the hand of every man we meet will be turned against us.'

Brynmaur looked grim. 'Exactly.'

'Exactly?'

'This Tancred wastes no time.'

'Him? But how could he get such rumours flying in so little time? Has he sent runners everywhere? Where would he get the men?'

Brynmaur tugged at his beard. 'No need for men. An idea comes into the world sometimes. You know how it is. Suddenly, one day, everybody everywhere is talking about it. Nobody knows exactly where it came from. It just *is*. Nothing uncanny about that. It happens. But this Tancred must have been loosing such ideas into the world on purpose, sending them out like a cloud of ink in a pond, runnelling everywhere. To do such a thing requires great *power*.'

Brynmaur shivered. 'Let's away from here and onwards. Fast as we can. Time is not our ally in any of this.'

They set off at the best pace their weary limbs would allow, detouring away from the direction the raggedy men had taken, onwards and up into the Heights.

XXVI

'Who do you reckon this Lord Jossa is, then?' Elinor said.

They had been working their way along a steep, stony incline, and had stopped for a breather. Day was well-advanced, and it was all uphill walking now – climbing, almost – and she could feel her heart banging in her chest still from the last steep bit of slope they had navigated.

They were come into the Heights proper, it was plain to see, and to feel in the long muscles of her thighs and her complaining knees. And she was panting all the time, it seemed. The pines were beginning to thin, alternating with stands of the slim mountain birches. More and more often, she could see the snow-gleamed teeth of the peaks that reared up in the distance all about them.

Brynmaur, perched on a bit of moss-cushioned stone, shrugged at her question. He took a drink of water from his flask, then rubbed at his eyes. 'Lord Jossa . . . Could be anybody. If such a man exists at all.'

'You think this Tancred just made him up, then? For some tricky reason of his own?'

'Who knows what schemes one such as he may be hatching.'

'Too true,' Elinor agreed glumly. Then, 'Brynmaur . . .' she started.

He shook his head. 'No more talk.'

'But . . .'

'What we need to do now is walk. Save your breath for that. The way ahead is steep enough to take it all.' He turned from her and set off once more, leaving Elinor no choice but to follow after. He had been like this all day, grim and withdrawn. It both irritated and worried her. He pushed himself so.

Elinor kept scanning their surroundings as she moved. There had been no sign of anything untoward since they had left the raggedy gang of men behind them, but she could not shake a queasy feeling in the pit of her belly. It felt as if there was something watching them – from the trees, the heights, the very earth itself, perhaps. Yet she could see nothing.

If only Brynmaur would talk. There were things she wished to know. This was no way to conduct a partnership – for they were become partners in this enterprise, whether they liked it or not. They needed to be able to depend upon each other . . . She could not help but think how it had been with Gyver, her sleek fur-man: friend, teacher, lover. There had been no such brooding silences between them. No . . . that was not altogether true. But they had come through such silences.

Poor Gyver . . . She saw him again in her mind as she had seen him last: sprawled upon the ground, his slim, furred chest punctured by stab wounds, one leg tucked under him at an awkward angle, the crossbow bolt sticking up out of it, one arm flung out as if he had been reaching for something, his blind, dusty-dead eyes staring into the empty morning sky . . .

Elinor shuddered. It did not bear thinking on.

Resolutely, she turned her mind upon the present moment, stilling the flood of old grief and older anger that welled up inside her, and walked on after Brynmaur.

Only when it was too grey-dim to see anything did Brynmaur finally slow. By then he was staggering like a drunkard.

'Brynmaur . . .' Elinor said, concerned.

He slumped down, gasping, his eyes glassy.

Elinor knelt by his side, 'Here.' She gave him her water flask to drink from.

He took it silently, drank, handed it back.

'What now?' she asked. 'We need a place to sleep the night.'

He nodded, silent still.

'Brynmaur?'

'Leave me be, can't you?'

She turned from him, too weary to want to be drawn into argument, and surveyed the land round about. They were on a steepish, high slope. The great, bare bones of the earth showed here, rising in sharp, stony crests out of the sod. The pines were dwindled to occasional, loosely gathered copses. Mountain birces abounded, but they were smaller trees, the biggest no more than twice a man's height. It was more open country than that through which they had been travelling, and the sky above them seemed huge. It lifted her spirits a little, to be here; in comparison, the thick dimness of the pines below had seemed constricting.

But it would be a cold night out here, high as they were, and there seemed little prospect of decent shelter.

And Brynmaur just sat as he was, head in his hands, panting softly.

'Brynmaur!' she snapped at him, exasperated. 'We have to find some shelter.'

'Fine,' he said. 'Find some, then.'

Elinor opened her mouth for a sharp reply, then closed it. Instead, she said, 'Why can't you just be nice?'

He looked up at her, surprised. 'I—'

'We've been thrown into this together, whether we like it or no. It's clear you have little liking for me, but can't you at least try to be civil about it?'

He shook his head. 'No, I . . .'

He looked so vacant that she felt suddenly out of patience with him entirely. A man of knowledge he might be, and one of the deep Curers, but at moments like this she felt like strangling him. 'There's what might be a promising depression in that outcrop up there . . .' She pointed. 'I'm going to see if it offers any shelter.'

With that, she left him and went toiling up the slope, refusing to look back.

In the end, it was not much she found: a little cut in the side of a great rock-face. But it would have to do. They would be sheltered well enough from any prying eyes, and there was enough of an overhang so that, should it rain in the night, they would not get entirely soaked. And the ground here was thick with a dark green moss that would give them a more comfortable bed to lie on than they had had the night before in the cave.

By the time Brynmaur joined her, she had her sleeping blanket unrolled and was sitting, munching on one of the remaining journey cakes.

He came up silently, unrolled his own sleeping blanket, sat himself down – none too near her. Stiffly, he took out the little paring knife he still carried and sliced in half a piece of dried goat's meat he took from his travel bag. Popping one half into his mouth, he put the little knife away and offered her the rest.

She took it and passed him a cake.

They ate in silence.

'How did you lose the finger?' Brynmaur asked after a little.

'What?' she said, taken aback. She hid her left hand in her lap, self-consciously. 'What business is it of yours?'

'I . . . I'm trying to make conversation, to be . . . "nice",' he said. 'I'm only asking after your life. It was the . . . the first thing that came to mind, seeing you hold the cake so.'

Elinor looked at him. He looked her back, open-eyed, seeming genuine enough. She sighed, 'It was my own fault. I trusted a man when I ought not.'

Brynmaur raised one white eyebrow. She was still having a little difficulty getting used to this white hair of his. It made him look so *old*.

'It was in the wild lands, eastwards and south of here,'

she went on after a little. 'I was there with . . .' She stopped.

'No need to tell me if you'd rather not,' Brynmaur said. 'Your life's your own, girl.'

'Don't call me *girl*,' Elinor snapped at him. 'I hate it when people call me girl. You know that.'

He sighed. 'All right. My mistake. Forgive me. There, satisfied now?'

Elinor scrutinised him, suspecting him of making fun of her. But he seemed to mean it. She nodded. 'Apology accepted.'

Brynmaur smiled a thin smile. 'You think an awful lot of yourself, don't you?'

She frowned at him. 'If this is the way our talk is likely to be, I'd rather go to sleep.'

He made a placating gesture. 'I don't mean anything hard by it, gir—' He stopped, swallowed, shook his head. 'You bring out the worst in me.'

Elinor blinked. 'What?'

Brynmaur shifted position uncomfortably. 'There's that in you that disturbs me.'

'Such as?'

He shrugged. 'I'm not certain I wish to say.'

Elinor scowled. 'You are the *most* infuriating man, do you know that?'

To her surprise, he laughed softly.

'What's so funny?'

'You, me. I don't know. Everything. Nothing.'

Elinor shook her head. 'You're not making sense.'

'It's *you* who's not seeing the sense.'

Elinor took in a breath, let it out. She was not sure there was any point in continuing this. Brynmaur seemed half-mad, almost, this evening. Perhaps the long trek up here and all they had seen and undergone had loosened his mind a little. 'Sleep,' she suggested, 'is what we both need, I reckon. I'm going to turn in.'

He shifted over close to her and put a hand on her arm. 'I

never saw it in you till it was too late. And now you don't see it in me.'

'See what?'

He stood up then, placing himself a pace or two in front of her. 'Look at me. What do you see?'

She blinked. 'I see you. With your hair white now, and skinnier than you were when I first met you, if that's possible. You're still just as scruffy, though.'

'No!' he said. 'Look with better eyes than that.'

'Look . . . how?'

'Who am I? *What* am I?'

There was an intensity to him that went right through Elinor like a cold draught. 'You . . .' she began and then stopped, uncertain.

'Let me tell you what I see, then,' Brynmaur said to her. 'You are a gudgeon, one through whom Powers move.'

'And so?'

'And so you have had . . . experiences, felt yourself like a leaf in the wind, like a cork born upon some huge current, felt yourself *filled* with that great current – will you or nil you.'

Elinor nodded uneasily, more than a little surprised at how he had managed to catch it all so perfectly.

'One is born a gudgeon. As one is born with the *gift*. Men such as Khurdis hunger after such birth-gifts – so much so that it all but takes their mind from them and they become fatally obsessed. But you know as clear as I, being a gudgeon is curse more than blessing, for one becomes a . . . utensil, and one's life a shambles.'

Elinor felt a chill shiver sneak down her spine. 'How do you . . .' She stopped, licked her lip. 'I forget myself. You are a . . . a man of knowledge. Of course you would understand about such things.'

'Look more clearly at me,' Brynmaur said by way of reply.

Elinor blinked.

'Look!'

311

It came to her then, seeing him so thin and bruised-looking. There was an old soul-hurt upon him. 'You, too,' she said softly.

He nodded. 'I, too.'

Elinor wrapped her arms about herself, gazing blindly down at her feet. Too sudden, all of this. And far too unexpected.

'I was born such as you,' Brynmaur went on. 'A gudgeon *and* gifted with the far-sight that allows one to see into the world's depths.' He laughed, a soft, bitter laugh.

'My mother had a bit of the "sight". It ran in her family. And though she had no more of it than would let her scry the future in folk's palms, it was enough for her to perceive the hidden birth-gifts of her firstborn. She was . . .' Brynmaur looked away and sighed. 'She was . . . *so* proud of her small, doubly gifted son.'

Elinor did not know what to say.

'You had it thrust upon you,' he went on. 'I had it held up before me all the days of my childhood. "Here is my son," my mother would say. "Destined for greater things, he is. *Doubly* gifted." And her face would light with a kind of fierce glee and she would lord it over all the neighbours.'

Brynmaur sighed and sat down with a small *krump* on the ground. 'As a little lad, I rather revelled in it, doing more than my own fair share of lording it over the village children. But such only brought me grief, as it did for my mother in the end. And as I grew I became more and more sickened by the whole affair.

'I determined to be a smith as a young man – to forsake entirely all that had been laid upon me at my birth – and apprenticed myself to old Mortis, Stroud's father, as you know. My mother nearly had a fit. I remember, she came into the smithy one morning, shrieking . . .' Brynmaur sighed. ' "You can never forsake your birthright," she said to me. I remember it clear as if it were yesterday. "Run all

312

you want," she cried, "but you cannot outrun your own nature." She was right, of course. But I learned that the hard way.'

Elinor was beginning to look at Brynmaur with new eyes.

He sighed again. 'This is . . . is not easy to relate. But it's necessary, I think. I was gifted as a babe. But I am no hero from a wonder tale. I am an ordinary man, with an ordinary man's hopes and fears . . . and weaknesses. I had no grand ambitions.' He laughed a bitter little laugh. 'The world is so strange, sometimes. Here was Khurdis, desperate to have the very gifts that, to me, were misery.'

'Better to grant them to you than him,' Elinor said.

'Better for whom?'

'For the wide world, perhaps . . .'

'Ah . . . The wide world. Who amongst us knows what is best for the wide world?'

Elinor shrugged.

Brynmaur was regarding her uneasily. 'I have been a . . . a failure in many ways. I did not want the gifts that had been dropped upon me. Most wearying, it was, with the world's flow pushing me in one direction and me obstinately forcing myself in another.'

Elinor tried to imagine what that must have been like. She herself had had enough experience with the force of the world's hidden currents to know how hard it must have been, like toiling up a steep hill all the time with never a moment's rest.

'And then the lung sickness came to the Three Valleys. Folk looked to me for a cure – for all that I had refused to give them cause to think I could do any such thing. Whole villages died in that outbreak. My mother, my father, my only sister were amongst the dead. I watched them die, helpless, cursing myself most bitterly – and too late – for an ignorant, blind fool.'

Brynmaur looked away. 'Folk blamed me for that, thinking I had let those people die on purpose for some dark motives of my own. They had never believed me in my denials. My mother's boasting about me had stuck too firmly in their minds, you see. In the extremity of their grief, some of them tried to stone me to death – and nearly succeeded. I still bear the scars.' He pointed to a little pale star of scar tissue on his forehead at his hairline.

'Who knows what might have happened if I had allowed myself to follow the direction the world's hidden currents moved me in that early part of my life? But I did not. And folk died, with me powerless to help. And my life came apart like an old sack rent down the middle.' Brynmaur went silent then, staring blindly down at the ground.

'What did you . . . do?' Elinor asked.

He glanced at her quizzically.

'I mean . . . you clearly did become a man of knowledge and a deep Curer. How did you do so?'

'I took a sojourn in the lowlands and found myself a teacher.' Brynmaur smiled thinly. 'Maelcom, his name was. Old and bad-tempered as a goat, but deep as the green sea. I learned very much from him. And then, though I did not wish it, the world pulled me back up into the mountains.'

'The world's . . . current drew you back here?'

Brynmaur nodded. 'The last place in the world I wished to be, and where I had no welcome at all. A bitter draught to swallow. But I had learned the folly of resistance. I came.' He let out a long breath. 'The years began to go by, then, with no hint as to why I had been channelled back. I had taken Pawli in, and folk started to accept me, grudgingly, but I felt like some fish stranded on a dry shore waiting for a wave to return it to the water. I began to . . . explore. I had acquired the *talanyr*, you see, down in the lowlands – a tale in itself, that – and through it I discovered the Otherwhere and . . . Moreena.'

Brynmaur went silent for a little. Then, 'And so you descended upon me, to find me only half in the world, and poor Pawli left dangling.'

314

'And Pawli?' Elinor said after a little, for Brynmaur had gone quiet again. 'What of him?'

'Pawli has the *gift*, all right. It runs in the family.'

'And you simply . . . refused to bring it out in him?'

Brynmaur looked away. 'It brings too much of grief, this far-seeing. Curse more than *gift*, it is. Look what it has done to my life. I will not willingly visit the same upon Pawli.'

'For all that it is his dream?'

'What do you know of Pawli's dreams?'

'I am not blind, Brynmaur.'

'Pawli's hardly more than a lad still. His dreams are a boy's dreams. He'll get over them. Best for him he does it quick.'

'But if he is truly *gifted* . . . it will come out in him anyway, will it not? It did in you.'

Brynmaur shook his head. 'Pawli is no gudgeon. He can lead his life any way he wishes. Only if there is somebody to draw the *gift* forth from within him will it manifest itself. He is like . . . like a harper, say. Take some lad born to play the harp, put one in his lap, and he'll have it singing in no time. Never let him touch a harp, however, and he'll be just like any other lad.'

'But unfulfilled.'

'What do you know of it?'

'I only know that things are as they are.'

Brynmaur snorted. 'Philosophy is it, now?'

'You can be so utterly blind sometimes, it makes me want to slap you!'

He looked at her, eyes wide with sudden surprise.

'I am become the person I am,' she said, before he could have a chance to interrupt, 'because . . . because I *am* something.' She stopped, swallowed. That was a most lame way of expressing it, she knew. She tried again. 'We all are born into this world, each of us, with a history. You know the old verse: "many deaths and many lives, each of which the soul survives; growing deeper, knowing

315

more; fulfilling what has come before". We change, the great world changes, seasons come and go, our lives come and go, all of a great, shifting pattern. And we ignore *that* at our peril.'

Elinor held her hands out to him. 'You know all of this, Brynmaur. You *must*! If we don't find our own way, the world's movement often does it for us.'

Brynmaur frowned. 'Let the world bring the *gift* out in Pawli if it will. I will have no part of it.'

'Perhaps the world has,' Elinor said softly.

Brynmaur looked at her. 'Has what?'

'Brought the *gift* out in him . . . through this Tancred.'

Brynmaur started, half made to rise, then fell back and went still as a carving, staring sightlessly into nothing.

'Brynmaur?' Elinor asked.

He blinked, shuddered. 'You're right,' he said in a small voice. 'Of course . . . How could I have been so blind-stupid? You're *right*. What have I *done*?'

People were such complex, odd beings, Elinor thought. It had seemed so obvious to her, all this, and yet here sat Brynmaur, man of knowledge, deep Curer that he was, blind as any ignorant fool could be – so wrapped in his own complexities and fears that he failed to notice what lay right under his nose.

'Surely it's not as bad as all that, is it?' she said.

He shrugged, silent.

'Brynmaur?'

'My doing,' he murmured. 'My doing, all of this. Woburn . . . everything. How could I have been so completely *stupid*?'

'No,' Elinor said, trying to be soothing. She went to him and put a hand on his arm where he sat. 'How could you have known? You did the best you could.'

'Don't condescend to me!' he snapped, thrusting her away. 'I have made a stupid, terrible mistake. Have the courtesy to at least acknowledge the truth of that.'

'Very well, then,' Elinor replied, stung. 'You have made

316

a terrible mistake and have brought calamity into the world.'

He regarded her bleakly, his white hair a tangle about his face. 'I have.'

'What do you intend to do about it, then?'

Brynmaur's shoulders were hunched, his head down. 'I will do . . . what I can, what I must.' He paused, folded in upon himself. 'But I fear it may not prove enough, in the end.'

'Brynmaur—'

'Don't look at me like that, girl. You're too young. You don't know.'

'Know what?'

'I was like you once. You think you can never fail.'

'I *have* failed,' she snapped back. 'And at great cost. My life has been wrecked by what I am.'

'But you keep on, indefatigable, because, deep down, no matter how bad things get, you are convinced that your failures are only temporary, only transitory. It is the great delusion of the young that they believe themselves to be essentially without flaw and that their lives will, one day, prove a grand success.' Brynmaur ran a hand across his lined face. 'Well, I am no longer young, and cannot delude myself into believing I am unflawed. Nor that my life will ever be any kind of great success.'

'And so you want what? Pity?'

He shot her and angry look. '*No!* I am . . .'

'What?'

'You don't understand, girl.' He moved closer to her. 'I have done a terrible thing, brought about the Powers alone know what disasters into the world. But this realisation you have forced upon me actually changes little. There is still only the one thing for me now: to find Pawli and save him, if I can, and to bring Tancred down. But I . . . I truly am not certain I shall succeed.'

'A fine attitude,' Elinor said. 'You surely won't succeed thinking like *that*.'

'So speaks the voice of youth,' Brynmaur sniped back.

'I may be young, but at least I'm not *defeatist*! And besides, you can't be all that old. You talk like you're my grandfather or something.'

'I'm forty-seven,' he said. 'That *feels* old, sometimes. And this evening is one of those times.'

'Ah . . . old man Brynmaur,' Elinor crooned scathingly.

'Stop it!' he barked. 'Stop it and listen to me.' He frowned at her. 'I am going on, for good or ill. But this Tancred . . . I've been thinking on it. If he truly endured all that you described, we are not dealing with any natural man. No man could survive such an ordeal and have his spirit remain intact, not even one of the great Seers.'

'But he did survive, clearly.'

'No. Only part of him did. A core, if you like. I'm convinced of it. What survived is like a thing that has been hung out in the open on a sharp pole, desiccated, stripped clean of any excess by a hard wind. It is a . . . a node of intention, of reflex and habit and power, but no full man.'

'He conversed like a full man,' Elinor said.

'He is not, believe me. Cannot be. And that makes him both less formidable, perhaps, and more terrible. For he will tend to act out old habit patterns and be, to some extent, predictable, but he will also be . . . *strong*, stronger than you can imagine, for he is, in a sense, more pure than any ordinary man.'

Brynmaur shook his head ruefully. 'After all these years, I am finally born towards something, a true channelling, but it is one that I brought about myself through my own blind-stubborn resistance. I go to do what I must, then. But I am a small creature facing a larger – and a fiercer. Not a hopeless task, no, but one with slight chance of success.' He reached a hand out. 'But you . . . I do not think you can understand what it is you face. You can still turn back. You have a life ahead of you. You—'

'I will not run away, tail between my legs,' Elinor said.

'Don't be pig-headed! This is no bard's tale we face. It is death – or worse – that awaits ahead in this Tower. Death and defeat *happen*, girl. Tancred is no simple bandit leader you can take with your white blade as if he were some child. See things with your eyes open!'

'I am no less driven than you,' Elinor returned. 'I, too, go where I must, to do what I must. I, too, have learned the folly of useless resistance to the world's currents. And do you imagine that being who and what I am has left me innocent?'

'No,' Brynmaur returned softly. 'Not that. But you carry a weapon that fills you with too much. The glow of it blinds you at times. That which lies ahead is nothing that mere brute force can defeat. And you have a . . . a flawed ally in me.'

Elinor looked at him: white-haired and painfully thin, ragged and dirty and travel-stained, older-looking than his years, older than his years, perhaps, in experience, yet stubborn-ignorant at times. Not a man to inspire easy confidence. But for all that, there was still something about him. He seemed to her like a tough, half-aged tree, a little stiff, a little battered, but with the heartwood still intact, and roots that went down deep into hidden places. 'I will continue on with you,' she said.

'Are you sure, girl?'

'Yes. And don't call me *girl*!'

'Sorry,' he said hastily. 'Are you *certain* sure . . . Elinor?'

'I said I was, didn't I?'

He looked unconvinced.

Elinor held her hand out, formally. 'Partners?' she said.

He hesitated a long moment, then took it. 'Partners.'

'But no more sulking, all right?' she said.

'I don't sulk.'

Elinor laughed. 'You do a fair impersonation of it, then.'

He frowned, opened his mouth, then grinned a small, tired grin.

'Just talk to me civilly, right?' Elinor insisted. 'No more snapping. No more dark silences.'

Brynmaur agreed. 'As best as I can.'

'Good enough,' she said.

They looked at each other then, hands still clasped, and Elinor felt something jolt softly through her. Brynmaur's eyes were green as the moss under their feet, and deep as pools. His was a kind face, somehow, despite all, and one upon which lines of suffering were deeply etched. No ordinary man . . .

Their eyes met, held for a handful of heartbeats, slid away.

Brynmaur withdrew his hand from hers. He stretched, yawned, sighed, trying to make light of things – but she knew that he too had felt . . . something.

'Best set a guard tonight,' he said after a little. 'No telling what might be out there.'

Elinor nodded. 'Turn and turn about, then. I'll take the first watch.'

'No,' he returned quickly. 'I will. You get some sleep.'

'But . . .'

'No,' he insisted. 'I'm too weary to sleep yet anyway. My bones ache. I need time to settle. You sleep. I'll wake you to take the watch later.'

She looked at him uncertainly.

'Sleep,' he insisted. 'You look like you need it.'

She did indeed feel most tired. 'All right,' she agreed. 'But don't let me sleep too long. You, too, look like you need the rest.'

He nodded. 'Sleep now. I'll wake you. Go on.'

She did, wrapping herself in her blanket. The world was shrouded in shadows now, the twilight time between day and night. The sky was a washed blue-grey, cloudless, flecked with a handful of early stars, and absolutely huge overhead. Elinor sighed tiredly. The moss under her was comfortable-soft as any mattress.

'Sleep,' Brynmaur said softly.

She did.

And found herself struggling through a darksome forest, like the pine forest she had been traipsing through for so many days, save it was thicker and more sombre, with a dark heaviness to it. The trees were spiky and dry, rattling like old bones in a wind that felt chill. An eerie, red-ochre glow shimmered down from the sky and through the mangled webbery of the trees, shimmering on their dark trunks and sharp limbs like some unwholesome liquid.

Behind her, in the tree-ridden dimness, something hunted.

Hunted her.

Where she had to struggle, breaking a way through tangly, clutching thickets, the thing that stalked her glided silently, fluidly, easily. She could hear it *hiss* like a great serpent, the sound carrying through the dark wood above the susurration of the wind.

The spiky-limbed trees rattled. Her heart hammered. She fled like a panicked fawn, slipping and struggling and falling. The trees seemed to clutch at her, the ground to rumple and heave under her feet in unexpected ways.

And then, despite all her desperate haste, the hunter was upon her, leaping across her path from above, needle fangs dripping glistening ribbons of saliva.

She reached for her blade – but it was not there.

The hunter *hisssed* in malevolent satisfaction, raised a long sinew-and-bone arm, flexed black talons sharp as any eagle's. *Kleekk keek kleekk*, the talons went. *Kleekk keek . . .*

In the eerie red-ochre glow, she could see its limbs twist and shift in queer angles. It stared at her with red-glowing eyes. Its needle-fanged mouth opened. A white tongue flicked out. She saw the mouth working, opening and flexing, the sharp teeth glistening.

Hiss, hisssk . . . tsissssk . . . it went.

She scrabbled about desperately for some sort of weapon, a branch, a rock, anything with which to defend herself. But there was nothing. She had to face this fell, unhuman hunter entirely defenceless. She could feel her heart quaver.

The thing leaned in closer to her, stalking like a mantis. *Hiss hissssk . . .* The eagle-taloned hand reached for her.

In panic, she batted at it with a fist, feeling the dry, bony knuckles, the horn of the talons. It was like smacking a tree limb, so hard and unyielding was it.

Closer still it leaned, the needle fangs dripping, the white tongue flickering like a serpent's, laced with drooling saliva. She struck at it, screaming . . .

And came awake in a star-lit half-dark, soaked with chill sweat, Brynmaur's arm about her.

'Easy,' he said. 'Easy now.'

She lurched up to a sitting position. The wood in which she had been trapped seemed to hover about her still in some strange way. There was a shadow-flicker of shape, a spiky limb, the flash of needle teeth, the faintest of sounds, *hisssss . . .* She stared about her, open-mouthed, stricken. Her heart was beating frantically, like a terrified bird trapped in a cage.

'Only a dream,' Brynmaur said. He ran a hand across her brow, softly, soothingly. 'You're back. It's finished.'

Elinor let out a long, shuddering breath, another. She shivered with cold. Her blanket had fallen from her and the air was bitter chill. She could see the far eastern horizon awash with a soft, pewter glimmer . . . good wholesome, ordinary morning radiance, nothing like the eerie red light of her dream.

'What was it?' Brynmaur asked. 'Of what did you dream?'

She shuddered. 'It was . . . was one of those creatures,

the ones who killed and ate the Woburners and nearly caught us back at the cliff. It . . . it hunted me in a dark wood. I was . . . entirely defenceless.'

Brynmaur looked at her most gravely. 'As in my dream in the cave last night.'

'Yes,' she said in a small voice. She shivered. In the dawnlight, his face was all glimmering beard and shadow. A distant bird greeted the coming day: *tee wee hoo tee wee hooo.* 'Why did you not wake me?' she demanded. 'It's morn already, nearly. You ought to have awakened me.' She looked at him accusingly. 'Did you fall asleep?'

He shook his head. 'I did not. Sleep held little . . . appeal for me. I was afraid I would have another . . . visitation. And now *you* . . .'

Elinor struggled up, discarding the last few folds of the blanket about her knees. 'You kept awake all night by yourself?'

'It is all right,' he assured her. 'Sleep is something I have learned to do without, when I must. I slept most of last night, and have sat and rested through this one. It is enough. And better, perhaps, than the alternative.' He put a hand to her. 'I am sorry. I never reckoned they would be able to reach you. I thought it was me, and what I am, that drew them.'

Elinor shivered. 'Clearly not.'

'Clearly not,' he echoed her in agreement.

Elinor stood stiffly on her feet, trying to stretch the kinks out of her muscles. Her scarred leg ached. She felt irritated with Brynmaur for taking all the sentry duty to himself – but having experienced the kind of dream he had, she understood his reticence to sleep too. Best just to let the issue drop.

'I reckon we'd better get moving, if you're able for it.' Brynmaur said. 'There's no telling for certain . . . but perhaps those creatures can follow such . . . such dream sendings and use them to track us. The quicker we're away from here, the better.'

'I'm for that,' Elinor agreed.

It took them only a few moments to gather everything and pack up, and then they were on their way once more, traipsing upslope and onwards through the slowly growing light.

XXVII

By midday the pines were all but disappeared, and even the high-slope birches began to give way to open meadow, thick with new flowers, white and palest yellow, violet and red. Skeins of naked rock ran through the steep, flowery turf, like old bones showing. Above it all, the peaks reared, snow glimmered and tall, thrusting upwards like so many proud old men.

'It's like like another world,' Elinor said. It had been hard walking, getting here, and her knees and thighs and back ached from it. But she felt as if she had been released from some prison. The dream had hovered over her for much of the morning, like a dark cloud, but it was dissipating now, dispelled by the open distances about her. The air in her lungs was clean as clean, and brisk with the high-slope coolth.

Brynmaur nodded. 'I've always liked the heights. Cleans a person's spirit, it does, just standing here. The distance of it all . . .'

Elinor took it in. She had looked at mountains many a time, and wandered forests much like the pines they had left below them. But she had never yet been up this high on a rocky slope. The sky seemed so close. It was like drawing near to the world's roof.

Come on,' Brynmaur said after a little. 'Time to be moving. Along the edge of this vale here and then one more longish, steep climb and we ought to be near our goal.'

On they went, working their way upwards, weaving and zagging, looking for the easiest route along which to move and still make headway. Elinor felt her heart thumping. Her thighs burned with the effort of the climb. Step, step, step, over this rock, across that . . . step, step, heave up . . . Like a dream, almost. Walking, walking, walking . . .

She felt queerly light-headed. It seemed to her that this day might be any day, that Woburn might lie ahead as easily as this Tower they were headed for. Time seemed to have got all globbed up somehow. The world seemed to shimmy. She rubbed at her eyes. A shiver of dizziness shot through her and she thought she was suddenly going to be sick.

'It's the altitude,' Brynmaur said at her shoulder. 'That and all we've been though these past days. Never been up in the heights before, have you? Takes a little time to adjust.' He steered her softly over towards a humpy bit of ground. 'Here, let's take a bit of a breather.'

She sat down with a little *kwump* on mossy earth and looked across at him. 'And you? Don't you feel it?'

He nodded. 'But I'm not unused to it. And . . . I have ways of dealing with it. Here, let me . . .' He reached a hand towards her forehead.

Elinor shrank back. 'What are you going to do?'

'Nothing especially dramatic. Trust me.'

'Don't have much choice, do I?'

'No. You don't. Besides, we're partners, remember. In this much, anyway, I can be trusted. Close your eyes, Breathe easy. Relax.'

She did as he bid, or tried to. Her belly felt all knotted and her limbs were quivering in little ungovernable spasms. His hand, when it touched her forehead, felt surprisingly warm. She heard him humming something, but could not make out anything in the way of words. Perhaps there were no words . . .

She never knew what it was, exactly, that he did, for she seemed to swoon away somehow, drifting in a pleasant greyness until, abruptly, she blinked, snapped open her eyes and . . .

Felt perfectly normal again.

'What did you *do* to me?' she demanded, a little unnerved.

He smiled. 'I merely . . . aided your physical body in making the necessary adjustments.'

'But how did you . . .' She stopped herself. There was no point in asking such a question. Brynmaur did what he did. No explanation of his – even if he were willing to grant one – would ever make the process of it properly clear to her. It was something he had been trained for, but, also, it was simply his *gift*.

'Shall we get on?' he suggested, smiling still. He made an overly dramatic, bowing gesture, ushering her onwards with a sweep of his arm.

'Don't be so smug,' she said.

He laughed.

'The least you could do is give me a hand up,' she complained, but she could not stop herself from smiling.

He reached her up, and they continued onwards.

'What do you reckon on doing once we reach the Tower, then?' Elinor asked. Now that they were drawing near, she wanted to discuss it, work out some basic plan of attack, perhaps.

Brynmaur shrugged. 'We shall see.'

'But you must have some notion, no?'

'No,' he said simply.

'No?' Elinor echoed. 'But . . .'

'I have no idea what I shall or shall not do. Do you take me for one of those who can far-see the future?'

'No. Of course not. But you must have *some* sense as to what you—'

'None whatsoever.'

Elinor regarded him. 'Are you just having me on?'

'No. Not at all.' He was serious. 'I will do whatever is necessary. If I can. But that "necessary" will only become clear in the fullness of time.'

'So you just walk on blindly, then?'

'Just so,' he agreed.

It sounded crazy. And not. Elinor had had enough experiences to know that plans were dodgy things. The world moved in its own, deep ways, and they with it. And Brynmaur seemed to have regained his confidence again – that strange, unrufflable certainty he sometimes had.

'How far, then?' she asked, 'before we reach this Tower? At least you can tell me that, I hope.'

'No more than a day or so now, I reckon. Maybe less.'

So soon. And then . . . Elinor had no idea what might transpire. She could feel it still in her bones and blood, the disturbance in the world, the way she and Brynmaur were channelled along here. It made the small hairs along her scalp prickle.

'Come on,' Brynmaur called back to her.

She had not been aware she had slowed. 'Coming,' she replied, and hurried to catch him up.

The afternoon grew brilliant, with the sky a shimmering blue over their heads and a strong, enlivening breeze that filled the lungs with a delicious freshness. Elinor flung back her head and took great, long breaths of it, feeling the breeze tug at her hair, her clothing.

'Good idea,' Brynmaur said, eyeing the steep slope ahead of them. 'We're going to need all the breath we can get, to work our way up that.'

'That' was a steep, curving hillside, part-clothed in high-slope birch, but mostly humpy meadow and naked rock. Up above and beyond it, the jagged stone teeth of the peaks showed, tipped with snow that shone brilliant in the sunlight. They were up above the pines for good and all now. Behind them, Elinor could see the forest as a dark sea.

'Might as well start,' Brynmaur suggested, eyeing the slope before them with a noticeable lack of enthusiasm.

'Race you to the top,' Elinor dared him.

She did not know what had prompted her to say it.

Clearly, there would be no 'racing' up the hillside ahead – and they ought to go with some care, lest there be dangers about. But there was something about the brisk clarity of this incredibly spacious mountain setting that made her feel giddy. She felt it in her blood suddenly, like wine.

'Come *on*!' she cried, and was off, scrambling lithely up the slope like a goat.

'Elinor!' Brynmaur cried. '*Elinor!*'

She looked back down at him, laughing, her arm slung about the twisty bole of one of the birches, its pale green leaves twirling and whispering in the breeze. 'Come on, you slug!' she called.

'Idiot!' he called back.

She laughed.

The flash of a smile showed on his face, there and gone again. Then back. He shook his head. 'You may want to behave like a silly, rambunctious pup, but I—'

'Oh, don't be such an old curmudgeon.'

He bristled. 'Curmudgeon am I? And *old*?'

'Come on, then. Let the wind fill you. Don't you feel it?'

'Feel what?'

'The world's happy this day. It's in the air. Breathe it!'

Brynmaur took a great breath, another – she could see the way his thin chest expanded with it – and came up after her, toiling like an old hound, but making a fair job of it nonetheless.

'There,' he said, coming to a stop where she still stood next to the birch. He was puffing and panting, his face shining with sweat. 'Happy now? I've all but exhausted myself, and the climb's barely begun.'

She looked at him out of the corner of her eye. 'I reckon we need a few lightsome moments, now and again. Don't you agree, partner?'

Hands on hips, still breathing hard, he smiled. 'I reckon we do,' he agreed. 'But a little less athleticism would be more to my liking.'

She smiled at him. 'You provide the next light moment, then. How's that? Then you can ensure it's as safe and calm and non-athletic as you wish.'

'Deal,' he said.

They shook on it with mock solemnity.

'Come on, then,' she said, still holding his hand and tugging. 'Let's make short work of this climb.'

But it took effort and time to get to the hillside's crest. Their first flush of enthusiasm soon waned, and the steepness of the slope and the rough footing beat the breath out of them. The turf was full of half-buried rocks that could turn an ankle all too easily unless one paid close attention; the birches grew in loose-scattered clumps and provided no help at all. Two-thirds of the way up, found they were struggling up mostly naked rock, hauling themselves along hand over hand in spots, slipping and skidding and panting.

But in the end they did make it, all but crawling over the last bit.

They lay on their bellies on the bare ridge of the crest, too exhausted to move for a while.

'Beat you,' Brynmaur muttered after a little.

'What?' Elinor returned.

'I beat you.'

'What?' She still did not take his meaning.

'Back below. You dared me to race. It was *my* hand reached the summit here first. I beat you.'

Elinor looked at him blankly for a long moment, then shook her head and laughed. 'Easy to win when one cheats.'

'It was *your* challenge.'

She patted him on the shoulder. 'Very well, then. You win. Happy now?'

'Absolutely,' he replied, grinning hugely.

She could not help but laugh, he seemed such a boy at that moment. 'My turn next,' she said then.

'Turn for what?'

'For the next light moment.'

'I haven't had *my* turn yet,' he complained.

'You just did it,' she said. 'This was it.'

He blinked, then laughed with her. 'Have it as you will, then. But no more rushing about unnecessarily, I implore you.'

Elinor nodded. 'Promise.' Her pulse was still thumping a little, and she could feel the sweat cooling on her forehead. 'Come on, then. Let's see where we are.'

They had crested the slope on a sort of hogback, with a thrust of dark rock rearing slantwise ahead of them, the height of two men perhaps. Rising to their feet, they walked past this and, round the far side, got their first sight of what lay ahead.

The peaks stood on all sides, rough and strong and jagged, their snow-glimmered tips seeming to scratch the very sky itself. Closer to hand, there lay a bowl-shaped valley, filled with dark pines at its bottom, shading out to high-slope birch and meadowland and bare rock as the slope rose. A twinkling tributary stream fell down the far hillside, splashing in a series of bright waterfalls to join, eventually, a larger river flowing through the valley's core.

At the edge, near a set of flashing falls, just where the trees petered out, there reared a high, slender, dark . . . something.

'The Tower,' Brynmaur said softly.

From the description Tancred had given her in the Otherwhere, Elinor had been expecting something old and decrepit, perhaps with moss-eaten, crumbling stone walls and ruins all about. But this was nothing of the sort. The tower rose straight and strong, a solid, dark pillar. It was a farish ways off, and the distance made it hard to make out the fine details, but she could see no evidence of moss on the dark stone, and none of age, either.

'He has . . . refurbished it,' Brynmaur said.

Elinor could make out several dark shapes circling in the

air about the Tower's top. Crows, they seemed, but . . .
She shivered, recalling what she had seen in the sky
overhead the little cave they had slept in. They might be
any manner of monstrous beast circling the air about that
Tower.

Brynmaur was staring sombrely. 'Best we get started,' he
said, quiet-voiced.

'Doesn't seem any too inviting, does it?' Elinor said.

'No,' Brynmaur agreed. 'It doesn't.'

Elinor glanced at him, suddenly concerned. All the
lightness was gone from him. From her, too, for that
matter. For all that it seemed no more than a rearing,
simple column of dark stone, there was some disturbing,
subtle aspect to that tower that made one shiver. It
looked . . . She did not know quite how to express it. It
gave her the same sense she had had in the Otherwhere,
somehow, looking upon the ruins there. It was an old
place, this Tower, despite its new-furbished appearance,
old and creepy. She did not know what its builder might
have had in mind when constructing it, but it was not the
sort of place she could feel in any way comfortable with.

'Come on,' Brynmaur said. His tangled white hair was
blowing in the breeze and he pushed it back from his face
impatiently. 'The thing's still a ways ahead.'

Elinor nodded. 'It's downslope walking at least, for the
most part.'

Brynmaur was silent, his eyes still on the dark shape of
the Tower.

They started off together then, but slowly, not relishing
at all what lay ahead.

XXVIII

It took them all the rest of that day and the morning of the next to reach the Tower.

They slept during the night only in snatches, propped up shoulder to shoulder together, wrapped in their blankets against a mossy boulder, sharing the watch and keeping each other from falling into anything like a prolonged sleep, lest the dream-hunter find them. It seemed to work. When day came, they were tired but able enough to continue on, and had spent the night undisturbed.

They broke their fast on strips of dried goat's meat – the journey cakes being all gone by now – and set off. By the tag-end of morning, they lay on their bellies, side by side, having elbowed themselves up to the crest of a stony ridge. Below, finally, lay their goal.

The Tower was large, but not quite so large as Elinor had been expecting. Somehow it had grown in her mind to be a dark, high-soaring edifice. It stood thrice as tall as any ordinary house, perhaps a little more. But it was not that much larger around than a big manor house and, from where she lay, it did not look especially terrible: merely a tallish column of dark stone.

There was something about it, though, that went beyond the simply physical. It had a presence, a solidity – as if it were somehow far heavier than the bare stone it was constructed of.

'How old do you reckon it is?' she asked Brynmaur at her side.

He shook his head. 'There's no knowing for certain. Many lives of men, at any rate.'

Elinor tried to imagine what it must have been like in the olden time, when the structure was new, when the ancient Lords had vied with each other and Seers like that Tancred had ruled the land all about. Why had this tower been built here? Who had constructed it? There was no way to know anymore.

Whoever had once inhabited it was long gone – dead or killed or simply fled away – and the Tower had stood alone all these years by itself, tough and enduring as one of the great peaks themselves.

There were no outbuildings round about, no defensive wall, no moat. The country was entirely treeless. Between their vantage point and the Tower lay a hump of turfed ground, against which a scatter of lean-to shelters had been erected in a haphazard crescent. Raggedy folk milled around aimlessly.

'I don't see any sign of Pawli,' Elinor whispered. 'He might not even be here.'

'He's here . . . somewhere.'

'How can you know?'

'I know,' Brynmaur said simply, and there was that odd certainty in his voice again.

Elinor looked down at the shabby camp. The folk there were just close enough so that she could make out some of their features, but there was not a single familiar face amongst them, none from Woburn, none even of the men they had encountered back in the woods. There were no women either, she realised. And nothing to evince any sort of real order. 'Where is this Lord Jossa, then?' she said to Brynmaur. 'Isn't he supposed to be taking charge here?'

Brynmaur merely shrugged, his eyes fixed on the dark column of the Tower.

Elinor swung her gaze back to the camp. There was an eerie silence to it all. Closing her eyes, she could hear nothing, as if the place were utterly deserted.

'What's wrong with them?' she whispered to Brynmaur.

He, too, was regarding the camp now. 'Nothing easily put into words. This Tancred . . . is subtle.'

'Meaning?'

'As I said, nothing easily put into words.'

'But you told me that Tancred was a . . . a remnant of a person, and predictable.'

'That does not make him any less complex.'

'But you said—'

'I said he was . . . purer, not simpler.'

'Wonderful,' Elinor sighed. 'So what is he capable of, then?'

Brynmaur frowned. 'The ways of those such as the old Seers are difficult to explain. The world is . . . how shall I put it? The world is complex and mysterious, and we perceive no more than a fraction of the real depth of it. Most folk see only the surface reflections, like looking upon a still pond and only seeing one's own face and the sky and the trees behind one's back. But there are those, like this Tancred, who see into the depths. More than see. The ancient Seers – literally see-ers, those who see – were not only capable of perceiving the multiplex, hidden undercurrents of the world. They could *affect* them. They reached into the deep-hidden pathways of living flesh, for instance, to *change* things.'

Elinor had already heard of this. 'The humanimals,' she said softly.

'Amongst others.'

'But what of Tancred?'

Brynmaur plucked at his tangled beard. 'He was one of the great ones in his day. I do not know what he may or may not be capable of doing now. Still much, clearly.'

Elinor swallowed. 'Listen . . . you're like this Tancred, aren't you?'

He swung round, eyes suddenly hot. 'I am *nothing* like this Tancred!'

Elinor held a hand out placatingly. 'I only meant . . .' She stopped, took a breath. 'Brynmaur, I only meant that

335

you, too, are one of those who can . . . see beneath the world's surface reflections. You *are* that, aren't you?'

He frowned, then nodded. 'To some extent, yes. It's the main part of what makes me a Curer.'

'Then can't you . . . *see* something useful ahead for us?'

'It doesn't work like that. I have no skill to peer into the yet-to-be, and I cannot know anything certain about Tancred till we actually face him.'

'So we must walk in blindly, then?'

'That, or turn tail and creep away,' he replied.

They watched the Tower in silence for some little time after that. Elinor kept glancing up into the sky, but there was no sign of any flying thing, save a brace of ordinary black crows made little by distance.

'We're not likely to find much in the way allies anywhere hereabouts,' she said.

'No,' Brynmaur agreed. 'Nor much of anything helpful.'

'At least it isn't raining.'

Brynmaur smiled. 'At least that.'

Elinor gestured at the ragtag camp that lay between them and the Tower. 'Do you reckon you could do it again?' she asked.

Brynmaur plucked at his beard. 'Perhaps.'

'It's the only way I can see of getting in there. If we wait till dark when most of them down there will be asleep and out of the way, and then you do . . . whatever it is you must so that no eyes may see us . . .'

'It seems our only road,' he agreed.

As night came on, the inhabitants of the rough lean-to camp close about the Tower lit watch fires. The flames danced, casting uncertain shadows everywhere.

All to the good, Elinor thought. There were sentries set about the ragtag camp, but they looked none too eager for the duty. The night was growing cold, and most of them squatted disconsolately, their attention fixed with envy upon those gathered close about the fires' warmth rather than outwards to where any potential threat might lurk.

'Let's do it,' Elinor said softly.

Brynmaur nodded.

He did nothing obvious, no waving of arms or chanting of power words, but, as she had before, Elinor experienced a shudder of something most strange going through her. When she raised her hand before her face, however, it was perfectly perceptible. As was Brynmaur himself. 'Are you sure this will work?' she said uneasily.

He shrugged. 'Who knows what we will find once inside that dark place?'

'No, I mean the . . .' She did not know what words to use. 'The . . . un-seeing illusion, or whatever you have cast about us. Will it work? I can see you plain as plain. Myself, too.'

Brynmaur smiled. 'It will work. Seeing oneself is not the same as having others see one.'

'I hope so,' Elinor returned.

'Come, then,' he invited her. 'Let's put it to the test.'

Down the slope they went, walking slowly and carefully, for the footing was none too good in the dark. The nearest sentry was now no more than twenty paces from them . . . fifteen . . . ten. Elinor saw the man scratch himself under the armpit, heard him sigh. He glanced back over his shoulder at the fires and those gathered close to them, swung his head about towards Elinor and Brynmaur.

Elinor stiffened involuntarily. There was not a scrap of cover hereabouts. She and Brynmaur were entirely exposed.

But the guard merely scratched himself some more, his gaze missing them entirely.

'See?' Brynmaur whispered softly in her ear. 'Come on.'

They moved forwards slowly, walking within arm's length of the unseeing sentry. It was the strangest thing, to walk like this past such a wide-awake man and have him look everywhere but at her. Almost, she was tempted to wave her hand in front of his face to see the reaction.

They skirted the fires, cautious still for all that they appeared to be safely unseeable. The men here were as thin and raggedy-looking as the lot they had encountered in the forest. And so silent it made Elinor's skin crawl. There was something most decidedly *wrong* here. No ordinary, healthy folk went about like this, like so many wraiths creeping through the world. She could not hear so much as one voice raised.

Over the hump of turfed ground they went, leaving the camp behind. Elinor slowed, panting. It was suddenly an effort to breathe. The air seemed unaccountably thick and heavy. Something tingled uncomfortably against her sternum.

The Fey-bone amulet she wore came abruptly to life and vibrated with a stinging coldness – as it had back in the Otherwhere when Tancred had drawn near to her.

'Brynmaur . . .' she said uneasily, glancing all about.

'It is the shadow of his *power* you feel,' Brynmaur answered, soft-voiced. 'Only that.'

Elinor shivered. 'He's not . . . not *here* somewhere?' She had one hand to her breast now, feeling the pulse of the Fey-bone, and the other upon her sword's hilt.

'One such as this Tancred alters the world. Like a great weight flung into a pool. The waters shift and flow and curl. We feel that here, as we draw near to him.'

Elinor stared all about. They were entirely alone, or seemed to be. The Tower rose before them, but all around there was only empty sod, with the rise of ground they had walked over at their back. Tancred would have to be cloaked in an enchantment of his own for her to miss seeing him out here. Unsettling thought . . .

'What if he, too, can make himself invisible?' she whispered to Brynmaur.

'I would still be able to see him, I think. He has too much weight to be easily overlookable.'

Elinor nodded, relieved a little. But the Fey-bone still tingled unpleasantly, and she felt her heart thumping. 'He is close, this Tancred. I can feel it. Not actually within sight, perhaps, but *close*.'

Brynmaur agreed soberly. 'I sense it too. But we must go on.'

He was right. Elinor could feel the subtle pull of the world's slope before them. They must trust that. Their way led ahead; that was clear enough.

The Tower loomed before them, rising up into the star-flecked sky. Looking closely, Elinor saw that the large stone blocks of its wall still fitted together with exact precision. Whoever had built it had been – or had commanded – a master stone worker.

'There's a door somewhere,' Elinor said. 'Tancred said Khurdis found it the day he discovered this place.'

'Let us find it for ourselves then,' Brynmaur answered.

They padded around the base of the Tower, peering at it. This far from the firelight, it was hard to make out details. Unless one concentrated, the structure tended to become a solid, dark, seamless column. Elinor had a sudden notion that they would walk round and round and round like this forever, never finding any door, walking and walking until . . .

'Hissst!' Brynmaur breathed sharply in her ear. 'Be careful!'

Elinor blinked.

'Walk like this,' he said, showing her. He took a large step, then a small one, then two quick ones in succession, then a sliding step to the left. 'No pattern to it,' he said. 'Pattern is dangerous in a place like this. One such as Tancred can make use of any pattern you offer him. There will be wardings set about this place.'

Elinor felt a spasm of quick irritation go through her. 'Why didn't you warn me about this before?'

Brynmaur looked at her, surprised. 'I . . . I never thought . . .'

'Brynmaur!' Elinor hissed uneasily. There was a sudden, far-away glaze to his eyes. *'Brynmaur!'*

He blinked and looked at her. 'I had forgotten about such things,' he said softly.

'About *what* things?'

'Patterns and wardings and wheels and such.'

'Wheels?'

'I'm not sure I can explain so that you'd understand.' He stopped her with an impatient motion of his hand. 'Come on. We've got to find this door. It must be about here somewhere.'

'What about sentries?' Elinor asked. 'Once we find this door, will we be able to slip past them unseen?'

'There will be no sentries.'

'How do you know?'

'The warding is all the sentry this place needs. Be careful.'

Onwards they went, slowly.

Round and round and . . .

Elinor shook herself, tried to make sure her steps were random and unpredictable as possible, as Brynmaur had showed her.

It seemed to her that they had been walking for a long time round this dark stone mass. Surely they must have circled it completely by now. Did this door really exist?

Round and round . . .

Perhaps they should just . . .

And then, suddenly, Brynmaur's hand was on her arm, squeezing, and she saw it there before her: a smallish, wooden portal.

As Brynmaur had said, there were no sentries, only the door itself, shoulder-high, perhaps, set into the dark stone of the Tower. Elinor put her hand to it. It felt like ordinary, time-roughened wood, plain and unadorned. On impulse she put her hand – the left one – against the Tower's face next to the doorjamb. The stone felt cold. Her fingers tingled uncomfortably – including the fifth, the little one, that was no longer there. Hastily, she snatched the hand back.

Brynmaur shook his head. 'Be *careful*,' he admonished her.

'I just . . .'

But he had turned from her and was examining the door, murmuring to himself quietly.

Elinor felt a sudden cold shiver go through her for no reason she could make out. The Fey-bone pulsed. Her hand went to her sheathed sword's bronze hilt, and she glanced all about. But there was nobody here save the two of them. The camp and its silent inhabitants were hidden beyond. She could make out nothing more about her than empty sod and dark sky and the Tower itself. But she could not quite shake a feeling of something . . . *wrong*. The skin along her scalp prickled with uncertainty. 'Brynmaur!' she hissed. 'There's—'

He motioned at her for silence. 'Shush! The door seems locked.'

'But—'

'Ah,' he breathed. It swung open with a little soft protest from the old hinges. It was a narrow portal, and none too high, and the opening it left was dark as pitch. A cold draught sighed out of the Tower, smelling of dampness and cold stone and . . . other, less definable things. 'Come on,' Brynmaur whispered and stepped inside, ducking to avoid banging his head on the low lintel.

Leaving her no choice but to follow.

The interior had no light at all once they pulled the door shut behind them. Elinor stumbled into Brynmaur and nearly brought the both of them down.

'What do you think you're *doing*?' he hissed at her. 'Be more careful, can't you!'

She bit back a sharp reply. There was nothing to be gained by snapping at each other. 'Sorry,' she said softly. She wished she could unsheath the white blade and so

341

illumine their way, but it was clearly inappropriate to draw attention to themselves so.

Brynmaur reached back in the utter dark and fumbled along her arm till he found her hand. Taking it up, he said, 'Follow me. Carefully.'

'How do you know where to go?' she whispered, stepping gingerly after him. She could not tell if they walked through a narrow tunnel or a broad, open space, but she was afraid she would smack her head on some unseen thing in the dark and raised her free hand in front of her face.

'One way's as good as another,' was the only answer he gave her and led off, tugging her awkwardly with the random steps he took.

She bit back any questions and let him lead her on – there did not seem much other choice – but her belly was clenched tight as a fist now, and she could feel the blood-pulse hammering in her throat. There was something about this place that made her feel like a rabbit sneaking into a ferret's dark hole.

All about them, the Tower was silent as could be, save for the hiss of their breathing and the little scuffing sounds of their passage.

Onwards they went, slowly, blindly.

Brynmaur's hand felt sweaty in hers. She wanted to let it go for a moment, to wipe her palm on her leg, flex her fingers. But she did not.

It was like a dream this, almost, walking on and on through an endless blackness. It felt like they had crossed far more than the span of the Tower by now. But there was no clear way to measure distance here, nor time, either. Just the walking, made awkward by the shuffle-step Brynmaur insisted on maintaining.

And then, abruptly, there was light before them. After the utter dark, it was so bright it made Elinor's eyes water. She snatched her hand from Brynmaur's and rubbed at them.

Ahead stood a portal of some sort. The light came from beyond it.

Brynmaur, too, was fisting his eyes and blinking. 'Come on,' he urged softly and led the way on.

On the other side of the portal, they found themselves in a large chamber. Hissing globes the size of a man's head hung from the ceiling, radiating an unnatural, colourless light. Before them stood a pair of long trestle tables laden with all manner of peculiar oddments. Elinor glanced about quickly, her hand to her still-sheathed sword, but there seemed no sign of anybody here. Just the empty, silent room.

On the left-hand table, close to the doorway through which they had entered, there was a tall and intricate iron rack which held a series of slim, stoppered bottles of blue glass, each filled with cloudy liquid. Further along lay a heap of raw bone, laid out in a patternless array, some pieces scraped clean and white, other bits still thick with grey-red shreds of fatty meat. A yeasty, decaying scent clung to them.

Further along, there was a gleam of metal, and Elinor saw lengths of bronze sheathing, a mass of twisted copper wires like a torn spider's web. Beyond that lay a heap of wooden slats, the wood unlike any Elinor had ever seen, dark red like old blood, the flow of the woodgrain as starkly defined as if it had been inked on with a pen. Towards the table's end there was an array of glass tubing interconnected in complex ways. Elinor saw a small green flame burning steadily in a socket.

But it was the right-hand table that held Brynmaur's attention.

Several liquid-filled glass jars stood in a row there, large as barrels. Inside these jars there was something floating. Elinor went over for a closer look. They seemed almost like severed, pale hands, those floating things, but boneless, and with far too many fingers. They moved, squirming over each other restlessly in a way that Elinor found disturbing. This close, she could hear the little squishy-splashy sounds of their movement.

'What are they?' she asked of Brynmaur in a whisper.

For a moment, she thought he had not heard her question, for he stood bent over, unmoving, staring at the squirming jar-things. Then he straightened and shuddered. 'I do not know. But they are not natural creatures.'

'They're . . . *alive*, then?'

'In a manner of speaking,' Brynmaur replied. 'Best to leave them well behind us.' He made a curt, encompassing gesture. 'Let's get out of here. There's nothing in this room for the likes of you or me.'

Elinor nodded, agreeing wholeheartedly. The room made her feel a little sick, somehow. There was an aura of old things here, of dark mystery and a groping after . . . she did not know quite what.

They padded along past the tables – with Elinor trying not to look too closely at anything else – until they came to a closed door at the chamber's far end. Brynmaur lifted the iron latch-handle and pulled. The old hinges made a protesting squawk that sounded horribly loud in the silence.

They both froze.

Nothing untoward happened. They padded onwards to find themselves in another chamber, lit by the queer glow-globes, this time set in wall sconces like torches. It was all of bare stone, floor and walls, the ceiling vaulted with age-darkened wooden beams overhead. It had a deserted feel, the air thick with the smell of dust and mould, as if it had stood empty like this for many lives of men.

'This place is *old*,' Elinor breathed.

Brynmaur nodded. 'Old and grim. I shall be glad to be out of here.'

'Me too,' Elinor agreed. She could feel the hairs along her neck prickling. She hoped, indeed, that they *would* be getting out of this dark tower.

Onwards they went, slowly and carefully.

*

In the next room there was but a single glow-globe. A curving stairway led upwards into darkness.

Elinor gestured questioningly.

Brynmaur nodded and started up.

The steps were of stone, worn hollow by the passage of many feet. Elinor could not help but wonder who had walked this way before her. Had they felt anything like the same unease she did now?

It was not a particularly long flight of steps, and they emerged onto the next floor soon enough, finding themselves in yet another silent, empty chamber. Was this whole place deserted, then? But the Fey-bone still quivered disquieteningly at her breast, so Tancred must be about, somewhere.

There was no lighting here, but a wash of radiance flowed in from an open portal to their left. Carefully they padded along towards it.

The room beyond was lit by more glow-globes. The floor was stone, as all the flooring had been thus far, but in the centre of this chamber there was a largish circle constructed of intricately patterned blocks of varying colours – though the pale light of the glow-globes seemed to drain the natural colour from things, rendering the floor pattern in shades of faintly tinted greys.

Elinor stared at that patterning. At first glance, it seemed an intricate spiral, winding in from the circle's periphery to the centre. But it was not that simple, she saw. For there was also another spiral working outwards, so that her eye was drawn in the two directions at once. It made her shivery-dizzy.

'Don't look too close,' Brynmaur cautioned.

Elinor shook herself.

He put a hand on her shoulder. 'Come along.'

They started on, and Elinor walked across the edge of that patterned circle, it being in her path. As she trod upon it though, she felt herself drawn forcibly into a kind of stuttering half-step, her right foot skipping from one dark stone floor-slab to another, her left only on the lighter-coloured ones.

Brynmaur gave her a sharp shove, knocking her off the circle and breaking the rhythm of everything.

'Be careful,' he hissed. 'Remember what I said: pattern. All pattern here is potentially of this Tancred's ordering.'

Elinor shivered and nodded. Her feet were throbbing unpleasantly. 'What would have happened if you hadn't . . .'

Brynmaur shrugged. 'Nothing good.'

Elinor started onwards again, forcing her feet to keep a random step. Halfway across the room, she stopped, uncertain. In the centre of the circle there stood four columns of red stone, forming a square.

They had not been there when she and Brynmaur first entered. She was sure of that.

They stood there now, twice her own height and nearly as thick around as her waist. At first she had thought them round, but they were rectangular. Along the face of each there was an intricate network of bas-relief carvings. She started to go closer to look, but Brynmaur pulled her back.

'Do not go near,' he said.

'What are they?'

'I am not sure. I think . . .'

'Think what?'

'Come along,' was all he said, gesturing her to him. 'But carefully. We are drawing closer to the heart of this place, and to this Tancred.'

Elinor nodded, feeling it too. She followed after, trying to keep her attention on him rather than the room about her. Brynmaur seemed not to be having the sort of difficulties here that she did. He walked purposefully through, as if it were any ordinary series of rooms they traversed. She envied him.

Into the next chamber they went, and here, for the first time, they encountered normal lighting. A series of tall candelabra lined the walls, set in a sort of rampart almost waist-high that ringed the room like a fence. It was of dark wood, this rampart, and covered with a tanglewood of carved, serpentine shapes.

Like all the others, this chamber, too, was empty. The flickering candlelight danced their two shadows across the walls.

'Isn't there *anybody* here, then?' Elinor said softly.

Brynmaur made no reply. His attention was fixed on a sort of dais that lay before them at the chamber's far end. Upon this dais there was a large, ornate chair constructed of wood and metal and bone. It shone.

'*His* seat,' Brynmaur said.

The chair fit so perfectly into its setting that it had to be as old as the rest of this place, but it had been polished and carefully cleaned, and it gleamed now as if it were brand new.

Elinor glancing about uneasily. She did not like this. The room had an eerie feel to it. The Fey-bone vibrated uncomfortably against her sternum with increased force.

Brynmaur, too, was staring about uneasily. 'I think . . .' he began.

The room exploded suddenly with hissing light.

A sharp stab of cold pain went through Elinor from the Fey-bone and she cried out, her hand going to her sword's hilt. Her vision was filled with writhing serpents of light. A formless, murmuring sound rose and fell all about her. She shook her head, blinking furiously, trying to force sense upon her surroundings.

And then it all cleared and she saw Tancred/Khurdis seated there before them upon the chair.

He was dressed in a long, flowing garment of shining cloth unlike anything Elinor had ever seen before. It hung in scintillating folds from his throat down to his feet, with long, voluminous sleeves and a high collar. Only his head and hands showed clear.

Elinor blinked, shivering. The Fey-bone pulsed painfully.

Tancred/Khurdis smiled, his dark eyes burning bright and hard as he gazed at them. He looked like the Khurdis Elinor remembered from her encounter at Woburn Village, save that his head was glistening and hairless (as had been the head of Tancred/Khurdis as she had faced him in the Otherwhere) and his face was so gaunt as to be nearly skeletal. The face of a man in an extremity of fever, it seemed, pale and drawn. Yet for all that, Tancred/Khurdis looked down upon Brynmaur and her with the same supreme arrogance he had evidenced in the Otherwhere.

The more she looked upon him, however, the more convinced she became that there was something deeply wrong in the face he showed them. It twitched, as if another expression entirely were trying to break through the grim satisfaction she saw writ there. And though Tancred/Khurdis was sitting in what appeared to be a comfortable, confident pose upon the chair, his fingers were trembling noticeably and he kept shifting position in little jerks.

'Well . . .' he said. It was the voice of Khurdis as Elinor recalled, an ordinary man's voice. There was a subtle depth of threat to it, though, that made her recoil.

Abruptly, the lighting in the chamber dimmed. The air seemed to thicken and Elinor found herself gasping to get breath. A painful spasm convulsed her limbs. At her side, she heard Brynmaur grunt softly.

The light resumed. Elinor found herself on her knees, though how she had got there she could not seem to recall. Brynmaur was still on his feet, pale-faced, but standing firm.

'Well . . .' Tancred/Khurdis said again, eyeing him. 'You are a man of surprises.'

Brynmaur said nothing.

'But not too many surprises. You escape one prison only to come stumbling into another. You made my life simple, man. I knew you would come to me. I did not even need to entice you. Ahh . . . what it is to be such a predictable creature.'

Still Brynmaur kept silent.

Tancred/Khurdis shrugged. 'Have it your way, then, man. I hoped we could talk. But . . .' He shrugged again, then raised his hand in a sudden gesture.

From behind the waist-high wooden rampart that encircled the chamber, a crowd of armed men appeared.

For a long, unpleasant moment, Elinor did not know what to think. They seemed some fell host, somehow reanimated out of the far past, for they were dressed in fantastic garb, all glimmering scale-mail and monstrous helms and barbed and glinting blades. But no . . . It was, she realised, merely a gang of the same sort of rag-tag folk they had passed in the lean-to camp outside the Tower. The men's armour was ill-fitting, and they swung their weapons about with no skill whatsoever. She looked to see a leader amongst them, somebody of greater stature or skill, or better fitting armour. But there was none. Where was this Lord Jossa, then? Perhaps he was mere myth after all.

She could not help but wonder fleetingly if poor Pawli were not one of this group, but what with the helms and all, she could not tell.

Despite themselves, the armed men were still an impressive lot in their way. Their scale-mail armour might not fit right, but the metal of it had been lacquered different colours and cleaned recently, so that it gleamed blood-red and gold, emerald-green and glossy black, bone-white, deep blue, and half a dozen other hues in the dance of the candlelight. The helms they wore had been fashioned into the likenesses of snarling beasts, great cat and bear and hound, but also others less recognisable, dragonish and monstrous. Their blades were all barb and hook, intricate razor-filigree and embossed iron, glinting and flashing coldly.

Rattling their weapons across the walls, on the wood of

the rampart, against their own armour and shields, the men made a sullen, ringing racket. Shouts and jeers went up.

Tancred/Khurdis lifted a hand and they went abruptly silent. He smiled. 'I was expecting you, you see,' he said to Brynmaur and Elinor. His face twitched and he clamped his teeth together with such sudden force that Elinor heard them go *klikk!* quite distinctly. He gestured at the armed and armoured men. 'This is your welcoming committee.'

Elinor reached to draw her sword.

Tancred/Khurdis held up his hand. 'Wait. Let us not rush into unnecessary violence. There are other ways than the spilling of blood to resolve things here.'

Ellnor did not know quite what to think. She stood unmoving, her hand on the sword's dragon hilt. She glanced across at Brynmaur, but he had eyes only for Tancred/Khurdis.

'I offer you an . . . arrangement,' Tancred/Khurdis said. 'You are no true threat to me, you two. Your fang, girl, I can draw easily enough – as I once told you. And as for you, Brynmaur . . . Well, we both know you have neither the strength nor the knowledge to stand against me. So . . .' He steepled his fingers before him, elbows on the chair's arms. It was an attitude of power, but, as before, Elinor saw his hands tremoring.

'So . . .' he went on, 'being a merciful man, I will allow you to walk away from here, entirely unscathed.'

Leaning forwards, he fixed his attention upon Brynmaur. 'The girl here need only lay down her weapon. The two of you must swear never to cross my path again, nor my designs. Do this . . . and you may walk away. Free.'

'No!' Elinor cried. There was no hint here of the black, implacable bitterness against Brynmaur that had been so plain in the Otherwhere, but she knew it would be there. He was dissembling. 'Don't trust him, Brynmaur.'

'Quiet!' Tancred/Khurdis snapped.

350

Suddenly, Elinor found it hard to get breath. The Fey-bone flared at her breast. She clutched at her throat, gasping.

'That's better,' Tancred/Khurdis said, nodding. 'Now . . . where were we, Brynmaur? What do you say to my offer, then? Do you accept? The girl here is comely in a skinny, hard-boned way. You might take her as companion and live out the rest of your days quietly enough, causing nobody any grief. Your own self not least of all.'

Brynmaur said nothing.

'Come now, don't be foolish.' Tancred/Khurdis leaned forwards, beckoning. 'Khurdis remembers you well enough. You were never a man with big dreams. You can walk away from this now, safe and sound. No bloodshed. No hurt for anyone. Walk away and build a little cabin some-place new. You are a small fish, Brynmaur, drowning in a sea far too huge for you. You have not the strength to con-tend with me. You know it. I know it. Walk away. There is no other safe option. Walk away with my blessings. Walk away . . .'

'No . . .' Elinor managed to croak.

Tancred/Khurdis cast a venomous look at her. 'I told *you* to be quiet.'

Once again, Elinor felt the choking sensation. The Fey-bone pulsed painfully.

'Well?' Tancred/Khurdis enquired. 'What is your an-swer?'

Elinor saw Brynmaur step forwards. His shoulders were slumped and he looked old and most weary. By contrast, Tancred/Khurdis seemed all strength and confidence, a man in the prime of his years, with vision and ability, a man who could move the world to his own ordering, who could . . .

'You must cease all this,' Brynmaur said.

Elinor saw Tancred/Khurdis blink, surprised. 'Oh, really?' he enquired after a long moment.

'Really,' Brynmaur returned with quiet force.

Tancred/Khurdis smiled, but the twitch was back in his face again. His head jerked in a little spasm. 'And what if I . . . demur? Just how are you going to set about forcing your will upon me?'

Brynmaur shrugged, but he did not look away.

Tancred/Khurdis smiled again, a mere stretch of skin over teeth. 'You have no low estimation of yourself, man. Pity you cannot come up to your own expectations.'

Tancred/Khurdis rose from his chair. His long robe caught the light and shone like finely polished metal. The eyes in his haggard, skull-like face burned. Raising both his hands, fingers flexed in an odd manner, he brought them down in a hard, sharp motion.

Brynmaur's limbs convulsed.

Elinor felt the very air of the room dim and go cold.

Again, Tancred/Khurdis brought his hands down.

Brynmaur shuddered. He took a faulty step forwards, two back.

Tancred/Khurdis brought his hands down a third time, and Brynmaur dropped to his knees, groaning.

Elinor gulped air as best she could, feeling her own limbs shake. She reached for her sword, but fruitlessly. Somehow, every time her hand went for the hilt, it slid past and wound up flapping uselessly in mid-air. She bit her lip in anger. She would not – would *not* – let this Tancred get the better of her so easily.

Gathering every bit of will she could, she stared at her right hand, flexing the fingers purposefully, first one then the next and the next, making a fist, feeling the dig of her nails against her palm. Then, slowly, with all the deliberation she could muster, she reached for the bronze dragon hilt.

It was like being in a dream in which she attempted to do something but, try as she might, she could not . . .

But she was utterly determined that she *would*.

On instinct, she reached with her left hand for the Fey-bone underneath her shirt, still pulsing in response to

Tancred's presence. The hard little form of it felt good under her fingers . . .

She felt the familiar solidity of the sword's dragon-hilt brush her right palm. Slowly, fighting to keep focused, feeling the Fey-bone shiver, willing her hand, which kept trying to slip away and flutter off like some wayward bird, to keep still, she reached . . .

And then she had it.

There was nothing more wonderful than the welcoming thrill of the sword-strength as it surged up through her limbs. She whipped the blade through the air, the radiance of it shining like a beacon.

The scale-mail armoured men cried out in sudden consternation.

She saw Brynmaur on his knees before Tancred/Khurdis, struggling and defiant still. Tancred/Khurdis was hunched over him, his haggard face twisted up, his hands twitching.

'Enough!' Elinor shouted.

Tancred/Khurdis flung himself about, staring at her. 'You *dare*!' he hissed. He thrust at her with his right hand, as if he held some dangerous thing which he had thrown. She felt an impact upon her, like a great weight of sand. But the white blade came up of its own accord, it seemed, and cut through the air in an intricate pattern that was none of her devising. The unseen weight that had been upon her dropped away.

Tancred/Khurdis stared, his hands jittering spastically.

Brynmaur rose unsteadily to his feet. 'It is . . . *you* who have not the power,' he said hoarsely to Tancred/Khurdis. 'Look at you! You shake and quiver like one with the ague. The mortal body will not stand it, man. Can't you *feel* what you are doing?'

Tancred/Khurdis turned on him. 'What would the likes of you know about *power*? I can make this body do whatever I wish it to. It is mine, now and forever.'

But Brynmaur shook his head. 'It will never be yours

and you know it. Look at how your hands quiver. And your face . . . Listen to me! You must abandon this madness before you kill the poor man you have infested. Your time is *over*, Tancred. You must accept that. You can only bring more grief into the world through this unnatural action. Grief to yourself as well as others. You must not—'

'Be *QUIET*!' Tancred/Khurdis roared. 'You know *nothing*, you ignorant country lout! You have neither the strength nor the wisdom to—'

'*I* have the strength.' Elinor interrupted.

Tancred/Khurdis looked at her.

She took a step towards him, another.

'Jossa!' Tancred/Khurdis called out. 'To me!'

A man stepped forth from somewhere behind the chair at Tancred/Khurdis's back.

He was not an especially tall man, nor heavy. But there was a solidity to him that made Elinor think of heavy, hard rock.

He stood, feet apart, one hand upon the hilt of the sword that was belted to his waist. It was of simple workmanship, that blade, and somewhat at odds with the rest of his apparel, which was all spotlessly clean and very fine. He wore knee-high, black leather boots, tight-fitting leather leggings stitched with metal plating, a scale-mail hauberk. The leggings were a dark blue, like a last glimpse of evening sky. The scale-mail shone like purest new silver. His hands were gauntleted to the elbows, his upper arms and shoulders padded with leather-and-metal guards.

But it was the helm he wore that riveted Elinor's attention.

It was constructed of brass and horn and wood and iron, all intricately interwoven to form the visage of a great cat, mouth open in a snarling howl. So carefully crafted was it that virtually none of the face which it protected could be seen. And so perfect was the likeness the helm had been fashion into that, at moments, the very head of a great cat seemed to sit alive upon his shoulders.

It was most disconcerting.

'So . . .' he said softly, in a voice that rang like iron. 'Have you come to enter my service then, like the rest?'

Elinor stared at him. So this was the Lord Jossa. She wondered where he had come from. He was impressive enough in his own way, she supposed. She could see how the shattered men such as she had met would be drawn to such a one. But she felt the sword-strength thrilling through her and knew that she could take a man like this – no matter how impressive he might look.

'I have come to end your service,' she said. She stepped towards him, the white blade up.

He drew the sword that hung at his waist slowly, as if relishing the effect it would have. It was a little broader than her white blade, and a little longer, though not by much. And no ordinary blade at all . . . The length of it glowed a bright red, as if it had been lifted from the forge only scant instants before. The air about it shimmered in heat waves.

'Come to me, then,' he said, beckoning her. 'Come and be greeted by my blade.' He hefted the thing. The air about it *sizzled* softly. 'Blaze, it is named. A *special* weapon.' He held it in a two-handed grip and swung it hard through the air, leaving a smoking trail.

Elinor swallowed. In all her days wielding the white blade, she had never faced a opponent such as this. She wondered uneasily what would happen when her blade and his touched.

'Come, girl,' he said. 'Or are you afraid?'

She was. He was utterly beyond anything she had ever faced before. But she was not about to concede any such thing to the likes of him. Carefully, she padded forwards, the white blade up and ready.

He was upon her, then, in an astounding rush.

The dreadful speed and strength of it nearly undid her

entirely. His smoking blade was smashing against hers almost before she knew what was happening. Only instinct saved her from instant disaster. She could feel the searing heat of his blade upon her cheek, so close did it come to her.

But he was . . . clumsy.

He swung the red-hot blade as if it were a stick, smashing and thumping at her with no finesse at all. If it were not for the brute strength and unnatural speed of him, she would finish this easily. But for all his apparent lack of any real swordsmanship, he *was* unbelievably strong, and fast as thought.

The white blade made her stronger and quicker than any ordinary person. But this Jossa was quicker still, and far, far more strong. He danced and leaped about her, hewing and cutting in his clumsy way, but each hack *kerwanged* against her blade like a great hammer blow, the shock shivering painfully through the bones of her arms and into her shoulders.

It was like nothing she had ever experienced.

And he showed no sign of slowing. Beat and cut and hack, the blows fell upon her from all sides, and it was all she could do to fend them off.

Then, abruptly, he backed away and stood looking at her – or, rather, the snarling visage of a great cat looked at her, balefully.

Elinor took a gasping breath. Her arms were shaking and sore, her heart hammering wildly.

Jossa laughed. He leaped abruptly into the air and the uncanny vitality that filled him took him nearly his own height off the ground, the cherry-bladed sword smoking as it cut the air. 'I am Lord Jossa,' he cried, landing on his feet again. 'Look upon me and despair!'

Elinor swallowed and tried to brace herself as he came at her again.

This time she almost had him, for she was beginning to catch the weakness in his hack-and-hew style of swordsmanship. With every stroke, he extended himself to the limit, and at the apex of each stroke he left himself vulnerable for just an instant. She bided her time, fending off the terrible force of his blows until her opportunity appeared. Then, with a fast thrust, she had him in the side, in his ribs.

But the white blade skittered across the scale-mail he wore in a spray of bright sparks. Jossa roared, turning, and smashed her across the side of her head with a gauntleted hand.

It was only the back of his hand that hit her, but it felt as if she had been kicked by a horse. The sword went spilling from her hands and she collapsed, reeling.

Jossa laughed.

Tancred/Khurdis did. 'So much for your bright fang, girl,' he said.

Elinor stared about her, her head ringing. She could hardly believe it as Jossa scooped up her blade and handed it across to Tancred/Khurdis. She struggled up, trying to stop him, but the room reeled about her and she stumbled awkwardly.

'Take·her!' Tancred/Khurdis commanded.

The next thing Elinor knew, half a dozen men were upon her and had stripped her of rucksack and water flask and scabbard. Then they brought her hands up behind her back and bound them together tightly with thick cord. When they had done, they flung her to the floor in front of Tancred/Khurdis, who stood before the chair, the naked white blade in one hand, the crimson scabbard in the other.

She saw other men jerk Brynmaur's travel bag off him, take his water flask, tie his hands as hers were, and dump him to the floor.

Tancred/Khurdis swung the white blade in an inexpert, enthusiastic arc, his face alight with raw triumph and sword-strength. Then, quickly, he sheathed the sword and sat down. 'Old Cimon did good work,' he said.

Elinor only stared.

'I told you I knew the maker of this blade. He was . . . an interesting man.' Tancred/Khurdis lifted the sheathed blade from his lap and held it aloft. 'Mine now. A clever toy.'

Elinor stuttered.

'Oh, yes, girl. A toy. No more. Cimon was clever, but not *that* clever. I am quite capable of making my own version of such a toy. As you have seen . . .' He gestured at the cherry-glowing blade still in the Lord Jossa's hand. 'Sheath it now,' he ordered. Lord Jossa did.

Tancred/Khurdis shifted his grip upon the sheath so that the hilt came up, the bronze dragon's head of it gleaming in the candlelight. 'There is a . . . how ought I to put it for you? There is a . . . *presence* in the hilt here. Something alive and yet not truly alive. Not especially difficult to do if you know how.'

Elinor's head throbbed painfully. Her arms hurt. Her hands did, where the binding cords were beginning to bite. She still could not quite believe what had happened to her. On the hard stone floor near her, Brynmaur lay staring up at Tancred/Khurdis, teeth bared through his beard like an animal facing its death.

'And so it ends,' Tancred/Khurdis said. 'It was stupid of you to walk in here like this, lacking the strength to oppose me.' He shrugged. 'Even then . . . You ought to have taken my offer when you had the chance.'

'You would never have honoured it,' Brynmaur returned, his voice no more than a hoarse whisper.

Tancred/Khurdis shrugged. 'Perhaps not. But things might have gone easier for you.' He gestured, and the armed and armoured men gathered close about. 'Take them up,' he ordered. 'It is time to . . . *eliminate* them.'

Elinor was hauled roughly to her feet and dragged off, Brynmaur behind her. Tancred/Khurdis strutted ahead, the white blade hanging in its scabbard at his waist now, half-hidden by the flowing folds of the robe he wore. Out the door of the chamber he went, with Lord Jossa, the armed men, Elinor and Brynmaur and all perforce trooping after.

XXIX

The men holding Elinor were clumsy, getting in each other's way trying to push and haul her along. As they all squeezed through the doorway, she managed to bite one of them, hard, on the forearm. He swore and smacked her across the mouth with a gauntleted hand, leaving her with a split lip and making her sore head ring like a cracked bell.

The chamber into which they emerged was the one with the spiral-patterned circle and the four stone columns in the centre of the floor. Tancred/Khurdis halted several paces before the periphery of that disorienting circle pattern, Lord Jossa at his side.

Brynmaur was staring at the columns, shivering.

'Yes,' Tancred/Khurdis said. He smiled. 'It is a Bridge. Exactly as you fear.'

Brynmaur said nothing.

'I also knew the man who had this tower constructed, you see,' Tancred/Khurdis went on. 'Mantas, his name was. He, too, was a clever soul in his way. Though of limited vision and too small-minded. They were his passion, the lamellar thresholds.'

Elinor only stared. Brynmaur might understand what Tancred/Khurdis was talking about, but she did not. She had no clue how four stone columns could be considered a 'bridge', nor what 'lamellar thresholds' might be.

Tancred/Khurdis was gazing at the columns. 'They were never my speciality, the thresholds. All most fascinating, to be sure. But I had other plans, back then . . .'

He paused for a moment. A shadow passed across his face, and he doubled over suddenly, grunting, as if somebody had just kicked him in the guts. He straightened up with an obvious effort, fists and jaw clenched, gasping and jerking. Slowly his face settled again. 'It was . . . long and long ago,' he went on, as if there had been no interruption. 'All the plans I once nurtured came to naught.' His face clenched again momentarily.

'But now . . . now I have a second opportunity. And Mantas, who was no friend to me or mine back then, has supplied me with the means to pursue new ambitions.' Tancred/Khurdis clapped his hands softly. 'In fact, perhaps this has all worked out for the best after all. One never knows. The world is such a wayward, hard-to-predict place. There were restrictions upon me back in my old life. Now . . . well, there is none living now who can oppose me. There is no limit to what I might be able to accomplish. You have witnessed only the barest of beginnings.'

'You have done a terrible thing,' Brynmaur spoke up, 'using this Bridge as you have to bring such fell creatures as you have into the world.'

'I have done what I deemed necessary to create an . . . appropriate climate in the land hereabouts in order to bring men in to me. The Lord Jossa needs followers if he is to become great.'

'These are not followers,' Brynmaur said, gesturing with his bearded chin to the raggedy, armed men. 'They are slaves.'

'Not at all,' Tancred/Khurdis replied. 'They have all come here of their own free accord, in search of a man to lead them. The Lord Jossa is just such a man.'

The Lord Jossa stood like a statue, unmoving.

'Under the Lord Jossa,' Tancred/Khurdis went on, 'with me as his advisor, of course, these men will help create a great realm. The Domain of the Tower! Like one of the ancient Domains, it shall be, with all the greatness that once was, revered and feared by all for many, many lives of men.'

Tancred/Khurdis's face was clenched and twisted, his eyes burning with a dark, fanatic fire. Elinor shuddered. Brynmaur had said that Tancred would try to live out old habit patterns. Here was the proof before her now: the ancient Seer intent upon reproducing the world he had once known – with a blatant ruthlessness beyond anything Elinor had ever conceived.

'You're mad,' Brynmaur said. 'You cannot recreate the past.'

Tancred/Khurdis only laughed. 'You have the blinkered vision of a stunted soul. No wonder you have made such a useless mess of what gifts were granted you.' He lifted his arm, then, so that the long sleeve of his robe fell back and his hand and forearm came free. Holding the hand up in front of his face, he flexed and curled the fingers. 'I, however, know *exactly* what to do – and how to do it. What a wonderful, empty world to be re-born into, and such a nice, youthful form, too. And all thanks to you. If you had not driven poor Khurdis to an extremity of humiliation as you did, he would never have ventured as far he did, and I would not be standing here now, back in the world.'

Elinor felt sick at his boastings, his mad vision, at the way he took joy in lording it over them.

'And now,' Tancred/Khurdis said, fixing his dark gaze upon Brynmaur, 'the time has come to reward you for the service you have rendered me.' His face grew tight, and he twitched in a series of little spasms. 'Khurdis bears you little love, man, and I have no reason to protect you. You have no value whatsoever to me. So we shall send you . . . away. Only, this time, there will be no possibility of return. I have chosen your prison with some care. A hard place, yes, but one in which a man of your skills and knowledge can survive for a considerable long time. In fact, I am counting on you doing just that. For the . . . sport of it. I will be observing you whenever I can.'

Tancred/Khurdis smiled. 'As for your companion, however—' He gestured towards Elinor. 'This one may yet prove a useful tool.'

'Don't count on it!' Elinor snapped at him, glaring what defiance she could.

Tancred/Khurdis merely smiled the more. 'Such fire in her. Good! Nothing makes better raw material than a young, wilful soul.'

This was not the first time in her life that Elinor had found herself a helpless captive. But the process did not grow any easier with familiarity. She knew from experience how likely it was that she would be able to resist a man such as this Tancred. There were simply too many ways to break a person – pain and delusion and hope and fear. She would not fool herself with false optimisms. Which left . . .

She did nor know what. But she was determined not to allow herself to fall meekly into Tancred/Khurdis's ungentle hold. The Lord Jossa had been standing all this while at Tancred/Khurdis's side entirely unmoving, in a stiff stance that seemed far from comfortable – as if he were not a real man at all, but some man-sized marionette that moved only when ordered to. She shuddered, thinking of what might lie in store for her.

Tancred/Khurdis, meanwhile, had produced a slim, complicated metal contraption from out of his robe. Pointing this at the four stone columns, he muttered something under his breath. His features went rigid. The sinews on his neck knotted up. His face drained of colour. Thin blue veins popped into life on his temple and he began to tremor.

For an instant, Elinor's heart leaped with sudden hope. Perhaps he had attempted something too much for him. Perhaps he would . . .

But no.

A faint beam of blue radiance shot from the metal contraption in Tancred/Khurdis's hand. The air shivered. The stone columns came to sudden life, taking on the same manner of blue glow that had shot from the contraption in his hand. The chamber filled with a deep, throbbing *hrummm*.

'He built well, did old Mantas,' Tancred/Khurdis said with some satisfaction. 'All these long years; and everything still works as perfectly as one could desire.'

There was something like a curtain of blue light strung between the pillars now. It shimmered and danced, as if it were falling liquid – yet it was not liquid and it did not fall. The air close about it *krakkled* softly. The encircling pattern on the floor had become a glowing spiral leading towards it like a walkway; pulling at the eye and the mind.

Elinor still did not grasp how any of this could be considered a 'bridge'. The pillars seemed entirely self-contained. The light-curtain that hung between them seemed to shut them off from the rest of the room.

Tancred/Khurdis motioned to the men holding Brynmaur. They hauled him towards the leading edge of the blue-glowing floor path spiral. Brynmaur struggled desperately in their hold, but with his arms bound as they were there was little he could do.

Nor Elinor. The cords were so tight, she could feel her hands beginning to go numb.

The *hrumming* noise filled all the room now, making Elinor's teeth vibrate uncomfortably. The blue radiance washed over everything, staining face and blade, cuirass and robe, all the same tint. The armed gathering of men stood staring, faces wide and awestruck, weapons all but forgotten now in limp hands.

The four columns were grown brighter and brighter, the *hrummm* more encompassing. The curtain of blue light that linked them jumped and spilled, like a sheet of palpable liquid plummeting out of, and disappearing into, nothingness.

'Closer!' Tancred/Khurdis ordered the men holding Brynmaur. He had to shout to make himself clear. 'Take him to the pathway!'

The *hrummm* was becoming more high-pitched now, painful to the ear and the bones of the skull. Elinor could feel her hair begin to lift. Green-blue sparks leaped from one man about her to the next. There were yelps and grunts and little shrieks. Several dropped their weapons on the stone paving of the floor and fled the room.

Tancred/Khurdis was laughing. He did something with the metallic contraption he still held in his hand, and the blue curtain of radiance about the columns leaped up in a flare of such bright suddenty that it left Elinor momentarily white-blind, all detail submerged in a painful blue-white after-image.

'Propel him along the pathway!' she heard Tancred/Khurdis shout.

Then, a few moments later, 'Do it, I say!'

Blinking furiously, her eyes streaming, Elinor tried to make some sense of what was happening.

Brynmaur and the four men guarding him were locked in a tangle on the edge of the floor-circle facing one of the streaming light-curtains that connected the columns. The men were attempting to thrust him onto the spiralling pathway. He was resisting with a desperate strength.

'*Do it!*' Tancred/Khurdis shrieked.

Brynmaur struggled, kicking and biting, but Elinor could see it was no use. He simply did not have the strength to resist the combined force of four men.

All about her, men were gazing, transfixed by the scene: the struggling figures silhouetted against the bright curtain of blue, the columns themselves, glowing and humming like live things almost, the very air in the room acrackle with a raw . . . something. Elinor's hair danced crazily about her head, and the tiny hairs along her arms prickled.

From their looks of frightened amazement, she was sure none of those gathered here properly understood what was happening. She herself did not. But if those columns truly formed some manner of 'bridge', then Brynmaur was somehow being *sent* somewhere.

'Force him onwards!' Tancred/Khurdis cried. 'Fools!' He twisted the contraption in his hand so that the spiral pathway blazed and the columns began to vibrate until they fairly sang, a rising, shrill pulse that hurt so it felt to Elinor as if somebody were driving a spike through her skull from front to back. She screamed. Everyone in the room screamed.

She felt the grip of those guarding her slacken.

With a desperate heave, she burst away from them and staggered towards the columns, hands still tight-bound behind her back. She could make out the glitter of naked blades, the shimmer of the too-bright blue radiance on polished helm and breastplate. A man came at her, spear out. She ducked his clumsy thrust, shouldered the spear aside, and kicked him as hard as she could in the groin. He folded, clutching himself, groaning.

Twisting round in furious haste, she half-fell, clutching the spear head and slicing it clumsily across the cords that bound her wrists. The ropes shredded away, and she grabbed up the spear shaft as best she could in her numbed hands.

She charged on, knocking two men down, thwacking another alongside the head with the spear butt. It was a disturbing-strange sensation to be fighting thus without the aid of the sword's strength. She felt clumsy and weak-limbed and slow. Her heart was hammering fit to burst and her lungs burned.

A new man leaped towards her, shouting, and she stabbed at him, taking him in the belly with a hard *thwonk!* The scale-mail cuirass he wore stopped the spear's blade from doing any real damage, and the force of the blow nearly tore the spear from her hands – she had inadvertently cut herself when severing the cords, and her hold on the spear shaft was now blood-slippery. Only just did she manage to hang on, spinning round, stumbling away . . .

And then she was nearly upon Brynmaur and the men trying to force him onto the blazing pathway.

'No!' she heard Tancred/Khurdis cry. 'Stop her, you idiots!'

The anxious fury in Tancred/Khurdis's voice goaded her to more effort, and she sprinted the last few feet.

The light-curtain was so blindingly bright now that she could hardly make out more than vague, shifting shapes ahead of her. Spear up like a staff, she charged, howling.

She had intended to smash into them obliquely, spilling them aside and thus freeing Brynmaur, but she had gained more momentum than she thought, or the spiral floor-patter somehow betrayed her, pulling her steps, or something . . . for she hit the clustered men straighter and far harder than she had anticipated, propelling them all backwards in a tumbling mass – them and herself and Brynmaur, too – across the floor-circle's threshold.

The blazing pathway sucked them all along like a river, delivering them to the *krakkling* blue barrier strung between the closest pair of pillars. For a long, hanging moment, they struggled on the brink there, a tangle of arms and legs and weapons, shouting and shrieking and grunting.

And then they broke through coruscating, blinding radiance and were plunged irrevocably *beyond* . . .

XXX

It hurt more than anything Elinor had ever experienced.

Like having each and every sinew stripped individually from her limbs and replaced with white-hot wires. Like having her muscles torn out in long, ripping flaps. Like having molten metal poured through the marrow of her bones. Like being boiled in a great kettle till the meat began to shred from her steaming skeleton. Like . . .

Somebody was screaming.

Aieieeeeee!!!!

Her skull felt as if a sharp iron wedge had been driven into it. She shuddered, gasped, tried to open her eyes and make some manner of sense of her surroundings.

There was darkness all about, a faint greenish radiance off up above somewhere.

Aieieeeeeeee!!! the screaming went on. There was a scuffling sound in the dark, a deep grunt.

Aieieeee! eeeeee—

Silence.

She heard somebody moan, very soft.

'Wha . . . what happened?' a voice said hoarsely.

And then, 'Elinor?'

'Brynmaur!' Elinor felt a wash of relief go through her. 'Where are you?'

'Here,' he responded weakly in the dark.

She was on her back, she realised, sprawled upon what felt like chill, coarse-grassed ground. She tried to get up and found that each movement provoked a flare of agony in her limbs. She heard the little sounds of others trying to move, grunts and curses and the pop and crack of ill-used joints. 'Brynmaur?' she said softly.

'Over here.'

On her hands and knees, she felt about, bumping into one man but knowing him for one of the guards by the feel of the scale-mail that clothed him. Then Brynmaur was before her, all but unseeable in the dark, but she could feel his bound hands and knew it for him.

She had left the spear behind somewhere and had to go back for it, scrabbling about in the darkness with her sore hands – cut and blood-wet still from where she had hacked away the chords that had bound her – muttering curses, till eventually she felt the shaft under her fingers. Working with clumsy care, she managed to saw the ropes off Brynmaur's wrists and set him free.

He groaned and sighed, rubbing his hands.

'What's happened?' she asked him, whispering, for there was something about this dark place that made her want to attract as little notice as possible. 'Where *are* we?'

'In some . . . *other* land,' he answered softly, confirming her fears.

There was a sudden scuffing sound, and they froze.

'Tha . . . that you, Kyllie?' one of their erstwhile guards asked out of the darkness in a shaken voice.

'No,' came the reply. 'It's me, Tuck. I'm over here, against the rocks.'

'What rocks?'

'Here, you fool!'

'It's black as pitch here. I can't hardly see my own hand in front of my face, never mind your stinking rocks!'

The guards did not keep their voices down, and though Elinor could see nothing more of them than mere, half-guessed shapes in the darkness, she could hear them plain as plain

'Where's Borth gone, then?' one of them demanded.

A third voice, hoarse and shaken, replied, 'Something took him.'

'What do you mean . . . something *took* him? Kyllie, that you? Where are you?'

'Didn't you hear him screaming? Some . . . *thing* came up out of the dark and took him.' The man's voice was grown quivery-high and strained. 'Like . . . like some great hairy lizard, it was. With eyes that glowed. I only saw it 'cause of its eyes. Nearly took *me*, it did. Went for poor Borth at the last instant. Over the rocks and into the dark out there, with him screaming so . . . Wha . . . what manner of place *is* this?'

'Now, Kyllie, you sure Borth isn't just—'

'Borth's taken! I swear it, I do! There was this huge, horrible . . . *thing* that came and took him away.' The man sobbed. 'Didn't you *hear* the poor bastard screaming?'

'Where are we?' another of the guards put in querulously. 'What's *happened*? I feel . . . *strange*.'

Indeed, Elinor felt none too steady herself. Her limbs were all quivery, as if she were running a fever, and she seemed to be finding it hard to keep her thoughts together.

'We have been sent to . . . to another land,' Brynmaur said, loud enough for them all to hear clearly. His voice was cracked and exhausted.

Shocked silence from the guards.

Then, 'It's *him*!' one of them said.

'Stay away from me, you,' another declared.

Elinor heard the soft rasp of metal.

'I've a good sharp blade here. Come anywhere near me, sorcerer, and I'll stick it right through you. So help me, I will!'

Brynmaur laughed a soft, shaky laugh. 'I'm the least of your troubles, man.'

'Don't trust him, Tuck,' a voice said. 'You remember what Lord Jossa's Seer said about him.'

'I remember all right. Won't find me trusting the likes of him. No fear of that.'

Elinor could hear the three men shuffling about in the

dark – drawing together for protection, she presumed. It was almost funny. 'Brynmaur's right,' she said, trying to reassure them. 'We mean you no harm. All we . . .'

'It's that *witch*, too!' one of the men hissed.

'It's *her* fault, all of this. She flew at us. Remember?'

'Keep her back . . . Here! Put your shoulder to mine. You, too, Kyllie. There now. She'll never take us unawares now.'

'Stay clear of us, witch! We're ready for you now. Just stand clear!'

Elinor turned to Brynmaur at her side, finding him by touch. 'What ought we to do about them, then?'

He laughed weakly. 'Do? There's nothing we can do. Leave them. They'll come to their senses. Or not . . .'

Elinor gripped the blood-slippery haft of her purloined spear. 'But we can't just . . . What if they decide to . . . to attack us?'

'Leave them be,' Brynmaur said. 'They're not the problem.'

'You think something really attacked that guard, then? Dragged him off as the man said? That screaming . . . I heard it. Did you? What if there was some *thing* that came and took him? Will it come back?'

Elinor gripped her spear tight, her mind filled with the image of some great hairy lizard-thing – as she had heard the guard describe it – stalking silently through the darkness, fanged and clawed, saliva drooling from its fearsome mouth, slimed with the blood of the guard it had dragged away and consumed. She could see the poor man, limbs flailing, shrieking in the clutch of the thing's great jaw . . .

'Elinor . . .'

The long razor teeth shearing through his flesh. The blood gushing. The horror on his face as he watched his life pour out . . .

'*Elinor!*'

She shuddered.

Brynmaur's hand was upon her arm. 'Get yourself together.'

Elinor could feel her heart banging. 'What if that *thing* returns?'

'It is not the problem.'

She could sense the impatience in his voice, and it stung her. She shook herself. 'What *is* the problem, then?'

'This place. This . . . world.'

She felt him tremble through the hand that still gripped her arm. She was shaking, herself. The sensation she had felt upon her first few moments here – as if some manner of fever had gripped her – was not dissipating. Her muscles ached; her head throbbed painfully. Every bend and twist brought a surge of pain in her lower back. Her mouth felt dry as shoe leather, so that she yearned for the water flask that had been taken from her. And her mind seemed fogged, somehow. It took an effort to keep her thoughts in place. The horrific scene she had envisioned of the dying guard tried to come creeping back into her mind.

'There are worlds such as this,' Brynmaur was explaining. 'Our kind does not thrive here. The very air is like an infection. It's as if little beasts are nibbling away at our muscles, minds, memories . . . The mind weakens and wanders. The body falters.'

Elinor swallowed, shook her head – and then regretted it, for a pulse of agony rippled across her scalp, as if somebody were tearing the skin off in a long flap. She groaned. It was so real-feeling that she put her hand hesitantly to her hair, expecting her fingers to come away soaked with fresh blood.

They did not.

She scrunched her eyes up tight – which, for some reason, seemed to help. The pain came and went in little sharp waves. Her fists were clenched and she could feel the cuts on her hands stinging. The air seemed almost . . . she was not sure. Sulphurous, was it? It was far from warm here (part of her shivering, she realised, was simple cold) but the air had no freshness. Each breath she took was an effort. Her lungs hurt.

She tried to take hold of herself, straightening her aching spine, to focus, to look about. Brynmaur still kept his hand upon her arm, and the touch of it was blessedly anchoring.

There was darkness . . . darkness everywhere, save for the faint, greenish glow she had noticed upon first coming to awareness here. The source of that glow lay above her right shoulder. Peering upwards, she saw a shadowy mass of what looked like – and yet did not really look like – tree limbs. And beyond them . . .

For a long few moments, she could make no sense of it at all. A green face, it seemed. Then a hovering globe in the dark. Then . . .

A moon.

But not like any moon she had ever imagined. It was half the size it ought to be, a round lump of green-glowing strangeness – not at all the wholesome silvery-white of her own familiar moon. She felt repelled by it, and yet also somehow a little drawn at the same time. Craning her head back for a better view through the tangle of 'branches', she made out a sort of face upon it, like the face of the Man in the Moon she knew, and yet totally unlike it. This one had only one eye, a pronounced beak of a nose, a slash-mouth that seemed to leer crookedly. A bilious face.

And beyond it and all about it . . . stars. Masses and masses of stars in a great complicated sweep. Yet dim as well, as if they were all far, far further removed from this place than were the stars of her own world.

The strangenesses of it all seemed too much, suddenly. She closed her eyes and hugged herself, rocking. She could no longer feel Brynmaur's hand upon her arm – though when he had removed it she did not know. She felt as if her insides were seeping out through her pores and into the ground. She felt . . .

'Elinor?'

Brynmaur's voice. She opened her eyes, blinking. There seemed to be a faint pulse of crimson radiance all about her. She blinked hard, rubbed her eyes, blinked some more . . . but it did not help. Everywhere she looked, her vision was filled with the same faint pulse of light. 'Brynmaur,' she breathed. 'Do you see? I don't . . .'

'It's the coming of day,' he said.

Elinor almost laughed. Not her vision at all, then. The world itself was lightening. This world . . .

It began to make something almost like familiar sense to her, day dawning, the small green moon sliding away towards the horizon. They must have *emerged* here just in the darkest time, on the cusp of the morning.

Brynmaur, she saw now, was sprawled against an upthrust of waist-high rock. Behind it, there grew some manner of plant, with a thick-straight stem, ribbed and mottled. The height of a tall man, perhaps. Branches layered out from it, ending in drooping, pale leaves, each of which was divided into a number of oddly angular sections. As she looked at it, the plant seemed to take on a sudden life, seeming almost as a sort of glowing torch, the ribbed stem shimmering white, each petal of each leaf haloed in a coruscation of faint light.

She blinked and rubbed at her eyes furiously, willing it to pass. Her fingers felt like fat sausages, her knuckles queerly too large. She tried to ignore the sensation and force her perceptions – and the world – into something like normalcy.

She heard something move and started, her hand going, by long reflex, to her sword's hilt. But the sword was not there, of course. She remembered how it had manifested itself in the Otherwhere, and felt a fleeting pulse of hope. But this was no soul journey she had made. She was here in the flesh – her aching, quivering flesh.

Brynmaur rose to his feet. 'Come along,' he said hoarsely. 'We need to be away from this spot.'

Elinor shook herself. She licked her lips, which were

cracked and dry, and tried to swallow, and almost could not, so parched was her mouth. She ached for a dip of cool water. 'I don't . . .' she began.

'Come *along*,' Brynmaur urged, reaching a hand to her. 'This is not a good spot in which to rest. Can't you sense it? We need to be gone from here.'

With his help, she got up, feeling dizzy and weak, the spear still clutched in one hand. It felt clumsy-heavy as a lump of stone.

'Come *on*,' Brynmaur said, pulling her along.

'Whe . . . where are we . . . going?' she stammered.

'It matters not. We just need to get away from this place.'

Elinor glanced about. They were surrounded by a mass of . . . she was not sure what to name them: trees, she supposed. But not like any true trees she was familiar with. Tall and twisty-limbed and dense, yet too sleek, somehow, and too bendy. Their 'leaves' hung down in sheaths, like so many horses' tails, all raggedy and spiky and twisted. Interspersed amongst them were the sort of rib-stemmed plant Elinor had seen glowing. And other sorts, too: pulpy-looking and squat, some of them, while others reared up thin and straight as the spear shaft in her hand, to end in a burst of what seemed softly fluttering gossamer.

With every heartbeat, more light was filtering softly into the world, a creeping red radiance that seemed to stain everything, yet which also rendered it all the more clear.

The 'wood' stood back beyond an encircling perimeter of pale rock, like a jagged fence, waist-high and higher, which formed a rough circle of cleared ground about ten paces across. In the middle of the circle, a humpy mound of stone rose up, the crest of which had been roughly carved into (or had the natural form of) a sort of face, eyes and nose and mouth, the mouth open in a howl, or a laugh, or a wide-mouthed contortion of agony, or ecstasy – it was impossible to say which. Coarse grass (or something very like it) grew in the open space round about that face, marked by a complex, twisty series of thin pathways. Clearly, some creature, or creatures, had used this area for some time.

'What *is* this place?' she said softly to Brynmaur.

'No place for the likes of you or I,' he replied soberly.

He was urging her onwards and away. But as she glanced back for a last time, she saw the three guards who had been plunged in here with them, huddled together against the stone perimeter at the far edge of the clearing, white-faced and twitchy and terrified.

'What of them?' she said. 'We can't just abandon them.'

Brynmaur stopped. 'It's not . . . This place is—' He ran a hand over his eyes. 'Very well. But don't be surprised at what happens.'

Taking a few steps towards the huddled men, he called 'Hoi!' softly.

They started, staring at Brynmaur as if he had materialised before them out of the very air. In the growing light, Elinor could make them out properly now. There were only three, clad in scale-mail hauberks, white-knuckling blades – two with curved swords, the third with a short, intricately bladed halberd.

'You must come away from here,' Brynmaur urged them. 'This is not a safe place.'

'It's *him*,' one of them said hoarsely. The one with the halberd, it was, a thin man with a haggard face. His hands, holding the halberd's haft, shook.

'Stay close, Kyllie,' one of the others cautioned him, a man larger-boned and beefier than the other two. 'No telling what the man might try to do to us.'

The three of them drew closer together, weapons up in a glinting hedge, staring at Brynmaur as if he were some huge serpent come to devour them.

'We need each other's help in a place such as this,' Brynmaur said softly. 'You have nothing to fear from me.'

'Don't trust him, Tuck!' one of the men said, the other swordsman, short and balding.

'I don't,' the beefy one responded. 'And I won't, neither. No matter what he says. We all know what he did back in the Three Valleys.'

'I mean you no harm,' Brynmaur said, holding both his hands out, empty. 'Truly.'

But, 'He's trying to cast a spell upon us,' the one with the halberd cried out. 'Don't look him in the eye. Don't look at how his hands move! He'll weave you into some manner of delusion or other.'

'No,' Brynmaur said, stepping towards them. 'No! I only want—'

'Stay back,' the beefy one blurted. He waved his blade about. 'Stay back or, so help me, I'll run you through!'

'Go away!' the other swordsman shouted. 'Leave us be!'

'Keep your voice down, man,' Brynmaur cautioned earnestly. 'There's no telling what manner of creature you might attract, yelling like that.'

Elinor stepped forwards, hoping to help. 'Listen to him,' she said. 'Brynmaur knows what he's talking about. This is a *strange* place. You must—'

'Keep back, witch!' the halberd-man shrieked.

Brynmaur sighed and turned away. 'It's no use,' he said to Elinor. 'They cannot see past their own fears. This place . . .'

Elinor shivered. She could feel the strangeness eating into her bones.

'Let's be gone from here,' Brynmaur said. 'Quick as can be.'

Elinor nodded.

Brynmaur was shivering in long, wracking fits. She could hear his teeth rattle. He tried to clamber over the stone perimeter, but did not have the strength. Elinor helped heave him over, then struggled after herself. Halfway over the stone, she fumbled the spear and had to stop and return for it. She did not know why, but the moment her foot touched the ground on the inside again, she felt a sudden, terrible panic in her bones. Her heart nearly came up out of her throat. Grabbing up the spear where it had fallen, she scrambled over the stone perimeter as if a pack of demon wolves were at her heels.

'Come!' Brynmaur urged her hoarsely. He was on his feet, shaking, his face clenched. 'Quick as can be!'

Together they fled as best they could, limping and shivering, weaving a staggering way through the 'wood'.

'What *is* it?' Elinor asked, gasping. She could feel the unaccountable panic still filling her. She pulled on Brynmaur's arm, slowing him. 'Brynmaur! I need to know. What *is* it I'm feeling? Is just it me? Or . . . what?'

'Something . . . arrives,' he panted. 'Now come along. Fast as you can!'

They fled through the 'trees'.

It felt like a nightmare version of all the walking they had been doing through the pine forest, save here the 'trees' were twisted and bloated and attenuated and strange, the ground littered with pale, pulpy growths that went *squersh* underfoot in a manner that made her belly heave.

On they fled, running when they could, limping along at a walk whenever the effort was too much. At one point, Elinor put a hand to a 'tree' bole for support. The 'bark' of it stung like fire, and she jerked back with a yelp.

'*Quiet!*' Brynmaur hissed.

Onwards again, gasping and staggering. Elinor felt her lungs ache hotly. There was a metallic taste in her mouth. Her knees arced fire with each step. She blinked and slowed. Red light was filling the world, like watery ink being poured into a complicated bowl. The whole point of this mad dashing about seemed to elude her suddenly . . .

'There!' she heard Brynmaur say.

Ahead, there was a gap in the 'wood'. Elinor shook herself and hastened for it alongside Brynmaur. Stumbling past a last clutch of 'trees', they found themselves on a sort of open hillside. There was the same manner of 'grass' here as there had been back in the stone-encircled clearing.

Very much like true grass it seemed, save coarser and paler.

'This way,' Brynmaur panted, pointing. Near the crest of the hill ahead, there was a great tumble of stone, cracked and shattered and ancient. 'We can take shelter there.'

Across the hillside they struggled, the 'grass' rasping *shrush shrush shrush* underfoot. Elinor glanced behind, for she still felt the panic in her guts. But there was nothing to be seen.

The tumble of stone, once they reached it, proved to be an upthrust nearly thrice a man's height at its tallest point and at least fifteen paces along. It was composed of flaky rock, filled with crevasses and shattered shelves and such. Together, they scrambled over and behind a large spur along the closest side, nearly thigh-high, and flung themselves belly down on the 'grass'.

'What now?' Elinor asked in a pant. Her breast was heaving so she could hardly get the words out clearly.

'We . . . stay . . . hid,' Brynmaur replied, gasping for air himself.

For a time, it was all Elinor could do just to lie there, breathing, concentrating on keeping her mind held self-focused. Her heart seemed to refuse to settle, banging away under her ribs as if it had a life of its own. Her spine was on fire. Her hands stung. Her head throbbed. Her mouth was so dry, it felt as if her tongue were separating apart painfully in little parched fissures. She groaned, trying to get proper breath.

After a little, the pains eased a bit. Her breath came more properly, and that seemed to help. When she was able for it, she half-rose to one knee and peeped out through a vertical crack in the spur of rock behind which they were hid, giving her a fairly good view of a slice of the landscape.

It was, she saw, well into morning by now. All trace of the stars was gone, and a sun was risen above the horizon before her – but a sun that was too large and too red. The landscape about them seemed washed in blood. The 'wood' reared up like a solid, dark wall, prickly and twisty-strange. The hillside upon which they were perched rolled downwards and away, past the forest, to a great, open expanse beyond clothed in the coarse 'grass', a rippling seascape that glowed a pale ochre-red in the sunlight. Off in the distance, there was a bright, reflective glimmer that she took to be body of water – a lake of some sort, perhaps.

She ducked back down behind the rock and turned to Brynmaur, wincing at the flare of pains such movement provoked. 'What do we do now?'

He shrugged.

'Brynmaur?' she said concernedly. He looked none too good, his face grey-green in the red-dawn light, his breathing harsh and irregular.

'I'm all right,' he insisted. 'Tancred said this was a land where the likes of me could survive, remember?' His bearded lips stretched in a thin attempt at a smile. 'I'm not about to prove him wrong so quick.'

Elinor put a hand lightly on his arm. She did not know what to say, what to do. She licked her dry lips with a dry tongue. Brynmaur's lips, too, she saw, were dry-cracked. At the very least, both of them must have water. She looked about, but there was nothing to be seen save the coarse 'grass' rolling on past the hump of the hill and the stone against which they were hid. The harsh air hurt her nose as she breathed and made her mouth sting burningly.

From the other side of their rock hideaway, there came the sudden sound of human voices. Elinor got to her knees again and peered over the stone.

The three guards were fleeing from out of the 'wood', stumbling in a clumsy group. Impulsively, Elinor stood up and waved. 'Over here!' she called.

They heard her all right, for they stopped dead and stared. But instead of veering towards the rocks, they shot off in the other direction, skidding and tumbling down-slope towards where the lake – if, indeed, it was a lake – glimmered in the distance.

Brynmaur was tugging at her sleeve. 'Fools,' she muttered, sliding back down behind the shelter of the stone.

'Fool, you,' Brynmaur said, 'to expose yourself like that.'

She looked at him then looked away. More sounds could be heard from the stone's far side now, a sort of high-pitched chittering – not at all like the sound of human voices. Elinor began to get up.

'Careful!' Brynmaur hissed. 'Don't let them see you.'

'Don't let who see me?'

'Whatever it is making that noise.' He tugged at her. 'Lie down and keep quiet. None of this concerns us any longer.'

But Elinor could not just look away. She knelt against the rock and put her eye carefully to the crack she had peered through before.

At first, all she could make out was movement. The coarse, sun-reddened 'grass' seemed all astir, as if a mass of great insects were squirming across it. She blinked and tried to focus more clearly. Slowly, what was happening out there resolved itself into detail.

The three guards were fleeing for their lives.

Behind them came a horde of . . . she was not quite sure what. They had the general appearance of men – arms and legs and head, eyes, nose, mouth. But they were far shorter than any man, no more than waist-high, perhaps, and their limbs, their hands and feet and fingers and toes all seemed far too long and their heads too narrow and snoutish.

They were entirely without clothing or adornment or weapon that Elinor could see, and though it was difficult to make out colours in the crimson wash of the big red sun, they seemed pale and greenish, with scaly skins. Their fingers and toes ended in dark, hooked claws, she noticed, and needly teeth filled their mouths. They moved with a kind of darting, snap-limbed, lizardish quickness, leaping and prancing in the fleeing guards' wake, throwing their snouty heads back and giving vent to shrill, chittering cries.

One of the guards fell. The other two kept on for an instant, then skidded to a halt and rushed back. The horde was upon them by then. The guards tried to form a defensive block, their backs together, blades out, the beefy man shouting orders and encouragement. But as the swirling, chittering, menacing mass of creatures welled up about them, the halberd wielder flung his weapon down in blind panic and fled, shrieking.

The creatures flung themselves upon him like a wave, and he went under, screaming and thrashing.

The other two tried to make a stand, back to back, the bald one and the beefy, blades ready. But one of the creatures somehow came in quickly under the bald man's guard and swarmed up his torso, clinging to him like a leech. He shrieked, flung his blade down, and tore at the creature with both hands, trying to dislodge it. In a heartbeat, he was overcome by a dozen others and went down. Elinor heard him cry out in terror.

Which left only the beefy swordsman standing.

Elinor saw one of the creatures spitted upon the man's blade, lifted high and flung away, shrilling in agony. But three more took its place, grabbing with their claw-fingered, too-long arms, chittering like mad things, swirling and leaping and reaching, and he, too, went down, shouting and cursing, submerged under a writhing mass as the other two men had been.

After the brutal scenes she had witnessed in her own world, Elinor expected these swarming, humanesque creatures to rip the poor guards to bloody shreds and devour them on the spot. But no such thing happened. Instead, the three men were carted away, alive, each held aloft by a struggling, chittering raft of creatures clutching him from beneath. The men thrashed and screamed and wept and struck, trying to break free, but there were too many hands upon them.

Across the hillside the creatures bore their prizes, and into the dark mass of the strange 'wood'. The last Elinor saw of the men was one of the guard's faces, tilted back, his eyes wide and white with horror. She shuddered. Somehow it was worse than if they had been killed on the instant.

Most of the mass of creatures had gone streaming into the 'wood', but not all. A considerable number still swarmed along the hillside, casting about like so many hounds in search of a scent. Some of them began to work their way upslope towards the rock upthrust behind which Elinor and Brynmaur were hid.

Elinor ducked back down, away from the spy-crack she had been looking through. 'Quick!' she said to Brynmaur, 'can you do it? Can you make us unseeable here?'

Brynmaur was on his knees. He, too, she realised, had been watching events – despite his insistence on not doing so.

'Can you do it?' she repeated. The chittering sounds were growing louder from the other side of the rock.

'I'm trying!' he hissed. 'I'm *trying*! Be quiet and let me concentrate.'

She hunkered down, pressing herself against the chill face of the rock, and reached up her spear. She could hear a *scrit scrit* sound now – small clawed feet on the stone.

A snouted face appeared above her. She heard the soft *shish shush* of the thing's breathing. It put a hand down to steady itself less than an arm's length from where she crouched. She readied herself for a fast, hard thrust with the spear, her heart banging, her vision pulsing uncomfortably.

Brynmaur had felt himself unable to hide them from the insectile pack that had hunted them back in the pine forest. She did not know what the chances were of him being able to do so now. Her mind ran through a quick scenario: take the one above her, fast as could be, then

383

move further along the rock outcropping to where it rose higher and might provide a better opportunity for defence. The three guards had had nothing against which to put their backs save each other and that had proven the quick undoing of them – that and the fear which had broken them. If she and Brynmaur could manage to keep the rock safely behind them, and she could keep the spear from being torn out of her grasp – she shifted her grip, feeling the betraying slipperiness of the blood-slicked shaft – and if they could keep the things at bay long enough . . .

The creature coming over the rock was close now. She could put the blade of the spear between its ribs in one quick motion. There were others of its kind coming over the stone outcropping at various points down the length of it. She would have to be fast. She tensed, took a breath.

The nearest creature came over the stone ridge and vaulted lightly to the 'grass'. She could see two slits above its snoutish mouth quivering – nostrils, she reckoned. Its eyes were dark and round, set far apart and high in its head. Its glance flicked about here and there, quickly. She could hear it chittering softly to itself. For all the world, it looked like a creature who knew there was something suspicious going on near it, but it clearly could not quite fathom what.

Elinor let out a most careful, relieved breath and glanced across at Brynmaur. He was crouched on his knees, eyes tight shut, face screwed up in concentration. She stayed as she was, unmoving, keeping her breath soft as could be.

The creature poked about a bit, clearly suspicious still, but then gave it up and leaped back over the rock and out of their sight. Elinor heard it give a thin call, which was answered from several points. There was a general scrabbling and chittering, and then the sounds dwindled away.

Silence.

Brynmaur let out a long, weary breath.

'Not bad,' Elinor said, trying to smile.

He stared at her, his breathing ragged and uneven.

Elinor slid over along the rock face and sat beside him. 'What do we do now?'

But Brynmaur made no response.

'Brynmaur?' she said concernedly. She poked him softly in the ribs. 'Bryn?'

He shrugged away from her irritably. 'Leave me be, can't you?'

'I only . . .' Elinor took a breath. She tried to gather herself, to ignore the pains and aches. 'We can't just lie here. What do we do now?'

'How should *I* know?' he snapped.

'But . . .'

'I'm sick to my very bones, girl. Those creatures came *that* close to seeing us. I don't know how they ever missed us. And if they return . . . Well, I'm not able for it again.'

'But . . .'

'Just let me be. I'm sick and I ache like somebody's been at me with a hammer. My mouth is so dry I can't even swallow properly. My head hurts.' He groaned. 'This foul place . . .'

Elinor shuddered, agreeing silently. She felt sicker than she had ever been in her whole life. Her mouth was so parched, lips so dry-cracked and sore, that talking was a minor agony. They must get to water. That had to be their first priority. But . . . *was* there water here to drink? They had seen none so far. She thought of the far-away glimmer she had seen that might be a lake. Could they make it?

She shifted position a little, trying to ease herself. Her spine felt as if it was about to come apart in pieces. Each movement she made provoked some new hurt in joint or muscle or bone. Her head throbbed naggingly. Waves of shivering went through her, rattling her teeth and sending stutters of pain everywhere.

'We've got to get *out* of here,' she said, gritting her teeth to stop them from chattering.

There was no response from Brynmaur.

385

'We *can* get back, can't we?' she said, trying to be resolutely positive. 'I mean . . . there has to be *some* way to break out of this land and return . . .'

Brynmaur looked at her, looked away.

'Brynmaur?'

He shrugged wearily. 'There were many worlds Tancred could have chosen to strand me upon. He chose this one.'

'And so?'

'A world such as this . . . there is no way back. Not for the likes of me. Not without aid from . . . *outside*.'

Elinor stared at him. 'So that's *it*, then?' she said, shocked. 'We . . . we're stranded here forever? Till we go mad or die in a fit of agony or . . . or whatever?'

'It's the end for us, girl,' Brynmaur replied exhaustedly. 'We have to face it best as we can.' He put a shaking hand out to her. 'I . . . I'm sorry.'

Elinor blinked, swallowed. 'No!' she said, refusing his hand. 'I will not believe it. There has to be something. There has to be *something* . . .'

Brynmaur merely slumped in on himself.

Elinor shuddered. It seemed impossible. Like a bad dream. To end her days here in this horrid, *other* place. She could feel her mind faltering, as if something were trying to pry at it, loosening all the connections. She saw Gyver, his familiar, dear, furred face, weary-seeming and sad. He was looking at her, shaking his head.

She rubbed her eyes, dispelling the vision – if vision it had been. It took an effort to keep her thoughts clear. Madness and pain. That was what lay in store for them here. Till the final release that death would bring. And then? What would happen to the soul lost in such an *other* world? Would there ever be any peace for it? Ever any new incarnation into natural life again?

She shuddered. There were tears in her eyes, blurring her vision.

To have Tancred triumph like this . . .

It galled. It made her feel so angry she thought some part of her might burst. There had to be some manner of escape. There just *had* to be . . .

But what?

What?

She looked about, desperate. There were little trails of faint light now, every time she turned her head, like radiant worms. Against her back, the stone felt cold and jagged-hard. The hillside went up away from her, the coarse 'grass' like an undulating carpet. The sky above her was turning a brilliant orange as the day advanced. Faint yellowish clouds formed a high, scattered, wavery pattern, like sand on a beach. Some flying thing soared way, way off in the distance.

There was nothing in any of it that might help.

Her head hurt. Her dry mouth did. She felt utterly, utterly weary.

A sort of swirling squiggle caught her attention. Up in the orange-glowing sky it was . . . huge, moving in a slow drop sideways and leftwards . . . And then she blinked and it shifted suddenly and she knew that the image was in her sight, not in the world.

'Brynmaur . . .' she moaned. But when she looked at him he was slumped against the rock, passed out . . . or . . . dead. She tried to reach to him, but could not. She was too weak.

'Brynmaur!' she tried to call once more. But her mouth was too dry, her breathing too uncertain, and her voice came out as no more than dull croak.

The world darkened.

Lightened.

Darkened . . .

She could feel her heart pounding against her ribs as if she were running hard. Her eyes stung. She blinked – darkness shot with squiggling snakes of light – and tried to get a proper breath. She struggled to keep herself focused and intact, but it was like a clod of earth struggling to hold itself together in deep water. She could feel herself slowly coming apart.

No! she cried silently. This could not . . .

be . . .

the end . . .

XXXI

Trees . . .

There were trees all about her. Pines. Blessedly familiar and wholesome. The lovely, astringent scent of them filled her nostrils. She did not know how it could be so, but it was. Her heart filled with joy. They were saved! They were back. She looked about wonderingly. It was her own world. No doubting it. Blue morning sky, the soft *shrush* of a breeze in the pines, the gurgle of a dancing brook nearby. Against all expectation . . .

And then, from behind her, she heard a soft *hissss*.

Turning, she perceived a figure approaching through the trees. At first, she could make no clear sense of it. Then she saw: insectile body, all sinew and bone, mere slit of a nose, long, tapering muzzle, thin white lips, wet, needle points of ivory-yellow fangs, glowing red-jelly eyes . . .

For a long, frozen instant, she just stood there. The home-coming joy that had been welling up inside her died. She did not understand . . .

The creature stalked towards her, moving with that terrible, insectile, predatory grace that marked its kind.

Elinor turned and fled. She could hear the crackle of pursuit behind her as it broke through the trees. She ran desperate-fast as she could, leaping over roots and caroming off tree boles, her poor lungs on fire, her limbs shaky-weak.

No use, of course.

The thing gained on her as if she were standing still. She stumbled to a halt and turned, unable to run more. Desperately, she glanced about, ready to put up a last defence any way she could. But there was no weapon to hand – no bright-shining sword, no spear, not a little paring knife . . . not even a stout branch.

The hunter was upon her.

Suddenly, she was not alone. Brynmaur stood at her side. She reached for him, hoping against hope that he could hide the two of them from the hunter's sight. He took her hand in his. She felt him shaking. She felt him tense as a hound.

The hunter *hisssed* at them.

Do it, Brynmaur! she willed silently. *Make it so this creature cannot see us.*

Brynmaur strained – she could feel it, feel each shift of sinew and muscle, heart and will, as he struggled to turn the hunter's attention from them.

To no avail.

The hunter came for them. Elinor swatted at it desperately, bare-handed. It grabbed up her naked hand in one of its three-fingered, taloned ones. The strength of it was like iron. She struggled and wrenched, but it was no use.

She heard Brynmaur moan, and saw that he, too, was taken, held in one taloned hand, like she.

There was nothing they could do.

Slowly, the hunter bore them to the ground.

Elinor felt herself filled with an impotent rage. It was all too terrible, this. To falter and fail in that *other* land, to feel herself returned and saved, to have to face this too-strong hunter . . . the implacable persistence of such a creature shook her, that it would pursue them across the terrible thresholds between worlds . . .

This close, she could sense a cold, enduring rage coming from it, like the chill aura off a chunk of ice. The talons were sinking into her now, like hooks into her guts. She shrieked and writhed, but there was no getting free of it. Deeper and deeper the talons went. She heard Brynmaur cry out . . .

The creature made a soft *hroomming* sound in its throat. There was a strange murmuring, a sort of hum that Elinor could feel through the marrow of her skull rather than her ears, like a far-away echo in a wood. She thrashed and shuddered powerlessly, feeling the hunter's rage encompass her, her own helpless outrage flare. The creature's eyes were before her, pulsing globules of unhuman, reddish jelly set in spiky bone orbits.

The talons . . . opened her.

She felt a sudden flush of warmth at her breast . . . The Fey-bone. Somehow she had forgotten all about the Fey-bone. It came to life now with an unexpected pulse of comforting heat.

As it had once before . . .

Peace, child, something said.

Peace.

Elinor did not understand.

And then, suddenly, she did,

'Moreena!' she cried. Elinor gazed up into the terrible face above hers. Against all hope and expectation. 'Can it really be you?'

'*It is me, child,*' the voice replied.

It was not the same manner of communication they had shared in the *other* place. Elinor did not know quite how they were 'talking'. It did not matter. Somehow, she knew this for Moreena's voice. 'But how—'

You are a most difficult soul to reach. Moreena said. *You and Brynmaur both. I have been trying for long and long.*

'It was . . . you, then, all along? *You?* And not the pack come hunting us?'

It was me.

'But I don't . . .' It was like a knife through her: all that might have been avoided, that might have been saved, if only she and Brynmaur had been less fear-blind. It was almost too much for her, all this – too much, too bitter-sweet, too suddenly.

She took a breath, felt herself shivering. 'How*ever* did

you manage to reach us? And where . . . *are* we? Is this a dream, or . . . or what?'

That would be long to tell, child, and we have not the time. Your bodily selves are dying. We must act quickly!

'Can you help us to return to our own world, then?' Elinor asked eagerly.

Yes, child. You must return and pull this Tancred down.

Elinor felt a flush of rage emanate from Moreena at the mention of the Seer's name. Perhaps it was the dream-state she was in – if this was, in fact, a dream she lived – but she experienced Moreena's anger as a relentless, cold wave, deep beyond measure, which came up all about her, inundating her. She felt her heart race.

Calm, child. Calm. The wave receded. *My apologies. I ought to have better control. But the man . . . ANGERS me.* There was a little burst of fury again, then calm. *Come, we must act. You and Brynmaur must return to your own land. I will . . . facilitate it.*

'Do it, then,' Elinor said eagerly. 'Anything!'

There is a problem.

Elinor's heart cramped. There always seemed to be a problem. 'What?'

A taloned finger pointed towards Brynmaur. *Him.*

Elinor could feel Brynmaur struggling, like a hooked fish thrashing on the line. He was moaning, trying desperately to push away the taloned hand that held him fast.

I cannot reach him, Moreena said. *You must help.*

'Yes!' Elinor agreed. 'Of course. Anything! Just tell me . . .'

We must . . . open him.

'How?'

An abrupt and terrible pain went through Elinor, as if her insides had been torn completely out. The dream-forest about her winked away and she felt herself like a mote of liquid, floating, floating . . .

And then there was Brynmaur.

It was almost as it had been once before, in the *other*

place of the flying pack, with Brynmaur encased in a hard, protective shell. She had to get through to him. She knew, somehow, that everything depended upon this.

But how?

He seemed impervious, locked away behind his hard shell.

She pushed and strained, trying to reach him, but it was no use. Might as well attempt to soak through solid rock.

Which left . . .

She did not know.

She felt a terrible sense of time slipping past, of her very life slipping away. On the horizon of her sense, there was a chill shadow hovering that she knew, somehow, was her own death. There had to be some way for her to reach Brynmaur. Stubborn fool that he was. There *had* to be some way!

Moreena! she cried out wordlessly. Moreena had somehow set all this up. Surely she would have some manner of aid to offer. *Moreena* . . .

But there was no sign of any help. She was utterly alone.

And failing. She could conceive of no way to force a path through to Brynmaur. He was simply too shaken, too fearful, too cut-off and well-protected. And she too weak.

If she had had anything like an ordinary body, Elinor would have flung herself at him, pounding with her last strength at his defences with her fists, and then thrown herself down and wept – with frustration, anger, despair, fear, half a dozen other feelings all tangled up together into a hard, complex lump. But she had no body, nothing with which to pound or weep. She merely hovered helplessly, uselessly, like a globule of abandoned liquid, alone and hopeless and feeling the chill current of final despair begin to seep into her – and, beyond that, the cold dark of her own death, like a bottomless chasm creeping closer and closer. After all the struggles she had endured in her life, after everything done and not done . . . to end it here, like this, failing . . .

No! She would not give in.

But there was nothing she could feel to do. No way into Brynmaur. No way back. No way forwards. No way . . .

A gossamer touch . . .

Elinor started.

Again, that faint, oh-so-tentative touch of something. Moreena, was it? No. She did not think so.

Brynmaur.

Something was seeping out through the hard-shell casing that encompassed him, like a soft liquid, moving most slowly, most uncertainly. Elinor slipped forwards, desperate and intense and frightened to move too quick, for she could sense Brynmaur's terrible indecision: to reach out, to pull back . . .

She reached to him, and he withdrew in a hasty flurry, like a great, complex snail whipping back inside its shell.

No! she cried silently. But it was no use. He could not – or would not – perceive her.

But even as she hung there, desperate and agitated, he began to seep out once more, feeling towards her in his oh-so-tentative manner. She held herself still, quivering, waiting . . . For she suddenly realised that it was the very weakness in her, the blank despair that had begun to overwhelm her, that drew him. He . . . *felt* for her.

Delicately, he touched her, pulled back, touched her again. It was like a slow wave of cool-warm liquid . . .

And then, somehow, some barrier that had been between them was gone, and Elinor became aware of Brynmaur from the inside.

The absolute intimacy of it was painful, like exposing tender flesh to a clumsy touch. Brynmaur had old, old hurts on him; she had known that. But she could feel them now as if they were her own hurts, almost – fear and pain and loneliness . . . such abysmal loneliness. And the pressure of the world upon him all those years . . .

She knew his child's memories: of folk staring at him, of his mother staring at him, her face filled with a terrible pride and an even worse expectation, of him knowing himself different, always different from other children, and *strange* . . . and she knew how the first stirrings of man-hood in him had shaken him so, his fruitless yearnings, the horrible embarrassment of it all when the girl – the beautiful round-faced, large-eyed girl, her hair glossy-dark as any raven's wing, her breasts showing in a soft curve under her dress – had laughed at him and called him little pig-boy.

And she knew the terrible time of sickness, when all Brynmaur had loved was taken from him . . . and how he had come to hate death, and killing, as a man might come to hate a personal enemy. And she knew his time of exile, him struggling to make sense of what he was become, and to become . . . And then Pawli – dear, *gifted*, worrisome, mule-willed Pawli – and Moreena . . . how Moreena's winsome beauty had been like a knife thrust at times, it was so painful. How she had terrified him and thrilled him beyond all reason. How she had been a haven for him – the very first in his life – and how he had hungered for her, loving the luscious scent and the warm wet feel of her sensitive, woman's places as they had come together in the Otherwhere. How, in that *other* realm, Moreena and all had been bound up in an intricate tapestry of purest wonder . . .

And herself . . . how he admired and despised her, needed her and wanted her gone from his life, for she was like a stinging insect, goading him to action, to awareness, to new life . . .

But it was a two-way process, this intimate perceiving, and as she knew him, so he knew her as well . . . her own silly girlhood yearnings, the desperate struggle to make a life for herself back in Long Harbour, that intricate, filthy-lovely city in which she had spent her childhood . . . her faithless father, who had abandoned her mother and her in her tenth year, and whom the girl in her still loved desperately, despite all; faithless Annocky, who had betrayed her; Dame Sostris and old Mamma Kieran and the hard route she had taken out of Long Harbour . . .

And all her strange life since: mad Lord Mattingly, who had gifted her with the white blade, faithless Rannis, Margie Farm and Gillien and Hann and Collart and the rest . . . Power-crazed Iryn Jagga and the his dark, mad-violent Brotherhood; Scrunch the bear and little Spandel and Otys the crow and all the other humanimals who had been such a part of her for so long . . . the strange presence of the humanimals' Lady (would she ever see again the image of her that had been branded into her palm with such pain?) . . . Ziftkin the Songster; and Gyver, poor dear, dead Gyver . . .

All gone, dead or taken or dropped behind, leaving her to wander on, moved irrevocably by the great, invisible press of the world's deep currents, will she or nil she, alone . . .

As was Brynmaur.

A flawed vessel. Alone.

Elinor felt shaken to the very deepest root of what she was. What had Moreena done to them? She had never experienced – never imagined – knowing another human being in such terrible, poignant intimacy. She knew the whole sordid, painful, struggling, mostly joyless life Bryn-maur had led. As he knew hers. She knew the shape of the shell he had created for himself as a protection from the world. He knew her innermost angers and regrets and hopes. It was most utterly confusing, with memories uncertain, for she did not, for the moment, quite know what was his and what hers . . .

She did not know if she could ever face him, knowing what she now did, if they should ever again return to anything like normal life. It would be like seeing him always naked.

If they were ever to return . . .

She felt something shiver through her then, another presence . . . something huge and utterly strange.

Brynmaur cringed and tried to draw away protectively.

It was Moreena. Elinor knew it. Brynmaur knew it, too, and feared it greatly. For her, Moreena represented nothing truly terrible, but for him, Moreena was the very epitome of how his life had gone: the world too wonderful and too dangerous, all that was most dear ripped from him . . . and now transformed into very nightmare.

But though Brynmaur contracted, he did not altogether withdraw away into his hard shell. Perhaps it was that he could sense Elinor's own non-terror in Moreena's presence; or perhaps Moreena herself was able to do something; or it might have been that the choice was so clear: accept or die – for they could both feel the cold dark of their own deaths on the horizon, and Brynmaur, for all his convoluted defensiveness, was still a man of more-than-ordinary awareness.

Elinor never quite knew. But somehow, at that critical instant, Brynmaur was able to open himself just enough.

Elinor felt something rush past her, felt herself being washed back as by a great wave. Then she was falling away, dragged down and down into a whirling, sucking drain that spewed her into a dark and painful, aching place . . .

Orange sky, yellow skeins of high-away cloud . . .

Elinor blinked, groaned, struggled to sit up. She tried to swallow and nearly could not, her mouth was so horribly dry. Her heart was banging hard, as if she had just flopped herself down after a too-long, too-fast run.

She looked around. Brynmaur lay on his side, eyes open, regarding her uncertainly.

She did not know what to say.

Their eyes met, and all the memories they had shared so intimately flashed between them. 'I . . .' she began uncertainly.

But there was something else with them, a hovering, amorphous shadow-shape that hung above Brynmaur protectively.

Moreena! Elinor was not sure how she knew, but the knowledge came to her with a blood-deep certainty.

'We must return to the place in the forest where we entered this land,' Brynmaur said. His voice was so hoarse and cracked, Elinor could hardly make out the words. 'Quick as we can before we become too weak to move. Tancred erred in sending us here. It is no place we can survive in for any length of time.'

'Bu . . . but—' Elinor stammered. 'Go back into that wood? Why?'

'The Bridge will be opened for us if we can reach it in time. *She* will ensure it.'

'*She?*' But Elinor knew who it was he referred to. Above him the shadow shape moved, like a drifting curtain, as if to beckon them on.

Brynmaur struggled weakly to his knees, grunting. 'Come on,' he said. 'It is our last . . . our *only* chance.'

Elinor stared at him, at the Moreena-shadow above him. There were a score of questions she wanted to ask. But there was no time. She could feel her own weakness, like a disease, eating into her. She nodded and dragged herself to her feet.

Over the upthrust of stone behind which they had hid and back down the hillside they went, stumbling and uncertain, leaning against each other for mutual support through much of it, using Elinor's purloined spear as a combination walking staff and crutch. Elinor felt like a very old, very sick person on her last legs. Brynmaur looked it. The coarse 'grass' over which they walked was slippy underfoot, and he fell once, heavily. Lifting him to his feet again proved almost too much for her. Her lungs ached, her chest did, trying to get some goodness from the air. Her vision kept threatening to fall away into squiggles of darkness.

Only the hovering shadow-shape above them kept them going – it was so palpably the shape of hope.

In amongst the 'trees' they stumbled. Elinor's weary heart misgave her and she stopped. Time had passed while they were in the dream-state with Moreena. Day was on the wane now and the 'wood' was woven with shadows and obscuring darkness. But the Moreena-shape drifted irresistibly on above them, and they followed limpingly, gasping and shaking.

With the light dying as it was, their vision was most uncertain. Twice Elinor started, thinking she had seen some creature or other stalking them in the dimness. 'How much further?' she said after a little.

'Not long now, I reckon,' Brynmaur said hoarsely. 'We've come a farish ways already.'

'So long as we aren't lost.'

Brynmaur looked above him at the still hovering shadow-shape. 'We're not lost.'

Elinor felt a little stab of jealously. How was it *he* could feel so clearly what Moreena intended? To her, Moreena was no more than a vague, silent shape. It seemed most unfair, somehow. Or else . . . what if it were all mere illusion anyhow? The meeting with Moreena and all of it no more than a manifestation of how her mind was crumbling. What if . . . She stiffened. That could mean they were walking directly into a trap.

'It is no trap,' Brynmaur said softly.

Elinor blinked. 'How did you . . .'

He smiled wearily at her. 'I could see it writ clear enough on your face. It is *her*, truly. *She* has come to us and will lead us free of this foul place.'

Elinor shivered. She did not like the way he said that word 'she' – like a word to conjure by. And how could she believe anything he said, anyway? If any of this was dangerous illusion, then *all* of it was. It was madness to walk thus blindly into the clutches of the dangerous creatures that had taken the poor guards. Better to flee back into the open hillside and search for water so that she could . . .

Without warning, there were three of the small, snout-faced creatures before them.

Elinor stared, her heart coming up in her throat.

'Start walking,' Brynmaur said softly. 'They will sense Moreena's presence about us. We are safe.'

Elinor stood frozen. Slowly, she raised the spear in her hand.

'Elinor!' she heard Brynmaur hiss. 'No! No bloodshed.'

She flicked a quick, sideways glance at him: dirty, tangle-haired and haggard, his eyes burning in his face. It would get them killed, this enduring insistence of his against violence of any sort. The creatures before them were *dangerous* . . .

'Lower your spear,' Brynmaur said.

It was like going down a cliff face with Brynmaur above, holding the rope. She either trusted him – or not. He would either hold her safe, or she would plummet to the bottom to be smashed like a bowl of eggs upon the rocks below.

'Come,' he said hoarsely. 'Walk forwards with me.'

The three creatures were stood directly ahead, silent and staring. There was something about them that was terrifying beyond all proportion. So human-looking and yet so not, childlike, almost, and yet starkly menacing at the same moment. Their dark eyes were unblinking and . . . hungry.

Nearly . . . very nearly, she flung the spear at them and then turned and fled. But she remembered with stark clarity the way fear had undone the three guards, and she stood her ground, letting the spear droop till its sharp point nearly touched the earth at her feet. She felt Brynmaur pry the fingers of her left hand away from the spear shaft and enclose her hand in his. He took a first, slow step, straight forwards, bringing her with him, spear trailing one-handed. Then a second step, a third, a forth . . .

The creatures slipped quietly aside to allow them to pass.

More of them appeared along their route as they continued on, like nightmare apparitions, then ducking away again, and they heard a chittering of many voices ahead. She and Brynmaur could not keep from stumbling now. Elinor slipped on a squishy, fungoid thing underfoot and cursed. She felt her nerves strung tight as wires. It still seemed the height of madness to be walking thus directly into the control of such frightful, unknown creatures . . .

When they finally reached the clearing, they paused on the outer side of the stone perimeter, gasping. Inside, the place was packed with such a press of creatures that they could not see the 'grass' that covered the ground. Elinor heard a weak, human moan of suffering. It took her a long few moments of peering about before she spied three quivering, human-looking shapes off to their left and close up against the inside of the stone 'fence'.

'They are beyond our help,' Brynmaur said in a soft, hoarse voice. 'Do not look.'

She tried not to, but could not stop herself from one glance: wet, puckered flesh, like raw red meat, staring, horror-filled eyes . . . She turned away hastily, shuddering, sick and shaken.

Slowly, awkwardly, they helped each other over the stone perimeter wall and inside. All about them, the creatures stirred and chittered uneasily.

'Walk to the centre,' Brynmaur said softly, taking her hand once more. 'Slow and sure as you can.'

Elinor felt such a villain, walking past the pitiful, half-dead guards. She still gripped the spear in one hand. Perhaps she could at least end their suffering.

Brynmaur pulled her on. 'No. The balance of things here is uncertain enough already. We are too late to succour the poor souls.'

'But how can we just . . .'

His expression was bleak. 'There is nothing we can do for them. Our only hope here is to press on, steady as we can.'

Elinor tried to keep her steps measured, though her heart was hammering. She felt the sickness of this place seeping into her like a thick, toxic fluid. The creatures were looking up at her, a myriad dark, alien eyes, staring, staring hungrily . . .

'Elinor!' she heard. She felt Brynmaur pulling at her. 'Keep walking.'

She had not been aware she had stopped.

'We're almost there now . . .'

They *were* there. The strange stone face – howling or laughing or whatever it was doing – reared up before them. All about, there was an agitated chittering of un-human voices. The air began to shimmer.

And then she felt a burst of searing pain, like a great burning blade thrust through her, and she and Brynmaur were . . .

Gone.

XXXII

Elinor came through as if she had leaped from a great height, rolling and tumbling on the hard stone floor till she fetched up on her belly, gasping.

But it was good, wholesome air she gasped, and, though her limbs ached, the terrible, debilitating dis-ease of that *other* land was entirely gone from her. She was returned to her own natural world! So might a hooked fish feel, thrown suddenly back into its own life-giving waters.

About her there was a sudden commotion of many voices. The Fey-bone was pulsing uncomfortably at her breast, a cold stutter.

They were returned back to the chamber in the dark Tower, she saw. There had been a procession of men marching out the door. But now they had stopped in consternation, clogging the entranceway. Tancred/Khurdis stood almost exactly where he had, as did the Lord Jossa at his side, maintaining his stiff and uncomfortable posture. In his hand, Tancred/Khurdis still held the metal contraption with which he had brought the stone columns of the Bridge to life. That Bridge glowed still, but more softly than it had, the curtains of blue radiance a faint pulsing rather than a hard glare. The contraption on Tancred/Khurdis's hand was gone dead.

Elinor did not understand. They had been gone the better part of a long day, yet here everybody was, as if only a double score of heartbeats had passed.

Tancred/Khurdis stared, wide-eyed, his arm raised protectively as if to ward off a sudden blow. 'No!' he cried. 'It cannot be. You . . . *cannot* return.'

Brynmaur was on his knees on the floor a little distance from Elinor, both of them outside the circumference of the spiral-pattern ringing the Bridge. He looked a right ragged and disreputable figure, filthy and tangle-haired. But there was something about him that drew the eyes of everyone in the chamber.

Slowly, stiffly, he rose to his feet.

'Seize him!' Tancred/Khurdis screamed. He brandished the metal contraption in his hand. Behind her, Elinor felt the Bridge leap into new life. 'Seize them both and throw them across!'

Elinor scrambled to her feet and grabbed up the spear which lay only a little distance off.

Men began to shuffle forwards, but with a noticeable lack of fervour.

'Quick, you fools!' Tancred/Khurdis screamed. 'Get them!'

But at that moment, the new-glowing Bridge flared into a sudden eruption. Behind the blue falling-curtain of radiance, a dark form took shape. Elinor could make out arms and legs, a torso, a head. It was not human; that much was clear. It seemed too tall and too thin, and the limbs bent in wrong ways.

Tancred/Khurdis stared, his face tight and stricken.

The apparition was stepping through the light-curtain now: insectile body, all sinew and bone and hanging skin, mere slit of a nose, long, tapering muzzle, thin white lips, wet, needle points of ivory-yellow fangs, dark, utterly unhuman eyes. Elinor felt the Fey-bone pulse with sudden warmth. The armed men in the chamber drew back in terror, weapons up.

Tancred/Khurdis snorted. 'Have no fear,' he announced, relief clear in his voice. 'It is merely one of the Shrags. A straggler, it seems.' He looked at the new arrival. 'You are late. And lost.'

The creature hissed softly.

'Go away,' Tancred/Khurdis ordered it. He raised one

hand and made a dismissive gesture. 'Back to where you came from. I command it! I have more important things to deal with at the moment than one of your kind.'

The creature stood as it was.

'I said *go*!' Tancred/Khurdis snapped irritably. He slipped the metal contraption back under his robe somewhere and raised both hands in a complex, dramatic pushing gesture. The air about his fingers seemed to glow sullenly. 'Go! Return from whence you came. I *command* it!'

The creature stayed, unmoving as a carving.

Tancred/Khurdis's skull-like face went tight. '*Go!*' he screamed.

The creature moved then, but instead of withdrawing back through the Bridge, it cut straight across the spiral-pattern on the floor towards Tancred/Khurdis. The men in the room spilled back away from it in frightened haste. Some threw down their weapons and fled the chamber entirely

'Stop it!' Tancred/Khurdis cried. 'Panicky fools!' He turned to the Lord Jossa, who had stood all this while unmoving. '*Kill* it!' he commanded. 'Quick!'

The Lord Jossa shivered, twitched, came abruptly alive. He drew the blazing sword in a quick arc of fire and leaped down to meet the advancing creature.

Elinor felt her heart lurch. That red-glowing blade would make short work of this newcomer – who had to be Moreena. Who else? 'Be— beware!' she cried, dry-mouthed and hoarse. 'The burning blade . . .'

But Moreena showed no sign of having heard. Perhaps she could not hear . . . Who knew what manner of senses might be natural for a creature as far removed from ordinary humanity as she was? This was the first time Elinor had seen Moreena actually in the flesh. Always before they had communicated in some spirit realm or other. But now . . . *was* there any simple way to communicate?

Moreena stalked towards the Lord Jossa, moving in the

strangely graceful, insectile manner of her kind, as if Jossa bore nothing more dangerous in his hands than a stick. Elinor clutched her little spear and tried to think what to do. She could see her own blade still dangling from Tancred/Khurdis's waist, half-concealed by the hang of his robe. If there was only some way for her to reach it . . . But there was not.

Jossa had crossed the distance between him and Moreena now and was almost within striking range. He looked like a very demon, his feline helm-visage seeming to roar silently. In a sudden desperate flurry, Elinor flung her spear at him. It took him in the side, in his ribs, and she heard him grunt. But the scale-mail he wore turned the blade and it fell to the floor with a dull *krunkk*. He did not even look round at her. She cursed herself for a fool.

The burning blade came up like a single fork of red-heat lightning, the air hissing and wavering about it.

'Do it!' Tancred/Khurdis screamed. He was jittering about, hands slicing the air in spastic patterns, little sparky shards spilling from them. 'Kill the thing!'

The Lord Jossa struck in a low, lightning stab, with all the super-human speed and power he had shown before, straight for the insectile belly.

But the creature he faced was faster. She side-stepped his stabbing rush and slipped by him, so that he stumbled forwards, unbalanced, and sprawled to his knees.

The men remaining in the chamber gasped.

'Fool!' Tancred/Khurdis shrieked. 'Get up. *Get up!*'

Moreena was moving towards Tancred/Khurdis now. Elinor could hear the soft *klak klik klak* of her talons upon the stone flooring.

'To me!' Tancred/Khurdis cried to Jossa.

The Lord Jossa scrambled to his feet and sprinted towards the advancing creature, glowing blade foremost, and drove her back with a series of flashing swings that set the air humming. He could not connect with any of his thrusts, for Moreena was still too quick for him, but he stopped her from advancing further.

Tancred/Khurdis had drawn the white blade by now. The two uncanny blades together in the room made the air fairly sing. Elinor felt the hairs along her scalp prickle.

'Let it come to me, then,' Tancred/Khurdis was saying now. With the white blade in his hands, his face had taken on a new expression, less tight, more leering. Elinor knew what he was feeling – the seductive strength of the sword. He moved forwards lightly, on the balls of his feet, swinging the blade in inexpert arcs before him.

The Lord Jossa stepped back a little, allowing the creature to pass, but he kept his own blade up and ready.

Tancred/Khurdis smiled a thin, arrogant smile. 'Come, then, creature, if you are so eager to meet your own death.' He gestured beckoningly with the sword. 'Come . . .'

But Brynmaur, too, had begun to come forwards now.

Tancred/Khurdis made a motion towards Jossa to allow Brynmaur on. 'You, too, then, man. My bright blade will drink your lifeblood as easily as this thing's.'

Brynmaur walked on with a steady, slow, weary step. Elinor found herself following after him, feeling a subtle pull she knew all too well.

Passing so close to the Lord Jossa's burning blade that she felt the unnatural heat of it, she stopped a few paces before Tancred/Khurdis, beside Brynmaur, who stood, in turn, alongside the insectile creature that was Moreena.

For a long few moments, the chamber was utterly still, the tensions held in uneasy balance, like some uncanny tableau.

'So . . .' Tancred/Khurdis breathed. His face was twitching. The hands holding the blade's hilt shook in little uncontrollable spasms. Elinor felt the Fey-bone at her breast quiver in hot/chill pulses. Her heart was banging. It all seemed craziness, this. What were they doing standing here defenceless, the three of them? Yet there was a kind of inevitability about it all . . . a momentum building subtly.

Tancred/Khurdis opened his mouth, closed it, took a ragged breath. A long shudder went through him. 'How shall you die?' he said. 'I think—'

Elinor felt a stirring from Moreena. She did not move physically, but there was . . . something.

Tancred/Khurdis's eyes opened very wide, then narrowed to slits. He stared at Moreena. A shiver went through him and he grunted. Elinor could feel the thrust and strain of something not quite palpable in the room. Her belly quivered and twisted with it. Tancred/Khurdis and Moreena stood face to face, their gazes locked – dark-troubled human eyes and implacable unhuman ones.

Tancred/Khurdis groaned. The sword quivered in his hold, began to slip. 'No . . .' He seemed to collapse in some odd manner for an instant. Then, 'No!' he shrieked again. 'NO! You will . . . not . . . do . . . this.' He was bowed over, shoulders hunched, as if a great weight were bearing down upon him. 'I will not . . . permit it,' he grunted, straightening himself slowly, head coming up.

He smiled, then, a flash of teeth in his skull-like face. 'I am far more than you deem, old one,' he said sneeringly to Moreena. And then, 'Oh, yes. I recognise you for what you are. Old . . . old and arrogant and purblind. For too long have you reigned over your little realm, unopposed. You might have stopped me once, but no longer. You might even, perhaps, have been able to stop me now . . . save that I have this,' he held aloft the white blade, 'to lend me strength.'

Elinor felt Moreena quiver, balked. Elinor's heart sank. It had all seemed so inevitable. She could not believe that Moreena could simply . . . fail like this.

But Tancred/Khurdis was grinning in nasty triumph now. He lifted the shining sword. 'What will happen to you, do you think, old one, when I set your spirit spinning loose? Will it ever return to its rightful place? I think not. A fitting punishment, that, for meddling in my affairs . . .'

Brynmaur suddenly stepped forwards. As with Moreena, Elinor felt a shifting of barely palpable, unseen forces.

But Brynmaur buckled almost immediately, going to his knees, hands to his throat, gasping and struggling for breath.

Tancred/Khurdis laughed. 'So much for you, little man. You are pitiful.'

Moreena started forwards, but Tancred/Khurdis drove her back with the white blade. 'Keep away from him!' he hissed. He motioned to Lord Jossa, who came across in three quick strides. 'Kill them if they move,' he ordered, motioning at both Elinor and Moreena.

Brynmaur, still on his knees, gasped and struggled for air, his face contorted.

Tancred/Khurdis watched like a cat, still grinning. 'How does it feel, man? Here, have a little breath.' Tancred/Khurdis lifted a hand and made an opening gesture and Brynmaur took a single, desperate, gasping breath.

'Only one,' Tancred/Khurdis said. 'Just to prolong . . .'

'No!' Elinor cried. '*Stop* it.'

Tancred/Khurdis looked at her. 'Oh, yes?' He laughed a soft, unfunny laugh. 'And just who are you to begin giving orders?'

'You . . . you offered us a bargain . . . before.'

'The time for bargains is well past, girl.'

'I think not.' She could feel the Fey-bone pulsing. 'I have something you want.'

He turned his full attention upon her now. 'What do you mean?'

'You took my blade from me, but there is something else . . . an object of power that you missed.'

He stared at her suspiciously. 'Such as?'

Slowly, she reached into her tunic and brought out the

409

little Fey-bone. It sat in her palm easily, a small, ochre-ivory length, the neck-cord dangling down from her hand. She could feel it pulsing. The intricate tanglewood of carving upon its surface seemed to writhe.

Tancred/Khurdis stared at it. 'What is . . .' He shivered. 'Where did you get such a thing?'

'Does it matter? The question is . . . do you want it?'

He laughed. 'I can take it from you any time I wish, girl.'

'I think not.' Elinor felt herself shaking. She did not know quite what she was doing here. It was the subtle pull of the world's current upon her.

Tancred/Khurdis regarded her warily. 'Give it to me, then.'

'First, we strike a bargain.'

'No bargains!'

'It will never be yours, then. Try to take it from me by force, and its virtue will be destroyed.' She had no idea if such a thing could be true, but it sounded well enough. 'My life, and the lives of my two companions here. Then it is yours. You offered us that once, to let us walk free if we agreed never to interfere with you or your aims again.'

Tancred/Khurdis was looking at the Fey-bone hungrily.

'It is a . . . *special* thing,' Elinor said softly, holding the Fey-bone out for him to see – still not knowing what she was about, really, feeling her way blindly, feeling her heart thump. 'A thing of *power*, old and strong.'

'Give it to me,' Tancred/Khurdis said sharply.

'Do we have a bargain?'

He paused. 'We do. Now give it into my hand!'

Elinor gestured at Brynmaur. 'Release him.'

Tancred/Khurdis frowned, nodded. He made a curt gesture and Brynmaur slumped, panting and groaning, but clearly breathing again.

Elinor stepped forwards gingerly. Lifting her hand, she let the Fey-bone slip from her palm and into Tancred/Khurdis's grasp.

He snatched it triumphantly, laughing. 'Stupid girl. Did

you truly think I would honour any bargain made with the likes of you? With this in my possession, along with . . .'

But there was something happening to him. His face blanched. 'No . . .' he breathed. 'No. It cannot be!' He tried to fling the Fey-bone from him but it remained tangled in his hand, the neck-cord wound round his fingers like a coiling serpent. He shrieked, flapping his hand hysterically.

Elinor did not truly understand what was happening, but in a sudden flash of comprehension, she grasped that it had to do with the mysterious Fey. It had been the Fey who had been responsible for Tancred's downfall long ago, she recalled. And now . . . She shivered, thinking on the incredible convolutedness of it all, her carrying the little bone all the way here . . .

Tancred/Khurdis was writhing, shaking and whirling as if he were roasting in invisible flames. The white blade went flying suddenly.

Before any could prevent her, Elinor dove for it and snatched it up. The familiar wondrous strength of it filled her and she threw back her head and howled for the pure perfection of it.

The Lord Jossa was there before her suddenly, his flaming blade *hissing* through the air. She parried, side-stepped, knowing him now, her limbs *thrumming* with strength. Tancred/Khurdis was shrieking. Jossa came at her in a wild fury, hacking and slashing till the air about them fairly crackled.

She held her own, but it would not last – for all the inexplicable clumsiness that marked his swordplay, he was too unbelievably brute strong, too uncannily fast.

And then, abruptly, he stumbled. There was a strange pulsing in the air, in the very walls and floor and roof of the chamber, it seemed.

Tancred/Khurdis was on his knees, sobbing. The Fey-bone had fallen from his hand and lay on the stone floor. His face was changed, somehow, the lines of it subtly altered.

Elinor saw Brynmaur struggle to his feet, move forwards. A groan seemed to go through the very stones of the Tower. The men in the chamber blinked and shivered and shook themselves.

'Brynmaur . . .' she heard Tancred/Khurdis speak – croak more than speak.

Brynmaur reached forwards. 'Khurdis?' he said uncertainly, his voice hardly much better that the other's.

'Me,' Tancred/Khurdis gasped. 'I . . .' A long, wracking shudder went through him. 'The . . . the bone . . . It drove him . . . away somehow.' He shuddered. 'I could not stop him. He . . . he was so *strong*. You have no idea . . .'

'It's all right,' Brynmaur said, reaching for the other man. 'It's over now.'

But Khurdis shook his head. 'No it is *not*.'

Brynmaur looked at him.

'I can feel him hovering. He was driven off, yes. But only temporarily. He is too strong, Brynmaur, and will be . . . back.' Khurdis broke into a sob. 'I cannot . . . endure more. He is so . . . *hard*. Like a great iron spike driven through me. It *hurts* so . . .'

Elinor tried to reach the two men, but the Lord Jossa rose before her, barring her way. 'Let me . . .' she started to say, but he struck at her, a little less fast than he had been, perhaps, but fast enough. The blow very nearly took her hand off. Only by a fraction did she manage to dodge away and parry.

'You must . . .' she could hear Khurdis say in a shaken voice. 'You must . . . end this, Brynmaur.'

'No!' Brynmaur replied.

'Yes! It is the only way.'

'*No* . . .'

'For pity's sake, Brynmaur!' Elinor could see Khurdis reach to Brynmaur in desperate supplication. 'For any affection you might once have had for me . . . Kill me, fast. Before it is too late. I can feel him drawing closer. The . . . bone will not banish him a second time. He knows what it is now, and will not be surprised again. You must *kill* me.'

But Brynmaur only shook his head. 'No! There must be some other solution. There *must* be!'

'Quick!' Khurdis gasped in desperation. 'Or it will be too late. *Quick* . . .'

Elinor tried to come at him. One quick strike with the white blade, and the issue would be settled once and for all. But Jossa would not allow it. He stood squarely before her, slashing and hacking in his clumsy-furious manner, keeping her at bay.

'Moreena!' she cried.

But Jossa had driven Moreena back, too, keeping the two of them from approaching anywhere near Khurdis. The only thing Elinor could do was keep Jossa as occupied as possible so that he could not turn and run Brynmaur through.

Which left everything in Brynmaur's hands . . .

'Kill me, Brynmaur,' Khurdis begged.

But Brynmaur remained frozen.

'*Please!*' Khurdis gasped. 'Before . . . before it . . . is . . .'

'Too late!' another voice finished triumphantly. 'I am *returned*! . . .'

But Brynmaur struck at last, weeping. He produced the little paring knife he had been carrying all this while and thrust it into Khurdis's ribs, once, twice, thrice.

Khurdis/Tancred shrieked, '*No!*'

And moaned, '*Yes* . . .' in desperate relief.

Brynmaur struck again, the little knife slicked with blood now, the front of Khurdis/Tancred's robe staining red. Again and again Brynmaur struck, weeping and crying, his face twisted into a wild rictus. The arms of Khurdis/Tancred flailed in desperation, thwacking Brynmaur across the chest, the face.

But it was no use. The little knife came down again and again, the flailing arms weakened.

Khurdis/Tancred groaned, collapsing. 'No . . .' he

413

moaned, deep and guttural and breathless. 'No! I cannot . . . *die*!'

A hard spasm went through him. Blood rose from out of
his mouth in a sudden, wet gush. He jerked, tried to rise,
collapsed back again for the final time.

And died.

A long, eerie, bodiless shriek went through the Tower,
high and wailing and furious.

And then it died, too.

Elinor took a gasping breath. Not a soul had moved during
those last moments. But now . . . Tancred might be gone
from them forever, but there was still Lord Jossa and the
armed men who remained in the chamber. They were
gathering at Jossa's back uncertainly, weapons to the
ready, those who had not already fled the room.

He would be a desperate man now, this Jossa, whoever
he might be – with all that he had worked for taken from
him so suddenly. And desperate men did rash, stupid
things. She did not think there would be any chance of
him responding to talk. Nor the men with him. They had
the look of so many furious-frightened animals. They
would see her only as a bitter foe. Which left . . .

More killing.

She shuddered at the thought, even with the white
blade's volatile strength thrilling through her. Why was it
always death that decided such encounters as these? She
could hear Brynmaur sobbing softly over Khurdis's still
form. There seemed precious little choice left her here, but
she felt sickened by the whole thing, suddenly, and
unutterably weary of it. Once again, she would have to
wade in and shed men's blood for . . . she knew not what,
exactly.

For the world's balance, she supposed. But it seemed a
far-away and quite formless notion.

The Lord Jossa stood with the peculiar stillness that he
had shown before, one arm half-raised, the blazing sword

up. She approached him most warily. The red-glowing blade slashed at her and she parried, skipping lightly back.

'No!' a voice cried.

Brynmaur threw away the dripping knife in his hand and came stumbling over. 'No, Elinor. Enough! Put away your blade.'

She was quite willing, in her present mood, but did not see how. Jossa stood there, a raw, palpable menace, his red-glowing weapon making the air shimmer and crackle softly. Behind him, the armed men gathered closer.

Brynmaur limped up till he came to stand before the Lord Jossa. 'Enough,' he said wearily.

The burning blade came up. Elinor tensed to leap in, hoping she could be fast enough, sure enough . . .

'Pawli,' Brynmaur said. 'Pawli, it's *me*!'

Elinor froze. *Pawli?* Could it be? How could Brynmaur possibly know? The face behind the helm's bestial visage was impossible to recognise.

But Brynmaur continued, 'Pawli, take off the helm. It's *over*. Take the helm off, now.' He walked closer, hands at his sides, utterly defenceless against any strike Jossa might make.

The Lord Jossa – Pawli – whoever it was – faltered. The glowing blade drooped.

'Pawli!' Brynmaur repeated. There were tears in his eyes still. He blinked them away furiously, reaching a hand forwards. '*Pawli* . . .'

The armoured figure stepped back, avoiding Brynmaur's touch.

'Pawli!'

The burning blade came up for the fatal strike.

Brynmaur stood unmoving, and Elinor leaped forwards, cursing herself, knowing she had left it too late.

But the burning blade did not strike Brynmaur. Instead, it went whirling end over end to splash against the blue-radiant curtain that still clung to the Bridge. There was a

415

burst of sparks, and then the blade went through, disappearing into nothingness.

Elinor skidded to a halt.

The helm went next, spinning through the blue curtain like the sword – a flash of sharp sparks that dwindled into nothingness.

'Pawli,' Brynmaur breathed.

It was indeed Pawli, haggard and thin-faced and stricken. 'Bryn,' he gasped and stumbled to his knees. 'I almost . . . Oh, *Bryn*!'

Brynmaur wrapped him in his arms. 'Pawli, lad. It's all right. It's over now. It's all right. It's *over*.'

XXXIII

But it was not over.

The armed men shuffled about, anxious and uneasy, eyeing Elinor as if they expected her to fly at them any instant. 'I am no threat to you,' she announced to them. 'There is nothing left here to fight over.'

The men stared, shivering.

From behind her, Elinor heard the sudden *klack klick klack* of sickle-claws on stone. Turning, she saw Moreena approach Brynmaur. Pawli flinched away, but Brynmaur held him firm, murmuring words of encouragement, though he was pale-faced himself. Moreena reached out a three-fingered, taloned hand, her queerly jointed arm extending with that slow, insectile grace she had. Pawli stared. Brynmaur lifted his hand out, tentatively. The two touched.

Nobody in the chamber moved; silence held. Brynmaur and Moreena gazed at each other – human and unhuman eyes locked – exchanging they alone knew what.

Until, eventually, Moreena turned from him.

Klack klick klack went her claws on the floor, softly. She lifted a hand to Elinor. Elinor took it in hers, feeling a surprising warmth, the slick hardness of the talons, the sinewy strength. She could just hear the soft *hisss* of Moreena's breath. This close, there was a scent to her, sharp and piquant, like some exotic herb, spicy and not altogether unpleasant, but strange. This time, there was no touching of foreheads, no mysterious mode of communication. She looked into Moreena's dark, utterly strange, utterly unreadable eyes and shivered.

And then, with a quick and unexpected leap, Moreena was gone across the blue light-curtain of the Bridge and disappeared.

The blue radiance that strung the stone pillars together flared up, flickered like a dying candle flame, sank . . . then came apart in a stutter of sparks, leaving the four columns silent and dull and lifeless.

Elinor heard Brynmaur gasp. She blinked, shook herself, turned . . .

Brynmaur was collapsed in a heap now, with Pawli in little better shape by his side. The gathered men stood still where they had been, weapons out, staring at her.

She did the only thing she could think to do. Slowly, with the eye of every man upon her, she walked over to where dead Khurdis lay. Gently, she shifted him so as to be able to disentangle the crimson scabbard from his corpse. It was wet with blood, but there was little she could do about that now. With slow deliberation, she lifted the scabbard for all to see and sheathed the white blade. 'There is nothing for any of us to contest over,' she said, feeling quivery exhaustion wash through her now that the blade was no longer feeding her. 'Put away your weapons. Let us have no more bloodshed.'

They hesitated, looking at her, at each other.

'How can we trust you, witch?' one of them demanded.

Elinor ran a hand wearily across her face. She did not feel able for any sort of argument. 'I do not especially care, man, whether you trust me or not. There is nothing left here to fight for. Any fool can see that. If you wish to be so stupid as to want to continue the madness that was given birth here – go right ahead. But I will have no further part of it.'

She sat down – half fell down – with the sword across her lap. 'Would any of you have such a thing as a flask of water about you?'

That flummoxed them, and they whispered and grunted and milled about in confusion.

'Water?' Elinor repeated. Her mouth and throat were so painfully dry she could hardly talk. 'Anyone?'

A man stepped hesitantly out from the group, then. Somebody tried to pull him back, but he shrugged the restraining hand off. Slowly he walked over to where Elinor sat and handed her a water flask he took from his belt. His hand, as he offered her the flask, was shaking.

The first taste of the water nearly took her senses from her, it was so wonderful. She swilled it about in her mouth, swallowed as slowly as she could, took another pull from the flask, a third. Cool water dribbled down her chin. Wiping her mouth with the back of her hand, she looked at her benefactor, who stood shivering before her, his hands white-knuckling a blade at his belt. 'You are a brave man,' she said, handing the flask back to him. 'I thank you for your kindness.'

He blinked, nodded, straightened. His hand came away from the blade. 'You are . . . welcome.'

Elinor gestured towards Brynmaur. 'He, too, is in need of water. We have . . . have made a far journey this day.'

The man hesitated, then turned and went to Brynmaur, offering him the water.

The rest still stared. Elinor was past caring overmuch. They would do what they would do. She was too spent to do much more than just sit here for the moment, next to dead Khurdis, and look about her vaguely. She felt numbed by all that had happened.

There was a face before her suddenly. How it had got there she was not certain.

'Ell— Elinor?' the face said.

She blinked. It was a man's face, a stranger to her, middle-aged and balding with bristly grey chin whiskers. 'Yes?' she said.

'We . . . that is, the men and I . . . we feel . . .' He jerked, took a breath. 'We feel you have the right of it. What is the point in more violence? We are willing to put down our weapons if you are.'

419

Elinor almost laughed. She did not feel at all able for any other option right at the moment. She gestured at the sheathed blade still in her lap. 'Mine is put away.'

The man nodded. He waved an arm in the direction of the clustered men. 'As are ours.'

It was true, Elinor saw. Where, before, every man had held some manner of blade to the fore, now there were none in evidence. 'Good,' she breathed.

The man leaned closer, twitching nervously. 'What?'

'Good,' she repeated, more loudly.

He nodded, clearly relieved. 'It is all right,' he called back to the rest.

Elinor sighed. She ached. She wanted nothing so much as a hot bath and a long, long sleep somewhere that was quite peaceful. But the men were milling about like so many lost sheep now, and Brynmaur lay comatose after his little drink, and Pawli too, and every man who had any wits about him at all was looking to her . . .

No, things were not yet over here by a long shot . . .

XXXIV

'*You* talk to him!' Pawli snapped, shaking his head. 'Bryn's as pig-headed as . . . as a *pig*!' Pawli was haggard, thin as a starved hound, and prickly-irritable.

As were they all. A single night's sleep and a wash and some hot food was nowhere near enough to make up for all they had endured. And she had been dealing with anxious, confused men ever since last evening, trying to keep things from falling apart here completely. Her back ached; her head did too.

'Talk to him!' Pawli repeated. 'He just *sits* there ignoring me.'

'I'll try,' Elinor replied.

'You've got to do better than just *try*! If Bryn doesn't—'

'Pawli!' Elinor snapped. 'Enough! Just shut up and let me go to him.'

Pawli opened his mouth for an angry retort, stopped, bit his lip. 'I'm worried about him, is all.'

Elinor nodded.

'*What?*' he demanded. 'What are you looking at? You've been staring at me all morning.'

'Pawli . . .' she began, not knowing how to begin. She was still not sure quite what had truly happened to Pawli. Tancred had made a tool of him; that much was clear enough. But by how much had Pawli been aware of things? How much willing? And what lasting damage, if any, might such an experience leave in him?

Pawli was shivering, his thin arms clutched across his chest. He had taken the armour off and was dressed in his old clothes, ragged and torn. 'You think *I liked* what happened? What he turned me into?'

'Pawli,' she said quickly. 'I don't know what happened. I . . . Why did you leave the sword?' The question just popped out. It had been nagging quietly at the back of her mind all this time.

Pawli blinked confusedly. 'What sword?'

'You left the white blade near the beginning of the forest up by Brynmaur's. After you took it, why just . . . leave it there for me to find?'

He hugged himself. 'I . . . How can I make you understand? Your blade was too . . . too brute powerful for me when I unsheathed it. It made me sick to hold it.'

Elinor nodded, feeling relief seep into her.

'Tancred was furious that I had abandoned it.'

'No doubt.'

'I brought the iron blade with me. He re-fashioned it into the red-hot glowing thing you saw me wield.'

'And how was it to wield such a blade?' Elinor asked.

Pawli looked at her a long moment before he responded. 'Both terrible and wonderful.'

'And now?'

'Now, what?'

'Would you wish to wield such a weapon again, given the chance?'

He blanched. 'Never!'

It was always difficult to be completely certain of another's innermost feelings, but Elinor thought Pawli was genuine in his response. It left her feeling considerably relieved, for she knew all too well the hunger that could arise in man's soul once he had wielded a weapon of great power. 'You have no temptation towards further swordplay, then?'

Pawli laughed, a tired little bark. 'It is not my gift.'

'And what is your gift, then?'

He looked at her, his eyes suddenly narrowing. 'What business is that of yours?'

422

'I have . . . How can I phrase this for you? I have a responsibility here. To these folk. To Brynmaur. You could be a . . . a dangerous man, Pawli.'

He laughed again. 'Dangerous? Me? Hardly likely.'

'You are no ordinary man,' Elinor said softly. 'No more than Brynmaur is.'

Pawli blinked, shivered. 'Go to him. Enough of me. Go see Bryn. He . . . *needs* you, I think. I do not know what has happened between the two of you, but Bryn is . . . changed.'

'I will go,' Elinor said, but she paused, shifting from foot to foot where she stood. She wished there were something she could say to bridge the gap between her and this young man. He troubled her. What path would he choose to walk from here on?

Pawli waved her off irritably. 'Go on, then,' he said.

Brynmaur, when she found him, was seated alone in a small window alcove on the Tower's second floor, staring sightlessly into the sky beyond.

'Morning,' she said quietly.

He said nothing.

She smiled tentatively. 'You look in need of a light moment.'

Nothing.

'Remember? On the slope when we caught our first glimpse of this Tower? My turn now, I think, to supply a light moment. If you—'

'Leave me be,' he rasped, still not looking at her.

'No,' she said. 'That I will not.'

He rounded on her then. 'Stay away from me, you hear. Just . . . just keep your distance from me.'

'Brynmaur . . .'

He ran a hand shakily across his face. His beard and hair were washed and clean now, and less tangled, but he looked none the younger for it. If she were seeing him for the first time, she would think him an old man. He looked thin and frail, his skin translucent almost, his face a fine network of lines and wrinkles. Knowing him as she did, knowing the hard course of his life, she felt her heart go out to him. 'Brynmaur,' she said softly.

He looked away from her. 'I . . . I *killed* him.'

Elinor blinked. 'Khurdis? It had to be done. It was . . . release.'

'Perhaps, yes. But . . . but I . . . In all my life I have never, never killed. I did everything I could to stop such madness. You know that. But this . . . I was . . . I was *glad* of it, when I killed him. I felt such anger, and such . . . such desperate satisfaction.'

'But you only did what you had to.'

'No. You do not understand. It is with me still, that . . . that dark satisfaction. I can still feel the solid *thwump* of my little blade as it bit into him, the hotness of his blood upon me. I . . .' He turned to her, finally, white-faced and shaking. 'I am no ordinary man, Elinor. I have abilities, as you know. I cannot go on with such an unhealthy appetite newly arisen in me. That way lies . . . disaster.'

'It's all right,' Elinor replied. 'It was only natural. You were angered. The situation was extreme. Now that things are returned to normal you can—'

'No!' he snapped. 'Easy for you to dismiss, you who have killed so many men you no longer can keep track!'

It hurt, that. She bristled.

'I cannot seem to let this thing go. I—'

'That was always your problem,' Elinor said. 'You never could let anything go.' As soon as she said it, she knew it for truth. His life fit into a sudden clear pattern for her.

He glared at her. 'Never let . . . How can you— You don't know anything about how I have been forced to live my life!'

'No, Brynmaur,' Elinor replied softly. 'I know *exactly* how you've lived your life. Remember?'

He made a clumsy pushing motion with his hands. 'Go away. Leave me be!'

But she would not, for she knew she had stumbled upon something that could be a key to prising him from the knot he had got himself into here. 'You've always clung on to everything, like a squirrel hoarding nuts. And the sheer heaviness of it all has weighed you down.'

'No!' he said vehemently. 'I never—'

'Let it go, Brynmaur. Let it all just go.'

'And *you* even do that, I suppose? What about that furman, whose memory you cling to so secret-desperately. And your father? A fine one to talk about letting things go, you are!'

Elinor took a breath, trying to calm herself. It was only normal that he attack her. Anyone would, in a circumstance such as this – it was natural defence. She had to get through to him.

'You're right,' she said. 'I am no paragon. But I have let things go enough to be here, now. My life opens before me as I go, and I live it as best I can. In the present. With memories, yes. But they are only memories. My past is gone from me. I am no longer the person I once was. As you well know. Why . . . until I left Long Harbour I had never said the word "you" in my life.'

He looked at her quizzically.

'In Long Harbour, we said "ye" instead of "you". I found it most strange adapting.'

'And most difficult, I'm sure,' he said scathingly. 'What could be more traumatic than re-learning how to pronounce your words?'

Elinor clenched her fists, took a breath. 'I am only trying to show how I have let things go. Not perfectly, perhaps. But enough. While you . . .' She sat down next to him. 'Look, if there's any real problem with this . . . "unhealthy appetite" you speak of, it doesn't lie with any such "appetite" itself.'

'Oh, no? With what, then?'

Elinor paused, trying to get her ideas straight. 'The more you dwell upon it, the more you worry at it and fight it, the more you loose sleep over it . . . the stronger this "appetite" will become. And, soon enough, it *will* become something that dominates you.'

'Now, listen, girl,' Brynmaur responded. 'Do you think me a witling? I know better than to—'

'Think of Pawli,' Elinor interrupted.

Brynmaur blinked. 'What about him?'

'You drove him from you and into that Tancred's ungentle hold because you would not relinquish your conviction that being *gifted* was a curse.'

'It *is* a curse!'

Elinor shook her head. 'It's nothing so simple as that. I know. You know, too, in your heart of hearts. But you could not just . . . let go. As you will not let go now. Why must you hold everything so tight to yourself? Why must you take up all the responsibility, all the worry, all the grief? Why must everything be *yours*?'

'Because I am . . . *different*,' he replied in a hoarse, angry voice. 'Because—'

'Because your mother expected it of you all those years ago.'

It shocked them both, that – the betraying intimacy of it, and the sharp-edged, painful truth.

Brynmaur looked at her, looked away, shuddered. 'I cannot—'

'The girl in me is still trying to live up to my lost father's expectations,' Elinor said, for the truth of it, and for the comfort of shared pain it offered.

There were tears in Brynmaur's eyes now. 'It seems to me that life is just a long series of separations, each more painful that the one previous.'

Elinor reached to him. She knew that feeling. 'We have been . . . *used* by the world, we two.'

He took her hand in his, holding it hard. 'I have no life left, Elinor. All has been taken from me, home, family, love, all . . .'

'Not quite all,' she said.

'What remains, then?'

'To breathe, to rise each morn, to go on.'

He laughed a sputtering, unfunny laugh. 'Oh, such sage advice. You have become a philosopher then, have you?'

Elinor bit her lip. 'There is Pawli. There are folk here who need you.'

He shook his head. 'Pawli? Pawli has gone strange. And nobody round here needs me. Have you seen the way folk look at me when they think I won't notice?'

'They need you, Brynmaur, whether they know it or not. It was no small feat, the vanquishing of such a man as that Tancred. How would you expect ordinary folk to look upon you? And what of this place, now, then? What of the Tower?'

'What of it?'

'Every man knows about it, now. Word will get around. Its location is known. What of the paraphernalia stored in here? Would you give every scoundrel who wishes it the opportunity to steal from here? And what of the knowledge and the power contained here?'

Brynmaur regarded her uncertainly. 'What—'

'This place needs to be decently . . . *humanised*, or it will draw misfortune and chaos into the land. This place needs a custodian.'

Brynmaur blinked. 'And you think I—'

'Who better?'

He ran a hand over his face, tugged at his white beard. 'But I . . .'

'There is no one else. None has the knowledge, or the wisdom.'

'Wisdom!' Brynmaur snorted. 'I have precious little of that.'

Elinor shrugged. 'You have enough, I reckon.'

He looked her straight at that. 'Do you truly, truly think so?'

There was something almost pitiable in the intensity of

427

his need in that question. It went to his greatest, most debilitating fear, she knew: that he should be proved too weak, too altogether unworthy of the gift that had been visited upon him.

'I truly, truly think so, Brynmaur.'

He let out a long, weary breath. 'I . . . I don't quite know what to say.'

'Say nothing, then. Or say . . . say something simple like "good morning" to me and "how about a bite of break-fast" . . . I'd guess you have not eaten yet this day.'

He smiled ruefully at that. 'You'd guess right.'

'And so?'

'And so . . . Brynmaur ran a hand wearily across his face, swallowed. '. . . I don't . . .' He went silent, looking at her. Then he smiled again, a mere ghost of a smile, and nodded slowly. 'Good morning to you, then, Elinor of the white blade. Would you like to share some breakfast with me?'

"T'would be my pleasure, sir,' she said with mock formality.

'Shall we, then?'

She nodded and stood up. He still held her hand in his – she had forgot – and there was an awkward moment.

'I . . .' he paused self-consciously. 'Thank you, Elinor. You have saved my life, I think, this morning. Thank you . . .' His eyes had become glisteny with unshed tears.

She nodded, feeling suddenly close to tears herself with the palpable intimacy still between them, the raw feeling of it.

He looked at her. 'I don't suppose . . . No. Never mind.'

'What?' she said.

But he had turned already. 'Come on, breakfast awaits us.'

She followed after, relieved for him, but feeling her belly flutter uncomfortably. The pull of the world that had been upon her, upon the both of them, was dwindled now, and they were free to go about their lives once more – if 'free' were the right word. But, truth be told, she felt more than a little like Brynmaur himself: too much had been taken from her in her life, and it did, indeed, feel like one long series of separations.

With yet another one looming ahead here. For Brynmaur, now, there might be a place here, a new life. But for her? More wandering, she reckoned. More of the open road and the dubious company of old memories.

It was not a prospect that exactly thrilled her at the moment.

'Elinor?' Brynmaur called back, for she had not moved.

'Coming,' she said quickly, and followed after him.

XXXV

'So . . .' Brynmaur said.

It was early morn, the air still chill, the sun hardly risen yet. Brynmaur, Pawli, and Elinor stood together at the Tower's foot.

'Are you certain sure this is what you must do, Pawli, lad?' Brynmaur said.

Pawli had his arms wrapped about himself. 'I cannot stay here, near this place.' He looked up at the dark column of the Tower and shuddered. 'And neither can I return to who and what I once was. I am doing no more than you did, Bryn, by walking away on a learner's journey.'

Brynmaur nodded soberly. 'True enough, I suppose. But promise me to be most careful, won't you? The path you are setting your feet upon is no easy one. You know all too well how nearly I came to grief through it.'

Pawli smiled, but it was a thin smile. 'I am not you, Uncle. Besides, I have your example before me. I'm not likely to make the same mistakes.'

'I most profoundly hope not,' Brynmaur replied. He stepped forwards abruptly and enfolded Pawli in his arms. 'Take *care* now, lad, you hear? The lowlands are a queer place.'

Pawli pulled himself back. 'No queerer than here, I'm sure. And besides, I'm not entirely . . . helpless.'

Brynmaur frowned. 'The *gift* is nothing to take lightly, lad. And it's still aborning in you.'

'At least now you'll admit it's there in me.'

Brynmaur sighed. 'Don't rub my previous confusions in my face, all right?'

Pawli smiled, more warmly than before. 'It isn't all that often that I get to be proved so right and you so wrong.'

Elinor felt a little shiver go through her. They were all much recovered, the three of them, but the scars of recent events still remained, and there were residual tensions between uncle and nephew. There was a distance to Pawli, as if he stood a little apart from the world. He refused to talk about what, exactly, had happened to him under Tancred's ungentle hands, but it had aged him, that was clear. His face had a set look to it, and his mouth was lined with pain. He had grown more and more restless, these past days; it was plain he could not stay near the Tower any longer. And Brynmaur, now, was established here.

So Pawli would go his solitary way down into the lowlands to search for a teacher to bring out the *gift* in him – as Brynmaur had done years ago. Brynmaur did not altogether like it, she knew, but he could not gainsay the younger man. He felt himself to have been too much in the wrong for too long where Pawli was concerned.

'Be careful, Nephew,' Brynmaur said softly. 'And come back to me one day.'

'I will, Uncle. Promise.'

Brynmaur turned to Elinor. 'And you . . .' He paused.

Elinor did not know what to say. Brynmaur had taken up his abode here and become the proper Thane of the Tower indeed – as if he had been born to it. Perhaps, in some way, he had.

And so he had found his place. And she . . . she was for the open road once more, keeping Pawli company for a time, then heading off on her own. Brynmaur had been so busy trying to set things to rights, they had hardly exchanged three words in the past week.

'Take care,' she said and turned to go. It was too much, suddenly, to say more.

Brynmaur made as if to reach for her, then drew back.

Pawli was ready. 'Let's be gone, then.'

Together, he and Elinor turned and walked off, leaving

Brynmaur standing at the foot of the Tower. All the men who had been gathered here at Tancred/Khurdis's calling had long since departed, and Brynmaur stood entirely alone, dwarfed by the Tower's height.

'I don't know whether to envy him or pity him,' Pawli said, looking back.

'Both, perhaps.' Elinor stopped walking for a moment. She raised her hand in a final salutation. Brynmaur raised his back. He was such a strange man. So many contradictions to him. So many strengths and weaknesses.

'I'll miss him,' Pawli said.

Elinor nodded. So would she. Perhaps she would come back one day. She turned and took a step, another, feeling the world under her feet, the familiar swing of the sword at her hip, the weight of the rucksack on her shoulders . . . feeling the road ahead waiting for her, knowing it would lead her on and on to places she could not now predict – and that the chances of her ever returning here were next to nil.

'Come on,' Pawli said. 'We've a long ways ahead of us.'

But Elinor could not do it. Instead, she turned abruptly back.

Brynmaur watched her in surprise. 'What is it?' he said as she drew near him.

She felt a fool. She was not sure why, exactly, she had returned.

He looked at her for a long, silent moment. 'I . . .' he began, coughed, swallowed, started again. 'I . . . we never had a chance to talk properly in the past few days, you and I. Not since you came to me when I was . . . well, upset.'

She nodded.

'I've been too preoccupied with everything. And if it wasn't for you, I'd never have . . . Thank you.'

She nodded again.

'Well . . .'

She went to him and gave him a quick, hard hug. Then turned and started to walk off again.

'Elinor,' he called. 'Don't . . .'

She stopped, turned.

'Don't . . . what?'

'Don't go,' he said. 'I . . . I need a companion in this big, empty place. Would you . . .'

She was not sure what, exactly, he was offering.

'No,' he said in a small voice. 'Of course not.'

'Of course not . . . what?'

'You would never wish to share your life with a man such as I.' He lifted a hank of his white hair. 'I look old enough to be your father.'

It was true. He did. But she knew him for a man lean as any greyhound, with a most human heart and a mind filled with many things.

Share her life with him . . .

It was something she had thought about, and refused to think about.

Share her life . . . Power and knowledge between them, she with her blade and he with his abilities as a deep Curer, and more. And a home such as this Tower – darksome now, perhaps, but surely a place that could be changed, a – she hardly dared think the word – a *home*.

'We are so alike, you and I,' he was saying.

It was true. There was not another human being in all the world she knew as well as he. Nor any other who knew her so well.

'We could make a life for ourselves here, the two of us.'

She looked at him. For all that they knew each other so intimately, there was no special connection remaining between them, no linking of mind to mind or heart to heart. The gulf that separated ordinary folk separated them, too.

'No,' he said. 'I do not blame you. I . . . I had to try, though. You understand?'

'You're a fool,' she said then.

He blinked.

433

'You never did have any true sense of your own worth.'

'Meaning . . . what?' he said.

But at that moment, Pawli came traipsing back. 'What's the matter?' he demanded of Elinor. 'Have you forgotten something?'

'No,' she said. 'No . . .'

'What, then?' Pawli said, clearly confused. 'Are you coming?'

'No,' Elinor said. 'I think not.'

'What?'

She stepped towards Brynmaur, her heart suddenly thumping. 'I think I'll be staying here, Pawli.' Softly, Elinor put her arm round Brynmaur's thin waist. He put his round her. She could feel his hand tremble as it rested upon her shoulder.

Pawli stared at the two of them as if they had gone quite mad.

'I've been on the road alone too long, Pawli,' Elinor tried to explain. 'We both have, Bryn and I. And I . . .'

She did not know how to explain it. She did not even know if she wanted to. She was not rocked by the tumbling passion that had marked her relationship with Annocky, the first man in her life, nor was she swept along by the wonder she had felt with Gyver, her fur-man. This was something else. She could feel passion for this man, she sensed that in the little soft flush of new warmth his touch was bringing to her. But there was more to it than that. They had shared so much, Brynmaur and she. They were so alike.

'We are of the same kind,' Brynmaur said.

It was true. Both . . . what was his word for it? Both *gudgeons*. Both too familiar with what it was to be lonely, with the weight of being . . . special.

Pawli was still staring.

'You're welcome to stay too, lad,' Brynmaur invited.

But Pawli shook his head. 'No.' He looked at Elinor, at his uncle, ran a hand over his face. 'My way leads into the lowlands. I . . .' He paused. 'The world is a most strange place.'

'That it is,' Elinor agreed.

'Fare well, then,' Pawli said finally, 'the two of you.'

'And you, lad,' Brynmaur wished.

They embraced quickly, the three of them, and then Pawli turned and walked off.

'I don't know whether to pity him or envy him,' Brynmaur said softly, watching Pawli slowly disappear in the distance.

'He said the same about you.'

'Did he, now?' Brynmaur replied.

Elinor smiled. 'I reckon he's still saying the same thing to himself. About the both of us, now.'

Brynmaur looked at her. 'Are you certain sure this is what you wish to do, Elinor? I wouldn't want you to . . .'

She nodded. 'Certain sure.'

He sighed. 'The world is indeed a strange place.'

'And we strange creatures.'

Brynmaur laughed, a soft, pleasant, easy sound. 'We are that,' he agreed. 'We are indeed that.'

They turned, then, and walked slowly back together towards the Tower, arm in arm.

PART THREE

XXXVI

Pawli stood high atop a stony promontory, looking back over the way he had come. Milky twilight faded the sky. The dark pillar of the Tower behind him was made small by distance now, but he could still feel the weight of it.

He felt the weight of many things: nightmare and dream warred in his soul, darkness and bright appeal. Too much pain . . . The person he had once been was gone forever, his innocence shrivelled away. He had been ridden like some beast – he burned, recalling it – and driven to things beyond his natural capacities. But he had been *opened*, too, by Tancred's ungentle treatment, and the shackles that had once galled him so were ripped entirely away.

All about him, he could hear the world *hroomming* deeply, singing its great, slow music.

Gazing back at the Tower, he felt a momentary spasm of envy for his uncle and Elinor. Bryn had finally got the belonging he had always hungered for. And Elinor had found sanctuary in that darksome place, as unlikely as it seemed. The very sight of it, for all that it was distant now, sent a cold shudder through him. His time there as the Seer's creature was like a nightmare, uncertain and terrible, that came back to haunt him in bits and stabs. These last few days had been torment, and he was most relieved to be gone from the place.

Yet the Tower would be changed now, he knew. Under Bryn's stewardship, it would enter a new season. And Elinor – who would ever have imagined she and Bryn together? – could settle in there like a ship coming to safe harbour.

He had never seen the sea . . .

Well, that was one of the things he might do, now.

Pawli turned and slipped over the crest of the promontory and away, leaving the Tower and everything else behind. He had not even bothered with a last look. What was the point? His life lay ahead now. There was only the one path for him. He felt like a small fish flushed out into the free ocean. He felt . . .

He did not know quite how he felt.

Except that he had come – was coming – into his own true being at last. That he understood with a blood-deep certainty. He could sense the world's subtle under-patterning more and more clearly, so much so that it seemed at times as if he waded through the world more than walked.

It thrilled him the way a rising wind must thrill a bird.

He strode on down a long, turfed slope towards . . . he knew not what, while the sky slowly darkened overhead and the great world turned. Empty-handed, he went, in pain and yet also in joy, alone, but feeling himself a part of greater things in the way he had always wished, missing Bryn already, happy to be travelling free . . .

Feeling *alive* as could be.